FAST FRIENDS

AN IRIS THORNE MYSTERY

DIANNE EMLEY

Originally published as *Fast Friends* by Dianne Pugh in 1997 by Pocket Books, a division of Simon & Schuster, Inc.

Cover design by Kimberly King

Arroyo Bridge
Books

Published by Arroyo Bridge Books, a division of Emley and Co., LLC. First Arroyo Bridge Books trade paperback edition April 2012.

ISBN-10: 0984784675
ISBN-13: 978-0-9847846-7-7

.:

PRAISE FOR DIANNE EMLEY'S

FAST FRIENDS

"Sharp and stylish. . . a multistranded complex of lies, betrayal, and desperation. . . that strips bare the politics of relationships. Clever and cool." —Val McDermid, *Manchester Evening News* (UK)

"A novel of suspense, romance, murder, and political intrigue on the richly detailed landscape of Los Angeles." —*Pasadena Star-News*

[Iris Thorne is] sleek, smart and refreshingly bitchy. . . Any heroine so ambitious and quirkily original that she'll sneak peeks into her associates' lunch bags for clues to their home lives deserves our undivided attention." —Dick Lochte, *Los Angeles Times Book Review*

"[Emley's] real achievement here is making every single person Iris is attached to look suspicious and guilty." —*Kirkus Reviews*

"There's action to spare here. . . . [Emley's] uncanny knack for using the perfect word to fit the occasion gives the novel a special quality, and her characters are complex and disturbing. . . . There is an almost erotic lushness to her writing..." —*Cleveland Plain Dealer*

"An engaging and page-turning blend of family psychopathology, financial and political shenanigans, and California entropy." —Jonathan Kellerman

"A tightly knit, unpredictable tale. With her bold moral compass, her appealing in-your-face attitude and unsettled romantic life, Iris is a compelling heroine." —*Publishers Weekly*

"As skillfully tangled as a Raymond Chandler or Ross MacDonald mystery. . . . Iris is a marvelous heroine. . . . [Emley] has developed a series full of humor and tension in a city teeming with glamour, disaster, and grit." —*The Herald* (Portsmouth, NH)

BOOKS BY DIANNE EMLEY

Iris Thorne Mysteries

Cold Call
Slow Squeeze
Fast Friends
Foolproof
Pushover

Detective Nan Vining Thrillers

The First Cut
Cut to the Quick
The Deepest Cut
Love Kills

For my father,
William M. Pugh

ACKNOWLEDGMENTS

Thanks to Rowland Barber for being a friend, fan, and mentor. My wonderful editor Linda Marrow for giving Iris and me a soft landing. Dana Isaacson for being my guardian angel. Jane Chelius for her early support of this book. Ann Escue and Mary Goss for commenting on the manuscript. June Pugh for sharing a memory. Charles for being there, as always.

.

One

Dolores Gaytan DeLacey knew she risked making her husband mad by straightening his newspapers, but if she just straightened them and resisted the temptation to throw any out, maybe he wouldn't notice. She never threw out anything that belonged to him anyway. She'd learned her lesson a long time ago—even though he'd accused her of exactly that as recently as last month. He had eventually made her understand that the newspapers weren't junk. He was going to read them when he had the time. And until he found the time, he'd keep them in his office, where she had no business being anyway. Why, just the other day, he told her, he'd taken one down and read it and had thrown it away when he was finished. So he didn't want her saying he never threw anything away.

Many of the piles of newspapers still had not been righted and lay where they had toppled over. Others listed to the side. It wouldn't take much to send them tumbling to the ground too.

She shoved the handle of her feather duster between the ties of her apron and leaned over to pick up a stack. She checked their dates to make sure she heaved them back where they belonged, then wiped beads of perspiration from her forehead and tried to catch her breath.

It had been an unseasonably warm and dry January for Los Angeles. Even though the thick adobe walls in the old part of the house kept the air cool, Dolly was hot. It didn't take much for her to overheat these days, but she didn't want to sit down and rest. She'd had enough of that.

It had taken her a long time, but she had finally made a navigable path to his desk. Of course he'd used his desk since the papers and everything else had fallen. He'd simply crawled over them with the ease of a much younger man. That's one thing Dolly could say about her husband. Nothing, not even age, seemed to slow him down. Crawling up and over was not an option for her, not that she had any business in his desk anyway. She had no business there at all.

She dropped heavily into his desk chair, the worn leather and old springs singing, and picked up the hem of her apron to blot her face. She looked out the small paned window that was cut into the adobe wall, and waited for her breathing to return to normal. The sun shone through lacy, dusty cobwebs strung across each of the corners. She wondered how she could have let her house go for so long. She told herself it wasn't her fault, not really, but she still felt it was. After all, this was her house. It would always be her house.

She pulled open the lower right-hand drawer of the old wooden desk and was glad to see that the metal box was still there. Grabbing its handle, she lifted it from the drawer, then carefully shoved the clutter on the desk out of the way to set it down. She opened it. It wasn't locked. Why would he bother?

The box held just two things. She took out the will, her will in which she'd left him all her worldly possessions. Those were the exact words: all her worldly possessions. She'd reread that phrase many times since she'd found the single typed sheet a month ago. The signature was shaky and infirm but it could have been her signature in 1971, twenty-five years ago, which was when the will was dated.

She had no recollection of making the will but she remembered very little from that time. It was during her amnesia. Of course, she didn't really have amnesia, but it was easier to explain things that way. Since then, some of her memories had returned, slowly creeping into her consciousness like creatures crawling from a dark cave. Most of the memories were joyful; some were not. Still, huge chunks were missing. Years and years. Vanished.

But there was one thing she never would have done, even then. She never would have left him all her worldly possessions. There was really only one thing he coveted anyway, and she'd promised her father that her husband would never own the remaining five hundred acres of Las Mariposas.

It was all that was left of the forty-three thousand acres granted to her great-great-grandfather in 1830 by the Governor of Alta California in payment for his services in Mexico's war of independence. Her great-great-grandfather had named the rancho Las Mariposas because of the swarms of butterflies he said he encountered when exploring the property. In reality, he had confused fields of golden poppies with butterflies.

Her husband said her father had specifically stated in his will that they were to own Las Mariposas jointly, but she still didn't know how that had happened. It was one of the things that remained hidden.

It would sort itself out. After all, her husband was twenty-two years older than she was. Certainly she'd outlive him. But things had been happening lately that made her uncertain. It had started with the baked chicken in mushroom sauce that he'd cooked. She was sick for two days after she'd eaten it while he remained healthy. Then there was the patch of flooring that had given way under her feet. She'd nearly dropped into the basement. One day she'd had a look around the garage and found all sorts of things that she'd never seen before. Rope, rat poison, saws. She'd only put it all together after she'd decided to stop taking her medication. It was as if a fog had lifted. Everything became crystal clear.

Reaching into the metal box again, she took out the other item it held: a gold wedding band. She held it up so she could see the inscription etched on the inside. *Gabriel y Isabella 14 Junio 1934*. She clutched the ring in her fist and her fist to her chest. The tears came immediately, forcefully. She felt the need to sink down, to get close to the ground, or to cling to something like the desk or a wall, but she fought it. She had to be strong. She had to keep her wits about her.

After calming down, she reached into her apron pocket, took out a square that she'd clipped from the neighborhood newspaper, the *El Sereno Sentinel*, unfolded it on the desk, and read it again.

SECURE WITH YOUR RETIREMENT PLANS? UNCERTAIN HOW TO PAY FOR YOUR CHILD'S EDUCATION?

I was raised in El Sereno and attended the local schools where I later taught hearing-impaired children. Now, as a senior investment counselor for McKinney Alitzer Financial Services, I'm in a unique position to understand your financial concerns...

Dolores looked at the small picture of Iris Thorne's face in the corner. She picked up the heavy metal receiver of the old telephone. Her father, Gabriel, had installed that telephone. It had been the first one in the house. She looked around the desk for something to help her turn the rotary dial that had round openings above each number, which were too small for her fingers. She used a pencil.

A recording answered. It told her what to do if she had a Touch-Tone or a rotary phone and Delores became confused and hung up. Her eyes again teared. She steeled herself and tried again and finally reached a real person, who put her through to Iris Thorne's number.

"Iris?" she asked apprehensively at the sound of Iris's voice.

It was another recording. Determined not to hang up, she clutched the telephone handset with both hands and listened carefully until it was her turn to speak.

"Iris! It's Dolly. Dolly DeLacey. I don't think he knows I know. I don't know who I can trust. He's turned my children against me. He knows everyone on the police department and at City Hall. I think he knows the governor and even the president and the president runs the FBI. Who can I turn to?"

She took a deep breath, trying to calm herself. She was getting hysterical. She knew firsthand that no one paid attention to a hysterical woman. "Iris, he's trying to kill me. Bill's trying to kill me. There's a rope in the garage and some saws and poison, Iris! It says it's for rats but there's a skull and crossbones on the box. It's deadly poison! Then in his desk I found a metal box with my will in it. But I don't remember it, Iris. How could I leave him everything? What about my children? And my father's ring is there, too…" She paused and listened. "It's him! There's his car. It's him. Oh my goodness!"

She quickly hung up, put the box back in the drawer, slid the drawer closed, pushed the chair underneath the desk, and with trembling hands tried to return the clutter on top of the desk to its original position. She started to leave the room, then rushed back to grab the ad that she'd forgotten on the desk. Hurrying out, she bumped against the stacks of newspapers. She felt more and more out of breath. Ducking into her bedroom, she closed the door and tried to compose herself. When she heard Bill go into the kitchen, just like she expected him to do, she began to calm down. Everything was going to be fine, she told herself. Everything was going to be fine because over the years she'd finally learned to think like he did.

He walked into his office and said, "Huh," when he saw that she'd straightened it up. Standing behind his desk, he reached down and picked up a small, carefully folded square of white paper that lay on the carpet. A self-satisfied smile crossed his lips as he wedged the paper between the desk and drawer, down low on the far side. This was the best location—confirmed via many tests—for it to drop to the ground almost unseen when the drawer was opened.

Two

Iris Thorne didn't pay too much attention to the man with the squeegee. Sure, she kept her eye on him, like any good city girl, while he squeegeed the windows of his beat-up old boat of a car in the bay adjacent to hers at the self-serve gas station. He was a bit tattered, with long, gray hair that brushed his shoulders. His pants were frayed at the hem, and he was humming tunelessly to himself. His beatific smile was in such sharp contrast to the defeated expressions virtually everyone else in the city had worn during the previous few weeks that Iris suspected he was either deranged to begin with or had been recently driven to that point.

She walked back to her give-me-a-ticket red 1972 Triumph TR6 after paying for her gas at the kiosk and saw the man now squeegeeing the Triumph's windows.

What the hell? she said to herself. She angrily unzipped her purse, suddenly pushed over the edge. *I can't take any more.*

As she fumbled to find a dollar, the man waved the squeegee, smiled warmly, and said, "Thought I'd clean yours too. I already had this in my hand." He shrugged diffidently, dropped the squeegee back into its dirty bath, humming all the while, then got in his car and drove away.

Iris watched him with her hand still jammed into her purse. *What was that about?* She inspected the TR for damage, calmed herself down, and drove away as well. She entered the eastbound Ten at its mouth in Santa Monica, passing the CHRISTOPHER COLUMBUS TRANSCONTINENTAL HIGHWAY sign posted at the entrance to the McLaren Tunnel.

It was 9:00, the end of the morning drive time, but traffic was still abysmal. The freeway was now dotted with the pickup trucks of carpenters, electricians, plumbers, masons, plasterers, landscapers, glass men, and fence installers, and with the sedans of insurance adjusters and government emergency personnel, and with large trucks carrying heavy equipment. Southern California's economy was on the move.

She normally left much earlier for her downtown L.A. office, but she'd had things to take care of at home. She'd finally managed to find a guy to board up her broken windows. With the demand these days, they were almost impossible to find. Glass men were even scarcer.

At first she'd thought she'd just leave the windows and French doors as they were, letting the Big One be her ersatz redecorator. At least she'd get light and fresh air. But one day last week she'd come home from work to find two teenage runaways in her condo, watching television and eating one of her Sara Lee butter pecan coffee cakes. They'd thought the building had been abandoned and turned out to be as afraid of her as she was of them. Iris felt sorry for them and gave them some money, but didn't sleep a wink that night, regretting her decision not to buy a gun.

Nothing beats firepower in strange times like these. Most everyone in postquake L.A. was being nice and cooperative and listening to their better angels, but there was always that other subset of the population.

She exited the Ten at the detour near Robertson Boulevard and joined the other drivers in gaping at the great fissure as they inched past it on the surface streets. The debris had been removed, the smaller pieces nabbed by souvenir hunters, and reconstruction was going full speed ahead both day and night. It still seemed impossible. The mighty Ten had fallen.

A bumper sticker on the car ahead of her said: CRISTO VIENE. ¿ESTÁS LISTO?

"Yeah," Iris said. "I'm ready for Him."

Finally reaching her twelfth-floor office, Iris pulled open the heavy glass door marked MCKINNEY ALITZER FINANCIAL SERVICES in raised brass letters. She let out a sigh of relief as she walked through the suite's plush mauve-hued lobby. Her priorities had changed considerably in the past few weeks. If she could get to work, get home, and manage to eke out a few hours' sleep between the aftershocks, it had been a good day.

She waved at the receptionist and swung left toward the sales department, her leather briefcase resting familiarly in her hand, her pump heels sinking into the thick carpet. She tried humming tunelessly to herself, like the squeegee man, to see if it changed anything. She altered her gait, adopting a long-strided, hip-swinging, loose-armed, above-it-all saunter, having learned long ago that appearance and consistency were essential to success.

She strode past the cubicles where the junior investment counselors were already at their desks, their telephone headsets plugged in, the lines open and ready for anything. Their voices were bright and clear and tinged with the urgency bred of hunger.

"Make money *and* pay lower taxes!"

"Every day lost is money lost!"

"Window's closing. Don't be left out!"

"Never too early to think about retirement!"

Iris could almost hear the snap of freshly written checks being pulled from their books. The day just might turn out okay after all.

She smiled at Warren Gray, who raised his eyebrows slightly in greeting. Both Iris and Warren had been with the firm for five years. After being neck and neck the first year, Iris's innate knack for the business began to shine through and she moved up quickly. She suspected that Warren resented her—many of the junior investment counselors did. It was a love-hate thing. They watched her not only to learn everything they could but to see if there was a way to topple her. She'd stopped caring about things like that a long time ago. It came with the territory.

She shot a smile at Sean Bliss, who was always immaculately groomed and tastefully dressed, who had pedigrees from the best schools, and who would have polite conversations with her at the same time as he lasciviously ogled her anatomy. Today he stared at her legs.

She intentionally brushed them together as she passed, making her stockings whiz rhythmically. *You're never gonna get it, Sean.*

She entered the range where she could see into Herbert Dexter's office in the northwest corner of the suite. The lights were on and she could see the reports he'd been going over, neatly squared on his desk. His desk chair was empty. One of his replica Remington sculptures, *The Wicked Pony*, was silhouetted against the bright sunlight that streamed in through his floor-to-ceiling window. The sculpture depicted a noble cowboy reaching up to grab the bucking horse that had thrown him. Dexter loved images from the Wild West. Even though the West they were living in now was about as wild as it gets, Dexter hid himself and his family in a gated community in a wealthy suburb. Iris and her cronies cattily noted that even the Dexters had been shaken by the quake.

A secretary from a temporary agency sat at a desk outside Dexter's door, brazenly going through the drawers. She was filling in for Herb's secretary, Louise, who had taken a few weeks off to deal with her quake-ravaged home.

Then Iris passed Kyle Tucker and mentally said, *Hi sweetheart.* She could tell he'd been calculating the proper moment to look up and greet her, not wanting to appear too anxious, which made him look all the more so. He was new to the industry, just barely out of graduate school, and was the latest in the firm's seemingly endless supply of fresh-faced, testosterone-fueled young men. He was cockier than most and gregarious and funny. The type of guy, Iris thought, who could tie the stem of his cocktail maraschino cherry into a bow with his tongue. He was rakishly good looking, with strawberry blond hair and an expressive, rubbery gash of a mouth that seemed to be always in motion, like a caterpillar.

During the few weeks that Kyle had been with the firm, Iris could almost see the wheels in his head churning as he tried to figure out the lay of the office political landscape. Now it was clear that he'd set his sights on cozying up to her. As she passed by, she smiled without showing teeth, a Mona Lisa smile, acknowledging him but remaining aloof. She'd seen them come and she'd seen them go.

She flitted her fingers at Amber Ambrose before turning to unlock the door of her office in the suite's southwest corner. Amber, an adult victim of parents who give their children cute names, was the only other female investment counselor at the L.A. office. She'd been with the firm for two years and was doing well. Amber flitted her fingers back as she continued her telephone conversation, displaying a perfect French manicure which made Iris conscious of her own uneven and broken fingernails.

"Top of the dung heap," Iris muttered as she unlocked her door and flipped on the lights. She stepped onto the carpet, which squished wetly under her feet.

"Son of a bitch." She dumped her purse and briefcase onto her desk, grabbed the telephone, and punched in three numbers with one hand dug into her hip and one pump toe tapping furiously. "Mario, Iris Thorne. I thought your guys were replacing my carpet last night. It's been clammy and cold in here ever since the earthquake and I've had it. *Today*, Mario!" She slammed down the phone.

She noticed Kyle cocking his head in her direction, his long lips held at a wry angle. She ignored him and jerked her chair away from her desk, grabbed a pair of athletic shoes from a drawer, flung herself into the chair, pulled off her pumps, and put them in the middle of the desk. "I'm not ruining another pair of shoes, dammit."

Amber came into her office and picked up one of the navy blue pumps. It had a slender strap across the arch. "Bally. Very nice."

"Thanks."

"Having a bad day?"

"It's been one *long* bad day since the earthquake three weeks ago."

"Maybe this will cheer you up." She leaned forward conspiratorially. "I have some dish."

"Oohh, tell, tell."

Amber closed Iris's door, then sat in one of the two chairs facing her desk. "I saw a fax—by accident."

Iris put her purse in the top drawer of a filing cabinet in the corner, took off her suit jacket, hung it behind the door, retucked her silk blouse into her skirt, and straightened her long strand of pearls. "By accident?" she said with a teasingly insinuating tone as she opened her briefcase on the credenza that stood against the western-facing window behind her desk. From the briefcase she removed several manila file folders and scribbled-on yellow pads and put them on her desk. She glanced at her phone. The red message light was not blinking. She thought it odd that she didn't have any messages.

"Well," Amber smiled coyly. "Accidentally on purpose." She abruptly leaned forward in the chair and announced, "Herb Dexter's leaving. He's going back to New York."

"No kidding." Iris flopped in her leather chair, her mouth gaping.

"It was from Garland Hughes *himself.* He said the district manager position in New York was waiting for Dexter and that he could be proud of the work he did getting the L.A. office back on track after the *tragedies* over the past couple of years."

"He actually used the T-word? How dramatic." Iris took her BUDGETS ARE FOR WIMPS mug from a desk drawer. It had brown coffee stains on the inside and the rim was smudged with a multitude of lipstick marks. "I never figured Oz for a long-termer anyway. Guess the earthquake put the last nail in the coffin." She smeared the lipstick with her thumb, trying to wipe it off, and raised an eyebrow at Amber. "Wouldn't that fax have come in on Oz's private machine in his office?"

Amber grinned mischievously.

Iris grinned back. "You're such a slut, Amber Ambrose."

"The paper on his fax machine jammed and that ditsy temp needed help." Amber innocently shrugged.

"Excellent work. I am *totally* impressed." Iris took some change from her desk drawer and stood. "I need caffeine. Follow me."

Warren Gray looked up when Iris opened her door. Amber followed her down the corridor past the investment counselors' cubicles.

"You taking ice princess lessons or something?" Warren asked Amber as they passed.

Amber gave him a cool look.

Warren turned to Kyle. "Just what we need. Two of them."

At the end of the corridor, Iris and Amber went inside the lunchroom, where they were again alone.

Iris poured coffee into her mug. "Did Hughes mention who they might put in Oz's place?"

"No."

"Hmmm." Iris looked thoughtful.

"What?"

"I could manage this office."

"They'd never promote *you*."

"Why not?" Iris asked warily. "Don't you think I'm promotable?"

"Of *course* you're promotable. What I meant was, they'll never let you manage *this* office. It's too hard to manage people who were your peers."

Iris didn't respond. She dropped coins into a vending machine and punched a button. A package of Oreo cookies slid from its wire holder and dropped into a metal bin with a brittle smack.

Amber said, "If you think you're ready, you should talk to Oz before he leaves or go straight to Garland Hughes. With your condo damaged the way it is, it's a great time to move. I know a lot of people who are moving to Oregon, Washington, Arizona…"

"*Leave* California?"

"Sure. Why not?"

Iris looked perplexed. "I don't belong anywhere else. I think I'd implode or spontaneously combust or something if I moved out of L.A." She took a cookie from the package, separated the two halves, and scraped the filling off with her bottom teeth, leaving pink lipstick behind. She offered a cookie to Amber.

Amber wrinkled her nose.

The lunchroom door opened and Kyle Tucker came in, holding the folded sports section from the newspaper in front of his face. "Hello, ladies." He walked across the room to the coffeemaker as Iris and Amber watched. He was long-waisted and tight-bodied and wore loose-cut Oxford cloth shirts that just hinted at the musculature underneath. There was a relaxed tension about him that made him always seem as if he was about to break into a run or a dance.

He picked up the pot and turned to face them as he poured coffee into his mug. Maybe he sensed they were watching him or maybe he was one of those guys who is not comfortable with his back to the door. His top lip wavered as he poured. Finally, both his thin lips spread across his face into a smile. "So. You decide to join my company softball team, Iris? First game's in two weeks."

"No thank you," Iris said.

"C'mon, Iris," Amber said. "I signed up. It'll be fun."

"You don't want me on your team," Iris warned. "I throw like a girl, I hit like a girl, I run like a girl, and I don't like getting knocked down or dirty."

"Aww, c'mon." Kyle stretched his lips high on one side of his mouth. "It's just for fun."

"I don't like to have fun," Iris deadpanned.

He chuckled, revealing his small square teeth. "Now *that* surprises me." He left the lunchroom.

"He's cute," Amber said.

"Adorable."

"He's not married, you know." Her eyes twinkled.

"He's too young for me."

"That's the new thing. Older successful women with younger men."

"Good Lord, am I an older woman?" Iris winced. "Anyway, it's my new policy not to get too close to anyone in this office. People come and go so quickly, it's like chumming up to the farm animals that might end up on your dinner plate."

"Well, he's certainly been asking a lot of questions about *you*. I overheard him asking Warren about the *tragedy* and the million in cash you're supposed to have stashed somewhere."

Iris pursed her lips and gave Amber a distressed look. "Won't that rumor ever die? Does anyone in their right mind think I'd be hanging around here if I had a million bucks stashed somewhere?"

"Oh, *I* know it's not true, Iris."

"Anyway, I'm off men. Have been ever since John dumped me to go back to his ex-wife."

"You ever hear from him?"

"Nope. I heard from a mutual friend that his house burned down in the brush fires last year."

"How awful."

"It's a shame. It was a great house. I guess the good news is that he couldn't have lost much in the earthquake." Iris crumpled up the cookie wrapper and tossed it in the trash. "Guess I better go move some money. Do you know if the phone mail is down? My message light wasn't blinking."

Amber nodded. "Everyone's messages are lost in the void somewhere."

Iris closed her eyes with exasperation. "Not again. The last time this happened, people left me messages and it took me three days to get them. What have you got going on today?"

"Cold calls." Amber sighed. "I wish I could be like you and have lots of established, wealthy clients who refer their wealthy friends to me, making me fat and happy."

"You're on the way to getting there, kiddo. Besides, there's something to be said for staying hungry. Otherwise you get lazy and forget to watch your back."

"I hate trying to convince complete strangers to give me their money."

"It's not so bad once you get the rhythm going."

"Easy for you to say. You were the cold-call cowgirl."

"Hee-haw!"

Three

Iris returned to her office just in time to answer her telephone, which was ringing in the polite tone she had programmed it to emit. She snatched a yellow pad and pen from her desk, crossed her legs, and swiveled her chair to look out her southern-facing window at the office tower on the other side of the street that blocked her view. If she pressed her cheek against this window, she could glimpse the rolling hills of Northeast L.A., where she grew up. It was only a handful of miles from downtown, but it seemed far away.

The telephone's display indicated the call was from outside the office, so she answered it formally, using her low-modulated, you've-reached-the-person-in-charge telephone voice. "Iris Thorne." She squeezed the cushion affixed to the telephone receiver between her ear and shoulder and poised her Mont Blanc pen above the yellow pad.

"Your mother said you'd done something with yourself. I wish I could say the same for Paula."

Iris leaned forward in her chair, her posture stiffening. She clutched the telephone receiver in her hand. The voice had thinned and quivered with age, but she immediately recognized it. It was just like him to assume she'd know who it was even after all these years and the thought made her bristle. "Mr. DeLacey. What a surprise. It's been a long time. How are you?"

She felt short of breath. She closed her eyes and tried to block the image of a man being beaten to death. It had happened twenty-five years ago, but the memory—in spite of herself— was as vivid as if it had happened yesterday. Through the years, she had tried to forget it and acted as if she had. Hearing Bill DeLacey's voice brought it all back.

"Yes, it has been a long time," he said in a way that seemed to sift the years through his fingers. "I could be doing better but I'm all right. I often wondered why you didn't call."

Iris angled her eyes toward the telephone receiver like one might eye a vicious dog while stepping around it. She was about to respond when she lost her opportunity.

"I guess you were in college the last time. Then your mother sold the house and all that mess and that was all she wrote. Would have thought your father might have called. After all, I was his employer for eleven years."

Eleven years under your thumb, Iris thought.

"Have to say he was the best handyman I had. Haven't heard from any of you Thornes except your mother every once in a while. Gave me your phone number. Said you graduated from college and taught deaf kids. I told her that was real nice. Then you went and got your MBA and I guess you stopped teaching to do this."

"Now I help people make the most of their money."

"Don't get defensive on me. The economy needs people to get their money out from underneath their mattresses. Where would I be without people with the moxie to take a risk? It was probably my example that gave you the idea in the first place. I'll take some of the credit for getting you down that road, anyway."

Why not take it all? Iris's face burned.

"Understand your sister's married and got a couple of kids. You never married, huh?"

"No."

"Huh. Well, like I always said, old Lily got the looks and Iris got the brains."

"That's what you always said," Iris responded flatly.

"You know Thomas graduated from that Yale Law School over there back East. He's still single. Getting married would be good for his political career, but he's going to do okay in this election without—"

"Election?"

"He's running for the City Council over here. Didn't you know that?"

"I live in Santa Mon—"

"Next election he should have a wife and some kids in the picture, plus I want someone to carry on the family name. Guess you know that Junior's still a bachelor too. Now, Paula, now I tried to get that Paula to go to college. Seemed like she'd do anything to defy me. Even when she was little…"

As Bill DeLacey talked, Iris pictured him sitting behind his desk in his cluttered home office where he ran DeLacey Properties. At one point, the mess on his desk grew so high that he draped it with an old plastic shower curtain and started a second layer on top. DeLacey Properties primarily consisted of low-income housing acquired to take advantage of federal grants and tax breaks. DeLacey turned a profit by not maintaining his buildings. He was a notorious L.A. slumlord.

"Where goes California?" DeLacey rambled on. "A businessman can't do business here anymore!" His voice was strident. "You got your high Worker's Comp insurance and your environmental regulations and your taxes and now you can't hardly hire the illegals, who are the only Mexicans willing to work. The native born think the world owes them a living. Let 'em go ahead and shoot the hell out of each other, that's what I say." He gasped several times with exasperation. "What's the small businessman to do?"

"It's a big problem." Iris plucked at her now damp silk blouse and glanced at a clock on her desk. He'd been talking for twenty minutes and hadn't yet arrived at the point of his call. She recalled visiting Paula at the ranch house on top of the hill that abutted the Thornes' property and getting trapped by Mr. DeLacey. She'd inch backward from him toward the door while he followed her, talking continuously, his body angled toward her, his index finger thrashing up and down with each ideological point made. Paula would follow him, making faces behind his back. Upon reaching the door, Iris would blurt, "'Bye, Mr. DeLacey. I hear my mother calling me!" and dart outside, hearing Paula's laughter fading behind her as she fled down the hill.

"Old Doc Grimes over at the Mayo Clinic did a study on manic depressives with paranoid tendencies and found that megadoses of vitamin C mixed with an amino acid found in corn husks given daily over a three-month period reversed the symptoms. Some years ago, I ground up some of this mixture and replaced Dolores's medication in her capsules…"

Poor Dolly.

Fifteen more minutes passed. Iris interrupted him in midsentence and lied. "Mr. DeLacey, I'm sorry to interrupt, but I have an appointment in a few minutes."

"Say! What do you hear from old Les?"

"My father?"

"He still living over in Azusa?"

"Last I heard."

"You don't talk to him either? You're not much on keeping up with folks, are you?"

"Mr. DeLacey, I really have to go."

"Oh, okay." He sounded dejected. "Well, I guess you know I don't make social calls." He took a deep breath.

In that moment of silence, Iris found herself imprinting in her mind the setting for the bad news that she sensed was coming. She became aware of her clothing, her tense, washboard-erect posture, the high, feathery, white clouds that streaked the warm January sky, the sliver of ocean that glimmered in the distance, and the telephone receiver that had grown slick with perspiration from her palm.

"Happened day before yesterday. Can't say I was surprised." He laughed in that way: rapidly inhaling and exhaling, as if about to hyperventilate. "Course, I thought she'd gone down there to take the Christmas lights off the trees with that extension ladder I bought from that new Home Depot they built over there. Now that's quite an operation. They've got plans—"

"Mr. DeLacey," Iris said sharply as if she was trying to wake him. "*Please*. What happened?"

He laughed again in apparent awe of himself. "I guess I tend to go off sometimes. Anyway, before Christmas she'd got it in her head to string lights up in the grapefruit trees there, the ones up close to the street."

"*Who?*"

DeLacey laughed again, sucking and expelling air, sounding more exasperated than amused. "Who? My wife! Who the hell else do you think I'm talking about? Are you even listening to what I'm saying here?"

Iris angrily opened her mouth but thought better of it and stuffed the smart-alecky retort she'd almost blurted. Instead, she calmly responded, "I'm all ears."

"She'd kinda been coming out of the fog she'd been in and was getting into things that she wasn't supposed to be getting into, so I told her to get the hell outside."

Iris was unable to remain sitting. She started to pace behind her desk and tried to goad him on. "Did she fall?"

"If you hold your horses, I'll tell you what happened. So, when she didn't show up around dinnertime...Thomas was coming over. He moved back into the district, you know. Bought himself a house over in Eagle Rock. Anyway, Junior went looking for her and there she was, hanging from a grapefruit tree. Made herself a noose from a rope I had in the garage. I bought that over at Home Depot too."

Iris wrenched her torso in response to a chill even though her office was warm. Suddenly exhausted, she flopped into her chair. "I'm stunned."

"Old Doc Vanderstaad was impressed with the knot she'd done up."

"Was she depressed again? Did she leave a note?"

"Note?" he shouted as if the suggestion was outrageous. "There was no note. Didn't expect there would be. She was never much on writing."

"That's not my experience. She used to always send me a card at Christmas with a little note in it."

"There was no note. I already told you."

"I thought she'd been maintaining okay."

"This was no surprise to me. If you'd bothered to keep in touch, you'd think the same thing. I always wondered why you turned your back on her."

"I did not turn my back on her."

"The hell you didn't. She practically raised you and your sister. Treated you girls like her own. I don't know why I should expect anything different from you, considering the way her own daughter acted. Both you girls thought you could go away and leave it all behind, but it don't work like that. It's too late to be sorry now."

Iris bolted from her chair. *C'mon, Iris Ann. Don't let him do this to you. You're not ten years old anymore.* She took a deep breath and regained her composure. "Does Paula know?"

"I don't know where she is. I don't want her regretting for the rest of her life that she didn't go to her own mother's funeral. It's tomorrow. You have to make sure she comes."

"Mr. DeLacey, I don't know where Paula is either. It must be twenty years since I've talked to her."

He paused.

After his seemingly endless words, the silence was unnerving. Iris worried her string of pearls.

"I thought you two girls were friends."

"We *were* friends, Mr. DeLacey. We…drifted. There was a fight and…"

"That's Paula for you. Always pushing everyone's buttons. I don't know where she gets it from. Her mother wasn't the smartest female in the world, but she had a good heart. Paula owes it to her mother to come to her funeral. Your mother said that if anyone could get Paula to come, it'd be you."

"My mother?"

"I told you she gave me your number."

Iris again started pacing behind her desk. "Like I said, Mr. DeLacey, I don't know how to contact Paula. Have you tried a private detective?"

"Is this too much of a sacrifice for you? Think you can do something for someone other than yourself for a change?"

Iris slapped her hand on her desk. "Mr. DeLacey, I'll do what I can to find Paula but the funeral's tomorrow. That's not much time."

"You could find her if you wanted to."

"I'll see you at the funeral." She hung up before he could say another word.

Just then, the message light on the telephone began to blink. Her phone mail had apparently been restored.

Later that afternoon, Iris looked around and realized she didn't know where she was. The bumper-to-bumper traffic on the Ten had put her in a somnambulistic state and she had lost track of her whereabouts. Her *Thomas Brothers' Guide to Los Angeles and Orange Counties* had sat open on the TR's passenger seat for the past few weeks to aid her in devising routes around the impossible traffic. Her office hours, from six in the morning to two in the afternoon— set to parallel the New York stock exchanges—used to give her a reprieve from the weekday rush-hour traffic. But the earthquake had shaken everything up. Today she was enjoying the traffic's monotonous predictability. It explained why she couldn't do anything else.

She drove with the Triumph's top down, slouched in the driver's seat with her head against the headrest, relishing the perfect seventy-five-degree weather that had prevailed since the earthquake. Southern California seemed to be giving her denizens a long, sultry look and a soft caress while knowingly whispering in their ears, "I'll rock your world and you'll love me anyway."

The weather reminded her of the warm skies that had prevailed after another earthquake—the San Fernando quake of

February 1971. The bloody events surrounding that quake had permanently changed the Thornes' and DeLaceys' lives.

A Jeep cut in front of Iris. Its vanity license plates taunted: R U FREE.

She flipped open her cellular phone, called her sister, and told her about Bill DeLacey and Dolly and Paula.

"Why is he so desperate for Paula to come to the funeral?" Lily asked. "He never gave a damn about her."

"And then there's Dolly's phone message."

"Sounds like she fell off her rocker for good."

"Maybe it would be convenient for Bill DeLacey if everyone thought that," Iris said dryly.

"Are you saying she didn't kill herself?"

"In her message, she said she'd found her will, in which she'd left Bill everything, by the way, and didn't remember writing it."

"If that's true," Lily said, "she could have blown his chances of ever building DeLacey Gardens."

"Bill said she'd been coming out of her fog. Maybe he was afraid she'd start to put together the missing pieces about everything that happened in seventy-one. If Dolly wanted to blow the whistle, building DeLacey Gardens would be the least of Bill's problems." Iris remembered the traffic and the Triumph. She glanced at its temperature gauge. The needle had moved close to the halfway mark but was still within the safe range.

"Why do you want to get involved with the DeLaceys after all these years?"

"Lily, it's the last thing I want after everything I saw back then. I still have nightmares."

"I know you do."

"It bugs me that I never said anything."

"You were just a kid. Mom told you not to say anything because she was afraid something would happen to you."

"I don't think she knows I told you."

"She does. I told her. You still haven't answered my question. Why get involved with the DeLaceys again?"

"Dolly said she didn't have anyone else to turn to."

"What about her children?"

"She felt they're against her, too."

"Sounds paranoid."

"I know." Iris eased into the next lane to avoid following a mammoth truck. "I guess I can hire a private detective to find Paula."

"How much will that cost?"

"I don't know. Couldn't cost that much, could it?"

"But the funeral's tomorrow. The whole thing seems weird."

"Consider the source."

"Leave it alone, Iris."

"I can't."

"Why not?"

"Because Bill's right. Paula should go to her mother's funeral. Dolly would have wanted it that way. It's the least I can do for her. When I was a kid, Dolly was kind to me when kindness was a rare commodity."

Lily said nothing.

"Besides, the great William Cyril DeLacey himself told me I might think I can run away from the past, but I can't. Lord knows I've tried."

"So you've decided what you're going to do."

"Yeah. Find Paula." At least she would try.

Four

The night air on February 8, 1971, was clear with a cool snap that sharpened the sweet, thick scent of the citrus blossoms—like ice enhances lemonade. The old trees had grown thick and gnarled and occasionally a dead one stood barren and ghostly among them. The fruit, rarely picked, stayed on the branches year-round, the rinds growing thicker and lumpier over time. Eventually the fruit blackened and hardened into small brittle balls that split when they hit the ground, revealing the bright pulp inside. The pulp eventually withered and the fruit was reduced to hard, black, hollow spheres that bore no resemblance to their earlier incarnations.

In the citrus grove stood a small house that was originally built for the ranch's workers. Now Gabriel Gaytan lived there alone, having given his daughter Dolores and her husband use of the large adobe house on top of the hill, which overlooked the grove, on their wedding day eighteen years ago. As another wedding gift, he'd given his daughter title to a small parcel of the ranch.

The workers' house had stood empty for years. Rancho Las Mariposas hadn't employed any live-in help since it had been divided between Gabe and his two brothers after Gabe's father died. His brothers caved into the land developers' promises of riches and sold their parcels before their father's corpse was cold. Gabe vowed that his five hundred acres would never leave the Gaytan family. Part of his strategy for keeping it in the family was to make sure his grandchildren were raised there, thereby bonding with the land. As for himself, he was content to spend the rest of his days at Las Mariposas. His funeral ashes were to be scattered over it. The land was the source of the Gaytan family's strength. Without the land, they would be nothing.

Since Gabe was a widower, the workers' house was plenty large for him. There his exotic birds could sing and screech to their hearts' content without bothering anyone. After moving into the workers' house, Gabe added a patio for his birds, pouring the cement and raising the slatted wood canopy himself. The cages for the black myna, the small green Amazon parrot, and a brilliant blue-and-yellow macaw were now shrouded with the sheets that Gabe carefully wrapped around them each night.

Normally the birds' tittering and clucking as they soothed themselves to sleep emanated from the sheets, but a groaning, sputtering mechanical sound now drowned out the more subtle noises of the ranch at night.

Fifty yards away, in the middle of the citrus grove, Gabe was building a wall. Les Thorne and Gabe's cousin, Humberto De la Garza, were helping him, although Humberto seemed to be doing more drinking than helping.

A makeshift scaffold straddled a six-foot-high, ten-foot-long wood frame. Steel supporting rods were set down the middle. It was a ramshackle thing with slushy wet cement oozing out here and there from between the loosely fitted planks. Gabe wasn't much on details. He was more of a big-picture guy.

Standing on a platform placed across the top of the frame, Gabe dug a shovel into an open sack of cement and flung the powder into a churning cement mixer. The platform bowed beneath the accumulated weight. A white powdery halo settled on his already caked skin, clothes, and black hair. He picked up a bottle of beer near his feet and sipped thoughtfully as he watched

Les pour water from a bucket into the mixer. They worked by the light of a butane lantern wired to the scaffold.

When the bucket was empty, Les tossed it to the ground, splashing water onto Humberto, who sat on the ground, leaning his back against a lemon tree.

"*Pince cabrón!*" Humberto cursed as he abruptly rolled out of the way, still grasping his beer bottle. He slowly stood, first checking to make sure his head cleared the branches above him. He was six feet five inches tall. His head was big and square and topped with an unkempt mop of thick black hair. Dense hair, too uncultivated to be called a beard, covered the lower half of his face and the top of his neck. His thick lips, shiny with beer, protruded through the facial hair like two moist slugs. He staggered, almost stepping on a black, shaggy dog.

"Watch it, *Gigante!*" Gabe said with annoyance. "Don't step on Perro."

Humberto raised his hand which dwarfed the beer bottle he still held, and pointed at the dog. His voice was deep and resonant and clumsy with alcohol. "Damn thing's always under my feet."

"Don't you think you've drunk enough of my liquor?" Gabe asked.

"What? You don't want to show your cousin a little hospitality?"

"Why don't you do some work? Help me with this."

"I wouldn't waste my time. That's not going to mean nothing to DeLacey."

"It will. Every day it'll remind him that beyond this, Bill DeLacey will *not* go."

"Looks like it's already going to fall over," Humberto said. "Probably won't even be standing by tomorrow morning."

"This wall's stronger than you think," Gabe boasted. "It's gonna be here a long time."

Les adopted a spread-legged stance on top of the scaffold and crossed his arms over his chest. His khaki work clothes, smeared with cement, and disheveled appearance did not obscure his blond good looks. His hair was clipped in a crew-cut style.

His chest and arms had been built up by years of manual labor. His skin was tanned, the creases in the corners of his eyes whiter than the rest from squinting in the sun. Standing six feet tall, he cut an imposing figure. He was smiling with closed lips, not because he found something amusing but because he felt uncomfortable.

Humberto raised his beer bottle in Les's direction. "What are you smiling at, Smiley?"

Les appeared embarrassed to be singled out. He drew his hand across his bristly hair and began opening another bag of cement.

"Let him be," Gabe ordered. "Bill DeLacey's going to give him enough problems when he finds out his handyman is helping me." He chuckled. "A handyman. Like DeLacey even bothers maintaining those rat traps of his. Well, he's not building one here. I don't care what promises he already made to investors. He can't build on land that isn't his. Fighting off developers is nothing new to me."

He sipped from the bottle and thoughtfully rolled the beer around his mouth. "Bill DeLacey. Comes to California without a pot to pee in. *I* give him a job. And what thanks do I get? He takes my daughter. A girl of sixteen and a man of thirty-eight. Old enough to be her father." Gabe pleadingly held his hands out. "Was it so terrible, living with me? She never wanted for nothing."

"There's no figuring women, *amigo*," Humberto commiserated. "At least he made an honest woman of her."

"What do you mean?"

"She was pregnant, *hombre*."

Gabe waved dismissively. "I didn't care about that. I would have liked raising the boy. I missed not having a son." He frowned. "Maybe I should have married again after her mother died. Dolly was only nine. A girl needs a mother." He shook his head as if there were no words adequate to express his thoughts.

"It's time to get over it, Gabe," Humberto said. "It's been eighteen years. She's had three kids with him."

Les tipped the cement mixer bucket and poured wet cement into the frame. "Gabe, it's gonna take you ten years to build this wall. We should build the whole frame and hire some cement trucks."

"This wall will make a statement to Bill DeLacey," Gabe continued as if he hadn't heard Les. "It'll say, you might have my daughter and you might think you have your hands on the land I gave her, but you'll *never* get your hands on the rest." He began to laugh, rounding the flat planes of his face. "Even if Dolly's stupid enough to give him her land, he can't do nothing with it! He don't have access to the street." As he laughed, tears sprang into his eyes. His face was red and flushed from emotion and drink.

Les climbed down from the scaffold and began gathering the buckets that were scattered on the ground. "I'm getting more water."

"Bring back some beer," Humberto ordered.

Humberto waited until Les's footsteps on the dry leaves had faded before speaking. "Why don't you do something about that DeLacey?"

Gabe frowned. "Like what?"

"C'mon. We could work it out, you know?"

Gabe rubbed his chin.

"Place like this, lots of things could happen to somebody."

The clattering of crickets became audible and the cement mixer's noise subsided to a hum as Les walked through the citrus grove to Gabe's house. The dog trotted beside him, stopping now and then to investigate a noise or mark a tree, the tags that dangled from his collar tinkling together. In the patio, Les dropped the end of the garden hose into one of the buckets, then twisted on the water spigot. As the ten-gallon bucket filled, he walked to a kitchen window at the side of the house, from which a light glowed. The screened window was open.

Dolly was in the kitchen, on her hands and knees next to a bucket of soapy water, feverishly scrubbing the floor with a steel wool pad held in her bare hand. The floor was covered with thick circles of soap, dirt, and wax intersected by two broad trails that Dolly had traced with her knees.

She was barely five feet tall and reed thin, never sitting still long enough to gain an ounce. In spite of her slender figure, there was a voluptuousness about her. Her lips were full, her teeth pearly, and her smile almost too broad. Her cheekbones were pronounced on her round face. Her nose was flat with large flared nostrils. Her thick black hair grew low on her forehead and was rolled into a dense coil at the base of her neck, where it was secured with a carved wood, mother-of-pearl inlaid, two-pronged pin. She was thirty-five years old.

She had pulled the wide skirt of her dress between her legs from behind and had tucked it into the front of her belt, turning it into loose pantaloons. The dress's scoop neckline hung away from her body, revealing the tops of her breasts, which jiggled as she scrubbed.

She frowned at the linoleum as she scrubbed and scrubbed. Her frown deepened as she worked at a particularly difficult, practically invisible speck. She bore down on the spot, grunting and whimpering, rubbing and rubbing. The room was quiet except for Dolly's mutterings and the wet metallic noise of the steel wool on the linoleum. A patch of dirty soap grew pink as she continued to scrub even though the steel wool had cut her hand.

Les watched her. He looked at her dangling breasts and her perspiration-dappled brow. As she leaned closer to the floor, he leaned closer to the window screen.

A voice from behind Les said, "What are you doing here?"

The words startled Les and he accidentally brushed against the screen.

Dolly wrenched herself upright and gasped, self-consciously grabbing at the neckline of her dress with her soapy hand and crinkling it close around her neck. "Who's there?"

She saw a shadow move outside the window and tried to scurry away from it. Her bare feet swam against the slick linoleum, not finding traction. Now in a panic, she tried to crawl out on her hands and knees.

"It's just me, Mom," eleven-year-old Thomas droned. He looked at Les and rolled his eyes. On Thomas, his father's angular, aristocratic features were softened by his mother's dark, sensual ones. He was handsome to the point of almost being pretty. "Les is here too."

"Sorry I scared you, Dolly," Les said.

Conscious of her disarray, she released her dress and smoothed it. She walked to the window and looked through the screen, peering at Les and Thomas, then squinting into the darkness past them. "Where's your sister?" she asked anxiously.

Thomas shrugged. "She and Iris went off someplace. They don't let me hang around with them."

She looked alarmed. "They're not with your grandfather and Humberto, are they?"

"They weren't there a minute ago," Les volunteered. "I'm sure they're fine, Dolly."

She stared at Thomas with intense eyes. "Come inside. It's too late to be out. It's dark."

"Aww, Mom…Stop being a downer."

"Thomas! Come inside now."

"No. I'm going to help with the wall."

"I'll watch him," Les offered.

"Let's go," Thomas said.

"She cleans a lot, doesn't she?" Les said as he walked away with the boy.

"I'm sick of her. She's always psyched out about stuff that might happen. I don't know what her problem is."

Suddenly the air seemed to resonate with small sounds. The caged birds tittered. The dog's tags chimed as he scratched behind his ear with his back leg. The songs of night birds in the trees were clear and radiant.

Les turned off the running water and cocked his head. "The cement mixer's off."

There were angry voices in the distance.

Thomas gasped excitedly. "They're fighting!" He bolted through the grove.

Les easily overtook him and the dog bounded ahead of both of them as they ran toward lights flickering through the trees.

Bill DeLacey's brand-new buttercup yellow Cadillac was parked next to the wall, the engine still purring. The driver's and front passenger's doors stood open. William Junior, seventeen, hopped from foot to foot in front of the car's headlights, dancing on his short, chubby legs and impotently wringing his hands.

Humberto was holding DeLacey's arms pinned behind his back. The posture emphasized the otherwise slender DeLacey's impressive belly, which hung over the top of his belt, testing the buttons of his white shirt and pushing down the waistband of his beige polyester pants, crumpling the fabric across his groin. He had a long face with high round cheekbones and a sharply pointed nose that was perennially sunburned. The large pink mole on his left cheek had turned crimson, reflecting his anger. He was fifty-six years old. "You goddamn good-for-nothing!" he snarled at Junior. "Do something!"

"William DeLacey Junior," Gabriel taunted. "Bill DeLacey's namesake." He held a broken bottle in his hand, business end out. He laughed maliciously and squinted at DeLacey. "I'll never understand what Dolly saw in you."

Les ran from the grove and grabbed Gabe's arms from behind. "Drop it!" He pinched Gabe's arms until Gabe was forced to let the bottle fall.

"So old Les still knows what side his bread's buttered on," DeLacey said. Even in his compromised position, he drew himself up before he began to speak. "No man can serve two masters..."

"Humberto, let him go," Les demanded.

"...for either he will hate the one and love the other..."

The giant grinned. "Get him to shut up first."

Thomas ran to Humberto and yelled. "Let my father go, you goofball!"

"Now there's a fine boy," DeLacey said. He twisted in Humberto's grasp to glance at Junior. "See your brother?"

Junior's chipmunk cheeks flushed.

"You're just trying to break him," Gabe said to his son-in-law. Then he turned to his grandson, Junior. "But it won't work, will it Junior? He's made stronger than you think."

"Break him? I'm trying to build him up." DeLacey's mouth went slack with disbelief. The world seemed to consistently surprise and dismay him. "You Mexicans." He paused, as if that explained everything. "That's what this whole thing's about, making a future for your grandchildren."

Gabe said, "Don't try to make this out like it's for the children. This is about saving *your* ass. It's not my problem that you took people's money and promised to build apartments here. My problem's making sure you don't get your hands on this land."

Les sighed. "Let's all go home." He leaned around to look into Gabe's face. "Have you calmed down?"

"Yeah, yeah. I'm fine."

Les released him.

"Let me go, Humberto," DeLacey said. "Party's over."

Humberto didn't move. He winked at Gabe.

Gabe snatched the broken bottle from the ground and began running with it toward DeLacey. Les lunged to tackle Gabe, but he slipped through his fingers. Thomas angrily ran after him. Junior froze while Humberto continued smiling sadistically, still tightly holding DeLacey. The dog barked frantically. A piercing scream cut the night. Gabe kept coming. DeLacey tried to double over to lessen the striking area. Reaching the wall, Gabe spun, missing DeLacey and smashing into the wooden frame. The wood cracked as it absorbed the blow.

The giant released DeLacey.

Thomas flung himself onto his father. Junior got inside the Cadillac as if to hide.

Gabe's laughter rang out. Humberto joined him.

Something white flickered in the car headlights. Dolly ran into the clearing. "Stop it!" Her hands were clenched by her sides, her arms were rigid, and the tendons on her neck stood out. "Stop this fighting. I can't stand it!"

"Thomas, get in the car," DeLacey ordered. "Dolly, come on."

Dolly ran through the trees. "I hate you both. My life's a living hell!"

"Hey, *primo*, look." Humberto pointed at a wet stain that had spread across the front of DeLacey's pants. His bladder had released involuntarily.

Gabe strutted in front of the car. "See, boys, see what the great Bill DeLacey is made of?" DeLacey released the Cadillac's parking brake with a thud and gunned the engine. The car skidded on the dirt road and veered unsteadily as it sped up the hill. When it rounded the bend, DeLacey and his sons finally lost sight of Gabe and Humberto behind them, standing in the middle of the road, pointing and laughing

Five

"Take some."

"I don't want any."

"Take some."

"I don't need that to get high. I get high on life."

Paula choked with laughter. Thick white smoke billowed from her mouth. "Right! Me too." She wearily shook her head. "Just living here is a trip. A bummer." She was fourteen.

They were in a toolshed that stood among the trees a hundred feet from Gabe's house. Milky moonlight filtered between gaps in the ill-built walls and shone brightly on the bare wood floor. The unfinished walls were lined with black tarpaper that had curled in the corners and torn in spots. Tools hung from nails in the raw walls. A tall wooden work table next to the door held cans of paint and varnish and jam jars containing nails, screws, and bolts.

Paula and her next-door neighbor, Iris, also fourteen, reclined on bags of manure and cement. Iris's mixed-breed German shepherd, Skippy, lay with his large body rolled against her. A votive candle on the floor twinkled in its molded glass holder.

"Did I tell you about when Mike and I were blasted on Boone's Farm and fooling around up behind the radio towers?" Paula leaned back on her elbows, stretched her legs out, and dropped one ankle on top of the other. She flicked her head, tossing her long, dark brown hair over her shoulder.

"We were humping, you know? And this guy comes *hauling* out of the radio station. He's all yelling, 'Hey! You kids!'" She laughed throatily. "It was brutal."

"I don't know why you get loaded so much. It's not gonna get you anywhere." Iris drew her nails across the thick fur on Skippy's head. The dog flicked his long tongue at her ankle, which was exposed underneath the hem of her jeans.

"So who wants to get anywhere?" Paula took another hit on the joint. "Did I tell you about Mike's friend who lives on a commune up north? They grow their food, make their clothes, everyone shares everything." She weaved her head up and down. "Sounds bitchin'." She slitted her dark brown eyes at Iris. "Think I'm gonna go. Blow this berg."

Iris ignored her. She'd learned to discount at least half of what Paula said. "So what's it like?"

"What?"

"Doing it."

"Sometimes it's okay."

"Is Mike the only one?"

"Nah."

"Was he the first?"

"Nah."

"Who? Jess?"

Paula shook her head.

Iris furrowed her brow. "Kenny?"

"I'd never ball Kenny. Just drop it."

"Manny?"

Paula's face grew dark. "Just forget it, Iris."

But Iris wasn't about to forget it. "Tell me."

Someone pulled hard on the block of wood screwed onto the door that served as a handle. The years of temblors had shifted the door so that it stuck in one of the corners. It bowed slightly before it creaked and scraped open. A diminutive figure, backlit by moonlight, stood in the doorway.

"Fucking Thomas," Paula said derisively as she quickly hid the joint. "Get the hell out of here."

He came inside anyway.

"Close the door," Iris snapped, trying to sound as tough as Paula.

"You missed the fight." Thomas sat cross-legged on the floor and began stroking Skippy's back. The dog acknowledged him by darting his tongue against Thomas's hand. "Grandpa was going to stab Dad with a bottle. Humberto was holding him." He glanced at Iris, trying to catch her eye.

Paula shook her head. "I wish they would kill each other."

"Mom came running out, screaming."

"Don't tell me she's losing it again."

"It's Grandpa's fault. He always starts the fights," Thomas said. "Dad says you can't stop progress."

"Kiss ass," Paula chided.

"Dad says he doesn't care if he has to fight with Grandpa over the land. If there's no struggle, there's no progress." Thomas pulled the dog's silky ear between his fingers over and over. "You've been smoking marijuana."

"I have not."

"I can smell it. Dad says—"

Paula kicked her sandal-clad foot at Thomas. "Get out of here, Daddy's boy. You make me sick."

"Don't get bent." He flirtatiously looked at Iris as he stroked the dog's ear. "She wants me to stay."

"Thomas likes Iris," Paula sang.

"I want you to go," Iris said.

He sharply twisted the dog's ear between his fingers.

Skippy yelped and gave Thomas a hurt look. Iris gasped and pulled the dog close to her. She looked at Thomas with horror.

Thomas shrugged. "So? I didn't do anything."

Paula kicked Thomas, hard. "Psychopath."

The kick brought tears to Thomas's eyes, but he just laughed. He left the shed, still laughing.

Through the open door, Iris heard a voice in the distance. "My mother's calling me. I'd better go before I get it."

It was late. The crickets were quiet and the air was soundless except for Humberto's drunken snoring. He had passed out under a lemon tree. He snored loudly, then paused, as if he'd stopped breathing. Then he gasped for air with a long, wet noise and partially woke up. "What did you say?" He changed the position of his arms and fell asleep again.

Gabe picked up two hammers from the ground, slid the handles between his belt and pants, then picked up a shovel. He looked at Humberto and pressed his thick lips together, his mouth forming a downward arc.

Les swung a pickax over his shoulder. "Is he gonna stay out here all night?"

"Why don't you take him to the house, then come back and help me clean up."

Les dropped the pickax, bent over Humberto, and tried to pull him up.

Humberto rolled his tongue around his mouth and dryly smacked his lips. "It's hot out here."

"You're drunk. Get up," Les said.

The giant struggled to his knees and Les helped pull him to his feet. After Humberto managed to raise his leg and take one unsteady step, he began plodding quickly as if, once in motion, he couldn't stop.

Les leaned against him, trying to keep him upright. "Just don't fall on me."

They disappeared in the grove.

Gabe hoisted the heavy pickax over his shoulder. Weighted down with tools, he walked through the trees to the toolshed, the dog gamboling behind. Once there, Gabe leaned the shovel against the wall and pulled hard on the door. It bowed and finally scraped open. He grabbed the shovel and stepped inside.

A triangle of moonlight from the open door cut across the wood plank floor. Perro ran ahead into the shed. Gabe let the pickax clatter to the ground. He pulled the two hammers from beneath his belt and set them on the work table. Walking to the back of the shed, he hung the shovel by its head between two nails in the wall.

The wood floor creaked behind him.

He turned around. A figure was silhouetted in the moonlight. The dog was wagging his tail.

"Who's that?" Gabe asked. He smiled, his lips parting to reveal his crooked teeth. "So you came to pay me a visit, huh?" He grabbed the pickax by its handle and dragged it across the floor. The noise masked the sound of the heavier of the two hammers being picked up from the table.

"What could you want this late at night?" His back was to the door as he hung the head of the pickax between two nails. "Cat got your tongue?"

The first blow of the hammer was not true but glanced against the side of Gabriel's head. Still, it stunned him and made his knees buckle slightly. He slowly turned. "Wha…"

The dog cowered and began to whimper.

The second blow hit Gabe squarely on the left side of his head, which cracked with a muted wet noise like an orange being trampled. He still didn't fall. He touched his head and his mouth contorted when his skull felt spongy and soft beneath his fingers. Then he collapsed straight to the floor like a released marionette. Bright red blood meandered across the wood planks.

The assailant slowly walked from the shed into the grove.

Perro frenetically pranced around and over Gabe, nudging his body with his nose. Then he ran outside the shed, raised his head, and began to wail.

Six

At 6:01 a.m., February 9, 1971, the shaking started.

Iris moaned, "Five more minutes, Mom." But the shaking didn't stop.

Her bed scuttled across the hardwood floor. A ceramic lamp on the nightstand rocked precariously back and forth on its base. Doorknobs and hinges rattled as they worked from their supports. Bottles danced on the dresser, slipped off the edge, and crashed on the floor. Windows clattered in their frames. The earth itself seemed to growl.

Iris wanted to steady the lamp, to get up, to hide, to wake up from this nightmare but—she could not. All she could do was lie flat on her back, clutching both sides of the mattress, praying for it to stop.

She envisioned her death: the daffodil-yellow plaster walls folding on top of her, as pliant as a sand castle, pinning her to the bed, crushing her, smothering her. She screamed. She started to cry. Then it stopped.

She tentatively put one bare foot on the cool floor. She tried the other one. As soon as she was standing, she was knocked to the ground by an aftershock.

"Iris, Iris!" Her mother, Rose, pounded on the bedroom door. A bookcase had fallen against it, holding it closed.

Iris got up and dragged the bookcase far enough out of the way to open the door a crack.

"Thank God you're all right." Rose nervously fingered the rigid pink plastic rollers in her short henna-tinted hair.

Iris wobbled past her into the short hallway of the three-bedroom, one-bath home and walked into the living room. "Was that an earthquake?"

The house was dark. Dim light filtered through the big picture windows in the living room and the smaller windows in the kitchen. The street lights were off. Birds, normally boisterous and clamorous at this time of the morning, were silent.

Iris's seventeen-year-old sister, Lily, futilely toggled a wall switch up and down. She turned on the television, which remained black, and continued walking through the house, flipping on switches. "There's no electricity!"

A low noise started somewhere in the distance and grew louder, rolling closer like an ocean wave. The house shuddered once before beginning to steadily tremble, rising to a peak that quickly waned.

"Whoa." Iris stood spread-legged in the middle of the floor. "Why won't it stop?"

Lily put the telephone receiver to her ear and then held it out as if its inoperativeness was visible. "The phone's dead too."

"Where's Dad?" Iris asked.

"Put your shoes on," Rose said. "There's glass."

"How am I supposed to call Jack?" Lily demanded.

"You don't need to be calling Jack."

"Dad's not here?" Iris asked.

Rose picked up two pieces of a broken decorative plate and fit them together. "Your father didn't come home last night."

Iris and Lily looked at their mother.

"You heard me."

"He's never stayed out all night before," Lily remarked.

Just then, Les Thorne opened the front door that led directly into the living room. His khaki work clothes were fresh and his hair and skin smelled of soap.

"Dad!" Iris exclaimed. "We had an earthquake." She ran up to him expectantly as if to hug him.

He just looked at her and said, "You shouldn't be walking around barefoot like that."

Iris's face fell.

"I told them, but they don't listen to me." Rose began pulling the rollers from her hair and slamming them onto an end table. She rarely allowed herself to be seen with her hair undone and her face raw. She looked uncharacteristically vulnerable. "Where have you been?"

Iris gave them both a fatigued look. "Great, a fight." She walked outside.

Les answered without looking at his wife. "I was at Sonja's all night."

Rose put her hand on her hip. "You admit it, just like that?"

"Rose, I don't want to talk about it."

Lily skeptically looked her father over. "At least he showered before he came home."

"I'm going to check the house." He walked back outside.

Rose followed him, her arms tightly clasped across her chest. "You think you're the lord and master of the house and you don't have to answer to—"

"The phones are back on!" Lily shouted exuberantly from behind the Venetian blinds over the kitchen windows.

Iris stood on the corner of the front lawn. "Skippy!" She whistled with several short breaths. "Here, Skippy."

Houses a few blocks away had electricity, the twinkling lights fading in the dawn. Neighbors wearing nightclothes had begun to wander out of their dark houses and onto their front lawns. Sirens screamed in the distance.

The couple who lived across the street stood on their lawn, listening to a transistor radio that broadcast thinly. "Everything okay over there?" the man shouted to Rose.

"We're just fine," she said gaily, self-consciously smoothing her hair. "Everything's a mess, of course. You?"

"We made out okay."

"Have you seen my dog?" Iris asked.

"Sorry dear, we haven't."

Jack Rossi pulled his pickup truck, the car radio blaring rock music, to a screeching stop in front of the house. Almost simultaneously, the screen door flew open and Lily, her freshly brushed, long, wavy blond hair flowing down her back, bounded down the cement porch steps, the wooden soles of her clogs clicking smartly. She was dressed in skintight jeans and a similarly tight T-shirt. A thin strand of love beads bounced on her braless chest. She ran across the grass and through the truck's passenger door in half a second.

"Let's go," she told him urgently.

"Lily!" Rose shouted. "Where are you going?"

"Just to see what's going on."

"What about school?"

"The radio said they're closed until they can check them."

Iris let out a whoop and ran across the lawn. "Wait up."

"Get lost, weirdo," Lily said. "Let's go, Jack."

"Iris, you have to stay here," Rose said. "Go clean up your room."

"I never get to go anywhere." Iris stomped up the front steps and stood on the edge of the porch with her hands on her hips. "When I get old enough I'm going to do whatever I want and *no one's* going to stop me."

Her mother warned, "Don't wish too hard for what you want, young lady. You just might get it."

"Why wouldn't I want to get what I want? That doesn't make any sense."

A black-and-white Los Angeles Police Department patrol car rounded the corner at the bottom of the hill and began to speed up it. All the neighbors walked to the edge of their lawns to watch as the police vehicles went into Las Mariposas.

Rose looked at Les. "What happened? Why don't you go see?"

Les shrugged. "I'm going to check my vegetable garden."

"You and that damn garden. If you spent as much time with your family as you spent…"

Iris went inside the house. While she was changing her clothes the electricity was restored, powering all the appliances that Lily had left on. Iris let the television blare and the blender churn and left the house via her bedroom window, disguising her departure by replacing the window screen.

She walked across the narrow strip of grass separating her house from the chain-link, barbed-wire-topped fence that encircled Las Mariposas, and crawled through an unfastened spot. In her backyard, she saw her father examining his garden, stooping periodically to check something, and her mother following a short distance behind with her arms folded across her chest.

The citrus grove was littered with a fresh blanket of white blossoms and fruit on top of the existing layer of dead leaves and tender, new wild grass. A pair of squirrels chased each other across the treetops. Sparrows tittered from the smaller branches. Crows strutted among the fallen fruit. The oily leaves of the trees clattered in the breeze, which carried the sweet smell of citrus through the air.

"Skippy!" Iris whistled three short notes. She walked many yards before the familiar sound of her parents arguing—her mother's screeching, her father's flat responses—finally faded.

Seven

"I didn't kill him." Tears streaked Humberto's cheeks. His thick beard was in disarray and he sorrowfully hung his big head. His hands were handcuffed behind his back. "I was passed out in the bedroom. I didn't wake up until the earthquake," Humberto wailed. "He was my friend!" The giant's clothing reeked of perspiration and sour beer.

Officer Gil Alvarez turned to Bill DeLacey. "What makes you think this man killed Gabriel Gaytan?"

"Old Humberto has a tendency to get violent when he drinks. I have several witnesses to that effect." DeLacey's fine brown hair was disheveled, exposing the bald spot that he usually tried to camouflage with artful hairstyling. He hadn't yet shaved and his whiskers were salted with gray. His white shirt was hastily donned, its tail partially hanging out the back of his pants. "Gabriel was going to throw him out. He's been freeloading here for a month. And this is the thanks poor Gabriel gets. Gets his head bashed in with a pickax."

"He's trying to set me up. He's the one who killed him! They were always fighting."

DeLacey raised his index finger like a baton. "Now I want to know why it took you men almost an hour to get here. Between the personal and business taxes I pay—"

"Frankly, Mr. DeLacey," Alvarez interrupted, "we made a special effort to get here as soon as we could because the call came from Las Mariposas."

DeLacey reached down to pat Perro, who was tethered to a short rope that he held. The dog recoiled. "Well, you fellows must be very busy today." He smiled, his broad cheeks drawing up into round apples. His long yellow teeth were glossy. "I guess I'm out of line."

"If I killed him, where's the blood?" Humberto asked. "Why aren't my clothes bloody?"

Alvarez considered that and looked at DeLacey.

DeLacey confidently replied, "He obviously changed his clothes. Once you start digging around, I'm sure you'll find everything you need."

A second officer, Ron Cole, was looking at the crime scene through the toolshed's feeble door which had been propped open with a broken cinder block. Dust particles danced in a wedge of sunlight. Tools had fallen from their places along the raw walls. Some of the jam jars on the worktable had fallen over and broken, spilling nails and screws. A can of paint on the table had tipped over, popping its flat round top and spilling white paint onto the floor. A stack of twenty-pound bags of manure against a wall tilted precariously. One had fallen from the top and split open, partially covering Gabe's head and shoulders.

"I'm confused about something," Cole said. "How did your wife know he was murdered? His body's half-covered. He could have been hurt in the earthquake."

"She came down *before* the earthquake."

"*Dios mio*," Humberto moaned.

"Will you stop your whining?" Cole snapped.

Alvarez said, "Let's review the chain of events. Mr. DeLacey, your wife came down the hill to her father's house at five this morning to get an early start on housework."

DeLacey nodded enthusiastically. "She's an insomniac. Doing housework relaxes her. I tell her to take vitamin C and B complex but…"

Alvarez rubbed his chin. "On her way to her father's house, she hears his dog crying and follows the sound. She looks in the shed, sees her father lying there, presumably dead…"

"She said his skull was bashed in," DeLacey volunteered.

"…then runs back up the hill to get you. You head down, by yourself, and while doing so, the earthquake hits."

DeLacey indicated his pants leg, which was stained with mud and grass. "Knocked me down. Must have slid ten feet."

"You come to the shed, have a look around, notice the bloody pickax, and then you go all the way back up the hill to your house to call us." Alvarez turned to Humberto. "Through all this, you said you were asleep until the earthquake. Then you got up and started looking for Mr. Gaytan."

Humberto nodded excitedly. "That's right. Why would I be looking for Gabe if I murdered him? When you came, you saw me calling for him. Why would I be doing that if I—"

"Knock it off!" Cole yelled. "If there's one thing I hate it's a loud-mouthed Mexican."

Humberto glowered at Cole.

A smile pulled at DeLacey's lips.

"Mr. DeLacey," Alvarez said, looking warily at Cole. "I'm confused about a few points. Why did you go all the way back up the hill to your house to telephone when your father-in-law's house is just a few yards away?"

"I was afraid I'd run into Humberto. After all, he bashed Gabriel's head in. How did I know he wouldn't bash mine in?"

"But I don't see anything here that connects Mr. de la Garza with this crime."

"The pickax!" DeLacey raised his index finger. "You forgot the pickax. Humberto de la Garza is the only one here strong enough to smite a man down that way."

"Couldn't be that heavy," Cole commented.

"Not for a healthy man, but a woman or a child couldn't wield it with the strength necessary to bring a man down." DeLacey avidly gestured toward himself. "Neither could someone like myself with my bad back. I've been under a doctor's care for years. Can barely reach down to tie my shoes."

"Can't you see through that?" Humberto cried.

"It's that pickax part I don't get," Cole said.

"Why's that?" Alvarez asked.

"C'mere," Cole said. "Have a look."

Alvarez walked to the toolshed, stepping on the rotting wood front step that creaked precariously. He bent over as if he were getting a closer look at something. He then left the shed, walking straight to DeLacey. "How did you see blood on the ax when it's covered with white paint?"

"Paint?" DeLacey said.

"Looks like a can of paint fell over in the quake. The head of the pickax is covered with it."

Humberto dropped to his knees and looked up at the indifferent blue sky. "He didn't look! He set it up and forgot to check it. Thank you, God. Thank you for the earthquake!" He began sobbing and laughing at the same time.

Alvarez and Cole exchanged a glance.

DeLacey put his hands into his pockets, which reached far down his thighs because of the low rise of his pants underneath his belly. A multitude of keys tinkled from one pocket and loose coins rang from the other. "You forgot the other thing. My wife *saw* Humberto running from the shed."

"You never told us that," Alvarez said.

"It was a detail I'd forgotten until now."

Humberto looked at DeLacey with horror. "She wouldn't say that. You couldn't get her to." He looked beseechingly at Alvarez. "The woman's not strong in the head. He'll never get her to say that."

"Maybe we'd better talk to your wife," Alvarez said.

DeLacey still jingled his keys and coins. "You can't right now. She's resting. I had to give her a tranquilizer. Humberto's right. My wife's not psychologically sound but she saw what she saw. You can't do better than an eye witness, now can you?"

"Oh Lord, no." Humberto, his hands still handcuffed, clumsily climbed to his feet. "This is not happening."

Perro began wildly barking, as if sensing an impending threat.

"Hey," Cole warned. "Just cool down, *amigo*."

"Can't you see what he's doing? I won't be blamed for this. I didn't do it!" Humberto ran. He bolted into the trees and was gone.

"Shit." Cole ran into the trees after him with Alvarez close behind.

"Skippy! Where *are* you?" Iris called despairingly as she walked through the grove. She stopped walking when she heard a rustling noise. "Skippy?" She whistled three short notes. Something was running, trampling the fallen leaves and fruit, and it was coming closer. She tentatively whistled three short notes again.

Humberto burst through the trees with Cole close behind him. Iris ducked behind a grapefruit tree and clung to it, pressing her cheek against the pebbly bark. She heard a moan and a thud and peeked around the tree to see Humberto on the ground, his hands still cuffed behind his back, and Cole on top of him.

Alvarez, out of breath, reached them. "You caught him. Good."

Cole tried to drag Humberto up by the handcuffs but he was too heavy. "Get up, you stinking son of a bitch." He drew his baton.

Humberto rolled over on his back and tried to raise himself to a sitting position. One of his big legs swung out and kicked Cole.

Cole reared back his leg and kicked Humberto in the side. "Fucking beaner!"

"Hey!" Alvarez shouted. "Cool it, Ron."

Humberto's face hardened and he pulled both legs toward his chest and let them fly at Cole's shins, knocking him backward.

Cole rolled on the ground, grabbing his legs.

Iris held her breath and tried to make herself small.

Humberto clambered to his feet and started to run. Alvarez drew his baton and swung it against the backs of Humberto's knees. The giant again went down face first. Alvarez, his face red with anger, whacked the baton against Humberto's shoulder blades.

"Stay down!" he screamed. He hit him again when Humberto tried to get up and then hit him two more times across the backs of his legs.

Cole got up, ran to the giant, kicked him in the head, hit him with his baton, and kicked him in the head again.

Humberto writhed on the ground.

"Stay still!" Cole yelled as he continued to beat him.

Alvarez stepped away and wiped perspiration from his upper lip with the back of his hand. He gaped at Cole as if he had just become aware of what was happening. "Ron, c'mon! Knock it off." He tried to pull Cole away.

The giant bled from his nose and mouth. He was mumbling, "Stop, please."

Iris held her stomach. She felt ill, but didn't dare move.

Finally, Cole stopped. He smoothed his wavy blond hair and took a few steps into the grove. He was out of breath and seemed dazed.

Alvarez looked at him with disbelief.

Cole stared back. He jerked his head to indicate Humberto, who was moaning on the ground. "The suspect resisted arrest. Guess he got pretty banged up on the rocks and bushes when he fell down the hill."

Alvarez shook his head. "What the hell got into you?"

Cole glared at Alvarez. "Don't you be talking about me. I saw you smack him too."

"Let's get out of here."

It took both of them to haul the semiconscious Humberto to his feet. They were half dragging him through the grove when Cole put his finger to his lips and hissed, "Shhh."

Alvarez cocked his head.

Cole whispered, "I thought I saw a girl when I first ran in here." He took a few steps in the direction of the noise. "C'mon out, honey. Don't be afraid." He drew his gun when he saw a shadow move behind a tree.

Skippy ran out in a flurry of dead leaves, spotted the men, and began to bark.

"Stupid-ass dog." Cole leveled his gun.

Alvarez said, "It's just a dog, man. What the hell's wrong with you?"

Skippy turned and ran.

They dragged Humberto to the toolshed, where Bill DeLacey was sitting on the step.

He climbed to his feet. "What happened to him?"

Alvarez said, "He fell down the hill when he was resisting arrest."

"It's flat over there. Looks like he's been beat up to me."

"I feel dizzy," Humberto wheezed. Blood streamed down his face, which had begun to swell and turn black and blue. "Bill, don't let them get away with it."

Cole looked evenly at DeLacey. "We attempted to arrest this man for the murder of Gabriel Gaytan. He fled, which to my estimation indicates his guilt. When in flight, he fell down a hill. You have a problem with that?"

Humberto lost consciousness. The two officers let him drop to the ground.

Alvarez said, "Look, DeLacey. I think you've got a very flimsy cover-up going. If you don't ask us too many questions, we won't ask you too many questions. Deal?"

Eight

The magnitude of the San Fernando quake was 6.6 on the Richter scale. Fifty-eight people perished and 2,400 were injured. There was $511 million in property damage. The quake's strong motion lasted only twelve seconds. Most of the L.A. city schools were closed for inspections and would probably remain closed for several more weeks. It was a windfall for Paula, but Iris was already bored.

She cleared hard, round acorns from the ground and sat among the cluster of eucalyptus trees that shared the crest of the hill with the adobe ranch house. The long, stiff, silver-gray leaves swayed lazily in the breeze, releasing their heady scent and clattering like wind chimes. The adobe ranch house, where Bill DeLacey and his family lived, was on the highest hill in the neighborhood. From there, Iris viewed her world. To the west were the towers of downtown Los Angeles. To the east, snow-capped mountains glistened beyond the rolling foothills. In between, modest homes dotted the hills and valleys.

Just beyond the eucalyptus trees, the chaparral-covered hill sloped down steeply. A narrow road was cut into the dry hillside and it spiraled around and around, growing increasingly narrow, until it ended at the ranch house at the top. Farther down the hill, where the slope became gentle, was the citrus grove. The workers' house, where Gabriel Gaytan lived, stood in a clearing in the middle of the grove. Iris could see its red-tiled roof and its covered patio.

At the edge of the grove was the chain-link, barbed-wire-topped fence that encircled Las Mariposas. Just beyond it was the Thorne property. In the backyard, Iris could see the neatly planted rows of her father's vegetable garden.

Skippy and Perro lolled near Iris, their pink tongues dangling from the sides of their mouths. In the two days since Gabriel's murder, Perro had taken up tagging along with Iris's dog. He seemed lost. Iris felt a bit lost too. Humberto had died of his injuries that morning. Iris would have liked to have talked to someone about it, but everyone seemed to have something else to do.

Paula was busy with her new hobby, Mike, and her old hobby, developing bad habits. Iris's father was at work and her sister was gone. Her mother was home. Iris could see her hanging clothes on the lines strung across the tiny backyard. But her mother sometimes made Iris feel as if she were underfoot.

Iris had told her mother about seeing Humberto being beaten. Rose insisted that Iris had simply seen Humberto being restrained when he resisted arrest. She warned Iris not to tell anyone about it anyway. Not because she believed Iris's recounting of the incident, but because she didn't want Iris to be caught spreading such a terrible rumor. It wouldn't look good. It occurred to Iris that maybe her mother didn't want to believe her. Maybe she already had too many things on her mind. But Iris took her advice and didn't tell anyone, except Paula, of course.

So Iris retreated to Las Mariposas. Unlike everyone else, Dolly always seemed glad to have her around. The ranch and its two houses were infinitely more interesting than Iris's house and yard. And from the top of the hill, her house looked small while the world looked big.

The DeLaceys' L-shaped ranch house was a stone's throw from the eucalyptus trees. Three bedrooms and a kitchen had been added to the original adobe structure, which remained as the front of the house. The adobe had low ceilings and tiny shuttered windows. Its thick walls were coated with a crust of limestone that had cracked in spots, revealing the clay and straw bricks underneath.

A detached two-car garage stood at the side of the house. In the driveway, Junior leaned inside the open hood of his Ford Falcon and worked a wrench at the engine's guts while listening to a transistor radio.

Bill DeLacey opened the ranch house's heavy wooden front door and let it slam closed behind him. He walked with his legs slightly bent as if a broad stance was required to support his belly. It gave him a crablike appearance. "Junior! Time to collect the rents. Then we've got to take Gabe's will to the attorney." He smiled his toothy yellow smile. "Not much longer now." Junior smiled back, a bit tentatively. He was always tentative around his father. He was much shorter than Bill, taking after his mother more than his brother or sister did. "When are we going to break ground on DeLacey Gardens?"

"The will's got to go through probate and now I've got to fill out some goddamned environmental impact report the goddamned liberals in Sacramento have got us into. Three months, I'd say. I think I can hold the investors off that long."

"They'll be happy to get their fifteen percent."

"I'll deliver the checks personally." DeLacey raised his index finger. "It's that personal touch that's important in this business, Junior. Never forget that." DeLacey smiled at Junior as if pleased with him.

Junior, elated but embarrassed by the unfamiliar attention, quickly climbed into the car and started the engine. It backfired twice.

DeLacey was still smiling when he said, "You call that a tune-up?"

The words slapped the smile from Junior's face.

"When I ask you to do something, I expect you to do it right. Or maybe you can't do anything right."

"I can," Junior protested.

"Well, you don't act like it and you don't look like it."

Iris then watched the car, its tires spitting loose gravel, round the first bend in the hill and disappear, though she could still hear its sputtering engine. The car reappeared farther down and disappeared again, only to reappear still farther down on the narrow spiraling road, which had no barrier separating the edge from the steep hillside. It rounded the last bend and traveled past Gabe's house before it passed the chain-link fence to the street.

Iris walked up the ranch house's brick steps, turned the old tarnished brass door handle, and pushed open the thick door with her shoulder. She never rang the bell here. She walked through the tiled entryway and into the living room. Squares of light from the small windows washed the delicate white-and-gold-leaf French provincial furniture with which Dolly had chosen to incongruously furnish the rustic house. Gold plaster angels and replicas of medieval tapestries hung on the walls.

Iris walked down the low hallway of the adobe section, the air cool and musty, and peeked in a small bedroom. Dolly, her hair done in a long thick braid down her back, sat at a sewing machine that faced a window. She was pulling a length of black fabric with both hands underneath the bobbing needle. The machine's humming reached an angry crescendo as she sped to the end of the seam. The room had been Dolly's childhood bedroom and was her bedroom still. She hadn't shared a room with Bill DeLacey in years.

Iris continued walking until she reached the newer part of the house, where the children's rooms were located. She looked inside Paula's room. It was in its usual disarray of clothes and record albums. The bed was made. That meant that Dolly had changed the sheets that day. That was the only thing that Paula allowed Dolly to do in her room.

Since no one was stopping her, Iris walked into Thomas's room, which was next to Paula's. His room always seemed chilly. Maybe it was caused by the excessive neatness. His bed was always made. Games and books were stacked in a bookshelf. On top, green plastic army men were arranged for battle. In his closet, the toy trucks and cars that he'd outgrown were lined up side by side. The old toys had been replaced by Thomas's new one. Mounted on the wall was the rifle his father had bought him for his last birthday. Also mounted on the wall were pelts from rabbits he'd killed, skinned, and stretched himself. Assorted liquid-filled jars on top of his dresser held snakes, lizards, spiders, mice, and other small creatures that had been unfortunate enough to cross Thomas's path on the hillside. Iris peered at them with macabre fascination.

Iris left Thomas's room and started to head back to visit Dolly when she noticed that Junior's door was open. He kept it padlocked unless it was Dolly's day to change the sheets. Dolly must have forgotten to lock the door after she left.

Iris looked stealthily from left to right down the hallway. Since she had still been undetected thus far, she decided to indulge in a rare treat.

Junior had several guns mounted to the wall; Bill DeLacey thought it imperative that his boys be familiar with firearms. There was a stack of girlie magazines in the back of Junior's closet and a cache of candy bars and potato chips on a top shelf behind some sweaters. But none of those were the reasons why Junior kept his room locked or what drew Iris there.

Positioned on a platform in the middle of the room, displacing his bed and dresser, which were shoved into the corners, was Junior's Lionel model train set. The tracks meandered through a fairy tale pastoral landscape of villages and farms, over hills and dales and through forests all handmade by the seemingly thick-fingered, dull-witted Junior. He spent countless hours and almost all his allowance on it yet never ran the train for anyone except himself. Paula told Iris that occasionally she'd be awakened in the middle of the night by the model train as it whistled and clattered around its track.

Iris stared at it without touching it. It was very seductive. She understood why Junior loved it and why he kept it under lock and key. It was a dream. It was an image that resided on the surface of a soap bubble and just as fragile. Exposing it to the light of day and the comments and criticisms of others would have ruined it. She understood. If she knew how to climb into that perfect little world and ride that perfect little train, she'd do it too.

Figuring she was pressing her luck, she turned to leave but spotted something in the bottom of the trash can near the door. She reached in and gathered the tiny torn squares of paper that had been a photograph. She squatted down and put together a few of the pieces on the floor. It was a picture of Gabriel Gaytan with one hand around his daughter, Dolly, and the other around Junior. None of them were smiling.

Iris tossed the pieces back into the trash and headed back down the hallway. She wandered into Dolly's room, where Dolly was still sewing.

Dolly raised the foot to release the fabric and pulled it between her hands to stretch the seam. She jumped slightly when she noticed Iris standing in the room.

"What are you making, Dolly?" Iris asked. She always called Dolly by her given name even though her mother had told her it wasn't respectful. Iris protested that that was what Dolly preferred. Iris wondered whether Dolly didn't like being a DeLacey.

"A dress for Paula to wear to her grandfather's funeral."

Iris watched Dolly sew up the opposite edge of the fabric. "I wish I knew how to sew. I think I'm going to take it at school."

"Doesn't your mother sew?"

Iris shook her head.

"She probably doesn't have time. I'm lucky I don't have to work outside my house."

Iris grunted scornfully. "My dad says she doesn't make enough money doing Mr. DeLacey's books part-time to make any difference anyway. She wouldn't have time for me even if she didn't work. She never has time for me. No one does anymore. Not even Paula."

Dolly tsk-tsked. "She's growing up too fast. Just like me." She took her foot off the pedal and stared out the old thick window glass, still clutching the fabric between both hands underneath the needle. "I thought I'd make everything different for my children." She looked at Iris ardently and said, "But everything's going to change now." She set her jaw defiantly. "It's up to me. I can do it," she said, almost to herself. "I can do it."

Iris walked to an antique dresser of dark wood against a wall and picked up a small box covered in tufted purple velvet and gold braid.

"I just have to stay very busy. My husband says that idle hands are the devil's workshop." Dolly continued sewing. "After I finish this dress, I'll teach you how to sew, Iris."

"Really?" Iris was about to open the box when Dolly spied her.

"Don't touch it," she warned. "That's my good jewelry."

"I've never seen you wear jewelry."

"My husband gave it to me. I'm saving it for a special occasion."

Iris put the box back and flung herself onto the taut chenille bedspread that covered the twin bed. She leaned back on her elbows and swung her legs back and forth, kicking the bed. "Did you really see Humberto kill your father?"

"No. I saw him running from the shed when I went to see why Perro was crying," Dolly said as if she was reciting something.

"I guess he really did it, huh?"

Dolly continued sewing and didn't respond.

"So where are you guys going to live when they tear the ranch house down?"

Dolly stopped sewing and turned to look at her. "What do you mean?"

Iris continued kicking the bed and disheveling the neat spread. "Just now, Mr. DeLacey was telling Junior that it'd be about three months. That there's some probate thing and some environmental thing to do first."

Dolly started rubbing her hands one inside the other as if she were washing them. "How is it possible? They haven't read my father's will yet. My husband doesn't even know where it is."

Iris shrugged. "After he and Junior got the rents, they were taking the will to the attorney."

Dolly slowly stood, still rubbing her hands. Now she began to rub and scratch her arms beneath the short sleeves of her dress, rending the skin with long red marks. She stared straight ahead. "He said he was taking the will to the attorney?"

Iris stood as well and frowned at her.

Dolly straightened the bedspread, pulling it taut again. "How did...? But he can't...Does he think...?"

"Is something wrong?"

Dolly left the room, walked through the house and out the front door. Iris followed. Once outside, Dolly ran. Instead of taking the road, she ran straight down the side of the hill, losing one of her slip-on shoes on the first tier.

Iris picked it up and ran after her with the two dogs loping ahead. She didn't have the guts to take the steep hill as fast as Dolly and lost her when Dolly ran into the citrus grove. She finally reached the grove and ran through the trees. "Dolly!"

At Gabriel's house, Iris walked onto the patio. The macaw was out of his cage, which lay on the ground where it had fallen in the earthquake. The bird had made a perch of the wood handle on top of Gabe's barbecue. His head anxiously bobbed and weaved as he danced back and forth and flapped his great wings, iridescent turquoise blue lined with brilliant gold.

The green Amazon parrot's cage was still upright. He frantically worked his strong beak at the lock on the cage door. The black myna bird's cage had fallen over and its decorative dome had rolled off. The smashed cage was empty. Thomas was sitting on the ground, holding the dead bird in his lap and stroking its shiny black feathers.

The sheets that had draped the cages had easily slipped off during the temblor and were salted with whole and halved sunflower seeds from the birds' spilled food cups. Shattered crockery from potted plants that had toppled from the patio wall was strewn about. The plants' exposed roots looked fragile and forlorn.

The parrot and the macaw jutted their chests out and reared their heads back as they watched the two dogs sniff around the patio.

"Look at this," Thomas said as he touched the dead myna bird's black eye. It shone dully beneath the partially closed crepey eyelid. "Isn't it bitchin'?"

"It's disgusting."

"It wouldn't let you do that if it was alive."

"Did you see your mother?"

"She went in Grandpa's house. You want to know a secret?"

"Sure."

"I can't tell you." He continued stroking the bird and looking coyly at Iris. "I'll tell you if you let me look under your shirt."

"Creep!"

Inside her father's bedroom, Dolly pulled open the door of the small closet. She cried out and covered her head with her hands as items stacked on the closet's shelf, which had shifted during the earthquake, spilled out. It seemed as if everything was against her. A tear rolled down her face. A second tear followed, too easily.

"You'll be all right, you'll be all right, you'll be all right," she chanted like a mantra.

She took a deep breath, reached between the few garments that hung from the rod, and spread them apart. The safe was on the floor behind them. She crouched down and spun the lock. The combination was easy. It was the day of her mother's birth, then her own, then her father's. Her father had made her promise not to tell the combination to her husband and she hadn't. Still, it was easy enough for him to have figured out for himself. That's what she was afraid of.

She took a stack of envelopes from the safe and rifled through them. One said: WILL. It held several pages of lined white notebook paper, handwritten with a blue ballpoint pen.

Dolly skimmed the document, running her index finger down the pages, mumbling to herself as she read passages aloud.

"'I, Gabriel Gaytan, resident of Los Angeles, California, declare that this is my will...I name Dolores Maria Gaytan DeLacey as my personal representative. I have one child, Dolores Maria Gaytan DeLacey. I have these grandchildren...If I do not leave property in this will to one or more of the children or grandchildren I have identified, my failure to do so is intentional. I give $15,000 to each of my grandchildren, my coin collection to my brother, Raymondo...' Here it is, here it is. 'To my son-in-law, William Cyril DeLacey, I give one square foot of Las Mariposas to be dug up and placed in a box so he can always keep what he wanted most in the world near him. I give my residuary estate to Dolores Maria Gaytan DeLacey. If Dolores does not survive me, her living children shall take my residuary estate.'"

Dolly refolded the papers and put them back in the envelope. She closed the safe and arranged the clothing on the rod to cover it. She looked around her father's bedroom.

"What should I do? Hide it. Hide it until I think of something."

A large framed picture had tipped over on a nightstand beside the bed. She picked it up. It was her mother's and father's wedding portrait. Her father wore a dark suit and a bow tie. His black hair was short and slicked close to his head. Her mother was wearing a white satin gown with a long train swirled about her feet. She held a bouquet of white roses and orchids. A crack snaked across one corner of the glass.

Dolly touched their faces and again involuntarily started to weep. She pleaded with an invisible assailant. "Please no. I have to take care of my family. *Please.*"

Her tormentor didn't listen and the weeping escalated to sobbing.

The tears flooding her eyes almost blinded her, but she managed to slide the velvet-covered backing from the old frame. She pressed the envelope next to the photograph and tried to replace the backing. It wouldn't go. The envelope was too fat.

She shoved harder and harder as she sobbed harder and harder. Suddenly, the backing slid over the envelope.

She stood the photograph on the nightstand and dropped to the carpet as if everything that held her body upright had failed her. On her hands and knees, she buried her head between her arms against the floor and sobbed, her body quivering.

Iris finally found her and crouched beside her. "Dolly?" She put her hand on her trembling back. "Dolly?"

Dolly didn't respond.

From behind her, Thomas spoke dispassionately. "She doesn't know you're there."

"But she was fine before. What happened?"

"Just leave her alone. Sometimes she's like that for hours."

Iris looked at him with revulsion. "We can't just leave her like this."

"Sometimes my father puts her in a cold shower. After that, she goes to sleep. But I don't think you and me could lift her. Just shine it on. You want to play a game or something?"

Nine

Iris was awakened by her parents' arguing. She could only make out occasional words unless she put her ear to the adjoining bedroom wall. Eavesdropping on their arguments used to be a fascinating diversion for her, but after learning that all they did was argue about the same things over and over—a curious discovery—she just tried to tune them out.

She folded her pillow over her head to cover her ears, muffling the familiar sound of her mother's high-pitched, relentless harangue and her father's terse monotone responses—when he chose to respond at all. Occasionally there was the thud of a small item—a book or shoe—thrown by her mother.

Through the pillow, Iris heard something bang against the wall, possibly the closet door being flung open. Dresser drawers were opened and slammed shut. She hoped it didn't mean what she thought it meant. She got out of bed, put on her worn bathrobe, spotted with egg yolk and hot chocolate, and slipped on her fuzzy blue slippers. She opened her door, tentatively stuck her head out, and looked at the closed door of her parents' room.

That closed door had always baffled her. It implied intimacy and closeness and private things. But so little of what went on between her parents was like that, so the closed bedroom door simply seemed like a ruse. Who were they trying to impress? There was sex, of course, but it was hard for her to imagine them ever doing it. It wasn't so much because they were her parents as because she couldn't see two people who were so discordant coming together in an act that she had been made to understand was an expression of true love, despite what Paula said.

The door abruptly opened, which was not unusual. Her mother liked to drag the arguments through the entire house and sometimes into the yard. Iris quickly hopped back into bed, still wearing her bathrobe and slippers, and pulled the bed covers over her. Her bedroom door opened and she recognized her father through the slits she had made of her eyelids. He set the suitcase he was carrying on the floor and walked to her bed, where he stood as if he didn't know what to do. When he returned to the suitcase as if he were about to leave, she startled him by sitting bolt upright in bed.

"You're leaving?" she asked in a wavering voice.

He scratched his crew cut and frowned at the ground.

"Why?" she wailed.

"Well, Iris. Your mother and I…"

"You're leaving to go to Sonja. Why don't you just say it? I know what's going on. I'm not stupid."

"I know you're not."

"Why do you like her better than us?"

"I don't, Iris. It's for the best right now. I know you don't understand."

Tears began to roll down her puckered face.

"Ohhh, c'mon, Iris Ann."

She glared at him, tears streaking her cheeks. "You promised! You promised you'd never leave again."

"Someday you'll understand."

"I want to understand now."

"I'll call you, all right? I'll come see you."

When he leaned close to kiss her cheek, his whiskers scratched her skin. She wanted to turn away from him in anger. At the same time she wanted to hold him so that he couldn't leave.

He walked out the door, closing it. She heard him briefly open Lily's door, close it, then open and close the front door. Her mother was quiet. Iris imagined her following a few paces behind him with her arms tightly folded across her chest and her jaw set. When she did that, it accentuated the lines down each side of her mouth and made her look startlingly old. It frightened Iris.

She heard the engine of her father's truck turn over, then a whizzing sound as he backed down the driveway. Now the truck would be poised in the middle of the street in front of the house and the transmission would clunk as he changed gears from reverse to drive. She heard the clunk. The tears began to flow harder. The engine accelerated as he drove down the hill, the noise fading at the same time as her heart seemed to be dropping farther and farther into a pit deep inside her, so deep that she couldn't feel it. She feared it might be there forever.

Suddenly, the front door opened and slammed closed. It opened again, slammed again.

Iris crept out of bed and walked down the small hallway, from which she could see the front door at the other end of the living room. Her mother opened and slammed the door again, leaning into the effort as if the door were heavy. She wore the same slacks and blouse that she had had on that evening, which meant that the argument had been going on for hours.

She opened the door again and this time pushed open the screen door and walked out, disappearing into the darkness. The screen door slowly suctioned closed.

Iris remained standing in the hallway, looking across the dark living room and through the door that opened onto more darkness. Her tears had subsided into convulsive hiccups. Something scraped against the outside of the screen door. It was Skippy, standing outside, pressing his nose against the screen.

She walked down the hallway to Lily's room, which was at the opposite end from her parents' room. She opened the door without knocking. "Lily?" she said quietly.

"What do you want?" She sounded angry and fatigued.

"Nothing. Can I come in?"

"I have to get some sleep. I don't care what Mom and Dad do. I'm sick of them. I've got four months. Four months until I graduate from high school and Jack and I get married."

"Oh." Iris closed the door. She went outside through the open front door, sat on the cement porch, and buried her face in the ruff of fur around Skippy's neck. "I don't care. Let 'em all go. I don't need 'em."

She went around the side of the house muttering, "Who cares about them anyway?" The dewy grass moistened her fuzzy slippers. Skippy trotted beside her.

The steady sawing of crickets sounded as if the night air was panting. A half moon was bright in the clear sky. The songs of invisible night birds sent fingers up and down Iris's spine. Instead of calming her mood, the night air heightened it, making it clear and brittle.

She neared the backyard, and heard labored grunting noises. A field lay beyond the small, groomed lawn which was bordered by pruned rosebushes in neat beds. Several fruit trees grew in the field—white peach, yellow peach, apricot, Santa Rosa plum, black plum and fig. Her father's vegetable garden lay next to the trees. In the moonlight, Iris saw her mother hacking the garden with a hoe.

Iris gasped. She shouted, "Mom!" but her mother either didn't hear her or didn't care. She just kept swinging the hoe.

Iris ran across the lawn and through the opening in the fence around Las Mariposas. She kept running. The terrain felt uneven through the thin vinyl soles of her slippers. Skippy ran a few yards ahead, stopped to wait for her, then ran ahead again.

"I'll show them. They'll be sorry."

She passed Gabriel's dark house and the toolshed. Both spooked her, but she steeled herself against her fears. She kept running. She looked up at the trees, evaluating them, then discarding them as not right for her purpose. At Gabriel's unfinished wall, she found the appropriate one, the giant's favorite lemon tree, which had strong branches she could reach if she stood on top of the wall.

The wall, its wooden frame and scaffold, the spilled bags of cement, and the cement mixer remained where the earthquake had left them. The yellow police ribbon that had circled the area now lay like a bright earthworm dredged up by a storm.

Iris climbed the scaffold and worked her way to the top of the wall. Steel supporting rods jutted through the top. She carefully stepped between them and stood up, spreading her arms to balance herself.

"They can't miss me here."

She pulled the belt from her robe and tied a loop at the end but it wasn't right. She tried again, wavering on the wall, almost losing her balance, the bulky slippers providing poor traction. Skippy sat on his haunches at the bottom of the wall and stared up at her with his ears pricked. She eased herself into a sitting position, dangling her legs over the side. She fumbled with the belt again and managed to make an acceptable loop. She slid it over her head and pulled it tight around her neck as a trial. It uncomfortably restricted her breathing. She removed it and felt the soft skin of her neck.

"This is stupid. They're not worth it."

She undid the belt and fed it back through the loops of her robe. Throwing one leg over the wall, she straddled it and began searching with her foot for the scaffold, when the earth began to tremble. She frantically waved her leg, trying to find footing, but lost her balance. She grasped one of the steel rods with her right hand but her left skidded down the front of the frame, tearing the sleeve of her robe and embedding wood splinters in her hand. The aftershock continued to rumble and Iris struggled to hang on while Skippy ran in circles and barked. Then it stopped.

She breathed a sigh of relief and began to climb down the scaffold. She spotted car headlights at the top of the spiraling road up to Las Mariposas. The white lights became red as the car rounded the curve and disappeared around the back of the hill.

Seconds later, the headlights again swerved as they rounded the bend and again turned red. Soon, she saw no lights but only heard the engine coming nearer. The car had reached the bottom of the hill and would soon pass through the citrus grove on its way to the street. The headlights loomed between the dark trees. It was Bill DeLacey's yellow Cadillac. Instead of heading toward the street, it jumped the road and barreled toward the wall.

Skippy began barking wildly and prancing back and forth. Iris dropped to the ground and clawed at the weeds and dirt, struggling to get out of the way as the car engine grew louder and louder. There was a din of steel crumpling and wood splintering. The engine sputtered and pinged as if it were in agony, then finally died. The car hissed steam and drizzled fluids.

Iris inched to the car. There was movement inside. She ran to the driver's door and struggled to pull it open. It finally gave and Dolly tumbled onto the ground. Blood from a gash on her forehead trickled down her face.

Iris leaned over her. "Dolly, are you all right?"

Dolly slowly clambered to her knees. She touched her forehead and looked at the blood on her fingers. She held onto the car door to help herself up.

Iris tentatively reached toward Dolly, who snapped her hand out and grabbed Iris's wrist. She started to run into the trees, still holding Iris.

Iris ran a few steps with her, then stopped, digging in her heels. "No!"

Dolly's grip on her wrist tightened. She wrenched her head around to stare hard at Iris. Her eyes were wide—alert and wild like a cornered animal's. "Run. He's going to get us. Run!" Iris cried, "Dolly, you're hurting me!"

"Humberto's dead! He's dead! We'll all be dead if we don't run!" She tried to pull Iris toward the trees.

Iris resisted, digging her heels, one bare and one slipper-clad, into the dirt. She was pulled along anyway, stumbling and tripping. She clawed at Dolly's fingers; they were like a vise around her flesh and white with the effort. Skippy snatched at Dolly's ankles and yipped helplessly.

Then someone grabbed Iris's other arm. "Let go of her." It was her mother.

"Run!" Dolly's lips were drawn back, baring her teeth. Her eyes were feral. "We have to run!"

Tears blackened with eyeliner and mascara streamed down Rose's face. "You're going to break her arm!"

Iris looked from her mother's face to Dolly's and down to her arm which she was certain would snap in two. Those three things took on a surrealistic presence. They were the only things that existed. Time stopped.

Rose began to shove and kick Dolly. Dolly suddenly let go and Iris tumbled backward onto the ground. Dolly ran into the trees. Skippy followed her, barking.

Rose fell to her knees and gathered Iris to her chest. "Iris, Iris! Are you okay?"

She stared at her mother, dazed and speechless.

"My baby! You're safe. I knew that if she took you I'd never see you again. My beautiful baby."

"I am?"

"Of course you are! What would make you say such a thing?"

Iris shrugged her shoulders and stared at her wrist, where purple bruises in the shape of Dolly's fingers were already starting to form.

Ten

Iris walked through the ranch house looking for Paula, who wasn't in her room. She left the newer section and entered the old adobe, where the temperature behind the thick walls dropped several degrees.

She guardedly peeked into Dolly's Spartan bedroom, the hairs on the back of her neck tingling, perhaps from the sudden chill in the air. Dolly was not there and she breathed a sigh of relief. Since that nightmarish night three weeks ago when Dolly had crashed the Cadillac, Iris had kept out of her way. She stood in the doorway and looked at the carelessly made bed. It was not made at all, really. The bedclothes were just pulled over the pillows and nothing was tucked in. The little embroidered decorative pillows that Dolly had made were scattered on the floor.

Iris continued down the hallway, to the room at the end, which Bill DeLacey used as his office. She peeked inside. An old wooden desk stood in the middle. On a corner of the desk was a big lamp with a dingy barrel-shaped shade trimmed with gold braid. Behind the desk, Bill DeLacey sat in an old, high-backed swivel chair. The remaining floor space was piled with newspapers, books, and all manner of things. There was an early cabinet-style television, a manual typewriter, a pull-handle adding machine, and various detached mechanical parts of indeterminate provenance. A radio was tuned to a station that broadcast string renditions of popular songs.

Several prescription containers of pills were lined up on the desk. Iris watched as DeLacey set one container down, picked up another, and flipped the pages of a large book. He tapped his finger on a page and shook his head. "I wouldn't have prescribed this."

When he reached to pick up another container, he spotted Iris. "What are you doing there?"

"I was looking for Paula." She started to back down the hallway.

"Come in and spend a minute."

Iris tentatively stepped into the room that she had never dared to enter before. She curiously looked around.

"Hear anything from old Les?"

"He called to see how we were doing."

"Guess you know he quit working for me."

A blueprint spread across several stacks of newspapers caught her attention.

"Funny thing for a steady man like Les to up and leave everything." DeLacey smiled, casually leaning back in his chair and crossing his legs in a relaxed pose that seemed calculated to put her at ease. His glossy yellow teeth made him look predatory. "Did he tell you why?"

Iris shook her head. "Is this DeLacey Gardens?"

"Supposed to be. Just one damned thing after another. Now they want this environmental impact report. Damn tree-hugging liberals. You'd think my investors would understand, but they're starting to want their money back. On top of everything else, our city councilman tells me he has misgivings about the project." DeLacey shook his head at the floor and panted laughter. "'Grave misgivings,' he says." He began wagging his finger. "I told him, this is an elected position, friend. I just may run against you. Then you'll find out how this city should be run."

Iris stepped backward as if driven by the force of DeLacey's wagging finger. Her heel scraped against a pile of newspapers. "I guess I'll go look for Paula."

"Now wait just a minute." He leaned farther back in his chair, the old joints creaking, and picked up a large spiral-bound checkbook from a pile of junk behind him. "You're planning on going to college, aren't you?"

Iris shrugged.

"Course, with the amount of self-education I've done, I should probably have earned a Ph.D. by now. But that's not the way it's going to be when you grow up."

"I might be a teacher. English or something."

He briskly shook his head. "Computers. In fifteen years, everyone's going to have a computer in their home. Mark my words." He wrote out a check, pulled it from the book, and held it face out across the desk. It was made out for a thousand dollars.

Iris's eyes bugged. She'd never had a check before, let alone that much money.

"You open yourself a savings account and put this check in there." He pulled the check away just as she reached for it. "Now you know there's no such thing as a free lunch in life."

She half nodded and half shrugged.

"That means everything has a price. The price of this check is that you'll tell me if anyone says anything about Gabriel Gaytan's murder. Your father, Dolly, Paula, Junior, Thomas, your mother, anyone. Deal?"

"What would anyone say?"

"Well, Iris, people don't like other people to be successful. People will try to drag you down, any chance they get. I just want a little help watching my back. Is that okay?"

"I guess."

"You can tell your mother I made a little donation to your college fund, but our deal will be between you and me. Can I trust you, Iris?"

"Sure."

"There's an old saying, Iris. If life gives you lemons, make lemonade. Never forget that."

She folded the check into her jeans pocket and left the room. As she did so, she saw Paula slip down the opposite end of the corridor and into her room.

Iris followed and knocked on the door.

"Get the hell away!"

"It's me."

"Oh. Come in."

Iris opened the door. The room was piled high with discarded clothing and record albums. Posters of favorite rock bands were taped to the walls. Paula was quickly stuffing clothes into a backpack on the bed.

"What are you doing?" Iris asked.

"Mike and I are splitting tonight to go to this commune up north. The one I was telling you about."

"Splitting? For how long? School's supposed to open soon."

"You don't learn anything in school. Anything worth learning you have to learn on the streets."

"What about your parents?"

"Hell, my dad will be glad I'm gone. My mother never gave a shit about me."

"Of course she did."

Paula suddenly grew angry. "Bullshit! If she did, she wouldn't have spent so much time being crazy."

Iris picked up an old framed photograph from Paula's dresser. "What's this? Your grandparents' wedding? Where did you get it?"

"That's what I'm trying to tell you. Three weeks ago, before they hauled her off to the loony bin, she came running in here with that picture, asking me to take care of it. I'm like, what? Take care of a picture?" She bitterly shook her head. "I'm getting out while I still can. People have a tendency to die around here. I'll end up being kicked to death like Humberto and no one giving a damn. Those cops'll get away with it, you know. Fucking establishment."

"Shhh!" Iris hissed.

"I haven't told anyone what you saw," Paula droned. "I'm not stupid."

"My mom says I didn't see what I saw. She says they were just restraining him. She says I have an overactive imagination. She told me to forget about it."

"You'd better."

"Do you really think they'll get away with it?"

"Police brutality against the underclass. Same old story. Course, after the revolution everything'll change."

The door opened and Dolly stepped into the room.

Paula threw the backpack off the far side of the bed. "Can't you knock?"

Iris gaped at the dark bruises that circled Dolly's arms and legs.

Dolly carried a photograph in her hand and was studying it intently. She put her index finger on each face, as if she were counting them, and then started over again. "I know this is Junior, this is Thomas, this is my husband, and that's you and that's me, but what's the occasion, Paula?"

Paula sighed, stomped over to Dolly, and wrenched the picture from her hands. "It's my graduation from junior high school. It was less than a year ago, Mom." She shoved the picture back at her.

Iris winced at Paula's cruelty.

Dolly peered at Iris. Her eyes, which before had glowed with a bright, persistent, restless light, now seemed dull and tinged with sadness. Her button-front dress had been extended at the waistband with safety pins to accommodate the weight that the usually hyperactive Dolly had recently gained. "Don't I know you?"

"This is Iris from next door for chrissakes." Paula picked up a brush and began angrily pulling it through her long hair. She threw it back on the dresser.

A tear sprang into Iris's eye. She prayed it wouldn't run down her face.

"I'm sorry, dear." Dolly rubbed her forehead. "I have this darn amnesia."

"You don't have amnesia. You had shock treatments." Paula flailed her hands at her. "Shock treatments, Mom!"

"I just can't remember things." She looked distressed.

Junior peeked in the room. "There you are. I was looking for you, Mom."

Dolly left the room with the picture. "I'm going to lie down. I feel tired."

After Dolly had left, Paula said to Junior, "Is that your job now, watching over her?"

"Someone has to, at least until she finishes her treatments and gets back on her feet."

"What a good son," Paula retorted.

Thomas wandered into the room.

"What is this?" Paula complained.

"Why is she all bruised like that?" Iris asked. "Why can't she remember anything?"

Thomas explained, "The shock treatments made her go into convulsions. She got bruised by the straps holding her down. She can't remember stuff because the treatments make people lose their memories. Usually they come back but sometimes they don't."

"Great," Paula said. "Now we have two fucking experts in the family. Thomas and Dad. And one nurse and one guinea pig."

"At least I care about her." Junior left the room.

Thomas followed.

Paula picked the backpack up from the floor and continued packing. She angrily shoved in clothes and shoes while Iris sat on a corner of the bed and watched. Paula finally stopped. She took a rumpled cigarette from her back pocket, straightened it, then lit it with a plastic lighter taken from another pocket.

"Why do you have to go?" Iris asked.

Paula inhaled deeply, blew out a long stream of smoke, then looked at Iris with eyes tinged with red. It was the closest Iris had ever seen Paula come to crying. "I'm afraid. I'm afraid that if I don't get away, I'm going to end up like her. I know it. I just know it."

She started to zip up the backpack, then impulsively snatched her grandparents' wedding portrait from the dresser and slipped it inside.

Iris sat with Paula in the eucalyptus grove while she waited for Mike to signal at the bottom of the hill. It was dusk. The sun was setting beyond the skyscrapers of downtown.

At the bottom of the hill, they saw car headlights start up the spiraling road.

"It's not him," Paula said. "He's not coming up."

When the car rounded the last loop, they saw it was a black-and-white LAPD sedan. It stopped on the driveway in front of the ranch house. Two police officers got out.

"That's them!" Iris urgently whispered.

"Fucking pigs," Paula said.

"I hope they don't see me."

Alvarez and Cole left the car and walked to the front door.

"Maybe they're going to arrest the old man," Paula said.

"Why?"

Paula regarded Iris with amazement. "The land, stupid." She arrogantly raised her chin. "Wouldn't that be cool? Gabriel and the old man." She snapped her fingers. "Boom. Both gone."

"You really hate both of them, don't you?"

Paula got up and dusted the back of her pants. "Let's see if we can hear."

Bill DeLacey had walked onto the front porch and was talking to the officers. Iris and Paula crept to the edge of the eucalyptus grove and lay on their bellies.

"It was decided that no further investigation into the death of Humberto de la Garza is warranted. It was ruled an accident," Alvarez said.

"Justice was served," Cole added. "Isn't that what this is all about?"

Alvarez eyed DeLacey. "You're one lucky son of a bitch. If it wasn't for an accident"—he shot a glance at Cole—"things would have turned out a lot different for you."

DeLacey jingled the keys and change in his pockets. "Do you know about the elephant?" He leaned back onto his heels, settling into his stance as if he planned on being there a while. "Now, the elephant can't do this." He waved his head from shoulder to shoulder as if he were indicating disagreement. "He can only do this." He nodded his head up and down. "That's what policemen should learn from elephants."

Alvarez moved close to DeLacey and said under his breath, "This case may be officially closed, but in my book, it's never gonna be closed."

"I don't care what you keep in your personal book, Officer Alvarez."

DeLacey went back inside the house and the two officers turned to walk to the patrol car when Cole noticed movement in the eucalyptus trees. He grabbed his flashlight and caught Paula and Iris in the beam. They scampered to their feet.

"What have we here?" Cole asked, walking over to them. He held the light so it shone underneath Paula's chin, and then did the same thing to Iris. "Haven't I seen one of you girls before?"

"I don't think so, but maybe you should take a closer look," Paula responded tartly.

"You're a feisty one, aren't you?" Cole said.

Paula looked at him salaciously. "Yeah."

Cole persisted, "Do one of you two young ladies own a dog?"

Alvarez grabbed Cole's arm. "Let's get out of here."

They climbed into the car and drove back down the hill.

"What did you do that for?" Iris asked angrily.

"Forget it," Paula said. "They're not gonna do anything to you. Case is closed, remember? Everyone's happy."

Iris and Paula waited silently in the eucalyptus grove for another half hour.

"Maybe he's not coming," Iris said.

"I hate him," Paula said, as if a thought that had been churning in her head finally spilled out. "I'll never forgive him for what he did to my mother. Bastard has to control everything. But not me, man. Not me."

A light flickered far down the hill on the city street.

"That's Mike." Paula got up, fed her arms through the backpack's straps, and started down the far side of the hill. "See ya around."

"Will you write or call?"

Paula glanced over her shoulder as she began to run. "Yeah. Sure."

Eleven

It was 7:00 Wednesday morning, the hump day, the numbing middle of the workweek, when unstructured time dangled like a carrot an entire Thursday and Friday away. Iris poured a cup of black coffee in the lunchroom of the McKinney Alitzer suite. She leaned into the employee refrigerator, her mug resting on top of it. She pulled off a slice of roast beef from a deli platter brought in the previous day for an employee's retirement party and shoved it into her mouth. She dipped in again for a piece of Swiss cheese and again for a couple of oily unpitted olives. As she chewed, she unfolded another employee's neat brown paper lunch bag and had a peek inside.

She never took anything from anyone's lunch. She just liked looking at them. The bagged lunches didn't reveal too much, but they revealed something. The sales assistant's Snickers bar showed she was cheating on her much-publicized diet. The newlywed male underwriter had started to bring in boxed frozen entrees instead of crisp sandwiches and assorted sides packed in Tupperware. Was the honeymoon over?

The lunchroom door opened and Iris sloppily refolded the bag with her oily fingers, guiltily slammed the refrigerator door, grabbed her mug off the top, and casually took a sip of coffee, her mouth full of olive pits.

Kyle Tucker sauntered into the lunchroom with his shoulders dipped back, his hips tilted forward, and one hand dangling at his side. It was his normal mode of movement. In his other hand he held the folded sports section from the newspaper almost against his nose. He lowered the newspaper and smiled as he opened the refrigerator. "Good morning."

Iris raised her coffee mug toward him and mumbled a greeting. She slipped to the trash can, discreetly spat the olive pits into her hand, and dumped them.

Kyle examined his soiled lunch bag. He angled his expressive, finely outlined lips to one side, revealing small, square white teeth and displayed the bag to Iris. "I don't get people. Someone was in my lunch and they weren't even careful about it."

"That would be me." Iris didn't know what compelled her to say it. Maybe it was because Kyle had been so obviously trying to suck up to her since he'd been hired or because his slick veneer seemed so implacable or because she was in a shit-eating mood and was looking to rattle someone's cage.

Those slender, rubbery lips conveyed surprise, then quickly recovered, telegraphing amused bemusement. "You?"

She figured he didn't believe her. She theatrically placed her index finger against her forehead like a TV psychic divining the future or what was contained in an audience member's purse. "Let's see…apple, orange, two sandwiches, carrot sticks, chips in a Ziploc bag. Did you make that lunch all by yourself or did your mommy make it?"

He angled a look at her in a way that he surely knew made him look very cute. It was unlikely that he'd be unaware of things like that. He ignored her question and asked his own. "You make it a habit to look in people's lunches?"

She ignored his question and smiled in a way that she knew made her look very unlike an ice princess. "It must be cheaper to bring in chips from the big bag than to buy the individual portions. Are we counting our pennies, Kyle?"

He laughed, his deep-set brown eyes crinkling at the corners. He reached in the bag, pulled out the apple, rubbed it on his shirtsleeve, and took a big bite. "Well, not everyone can be Iris Thorne."

She answered his first question. "Actually, I'm doing a sociological study. Believe that?"

"If you say so."

"Actually, I'm nosy."

"Aww, don't say that. You're just curious."

"Yeah, that's it."

He took another bite of his apple and offered her the contents of his bag. She declined.

"What's in your lunch bag?" he asked.

"I eat out."

He waved the apple up and down in her direction. "Why are you got up like that? Going to a funeral or something?"

They were into it now, that teasing, joshing, pushing-and-shoving guy thing. He'd later tell people that he didn't think Iris Thorne had a pole up her behind like everyone said. Underneath the facade, she seemed real regular.

She looked down at her gold-and-pearl-button black St. John knit suit, her black Anne Klein pumps, and sheer black stockings. "As a matter of fact, I am."

He almost choked on the apple. "I'm sorry. I just…"

"That's okay, Kyle. Make fun of me in my time of grief." She feigned affront.

"My condolences, really."

"Thank you." She fingered her short string of cultured pearls. "I feel like a freaking politician's wife."

"I think you look very nice."

"Thank you again. It's the mother of a childhood friend. I haven't seen either of them in years. The family stayed in the old neighborhood. I haven't been back since college."

He patted his straight strawberry blond hair, which was held in place by hairspray or something that made it stiff. "Where is the old neighborhood? No one seems to know much about you."

"Not much to know." She winked at him.

"I don't think it's hard to figure out. Let's see." He took another bite of the apple and chewed thoughtfully. "Professional family. Daddy's a doctor or attorney or something. Mom's in the Junior League. You went to riding camp in summer. Ski camp in winter…"

"Kyle, you are an astute judge of character." She wondered why in the world she was flirting with him. She sensed it was a big mistake. He probably thought he was in a position to score.

"One thing I can't figure out is why you went to UCLA instead of USC."

"Just a rebel, I guess." She sashayed toward the lunchroom door, knowing that the knit suit clung to her curves, clung too suggestively for the office but she'd worn it anyway. To hell with protocol. To hell with everything. Dolly DeLacey had hanged herself. Everything else seemed trivial. She opened the door.

"So what did you want to be when you grew up? Did you always see yourself moving large sums of money, holding people's financial future in your hands?"

She considered his question and thought about using him to float some preposterous rumors about herself through the office. That was always entertaining. But instead she answered truthfully. "When I was a kid, all I wanted to be was an adult."

She walked back to her office, stepping quickly and purposefully to convey the illusion that she had just left one important thing and was rushing to the next. Busy, busy. *What was that about Iris?* she asked herself. *He's cute. It was fun. Remember fun?*

She walked past the investment counselors' cubicles, past Warren Gray, Amber Ambrose, and Sean Bliss. Sean gave her a more piercing up-and-down than usual. She made sure her extra-sheer stockings whizzed together for his libidinous benefit.

Inside her office, the texture of the carpet changed when she walked across the new piece that the building maintenance had patched in to replace the water-damaged section. She flopped in her desk chair, picked up the telephone receiver, and punched in the series of numbers that would reveal her phone messages. She jotted them down on a yellow pad. Nothing special. A few anxious clients needing to have their hands held. A referral from someone Iris went to college with who worked for a city councilman. The councilman wanted financial guidance. The last message made her gasp and widen her eyes.

"Two thousand dollars," she exclaimed. "My ass!" She sure as hell wasn't going to pay that for less than a full day's work.

She leaped to her feet and angrily paced behind her desk. Then she walked to her floor-to-ceiling southern-facing window and leaned against it, pressing her cheek against the glass. It was a clear day and she could easily see the hills of Northeast Los Angeles. She spotted the one that she always fancied to be Las Mariposas, although she knew she couldn't really see that far. She directed her comments to Bill DeLacey, whom she imagined sitting at his desk there.

"Two thousand dollars for some crooked gumshoe to find *your* daughter. Bullshit! And the funeral's today. Just like you to expect the impossible."

Iris's mutterings attracted scant attention from coworkers outside her office. They'd grown used to this eccentricity of hers and had learned to stop asking, "Did you say something?" when she was in this mode.

"You don't care if Paula goes to Dolly's funeral. You're the one who said good riddance to bad rubbish when she left. So what's this really about, Mr. DeLacey?" She pulled her string of pearls back and forth between her fingers and scowled at the window.

"Hot out today, huh?" Amber stood in Iris's doorway, startling her.

Iris still wore her animosity toward Bill DeLacey on her face when she turned toward Amber but quickly caught herself. She loosened her rigid jaw and smiled. "Shake and bake." She returned to her chair. "Earthquake weather."

"Not according to the Caltech scientists."

"Everyone who lives here knows that when it's hot and dry during the day and cold at night, it's earthquake weather."

"I think with every earthquake, all the scientists find out is how much they don't know." Amber sat in one of the two chairs facing Iris's desk.

Iris tapped a pencil on her desk, sliding it between her thumb and index finger until she reached the eraser end, then sliding it the other way until she reached the lead. "Comforting thought." She lost her grasp on the pencil and it skittered off the edge of her desk.

"Something wrong?"

Iris nodded pensively. "Yeah. I'm going to a funeral today of a woman who hanged herself. The mother of a family who lived next door to where I grew up."

"How awful. Had she been depressed?"

Iris laughed wistfully. "I think there was always something wrong with her up here." She tapped her temple. "It baffled me as a kid. Sometimes she'd go on these crying jags. Other times she'd be manic, scrubbing floors in the middle of the night. Other times, she was just fine."

"Sounds scary."

"She had a nervous breakdown when I was fourteen. Her husband had her committed to a mental hospital where they gave her shock treatments."

"Shock treatments?"

"Calmed her right down. Boy oh boy, did it ever." Iris shook her head with dismay. "I guess they finally wore off or something." She leaned back in her chair and crossed her legs. "It's sad. She had plenty of her own problems, but she always had time for me when I was a kid. It meant a lot."

"Really? Why?"

Iris casually lifted and dropped one shoulder. She didn't like talking about her private life in the office. "I don't know. You know how things get out of proportion when you're a kid."

"What happened?" Amber probed, revealing a little too much enthusiasm, as if she had sniffed blood.

Iris had come to consider Amber a friend, but she still held something back from her, even though Amber hadn't given her any indication that there was any reason to. Also, Iris didn't like revisiting her past. And she found it hard to trust people completely. "Nothing to write home about."

Amber changed the subject, appearing to respect Iris's desire not to dwell on it further. "I'm having lunch with some of my old friends from Pierce Fenner Smith today." She stood and walked to the door. "Want to come? Might cheer you up."

"Thanks, but I have to bail out of here early to pick up my mom and sister."

Amber quickly stuck her head back inside Iris's office and loudly whispered, "It's Garland Hughes with Oz. Hughes must have flown in from New York last night."

Iris jumped to the window that overlooked the suite.

Herbert Dexter, the manager of the Los Angeles office, looked even taller and lankier than usual next to Hughes, his shorter, more solidly built boss. They were chuckling amiably. Hughes exchanged a few words with the temporary secretary and the three of them chuckled some more. Hughes chummily rested his hand against Dexter's back as they went through Dexter's office doorway. When Hughes turned to close the door behind them, he spotted Iris standing behind the open miniblinds and Amber in the doorway of Iris's office on the opposite side of the suite.

"Oops!" Iris quickly busied herself at the filing cabinet in the corner. Amber feigned interest in what Iris was doing.

Hughes waved.

They offhandedly waved back, as if they'd just noticed him.

"I think he's charming, don't you?" Amber asked.

"Definitely. He's strong and boyish at the same time—a potent combination for me."

Amber regarded Iris. "He's available, you know. He just got divorced."

"A recently divorced man. How delightful."

"I always thought he had an eye for you."

"Nah. He's just nice to everyone."

"He's probably here to talk about Oz's replacement. Everyone's wondering who it's going to be."

"I've been wondering that myself. I would kill for that job."

Amber looked at Iris incredulously.

Iris smiled cagily. What Amber didn't know wouldn't hurt her. Iris had lunch plans with Garland Hughes.

"You don't think you're a candidate, do you?" Amber asked sarcastically.

Iris was surprised by Amber's tone. "Sure. Why not?"

"Iris, you've really got to let go of this fantasy. They're not going to make you manager of this office. I'm not saying they'd never promote you, but you'd go to another office. I don't want to sound mean or anything, but I don't want you to get your feelings hurt."

"Amber, I didn't get where I am by being negative."

Amber looked aghast. "You got the corner office. You got the title. You got the raise. You got the good accounts. I think you've squeezed all you're going to from their feeling sorry for you."

"Sorry for me?"

"Sure. Because of the murders a few years ago."

"You're kidding, right?"

"You can't always get everything you want, Iris." Amber walked down the corridor and sat down in her cubicle with her back to Iris.

Iris stood in her doorway, stunned. "What the hell got into her?" She returned to her desk. "Iris Thorne gets everything she wants? Huh. Maybe I could if I knew what it was I wanted."

Twelve

Iris loitered in the cavernous lobby of the Edward Club, looking into the glass cases lining the walls that displayed artifacts from the club's history. Black-and-white photos honored the EC's bearded or mustachioed founding fathers who also had a hand in building Los Angeles. Engraved silver and bronze trophies celebrated the members' athletic triumphs over other members. Delicate pieces of crystal stemware edged in cobalt blue with a florid EC etched on each face were carefully displayed. A folded white card, solemnly lettered in black ink, stated that this was the club's traditional crystal and it could no longer be obtained. The passing of an era was mourned. In private, members mourned the passing of another era, when the membership was homogeneously white, Christian, and male.

Garland Hughes was fifteen minutes late. Iris had at first eagerly agreed to have lunch with him, considering herself to be truly anointed to dine tête-à-tête with her boss's boss at his club. After languishing for a few years, her career was again on the move. Big things were afoot. Momentum was building. Hallelujah.

Then she'd decided this might involve something more than just her career. It was a subtle, unstated thing. During his monthly visits to the L.A. office, she thought she detected something in the way he looked at her with his head slightly turned instead of facing her head-on and in the way his voice softened just a tad when he spoke to her. Even his eyes had seemed to soften. Once she suspected that his interest in her went beyond business, all the subtle little signs might as well have been flashing in neon. Not that she minded. She'd always found him very attractive. The combination of self-confidence, achievement, and power had an effect on her that she never obtained from eating oysters. And his chiseled features, piercing blue eyes, and athletic physique didn't hurt either. But he was her boss's boss, for goodness' sakes. Hadn't she already gotten into enough trouble at the firm?

Her black St. John suit meshed well with the ladies who were there that afternoon for luncheon and a fashion show. Usually her conservative business attire served to indicate that she wasn't on the lunching ladies' team. But twice while she was waiting, hosts from the front desk had tried to guide her toward the luncheon and twice she had politely explained she was here for a business meeting, holding up her briefcase as if it were some sort of badge.

Such a mistake used to irritate her to no end. After all, she'd worked her butt off for everything she'd accomplished and it offended her to have people assume she was some executive's pampered wife. But today the idea had an alluring, almost forbidden appeal. After all, she could pass for privileged. She'd fooled Kyle Tucker. It had taken a lot of years and a lot of tears to cover up those blue-collar roots. She'd done it the hard way, with lucky breaks few and far between and with plenty of so-called friends like Amber clinging to her ankles, trying to make sure she didn't get ahead, at least not any faster than they did. So what if she decided to let someone like Garland Hughes bring home the bacon? So what if she did?

It was an alluring proposition, as such things usually are. But like the teller's fantasy of robbing the bank and moving to Argentina, it was fraught with problems. Long ago, Bill DeLacey had told her there was no such thing as a free lunch. To get something you have to give up something. What would the price be? It certainly meant handing over some power and independence to another and trusting that the gifts would be honored and not abused. The very thought made her feel short of breath, as if someone had put a pillowcase over her head.

A man darted into the lobby with the air of someone who was very busy and who assumed the people he came into contact with would recognize this and not waste his time. His business attire was spit-and-polish perfect, caressing his athletic body in the easy manner of fine fabrics. However, his short, straight auburn-brown hair was askew on his head, the result of him frequently running his hands through it in frustration.

Garland Hughes spotted Iris and walked toward her, his thick-soled, expensive leather shoes resounding against the lobby's polished marble floor. He seemed to be glad to see her but there was also something of relief at having finally arrived and being able to mentally tick off one more item on the "to do" list.

"Iris!" He extended his hand before he'd reached her. "It's good to see you." His blue eyes, harried when he first come in, grew animated.

She took his hand.

He squeezed hers and looked into her eyes two seconds past business cordiality.

"Good to see you too, Garland."

"You look terrific."

That was proof. This lunch was personal. Iris couldn't stop herself from blushing. "Thank you."

They entered an old, wood-paneled and brass-trimmed elevator where they were alone. He gave her a look out of the corners of his eyes. There was something vulnerable and open in it that put her on guard.

"I'm sorry to hear about your loss," he said, meaning the funeral.

"Thank you."

"Let me know if I can do anything for you."

"You already have. I'm taking the afternoon off."

He laughed. She was glad. She didn't know how in the world she was supposed to act with this man.

"Actually, after lunch I'm going to follow up on a sales lead, a referral from a client, before I head over to the funeral." She wanted him to know she wasn't taking the entire afternoon off. He was still her boss's boss. No need to be unnecessarily cavalier. "I'm going to pitch one of the L.A. City Council members." It wasn't exactly name-dropping, but it wouldn't hurt if he knew she moved in high circles.

He glanced at his watch for a nanosecond. "I'm sorry our lunch got squeezed into an hour. I've got meeting after meeting during this trip."

"No need to apologize." That's probably how it would always be with him, apologies for the scarce time spent with her. Maybe that was okay. She wasn't much on clinging people anyway.

In the large, high-ceilinged dining room, the tall windows were draped with heavy burgundy velour tied with gold tassels. They ordered lunch and drank iced tea from the club's new crystal and gossiped about the firm.

"So how's the new hire, Kyle Tucker, working out?" Garland asked between bites of his flattened chicken.

She sucked in a few strands of linguine with scallops that hadn't made it completely into her mouth. It was a sloppy dish, which she was thoroughly enjoying but never would have ordered on a typical business lunch. Since he'd revealed a glimpse of his private, vulnerable side to her, she'd reveal something of herself to him—she could eat like a horse. "He's very determined to succeed. Seems bright. Has savvy."

"Good, good. He didn't have the experience we were looking for, but Herb felt very favorably about him. Since we needed someone who could come on stream quickly, I decided to take a flyer with him. I don't know if we'll ever get on top of this employee turnover problem at the L.A. office."

He seemed reflective as he ate another piece of chicken. Iris slurped some more linguine with equal reflectiveness.

Then he glanced at her in a way that made her hold her breath, as if he were about to reveal something else that was private. "Please keep an eye on him. If anything goes wrong, we've got to nip it in the bud."

Well, she'd called that one wrong. She took a deep breath and tried to relax. Maybe this was just a business lunch after all. She probably needed to start dating again and get out more. She was finding smoke signals everywhere.

He paused for half a beat, then continued, "How's Amber doing?"

"Fine. Great."

"Herb and I are close to getting Viagem's pension fund. We're thinking of giving it to Amber. You think she's up to it?"

"I think that would be quite a coup for her."

"Of course, you'd be my first choice to handle it, but you have too much on your plate as it is."

"I agree. Let Amber have a shot."

"Do you think she'd be too aggressive, that she'd gum things up trying to make a splash?" Iris sighed and looked out the window at a homeless man standing on the corner next to a bucket of soapy water and waving a squeegee, offering to clean windshields for change. She was reminded of the tattered man who had cleaned her windshield just to be nice. "Frankly, Garland, I feel uncomfortable talking to you about my coworkers. It makes me feel like I'm a mole for the other side."

"You're right." He rubbed his already disheveled hair.

She patted her lips with the napkin, leaving rose lipstick marks on the crisp white linen, then bought a few more seconds by picking flecks of lint from her black skirt. "I also feel uncomfortable about this lunch. Tell me if I'm completely off base, but did you ask me to lunch for personal or business reasons?" There. She'd said it.

His eyes softened and he gave her that sidelong look.

She'd hit the nail on the head. Her skin grew hot. She was blushing again.

"Good broker's instinct." His voice grew gentle. "I didn't know how to broach the issue with you, Iris, or even if I should, but I am very attracted to you." He reared back. "Of course, that's in addition to having the utmost respect for your intellect and your business acumen and your value to the firm."

"I'm very flattered." What else could she say? But it happened to be the truth.

"I've spent many hours wrestling with whether I should reveal my feelings. But nothing ventured, nothing gained."

"I've always found you attractive too, Garland."

"I hoped you'd feel that way." He slid his hand across the tablecloth and touched the tips of her fingers. "Would you consider going out with a beat-up, battle-scarred joker like me?"

She left her hand where it was. His fingers felt soft and warm against hers. It had been a long time since she'd had any contact of that sort. She hadn't realized how much she missed it. "I would love to, but potentially it creates a lot of problems. I don't want to put my job at risk."

"I understand." He took her hand between both of his and leaned toward her with his elbows on the table. "There's something that might mitigate the situation. I'm probably leaving the firm."

She raised her eyebrows.

"Some friends and I are putting together a venture capital group. I've been thinking about going out on my own for a long time and things finally seem to be falling into place. This is confidential, of course."

"Congratulations. That's terrific."

"It may be as soon as a few weeks. It may take a little longer. When it happens, I'd like to take you to dinner to celebrate."

"I'd love it." She smiled at him. She felt attractive and desirable. She felt good.

They finished their meal. As soon as she laid her knife and fork across her plate, it was swept away by a sharply attired middle-aged Latino waiter who had been chatting familiarly with some of the other diners.

Garland sat back in his chair, crossed his legs, and dropped his folded hands in his lap. His demeanor lost the softness it had acquired when they were talking about personal issues and grew tough edges. He seemed to have something on his mind. "Iris, there's another matter I wanted to speak with you about."

Iris's body temperature, which had returned to normal after their previous discussion, was again on alert.

"You might have heard that Herbert Dexter plans to move back to New York."

"I've heard a rumor."

He laughed. "It never ceases to amaze me how confidential news like this gets out."

Iris shook her head to commiserate but said nothing. Even though Amber Ambrose had been snotty to her earlier that day, she wasn't about to rat her out.

"Herb and his wife are old Easterners who never settled into the lifestyle out here. He feels he's accomplished what he came out here to do in terms of putting the L.A. office back on track and is looking for a new challenge. There's a position opening up in Manhattan that'll be a good move for him." He laced his fingers on the tablecloth. His eyes were intense and the message was brief. "How do you feel about managing the L.A. office?"

"Wow." She rubbed her forehead and looked out of the window. The homeless man was quickly washing a client's windshield before the light changed.

"You don't have to decide now." He studied her eyes.

"I want it," she blurted, as if she thought he might withdraw the offer. She ran her fingers up and down her pearls, caught herself, and folded her hands on the table. "I mean, I'd be really honored. I think I have a lot to contribute."

"Excellent. Herb and I already started discussing the transition earlier today."

Iris thought about Amber and smiled wryly to herself.

"You'll be sorry to know that you'll experience a significant salary increase." His eyes sparkled. "Iris, I'm suggesting you for this job because I believe you're absolutely the best person for it. It has nothing to do with any personal feelings I have toward you. After all, I still have a responsibility for the bottom line." He glanced at his watch. "I've got to run."

They walked across the dining room's polished wood floor through spots of sunlight that shone through the sparkling windows, descended the elevator, and left the Edward Club for the rude noise and activity of the street. Iris watched the hustle and bustle and today found it to be the most beautiful thing she'd ever seen. They stood on the sidewalk in front of the club.

"That was quite a lunch," she commented.

"Big changes ahead for both of us."

"Funny. You go along, feeling like you're in a rut, then there's an earthquake and all sorts of things start to happen." She held her hand out to shake his.

He took it and didn't let go. They were standing close together, close enough for him easily to kiss her, which she hoped he wouldn't attempt to do. He was still her boss's boss, soon to be her direct boss, and until that relationship changed, she told herself, they had to play it cool. With that decided, she impulsively brushed his lips with hers, spun on her heel, and began walking to the office, looking back to shoot a smile at him over her shoulder. He stood where she'd left him, looking as if he could be knocked over with a feather.

In a second-floor restaurant across the street, Amber Ambrose urgently jabbered to the women friends with whom she was having lunch. They all leaned close to the window to watch Iris, who was virtually skipping down the street. After she had passed beyond their view, Amber dropped heavily back into her chair.

Thirteen

Iris parked the Triumph in a lot near 200 North Spring Street. She walked up a long cement walkway that crossed the broad lawn in front of Los Angeles City Hall past scattered panhandlers who emitted a steady chorus of "Help me out? Spare some change?"

The thirty-story landmark, built in 1927, had long ago lost its status as the tallest building in Los Angeles. Since it now stood virtually empty, it was the seat of city government in concept only. The city bureaucracy that hadn't already relocated due to lack of room had been forced out to clear the way for a three-year seismic strengthening project. The building's most visible denizens, the mayor and the City Council, were the only ones remaining through the renovations, the official reason being that their offices were on the lower floors, making it easier to effect a rescue in the event of a quake. Unofficially, the top brass refused to be moved.

Iris walked into the tall, domed lobby, past the long fresco depicting the history of California, from the time of the Spanish occupation, to the era when missions were built by Franciscan priests to convert the Native Americans, to when the land was turned over to the Mexicans, and, finally, when it became part of the United States of America. Her heels clicked on the terra-cotta colored fired tile floor, and she questioned the wisdom of making a sales call in her snug knit suit.

She approached a guard at an information desk on one side of the lobby and asked for directions. He gave her what she interpreted as a knowing look; self-consciously she fiddled with the buttons on the front of her jacket. With a crooked smile pasted on his face, he directed her to a bank of wood-paneled elevators against a wall.

She thanked him and took the stairs instead. It was just one floor and it would be her luck to have an aftershock knock out the power, trapping her between floors when she had other places she was supposed to be. She exited the stairwell on the second floor and walked on old linoleum past people bustling to and fro, some engaged in urgent conversation.

The corridor was lined with doors, all inset with frosted glass embossed with thumbprint-sized depressions. At the end of the corridor was a door with GILBERT ALVAREZ, COUNCILMAN 14TH DISTRICT stenciled in black paint on the glass. She turned the polished brass doorknob and entered a front office furnished in masculine dark green leathers and plaid fabrics. A secretary sat at a large wood desk in one corner. Another glassed door led to an inner office from which muted voices emanated and dark shadows passed behind the glass. The musky low odor of cigar smoke hung in the air.

The secretary was young and pretty. She was a Latina and wore her dark hair, which was probably long, neatly coiled and pinned at the back of her head. She asked, "May I help you?" in a gentle voice that seemed modulated to please, that seemed to suggest that she was soft and accommodating and here to soothe and comfort. She dialed the inner office with the tips of her long acrylic fingernails and watched her hand as she did so, as if she were one of her favorite admirers. "He'll be with you shortly."

Iris sat on a leather couch and distractedly flipped through a magazine. Before long, the door to the inner office opened and a man poked out his head. He smiled broadly and crossed the small room with his hand extended. "Iris."

Iris stood and took his hand across the magazine-strewn coffee table that separated them. "Hi, Jeff. Good to see you."

"Good to see you too. I'm glad you were able to meet with Gil on such short notice."

"Have to strike while the iron's hot."

"That's exactly the attitude I like to see in my money manager." Jeff Rosen was in his late thirties but looked much younger, with unkempt dark hair that fell over his eyes. He was one of those men who would continue to look young until his hair began to turn gray or fall out. He exuded energy. Dressed in a suit and tie that looked out of place on him as if he were a schoolboy dressed up for a special occasion, he grabbed his tie as if to straighten it but left it with the tongue jutting out even more than it had before. "Come in and meet Gil."

Iris walked into the councilman's office. The wood-paneled walls were covered with awards, proclamations, and framed photos of Alvarez with the famous and the powerful, side by side with tempera paint-on-butcher-paper paintings from school children. Bronze trophies were scattered around the office along with objects that appeared to be handmade gifts from constituents.

A man rose from a leather desk chair and stepped from behind a large desk. He held a half-burnt cigar between his fingers.

"Iris Thorne, I'd like you to meet Gil Alvarez, councilman of the great Fourteenth District for the past twelve years."

Alvarez had been watching Iris or, more accurately, appraising her since she'd entered his office. He switched his cigar to the other hand and extended his now-empty right hand to shake hers. It was a warm, firm handshake, the handshake of a man who'd made a profession of it.

Rosen added, "We're bound to win a fourth term in a few weeks."

"So this is the great investment counselor, Iris Thorne." Alvarez's hairline receded far back on his forehead but he brushed his dark, wavy hair straight back anyway as if he had nothing to hide. He was of medium height, rotund, and wore a neat narrow moustache on his upper lip, which called attention to his easy broad smile. He appeared to be in his fifties.

"I don't know, Jeff. I don't know how comfortable I am trusting my money to such an attractive woman. I've had bad experiences with that before. You've probably read about it in the papers, Iris." He was still holding her hand.

As a matter of policy, Iris waited for him to release first—it was his office, his turf, his handshake, and she wanted his business—but it was reaching the point of ridiculousness. The gesture was entering the realm of flirtation. "No, I haven't."

Alvarez finally let go. Iris resisted expelling a sigh of relief.

"Gil's referring to his divorce," Rosen explained. "Frankly, I'm relieved to know there's someone in the city who hasn't heard about it. It even appeared on *Hard Copy* last night."

"I missed it," Iris said.

"Gil, I told you that Iris and I went to business school together. She's managed my money for years, brilliantly I might add, and recently we set up college funds for my two kids. I trust her implicitly."

"That's quite an endorsement," Alvarez responded. "My campaign manager doesn't give praise like that easily. Have a seat."

Iris and Rosen sat in matched well-worn leather club chairs. Her snug skirt rode up and she discreetly tugged on it, a gesture that didn't go past Alvarez.

Rosen squinted at something across the room, then snapped his fingers. "Iris, come to think of it, you might be from Gil's district. Aren't you from East L.A.?"

"El Sereno," Iris answered.

Alvarez spread his arms in an encompassing gesture, the burning cigar still stuck between his fingers. "A local girl. Where did you live?"

"On Lombardy Boulevard, beneath Las Mariposas."

"Las Mariposas?" He sucked on his cigar, then slowly blew out thick white smoke. "Then you must have known the DeLaceys."

Iris held her breath as the smoke wafted past her and tried to disguise her restricted voice. "I practically lived at their house."

"You know that Thomas DeLacey is running against me. Oh!" He made an overly dramatic apologetic gesture, putting his hand on his cheek and contritely looking toward heaven. "*Excuse* me. Thomas *Gaytan* DeLacey."

"He was Thomas DeLacey when I knew him. Gaytan was his mother's maiden name."

Alvarez said, "He doesn't want the voters in our predominately Latino district to forget his noble heritage as the descendant of one of the original Mexican landowners."

Iris smiled. "How ironic. Bill DeLacey wasn't proud that his kids were half Mexican and now Thomas is capitalizing on it."

"We're convinced that Gaytan DeLacey will stop at nothing to get elected," Rosen said. "Changing his name is the least of it. He sold his house in Brentwood and bought in the district. He changed his party affiliation from Republican to Democrat. Even though the City Council is nonpartisan, he knew the citizens of the Fourteenth would never elect a Republican. He's made it clear that he wants a career in politics and sees the Fourteenth District City Council seat as his first step."

Alvarez shook his head vehemently, "I've done everything within my power to get money for my district, to get projects, to do whatever it takes to improve the lives of the citizens of the great Fourteenth." His eyes teared. "I *love* the people of the Fourteenth. I *am* one of the people of the Fourteenth." He balled his hand into a fist. "I am the best candidate for this job. I won't be run out of office by some Johnny-come-lately who only sees the Fourteenth as a stepping stone to the mayor's office and a way to gain approval for his father's real estate development projects." He pounded his fist on the desk.

"You mean DeLacey Gardens?" Iris asked.

Alvarez's fist was still balled. "Bill DeLacey has pushed that low-income housing project to the City Council every year since I've been elected. It's rumored that he's tried to bribe members of the Planning Committee and that he's submitted falsified environmental impact reports. Now he thinks he can put his son in office and ram the damn thing through."

Rosen held his hand out to indicate Alvarez. "No one is better at forging compromises than this man. He tried to get DeLacey to modify the project to be a better fit with the neighborhood, but the man won't budge."

Alvarez added, "He says he can't scale it back. That he's lost too much money on it as it is. I don't know how he keeps finding investors for it. I think he might have a Ponzi scheme going where he gets money from this guy to pay the other and so on."

"Gil's platform has always been ideology free—potholes and police, no bull—and it's served him and his constituents well," Rosen said. "When Thomas Gaytan DeLacey came along with his blow-dried hair, Yale law degree—"

"People in the *barrio* aren't impressed by Yale Law School," Alvarez sniffed.

"—and no political experience, we weren't concerned. Frankly, we were caught with our pants down when Gaytan DeLacey did well enough in the primary election to force a runoff."

"Please don't take this the wrong way," Iris began, "but why did Gaytan DeLacey do so well in the primary if the citizens are happy with their current representation?"

Alvarez's expression grew stern. "Simple. By conducting the lowest, most vile smear campaign I've seen in all my years of public service."

Rosen turned to Iris. "Gil's alluding to his divorce. Long story short, it's been an ugly situation. Sure, there've been indiscretions on both sides, but the whole thing's been blown out of proportion by the press."

Alvarez leaned across the desk. "Look, I'm willing to own up to the fact that my personal life's been a mess lately. I've made my share of mistakes, but I've *always* put my constituents first. I welcome a good old-fashioned knock-down political fight, but I will not have my character assassinated in the press. Mr. Gaytan DeLacey is in for a surprise if he thinks I'm just going to lie down so he can roll over me. We have our own bag of tricks." He smiled knowingly at Rosen.

"The DeLaceys should learn that people who live in glass houses shouldn't throw stones," Rosen added.

"There's something I learned early in my political career. Help your friends and screw your enemies, then people will always know where you stand." Alvarez pressed his palm, still holding the cigar, against his chest. A large diamond ring sparkled on his pinky finger. "This whole situation breaks my heart. I hope I'm not offending you by discussing your old friend this way."

Iris shrugged. "I haven't seen the DeLaceys in over twenty years. Been at least that long since I've been back to the old neighborhood. I don't know if you're aware that Dolores DeLacey, Thomas's mother, passed away. Her funeral's today."

"Hanged herself," Alvarez said. "You'd think Gaytan DeLacey would try to keep something like that out of the press, but he's used it for all it's worth." He shook his head. "Poor Dolly DeLacey. She had a hell of a life, didn't she?"

"Did you know her?" Iris asked.

He nodded slowly. "Oh yes. Her father was murdered, you know." He gave Iris that appraising look again. "I thought I remembered a family by the name of Thorne. Was your father employed by Bill DeLacey?"

"Yes, he was."

"I interviewed him about the murder."

"Interviewed him?"

"I was a police officer. LAPD. Ten years before I quit to take a job as an aide to my predecessor in the Fourteenth. My partner and I were the first cops on the scene." He gazed at nothing and began to laugh. "Poor Gabriel met his demise sometime before the San Fernando earthquake. When we got there, stuff had fallen all over the crime scene. Never seen anything like it." He shook his head at the same point across the room. "Never seen anything like it in a lot of ways."

Iris gaped at Alvarez.

"Something wrong?" he asked.

"No, I was just...That was a nasty situation."

Alvarez stroked his moustache and nodded solemnly.

"Tell me"—Iris nervously tugged at her skirt—"what happened to your partner? What was his name?"

"Ron Cole. Still with the force. He's a detective now. Homicide. Due to retire soon." He shook his head wistfully. "Real tough guy, but a heart of gold." He tapped his fingers over his heart. His ring glittered.

Iris made a broad gesture of looking at her watch. "Is it that late already? I'm sorry, but I have to be going." She abruptly stood and breathlessly said, "Why don't you call me and we'll set up a time to discuss your financial situation? Here's my card."

Alvarez tossed the card carelessly on his desk. "Nothing to discuss." He began moving files and papers around, looking for something. He picked up a manila folder and handed it to her. "That's what the guy I've got now has gotten me into. None of it's worth a damn. Just put me into whatever Jeff's got."

"But...but Jeff's in a different stage in life than you are. He's planning to put kids through college, you're probably thinking about retirement. He's looking for growth, you probably want income."

"You work out whatever you think is best and we'll talk."

"I'm not the best person to handle your situation."

Rosen winced at her in disbelief.

She stammered, "My specialty is smaller, I mean, larger portfolios. Pension funds and such. I'm not skilled at...I mean I don't know..."

Alvarez spread his arms and bellowed, "Means nothing to me."

She opened the folder and glanced at the documents. "What I'm trying to say is, I don't really have any high-profile individuals among my..." She paused. The portfolio was worth several million. "Clients."

"What's more important is that I know where you came from," Alvarez said. "You're a girl from the Fourteenth. I know all about you."

She closed the folder, set her briefcase on the chair, snapped it open, slipped the folder inside, and snapped it closed. "I'll put something together and call you."

Fourteen

"You think your father will be there?"

"I don't know, Mom."

"He worked for Bill DeLacey for years. You'd at least think he'd pay his respects to Dolly." Rose Thorne frowned petulantly.

"You'd think so." Iris steered the Triumph through Lily and Jack's neighborhood in the San Gabriel Valley suburb of Temple City.

Temple City was like most any other valley suburb—flat, hot, smoggy, and far enough from L.A. to lose the benefits of big city life yet close enough for L.A.'s problems to slop over onto it.

The evenly subdivided streets were dotted with tiny houses separated from one another by hyphens. Most of the houses had been built thirty or more years ago by individuals with grandiose plans but limited resources who went in for dream houses in miniature on the blank canvas that was southern California. Small storybook-inspired cottages with turrets and recessed windows stood next to tiled, zigzag-roofed mock adobes, next to low-roofed, deep-porched California Craftsman bungalows, next to the boxiest of 1960s cracker boxes with tarpaper-covered roofs strewn with small white rocks.

"Course, your father would probably bring his new family anyway. Man his age having five more kids," Rose sniffed. "He acts like you and Lily don't even exist."

"We act like he doesn't exist, so we're even."

"Iris, you shouldn't be that way. He is your father, after all."

"Yes, Mom."

"I hear he spends a lot of time with this new family. I don't know what was wrong with the family I gave him."

Iris rolled her eyes. "Let it rest, Mom. You're dwelling on things that happened almost twenty-five years ago."

The six cylinders of the Triumph's baritone engine rumbled loudly on the quiet streets. Two boys playing in a yard stopped to watch the Triumph pass. It was a life-sized toy.

"So did you find Paula?" Rose asked conversationally.

"No."

Rose was silent for a moment, then, as if she didn't understand Iris's response, asked, "You mean you couldn't find her?"

"No. I didn't try. I'm not going to pay two grand to a private detective."

"But Bill wanted you to find her."

"I don't work for *Bill*."

"Iris, Bill DeLacey's done a lot for our family. I don't know what would have happened to us if he hadn't helped me out when your father and I were having our problems."

Iris set her teeth on edge.

"He's very upset right now. I called him right away when I heard about Dolly and invited him over for a home-cooked meal."

Iris closed her eyes briefly as if to block a horrible image. "I refuse to be used by Bill DeLacey. If he really wants to see Paula he can hire a private detective. That's probably what this whole thing is about anyway. He always was cheap."

"How can you say that after he gave you all that money for your college education?"

"All that money? He gave me a thousand dollar check. That didn't even make a dent. *I* paid for my education." She shook her head with incredulity. "That money had strings attached, did you know that? He wanted me to tell him if anyone said anything about Gabriel Gaytan's murder. Don't you find it odd that he would hire a little girl to be a spy?"

"He did not, Iris."

"He did too."

"Well, I refuse to believe it."

"Believe it or not, it's true. Why is he so desperate to find Paula anyway? When she ran away, he knew where she was. He didn't even try to go get her. She was only fourteen."

Rose grasped the large, square vinyl purse that was on her lap between both hands. "He wants Paula to come to her mother's funeral, that's all. Bill DeLacey has his faults like anyone else. You can't live your life looking for the bad in people, Iris Ann. You have to look at the bright side of life. That's what I've always done."

Iris rolled her eyes again. She parked the Triumph next to the curb in front of Lily and Jack's 1940s three-bedroom, one-bath home. The house had a Spanish Gothic flavor. A striped canvas awning supported by two cast-iron spears jutted from the porch. A pattern of swirls had been molded into the plaster, which was painted pale mint green. Trimmed bushes and showy flowers bloomed in beds that extended across the front of the house and down each side of the lawn. Frilly lace curtains hung in the large arched picture window.

A sprinkler attached to a garden hose waved streams of water up and down the hearty St. Augustine grass, splashing on the sidewalk on its downward swoop where the children of the house's first owners had scrawled their names and left their handprints in the concrete.

Assorted bicycles were in the driveway in front of the detached garage. Jack's pickup truck with ROSSI ELECTRICAL painted on the door was parked on the street. Lily's minivan was parked in the driveway in front of her eldest son, Vincent's, Volkswagen Beetle—a gift from his parents for his sixteenth birthday. The Beetle's doors were open and Vincent's legs extended from the front seat. Eleven-year-old Gerald stood like a sentinel next to the Beetle, holding assorted wrenches. When he saw the Triumph pull up, he dropped them on the cement driveway with a clatter and ran to the curb.

Rose frowned at Jack's truck. Fortunately for her, the world was replete with things to fret over. "Wonder why Jack's home. Don't tell me his work's slow again."

"I didn't know his work had been slow."

Rose lowered her voice, even though just the two of them were in the car. "Lily was afraid they might lose the house."

"Why didn't she tell me? I would have helped them out."

"Don't tell her I told you. You know how Jack is. Things haven't been that great between them." She put her hand on the Triumph's door handle, then turned to look at Iris.

Iris was busy brushing her hair in the rearview mirror and didn't immediately notice her mother's penetrating stare. "What's on your mind?"

"So what do you hear from John Somers?" she asked nonchalantly.

"Nothing," Iris responded curtly.

"He's a good man, Iris."

"He's a confused man, Mom," Iris answered with forced patience. "I don't need such a man in my life."

"He'll come around. He just needs some time. He really loves you."

Iris shouted, "Dumping me to go back to his ex-wife is a hell of a way of showing it!" She immediately felt guilty for yelling at her mother.

Rose clutched her purse more tightly to her chest and looked at Iris with hurt eyes.

"I'm sorry, Mom. I'm sorry." She patted her mother's shoulder.

"I'm surprised you have any friends at all, the way you go around losing your temper like that."

They ungracefully climbed from the Triumph, the only possible way while wearing stockings and heels.

"Hi, sweetheart." Rose hugged Gerald. He threw his arms around her waist, which expanded a bit each year. Rose was still an attractive woman looking younger than her years, but she groomed herself showily, as if that would compensate for the beauty that had faded. She dressed stylishly, wore glamorous makeup, even in the middle of the day, and fashioned her hair in a high auburn-dyed bouffant.

Gerald shouted, "Hi, Grandma! Hi, Aunt Iris! Did you bring me anything?"

Rose dug in her purse and presented Gerald with a Hershey bar.

Iris leveled a glance at her mother. "You know Lily doesn't like them eating junk food."

"I can spoil my grandchildren if I want to. These might be the only grandkids I'll have."

Iris pursed her lips as if she'd tasted something sour.

"Hey, Aunt Iris," Vincent said. "Why don't you let me take the TR for a spin?" His dark hair fell across his eyes and he jerked his head to flick it back.

"I can't today, Vince. I don't have time to go with you."

"Oh, go on, Iris," Rose said. "He'll be careful, won't you, Vincent?"

"*Mom.*" Iris glared at her mother.

Vincent smiled and nudged Iris with his shoulder. "Sure I will. C'mon, Auntie." His brown eyes sparkled.

Iris teasingly pointed at him. "You remind me of your father when he was younger."

"So you gonna let me drive it?"

"I'll think about it."

Iris and Rose walked down the short cement path that cut across the front lawn. The front door was open behind the screen door.

"C'mon in," Jack said from inside.

Iris opened the screen door which led directly into the small living room. Pop music was playing somewhere in the back of the house.

Jack walked from the kitchen into the living room, eating from a can of chili with a spoon. He was in his middle forties and handsome with black hair going salt-and-pepper. His features were beginning to lose their sharp edges. He wore dark blue work pants, a white short-sleeved shirt, and black work shoes. "Lily's still getting ready."

"How are you, Jack?" Without waiting for a response Rose said, "I'm surprised to find you home in the middle of the day. Your work hasn't been slow, has it?" She strolled to a wall and began straightening pictures that a recent aftershock had knocked askew.

"Heck no. Thanks to the fires and now the earthquake, I've got more than I can handle. I came home to pick up Vince. He's been helping me."

"I thought he was on the track team," Iris said. "Doesn't he have practice after school?"

"He's not going to earn a living running track."

Iris commented, "It's a shame to curtail his school activities. He'll have to start working soon enough."

He pointed the spoon at her. "I know how to raise my kids, Iris. Lily and I don't travel in the same circles as your hoity-toity friends who can afford to let their kids play all the time."

Iris was tempted to have the last word, but she resisted.

The pop music stopped. Thirteen-year-old Ashley bounded into the living room, closely followed by another girl.

"Hi! Hi!" Ashley waved at Iris and Rose. "That's my grandmother and this is my Aunt Iris," she explained to her friend. "My aunt gave me the birthstone ring for my birthday. It's a real emerald, Heather." She held her hand out so Heather could admire it. "I never take it off, Aunt Iris."

"Looks terrific, too," Iris said.

"Is it really a real emerald?" Heather asked.

Jack responded. "Of course it is. Think your aunt would buy anything but the most expensive even for a thirteen-year-old?"

"I like giving her things I never had when I was a kid," Iris said.

"She doesn't need expensive things like that," Jack said. "She'll start to put on airs."

Rose interjected, "You had plenty of nice things when you were growing up, Iris."

"Airs?" Iris asked. "What are airs?"

Jack said, "I'm just saying that I'm perfectly capable of providing for my family, that's all."

Rose pouted. "I might have gone without myself, but I made sure you girls had things."

"Come and watch us practice for cheerleading, Aunt Iris."

"Gladly." Iris walked out the screen door, brushed off a spot on the front porch, and sat down.

Ashley turned off the sprinkler. "We're trying out for junior cheerleader. Watch this. One, two, three. We came! We saw! We took the ball and conquered now! We came…"

"I think the Triumph could use some exercise, Aunt Iris." It was Vincent again.

Iris reached into her purse and tossed him the keys. "Twice around the block."

"Awesome! Thanks, Auntie."

"We took the ball…" The girls stopped when they noticed two boys walking down the street.

Ashley excitedly grabbed Heather's arm. "Look. It's Jason and Eric. They're *so* cute! Say hi to them. Say hi!"

"You say hi, you say it first!"

"No, you say it!"

"I'll just die! You say it!"

"Okay, okay!"

They giggled, flailed their hands, then recovered and casually strolled to the curb. "Hi." Ashley waved awkwardly. Heather then did the exact same thing.

Iris heard the screen door open behind her.

"I'm ready I.," Lily said as she walked down the steps, wearing a black jacket, black skirt, and a deep blue blouse, two sizes larger than she wore in high school. She dyed her short hair ash blond, recreating the color of her youth, and wore it permed and styled away from her face. She did it herself to save money and it had an over-processed, wiry texture. Rose followed her.

Lily tucked in a tag on the back of Iris's jacket neckline, then began fussing with her collar. Iris brushed at Lily's hand, turning slightly as she did so.

Lily noticed her face. "You crying?"

Rose grabbed Iris's arm and stared at her with grave concern, then tried to force a pink tissue on her. "What's wrong, Iris? Are you upset about Dolly?"

Iris shook her head. "It's nothing."

"Did Jack upset you?" Lily asked. "It's just that money's been so tight, he feels bad he can't afford to buy the kids expensive things."

"Oh, puh-leese. I wouldn't cry over Jack. It's nothing. Okay? Can we just drop it and go?"

Rose persisted. "But it has to be *something*."

Iris finally snatched the tissue that her mother had been waving and dabbed her eyes with it. The moment passed. She began to breathe easier. "I was just watching the girls and it occurred to me how young they are."

"Yeah?" Lily said. "And?"

"You're very young when you're thirteen."

"And?"

"And...that's all." Iris stood, brushed the back of her skirt, and looked at her mother and sister who were watching her curiously.

Rose asked, "Are you eating right?"

Fifteen

Iris, Lily, and Rose were crammed together at the end of a pew in the tiny crowded Baptist church. An ancient woman with a pronounced dowager's hump and a cloud of fine white hair was playing dreary music on an organ at the front. Sprays of flowers were arranged around and on Dolly's light blue casket.

"It's open," Lily remarked with dread.

"Casket looks like it's made out of plastic," Iris commented. "Bill DeLacey always was a cheapskate."

Rose sighed heavily. "She's better off."

Iris grimaced. "Why is someone better off dead? How do we know?" She squinted at the flowers. "I hope the flowers I ordered got here."

Rose looked at Iris with alarm.

"Yes, Mom, I sent them from all of us."

"I'm surprised he didn't cremate her," Lily said. "I remember a DeLacey lecture about how burying people is a stupid waste of land since we're all going to be dust anyway."

"She was raised a Catholic," Iris said. "They don't believe in cremation. What's she doing in this Baptist church anyway?"

Rose leaned across Lily to speak to Iris. "Bill wouldn't have that Catholic business in his house. That's for the Mexicans and people like that."

"People like what, Mom?" Iris asked.

"Iris, if you're insinuating that I'm race prejudiced…" She twisted the straps of her purse. "You know there's good and bad in all races."

"I guess Dolly was good enough for Bill DeLacey to knock up when she was sixteen," Iris retorted.

Lily nudged Iris in the side with her elbow.

"The Gaytans were the good Mexicans." Rose reversed the position of her purse on her lap. "I don't know what's gotten into you today. You're just determined to make me out to be wrong."

"Look at the crowd," Lily commented, changing the subject. "Dolly couldn't have known this many people. Wonder if it's because Thomas is running for the City Council?"

"That's exactly what L.A. could use right now," Iris snapped. "Snot-nosed, kiss-butt Thomas DeLacey on the City Council. The little boy with ice water in his veins."

"A lot of young women," Lily noted, looking around. "Must be his groupies."

"Groupies?"

"Didn't you see Thomas on *Hard Copy* last night?" Lily asked.

"No, why?"

"Let's just say that Thomas is all grown up."

"Went from punk to hunk, huh?"

"That opponent of his, that Alvarez, is something. He's been arrested twice for drunk driving and now his wife's accused him of beating her."

"Really?"

"Uh-huh. And there's some question about misused campaign funds or something."

Iris covertly glanced across Lily to spy on her mother. Rose had her hands folded on top of her purse and was humming along with the organ music. Iris leaned close to Lily's ear. "You don't remember who Alvarez is?"

Lily shook her head.

Iris whispered, "He was one of the cops who arrested Humberto."

"You're kidding!" she said, too loudly.

"Shhh…"

They both glanced at Rose, who was still caught up in her own thoughts.

"And that's not the half of it," Iris said. "I just met with him. I'm going to manage his portfolio."

Lily looked aghast at Iris.

"I know. I started to turn it down but it's worth a couple million bucks. I can use the money. The deductible on my earthquake insurance is sky high, plus everything else I have to shell out for repairs." She shrugged. "It's honest money. I think."

"Did he recognize you?"

"If he did, he kept quiet about it."

"I hope you know what you're doing, sister."

"What's the worst that can happen? If I don't make him any money, he'll just kick the crap out of me."

Lily patted her mother's leg. "What are you thinking about, Mom?"

"Oh, about when you girls were growing up." She became wistful. "I miss those days."

"You do?" Iris asked with surprise.

"They were the best years of my life." She cheerlessly plucked at her skirt.

Lily turned to look at the back of the church, following the gaze of some of the young women there.

A tall dark-haired man dressed in a dark suit entered the church and slowly proceeded to the front, stopping periodically to shake hands and kiss babies. A photographer who had been loitering around the sides sprang into action. His subject obliged by lingering while the camera was being focused.

Iris turned as well. "No!" she whispered.

Rose, roused from her reverie, leaned over Lily and solemnly pronounced, "He's not married, Iris."

"His personality couldn't have changed that much." Iris looked him up and down. "Nice suit."

Rose added, "He's an attorney."

Iris sarcastically circled her index finger in the air. "Big whoop-de-do." She scrutinized him again. "Maybe he is worth a closer look. Some people do change." She pressed her arms on the pew to raise herself and peered at his shoes. She quickly dropped back into place when he looked toward them.

"Mrs. Thorne," Thomas exclaimed in a sonorous voice.

Rose bolted up and threw her arms around his shoulders while he bent double to reach her. "Thomas!"

"I'm so glad you came. My second mom."

Rose held his hand. "You're so *tall*, Thomas." She pulled him into the pew. "You remember Lily."

Thomas clasped Lily's hand between both of his. "Lily, wonderful to see you."

Rose pulled him forward. "And of course you remember Iris."

He clasped Iris's hand. "Who could forget her? Boy, you've grown up."

"I was just thinking the same thing about you."

"See this tooth?" He pulled his lips away from his white teeth and ran his tongue over an incisor. "Reminds me of you, especially when I have to get the cap replaced." He still held her fingers.

She saw her mother glance at their hands and immediately slipped from his grasp. "I didn't know it had rocks in it, Thomas. Honest."

"*Sure* you didn't."

Iris explained. "I made him a mud brownie and he believed me when I told him it was real. I hope you're not still that gullible." She rubbed her fingertips where he had touched her.

"You set a precedent, Iris. It was the first in a long line of foolish things I've done for pretty girls." He looked searchingly into her eyes.

She blushed.

Rose picked up and patted his hand. "Thomas, I'm so sorry about your mother. She had a hard life. I know she's in a better place."

Thomas grew somber. "She experienced much sorrow in her life but my father always told me that no one's given a burden larger than that person can bear. People think of my mother and see weakness but they should see courage. I owe her everything." His eyes grew red.

Iris, Rose, and Lily dabbed their eyes.

He looked toward the front pew, where Bill DeLacey had just turned around and cast a gimlet eye at them. "I'd better get down there. Dad's giving me *that* stare." He touched the corner of his eye and looked at the tear that came off on his finger.

"I know *that* stare," Iris said. "I got it today myself. You've probably noticed that Paula's not here."

Thomas waved dismissively. "Don't worry about it, Iris. I told my dad not to involve you. Not attending her mother's funeral will be something she'll have to live with." He smiled. It was his mother's broad, white smile. "I hope you won't avoid me because of my dad."

Iris smiled back. "What was it he used to say about the sins of the father?"

"The iniquities of the fathers are visited upon the children."

"True?"

"Maybe we can discuss it sometime. Over dinner."

"I'd like that."

"I'll call you." He made his way to the front of the church, stopping to chat with guests before he took his place next to his family.

Lily mocked Iris, "Not little kiss-butt, snot-nosed Thomas. Not me. Not ever!"

"Shaddup," Iris snarled. "I do wonder about the propriety of making a date at your mother's funeral."

Rose leaned over Lily. "You could do a lot worse, Iris."

Iris angled a comment out of the side of her mouth to Lily. "I have."

During the service, Rose distributed pink tissues pulled from the seemingly endless supply in her purse to Lily and Iris, who wept freely, as did most of the other guests. Bill DeLacey droned on for a solid hour, little of it spent talking about Dolly. Thomas gave a moving and short eulogy. Junior remained seated in the front row, his shoulders shaking as he sobbed.

"Poor Junior," Rose clucked. "All those years he spent taking care of Dolly. Never got married. Devoted his life to his mother." She said it as if she thought Junior qualified for sainthood.

"You going to view the body, Mom?" Lily asked.

"My God, no."

"I'm going," Iris said. "Come with me, Lily."

Iris and Lily stepped over Rose and filed to the front of the church. Halfway there, Lily grabbed Iris's hand. After a few more steps, they caught a glimpse of Dolly's face. Iris gasped and squeezed her sister's hand. "Look how heavy she is."

Lily blotted her eyes with a damp tissue and frowned. "She used to be skin and bones. She never sat still. How did she gain so much weight?"

The queue moved quickly as people took a glance and moved on. Then it was Iris's and Lily's turn.

Dolly lay on tufted powder blue satin that looked garish and shiny. Her hair was still long and draped across the front of her body, its near-black hue now streaked with gray.

Lily gave a quick look, like everyone else, then began to walk, pulling Iris by the hand, but Iris didn't move. She continued to stare down at the body, transfixed, her hand pressed against her lips, her head shaking back and forth. A man behind Iris loudly cleared his throat and Lily gently tried to pull her away.

Iris didn't move but looked at the front pew, her lips pressed into a thin line. Thomas was there, graciously greeting well-wishes. There was a break in the procession and he pressed his fingers against his eyes.

Iris spotted Bill DeLacey on his way out, trailing after a guest he'd cornered in a conversation who appeared to be trying to escape. Junior lumbered after his father, then stopped in the doorway, turned, and looked at the casket as if torn between staying and leaving. Iris caught his eye. He took a step away from her. She continued to stare at him. He glanced out the door after his father, then, almost unwillingly, at the casket, then at Iris, whose eyes seemed to demand an explanation. He shrugged his shoulders and shuffled out.

Lily pulled harder on Iris's hand and they left the church for the bright sunshine.

"That son of a bitch, Bill DeLacey," Iris muttered. "He killed her. That son of a bitch killed her. And Junior knows it. Did you see the way he looked at me?"

"C'mon, Iris. A disturbed woman left you a weird phone message. That's all."

"Even if Dolly was suicidal, to choose hanging? Certainly she could have stockpiled enough drugs to do the trick. But, no. Instead, she made a noose, carried a ladder into the grove, climbed it, put her head in the noose, and jumped. Really."

"I don't know, Iris. Some things are better off buried."

Iris clenched her fist. "He is *not* getting away with this. He got real lucky when Gabriel Gaytan was murdered. Those cops were lucky too. Twenty-five years ago, beatings like that were a lot easier to cover up. Videotape didn't exist. I was just a kid and I was terrified to say anything. But if I let him get away with killing Dolly, I won't be able to live with myself."

"We're being summoned." Lily jerked her head toward their mother, who was standing with Bill DeLacey and Junior. Rose was merrily waving for Lily and Iris to join them.

"Here we go." Iris adjusted her purse strap on her shoulder and began walking with solid, assertive steps.

Bill DeLacey was talking. "Old Doc Vanderstaad said she never knew what hit her. You know, when the rope hitches up, your nerve endings get overstimulated and you don't feel pain. She had this look on her face like…"

His scalp, pink from the sun, was visible through the few strands of hair he brushed over the top of his head, which didn't hide his baldness but only accentuated his broad forehead and long face. He was wearing what were probably dress clothes—a snagged, ribbed, light blue polyester shirt and dark blue polyester pants that were slung low on his hips and belted beneath his large belly. A rigid thick tie circled the area under his fallen chin. He stood with his legs staggered as if he were in pain or bearing a great weight. His eyes were hidden by dark green clip-on shades.

"Well, look who's here," DeLacey said joylessly.

"Junior, my condolences." Iris hugged his big shoulders, which were broad with both muscle and fat.

Junior's shirt collar was snug around his chubby neck. The rim was wet with perspiration. He gave Iris a limp hug back.

Iris held her hand out toward Bill DeLacey. "Mr. DeLacey, I'm so sorry about Dolly."

He was holding a brown paper grocery bag by its rolled-down top in his rope-veined worker's hands. He shoved the bag toward her open hand. "Here. This was for Paula but it looks like you couldn't see to bring her, so you take it."

"Thank you," Iris said dryly as she accepted the bag.

Her response seemed to amuse DeLacey. He began laughing in that inhaling, exhaling way of his and shaking his head. "That's all you have to say?"

"What would you like me to say, Mr. DeLacey?"

"Iris, tell him how you tried to find Paula." Conflict made Rose uncomfortable.

"I called a private detective, decided it was too expensive, and ran out of time to do anything else."

"A private detective?" DeLacey exclaimed.

"I told you I don't know where Paula is, or don't you believe me?"

Junior nervously took a package of cigarettes from his breast pocket, shook one out, and lit it with a match from a book. "Now what are we going to do, Dad?"

DeLacey scowled. "Junior, just shut your fat mouth."

Junior seemed to sink as if enduring the force of a blow.

Iris said, "Mr. DeLacey, why don't you be straight with me?"

He gave her an exasperated, open-mouthed look. "Be straight?" He settled back on his heels and raised his index finger, making an arc in the air. "Now all I asked is—"

Iris began to speak loudly, drowning him out. "Dolly left me a message a few days ago saying she was afraid you were going to kill her. Now she's dead. Then you try to use me to get to Paula for reasons that apparently have nothing to do with the funeral. Would somebody like to tell me what the hell is going on?"

Junior nervously rolled the cigarette between his fingers.

DeLacey's voice grew soft. "Now, you know Dolly was mentally ill—"

"Iris!" Rose interjected. "Don't tell me you *believed* her?"

"Just because Dolly was crazy doesn't mean she didn't know what she was talking about. I'll be waiting in the car." Still holding the bag, Iris walked away, the sound of their concerned voices fading behind her.

She crossed the church's front lawn, waving at Thomas, who was still making the rounds. She began to cross a basketball court where the old blacktop was buckled from earthquakes when she sensed someone approaching her from behind. The footsteps fell into sync with hers.

She cast a glance to the side and saw a man she didn't recognize. She started walking faster. So did the man. After walking faster still, she abruptly stopped and faced him. "What's your problem? Why don't you just buzz off!"

Iris frowned at the intruder, then began to laugh, mostly at herself.

Paula smiled. She was well disguised in jeans, a loose Hawaiian shirt with the square hem out, a Panama hat with her hair pulled up under it, and dark sunglasses. "You've turned into a real bitch, girlfriend."

"I had early training by one of the best."

Paula bobbed her head appraisingly.

"Did you know everyone's looking for you?"

"I didn't know I was lost." She flicked the ashes from her lit cigarette by snapping her middle finger against it with the mien of someone who'd spent a lifetime copping an attitude. She looked at where her family was standing. "They all look like shit, except for the golden boy of course and you. Guess they had to get the old lady an extra large coffin. Glad to know she hadn't missed any meals."

"How did you know about the funeral?"

"The old man told me. I'd better go. He's got a sixth sense. Look, meet me tomorrow. I need to talk to you. There's a bar down in Hollywood. The Last Call. Two o'clock?" She started walking, leaving the blacktop and crossing the lawn.

Iris followed her with difficulty, the heels of her pumps sinking into the grass. "Wait."

Paula walked to an ancient four-door Oldsmobile that was parked at the curb. Its metallic midnight blue paint was faded in spots, acquiring different hues according to the amount of wear. Some patches had worn away completely, revealing rusted bare metal. The car's roof had a badly peeling landau top. A man waited in the driver's seat. He appeared to be tall, with long, kinky light brown hair held in a thick ponytail by a rubber band. Another man sat in the rear. He had shoulder-length straight black hair.

Iris finally caught up with her. "What do you mean, the old man told you about the funeral? Someone around here's going to start answering some questions."

"Don't get your panties in a wad." Paula opened the passenger door, smiling smugly. "Meet me tomorrow and I'll explain the facts of life to you."

"Three o'clock." Iris made a mental note of the Olds's license plate number as it pulled away. Suddenly she remembered she was still holding the bag that DeLacey had given her. She futilely raised it in the direction of the Olds that was rounding the corner at the end of the block. Iris didn't see Junior standing on the curb a few yards from her, also watching Paula drive away.

Sixteen

Iris drove the Triumph up *the hill that led to the Las Mariposas ranch house. The road didn't spiral around the hill like it did in reality, but cut and switched back across the face, zigzagging at a treacherous angle. The hill was a tall jagged mountain and the house a tiny dot at the top. It was raining hard, sheeting down, pounding on the TR's rag top and dripping through its faulty seals onto her. The normally dry, golden brown chaparral looked sadly out of character, like a wet cat. The unpaved road was thick with mud.*

Iris drove and drove, the TR's six cylinders roaring in a low gear, but the more she drove, the taller the hill seemed to get. She kept going. Finally, the house loomed into view. Paula stood at the top of the road. Her proportions were too large for the surroundings, like a big doll in a small doll house. She was perfectly dry. Her long brown hair whipped about her face as if a Santa Ana were blowing. She smiled broadly in that way of hers, as if she had the goods on you but she'd never tell. Iris was elated to see her and was waving through the windshield and Paula was waving too when the Triumph began to slip backward. Paula continued to wave as if nothing had happened, her figure quickly growing smaller as Iris went faster and faster straight down the hill. She saw Gabriel's wall looming closer in the rearview mirror. Bodies in various states of decay were layered in the wall like a catacomb. Some were skeletal, some had flesh that was sunken and dried like jerky, some were new, with bloated and oozing skin. The Triumph accordioned when Iris hit the wall. The impact sent the bodies flying into the air. One of them spun to face her. Humberto opened his eyes in his decaying face and stared at her accusingly.

Iris bolted upright in bed, gasping. She clutched at her heart and looked at the clock on the nightstand. Its green numerals glowed: 3:45 a.m.—half an hour before the alarm was set to go off. It was dark, but the room had been dark since she'd had the shattered windows boarded up. That was about to be remedied. She'd found a glass man to whom she was more than willing to pay a premium.

She walked into the adjoining bathroom and slipped on her terry cloth bathrobe. Plaster had dropped from the bathroom ceiling, revealing a dark hole full of pipes and conduit. Many of the ceramic floor and shower tiles were cracked. She'd thrown away the worst ones, leaving square patches of gray sealant behind. She put on slippers. She didn't dare walk through her home barefoot anymore.

She walked past the second bedroom, which she'd set up as an office, and past the smaller guest bathroom and into the living room. Water from a broken ceiling pipe had buckled sections of the hardwood floor and ruined her imported wallpaper. The Oriental rug had had to be thrown out along with the raw silk couch and the coffee table, after the insurance adjuster had taken pictures of the mess. Her brother-in-law and nephew had dropped the furniture from the terrace that ran the length of the living room to the ground below. The custom-made French doors had popped from their frames, making the job easier. By the time they had gone downstairs to straighten things out, some of the furniture had already been carted off, one person's tragedy becoming another's good fortune.

She used to love her condo and all the special touches with which she'd decorated it. Her home had been a source of pleasure and comfort to her. Now everywhere she looked, something grated on her nerves.

In the kitchen, the automatic coffeemaker had just switched on, its red light glowing dumbly and faithfully in the dark. She was always glad to see it. She pulled out the carafe and poured the few drops of coffee that had brewed into a plastic mug and drank them steaming hot and black. She stepped around two garbage bins. One held her broken china and everyday dishes and the other her crystal. She'd replaced everything with plastic. The insurance company would have paid for a like replacement, but when Iris went to the store and held the fragile pieces in her hands, she just couldn't bear the thought of owning them. But she couldn't part with the bins either, not just yet.

An aftershock rumbled through. It started with a gentle nudge, which grew more insistent until the building's joints creaked and the broken china and crystal tinkled. Iris braced herself against the kitchen counter until it stopped.

"Three point…two, three point three," she announced.

She wandered to the dining room windows, the only ones that hadn't broken, and looked out. The buildings on her street had sustained heavy damage in the initial shaker, but one street over, there was hardly any damage at all. Even within Iris's street, a building that had been hardly touched stood next to one that had been red-tagged. It just happened that way.

The tags were notebook-sized pieces of construction paper, color coded according to the level of damage, affixed by officials who were surveying all the buildings in the city. A green tag meant the building was safe. Yellow meant significant repairs were required. Red meant it was unsafe—damaged beyond repair.

The tags had a psychological effect upon the city's residents. Green made people feel confident and happy. Yellow was sad but still hopeful. People gaped at red-tagged buildings like one might rubberneck at a traffic fatality—horrified but unable to look away.

Across the street from Iris's green-tagged building, a butane lantern glowed in a tent set up on a building's front lawn where some of the residents preferred to sleep, at least until the aftershocks subsided. There had been several the previous night, which had jolted her from an already light sleep. She wondered if this was what it was like to live in a war zone. Misfortune could come crashing down at any moment, rest was fleeting, yet life went on.

She showered, dressed, and drove to the office. She left much earlier than normal, which was okay since traffic had been so goosey with the Ten being down. At the corner, she passed an abandoned, red-tagged condo complex that had shifted off its foundation, the walls tilting precariously to one side. Someone had spray-painted a message across the front: THE FAT LADY HAS SUNG.

Finally arriving downtown, she took the elevator to the twelfth floor. She pulled open the heavy glass doors of the McKinney Alitzer suite and strode across the thick mauve carpet. She was early and the investment counselors' cubicles were mostly empty. She glanced toward Herb Dexter's office, as she always did whenever she walked into the sales department. He sat behind his desk, studying a report, his elbows on the desk, his long fingers pressed against each temple.

He looked up just then, the fluorescent light reflecting from his round, tortoiseshell-framed glasses, and somewhat regally called her to his office with a wave of his bony, fragile-looking hand. People unfamiliar with Dexter sometimes made the mistake of assuming that his nerdy appearance implied weakness. But Iris had seen Dexter eat those types for breakfast with cutlery so sharp that it took them a moment to realize their entrails had been severed and presented to them on a fine china plate. It wasn't a side he revealed often, but then he didn't need to.

"Iris, you're here bright and early."

She stood inside his doorway. "The aftershocks gave me an early wake-up call this morning."

Dexter knowingly raised his eyebrows. "My wife and I are both eager to load up the moving van and head east. Between the riots and the fires and the earthquakes, not to mention the economy, the immigration issue…"

Iris regarded him with fatigue.

Dexter adjusted his glasses. "Well, I'm sure things will straighten out eventually. I just got off the phone with Garland Hughes. We're anticipating announcing your promotion first thing next week. I'm delighted that you want to jump into this. It's a good opportunity for you and an excellent move for the company."

"I'm pleased as well. Thank you."

She looked at the replicas of Remington sculptures that cluttered his office. The cowboys on their trusty steeds mastering the frontier created an aura of macho activity that was dichotomous with Dexter's quiet mental churnings.

"The firm still has some concerns about promoting someone to manager within the same office. But if you feel confident you can handle any fallout from your former peers, we'll trust your judgment."

"I'm confident I can."

"Good. L.A. can use a manager who not only understands this marketplace but this office as well. The manager's training class starts in New York in three weeks. I'll be staying on until you finish your training and get your feet wet in your new position." He stood. "Of course, this is all confidential, although I'm told that rumors about my returning to New York have been circulating."

"I've heard some water-cooler gossip," she conceded without revealing the source, knowing that Dexter would have the grace not to ask.

"I'd hoped to keep the news between us until I could make a formal announcement, but I guess the slightest hint of change sets tongues to wagging."

"Change makes people nervous."

He extended his hand.

When she took it, he grasped her hand more firmly than usual and smiled into her eyes. This was different. She was one of them now. She left his office and virtually bounced across the suite to her own. Warren Gray, Sean Bliss, and Kyle Tucker had arrived and were in their cubicles. Amber was walking in. They had been shooting glances at her while she was in Dexter's office, trying to catch a snatch of conversation. She unlocked her office door and mulled over what they might be thinking.

"Who cares?" she said aloud.

None of it mattered. The time of trying to encourage their friendship had passed. Now her job was to earn their respect.

She turned on her calculator and busied herself in her favorite time-waster—counting her money. She calculated how much more she'd net after her raise and how much her cut of the office's sales would bring her, especially after she started to put the squeeze on her sales staff. She then played with different distribution scenarios between stocks, bonds, and cash, and between retirement and current funds. This was great. This was better than sex. This was what she wanted, what she had worked for all those years and shoveled all that excrement to attain. She was loving life.

Her phone rang. The display indicated it was an outside call. She answered, "Iris Thorne," using a low-modulated but assertive tone, tasting the sound of her own name, which was now worth more, which now carried more weight in the world. She was the manager of the L.A. McKinney Alitzer office, the only female manager of one of the firm's major metropolitan offices. She was important.

"Good morning, Iris. It's Thomas Gaytan DeLacey."

"Hi, Thomas! Good to hear from you." She was effervescent.

"I know this is short notice, but I so enjoyed seeing you the other day, even though the circumstances were unpleasant. I wondered if we could get together for dinner tomorrow night."

"Tomorrow?" Iris loudly turned the pages of her Day Timer, even though she knew she didn't have any plans. "Let's see...Umm...Tomorrow looks great."

"Terrific. If it's okay with you, why don't you head out to my side of town. I'd like to show you my campaign office and I know a lovely place in Pasadena where we can have dinner."

"Sounds wonderful."

"Great. By the way, I wanted to let you know that your dad sent a nice spray of flowers to my mother's funeral. I hear that you and your sister's relationship with him has been strained since he remarried."

"To put it mildly."

"He's distanced himself from my family as well. I've always wondered why." He fell silent.

Iris also remained silent until she suspected that this was her cue to speak. "I have no idea. My father is an enigma to me. He never seemed happy with what he had or where he was." "I just wanted you to know that even though he didn't come to the funeral, he did acknowledge my mother. It was very kind."

"Thanks for letting me know."

They finished planning the time and location of their date. She hung up, grabbed her mug, and went into the lunchroom. Amber Ambrose, Warren Gray, and Kyle Tucker were huddled in a tight group, talking. They stopped when they saw her.

"Hi," Iris said cheerily. She poured coffee into her mug.

After a few painful beats, Warren awkwardly resumed talking. "Could you believe it when he blew that free throw?"

"I know," Kyle commiserated. "It was all over."

"Totally," Amber said.

Iris turned to face them. Amber and Warren were watching her. Kyle seemed ill at ease and looked at the floor.

"Amber!" Iris exclaimed with surprise. "I didn't know you were a basketball fan."

"I'm not really but occasionally I see something to watch that I find interesting." She gazed at Iris haughtily.

Warren and Kyle shot alarmed glances at Amber.

Iris quizzically looked from one to the next. "What's going on with you guys?"

"Nothing's going on," Amber said. "We're just talking about the game."

"Oh-kay." Iris left the lunchroom, feeling their eyes on her back. *They're not ruining my good mood. The hell with 'em.*

Iris worked hard all afternoon with renewed vigor, spending time following up on sales leads that she would soon be able to turn over to her subordinates and tying up a few loose ends before she left to meet Paula. She flipped through her Rolodex and found Gil Alvarez's number. After punching the number into her telephone keypad, she spun her chair to face her western window as she waited for the ringing phone to be answered. The days continued to be unseasonably hot and the sky had lightened to a pale blue-white as the afternoon peaked.

The secretary with the soothing voice answered and explained that he was out of the office.

"Please let him know that I've looked through his holdings and would like to sit down with him and share my ideas."

She distractedly flipped through her Rolodex as she spoke, lighting on the card with her father's number. The paper had attained a yellow hue with age. She'd written that card when she first got the Rolodex after starting her job with McKinney Alitzer. She'd put in his number though it had been years since she'd spoken with him even then. Each year, she purged old cards and each year she pulled this one out and looked at it. First, she'd feel angry and toy with throwing the card away. Then the anger would transform into something less easily borne—hurt— and then, worse still, remorse. Finally, a ray of hope would glimmer and she'd slide the card back into its spot under the T's for Thorne, having long ago moved it from the D's for Dad. But she still put it back. It was a slender connection, but it was something.

She left her name and number with Gil Alvarez's secretary and pressed the button that disconnected the call. She immediately started dialing again. She had to do it now. She couldn't stop to think about it. After four rings, the phone was answered by a young voice. Iris couldn't tell if it was a boy or a girl. She heard children yelping in the background.

"Is Les there?"

"Yeah. Just a minute." The phone was clumsily put down. "Dad!"

The word startled her.

"Dad, some lady wants you on the phone."

Suddenly, her eyes grew hot and her chest felt empty. She grew short of breath.

The phone was picked up. *"Yellow,"* Les said in his countrified way.

Iris hung up.

Seventeen

Iris negotiated the maze of intersecting freeways in downtown L.A. known as the cloverleaf until she managed to get on the 101 north, which led into Hollywood. She thought about the last time she'd seen Paula. She'd been a freshman at UCLA and living in a dormitory. Paula would occasionally appear on her doorstep, sometimes with some guy, sometimes alone. The last time, Paula had arrived alone.

They had gone out that night. John Somers, Iris's then boyfriend, drove them around in his beat-up MG with the brakes that were almost gone. John had worn his college uniform of Levi's button-front shrink-to-fit jeans, a Levi's work shirt, and Adidas tennis shoes. His hair was thick, wavy, red and reached well past his shoulders. His beard was full and roan-hued. The abundance of hair made him look imposing, even dangerous, like a wild man who had crawled out from the foothills. The hair added substance to his already large frame and, perhaps intentionally, obscured his more delicate, almost fragile features—his Cupid's bow lips and sensitive green-flecked hazel eyes.

Iris and Paula had crowded into the MG's single passenger seat and took turns pulling the emergency brake to stop the car. The three of them were having fun, the kind of fun that came from being old enough to have a little money and transportation and to know where the action was, but young enough not to dwell on any consequences. Paula, of course, was a catalyst.

She had got them into the Whisky on the Sunset Strip even though they were under age, because she knew the band. She turned heads as she walked through the club and she relished the attention. She was exotically beautiful with her mother's lush lips and dark coloring and her father's height, which she accentuated with platform shoes. Her skin-tight bell-bottoms had hodgepodge patches stitched over threadbare spots in the rear and knees. Her braless breasts peek-a-booed through the open weave of her crocheted top, a tease which she accentuated by flipping her hair over her chest. Several slender gold S-link chains glittered against her deeply tanned skin. A charm dangled from each chain: a crooked Italian horn, the word SEXY, and a tiny, long-handled spoon used for dipping cocaine from vials.

Paula was an intoxicating cocktail of glamour and urbanity with a splash of jadedness. Iris was in awe of her. Paula seemed to know something about everything and seemed to have something on everyone, even if she didn't. Her charms weren't lost on John Somers, who was amazed that she and Iris were friends. Paula was so unlike Iris's other friends.

Cocaine was just making inroads as the new glamour drug and Paula had been singing its praises. "It's like champagne. There's nothing like doing some lines then fucking." She gave them a knowing small smile, which she focused a shade too long on John.

He was enthralled. "Can we score some?"

"Sure," Paula responded. "Got any dough?"

After many promises to pay her back, John and Paula got Iris to dip into the cash that she'd set aside to buy textbooks. Paula procured the coke, as promised. They went to John's apartment, where Iris refused to partake.

"C'mon, Iris," John chided. "Stop being so straight. It won't kill you."

"One strawberry daiquiri is her limit," Paula teased.

After watching them get high, which Iris found an almost clinical experience, she went into John's bedroom and fell asleep in her clothes. It was still dark when she woke sometime during the night. Small noises emanated from the living room and the soft light of candles flickered. Iris tiptoed toward the living room, fearful of what she might see but having to see anyway.

Paula saw Iris first, but not immediately. John didn't notice. He was engaged in a passion that was hungry and brutal and so different from anything he had shown Iris that she barely recognized him. She was both horrified and fascinated as she watched his broad, straining, sweat-covered body and his contorted face. All of a sudden, as if he'd been shaken from a spell, he noticed her. He didn't say a word, but his delicate eyes and mouth peeping through his hair betrayed him. He was sorry and his expression seemed to acknowledge that he recognized it didn't matter.

Paula also said nothing but predictably, her gaze was arrogant, as if to say, "It's your fault."

Iris quickly got her shoes and walked home alone in the dead of night. The next day, Paula returned to Iris's room to get her things and Iris told her she never wanted to see her again.

Paula snapped, "No problem," and left.

Later, Iris discovered that the rest of her textbook money was missing.

The Last Call was on a street off Hollywood Boulevard near Vine, an intersection that wore its faded glamour like a forgotten ornament clinging to a discarded Christmas tree. The cops and the City Council had done an admirable job of moving the party girls, bun boys, and drug dealers away from the main strip. The tourists, in bright shorts, Hawaiian shirts and cameras, could now travel the Walk of Fame, pointing at their favorites among the brass-trimmed, pink granite stars, and try their feet and hands in the cement imprints in front of the Chinese theater with a false sense of security.

Iris parked across the street in front of the bar and expected never to see the Triumph again. A couple of teenage boys sat on the back of a bus stop bench nearby. They had the street-wise, tightly coiled attitude of runaways, as if they were perennially waiting for something —friends, enemies, or for the life that they had run away for to start. They barely glanced at Iris, who must have seemed to them to be nothing but a predictable, monied adult, but they lavished covetous attention on the shiny, fire-engine-red Triumph.

Iris walked up to them. "You guys want to earn ten bucks?"

"To do what?" one of them said unenthusiastically, apparently having been approached to do things for money before.

"Watch my car? I'll give you five now and five when I come out."

"Twenty," the other said.

"Fifteen," Iris responded. "Five now and ten when I come out."

"Deal."

Iris fished a five from her purse, gave it to one of the boys, and walked across the street, carrying the brown paper bag that Bill DeLacey had given her. She noticed the faded midnight blue Oldsmobile parked on the street near the bar.

The Last Call was in the middle of a row of single-story shops with a fortuneteller on one side and a Thai restaurant on the other. All the shops had black metal security bars across their doors and windows. Some of the bars were molded into swirls and twists in the manufacturer's valiant effort to make them appear decorative. Others with no such pretensions had finished the tips of their bars with vicious spear-like appendages. Just keep the hell out.

The Last Call's front door was open, but a wood panel six feet tall, four feet wide, and painted a dull black stood just inside it to discourage people from casually peeking inside. There were windows on either side. In one, a neon sign advertising Coors beer shone pale yellow through the grimy glass and the security bars. In the other, NO ONE UNDER 21 ADMITTED was barely visible through the dirt. A neon sign with THE LAST CALL in tall letters and a martini glass holding an olive leaned into the street from the roof. The strains of a Led Zeppelin tune filtered onto the sidewalk.

"Thank you for this lovely adventure, Paula," Iris muttered to herself as she clutched her purse close under one arm and the paper bag under the other. She stepped through the doorway and around the panel. The air smelled stale and faintly odorous, suggesting sources that she preferred not thinking about. The light was dim and she stood just inside the door waiting for her eyes to adjust. The song was over and the music stopped. The lights of a jukebox shone against a far wall. She could make out a dark shape standing in front of it and then heard coins rattling through the mechanism.

She felt people watching her, although she couldn't make out much more than dark shadows in the gloom. She heard them rustling. She imagined them wondering what a well-dressed woman was doing in such a place and speculating about what she could want from them or what they could get from her. The clack of billiard balls resonated from somewhere in the back.

A country-and-western song came on this time and the person in front of the jukebox started clapping with the music and doing line dance steps.

Cursing under her breath, Iris began walking toward the end of the bar, where she'd spotted some empty stools far from the other patrons.

Paula Texas two-stepped behind her, singing along with the jukebox. "You promised you'd never leave…" She grabbed Iris's hand, put her arm around her waist, and tried to dance with her. "Now you're sayin' you're never comin' back. Well, baby, don't let the door…"

When Iris remained frozen, Paula continued dancing on her own. "Who would have thought? An old rock-and-roller like me into country."

"I left the office early to meet you."

Paula puckered her lips. "What a sourpuss. Don't tell me you haven't had any fun since I've been gone."

"Oh yeah. Life with you was a barrel of monkeys. Remember when you slept with my boyfriend and stole my money? Gee whiz. I can't remember the last time I had so much fun."

Paula theatrically hunched her shoulders and tiptoed past Iris toward the bar. "Would Madame like a drink?"

"Madame would like to know why the hell she's here."

Paula continued tiptoeing, casting mock tentative glances at Iris, who was growing more irritated by the minute. They walked to the end of the bar, passing men hunkered over their drinks who could have been anywhere from twenty to fifty years old. They wore jeans and T- or flannel shirts and long hair—the rock and roller's uniform of the past three generations. Posters from 1960s concerts given by the Grateful Dead, Jimi Hendrix, and the Jefferson Airplane were hung behind the bar. An extra-large bottle of aspirin stood next to a heavy, old, steel cash register. Scattered bottles of booze with few premium brands stood on shelves that were backed with mirrored panels.

"Strawberry daiquiri?" Paula grinned. "Or have you moved on to something stronger? Seems like everyone I knew who was as straight as you has gone wild and the people I knew who were wild-ass crazy have found Jesus or something." She threw her head back and laughed. "Or they're dead."

Paula's voice was the same, loud without effort and clipped in a way that was accusing and demanding at the same time. Her hair, always lush and wavy, reached the middle of her back and was still dark chestnut brown. The color looked unnaturally uniform, as if she might be using a rinse to cover gray. Her figure had filled out from the voluptuous twenty-year-old that Iris knew. She looked much older than her years. "Except for me. Though it wasn't for lack of trying."

Iris brushed off a stool before sitting down. "I'll have something in a *sealed* bottle."

"Toby, two Coors in bottles, please."

Toby, the bartender, had deep vertical lines in his face. His long gray-streaked hair was gathered at the nape of his neck with a rubber band. A gold hoop earring dangled from an ear. He jerked the bottle tops off with an opener bolted to the side of the bar, the caps clattering when they hit the many others already on the ground. He set two dewy bottles and two milky glasses in front of them.

Iris pushed the glass aside, wiped off the bottle with her hand, and drank straight from it.

Paula lit a cigarette. She puckered her full lips and frowned as she dragged on it, accentuating the wrinkles between her eyebrows and the vertical lines on her lips. She still wore the heavy eyeliner and mascara that she'd worn at twenty and the effect was harsh against her older skin. The gold chains were gone but each ear now displayed three pierced earrings in ascending sizes, ending with big gold hoops.

Iris swatted at the smoke.

"Iris, you started out this way the other day. You're just determined to be a pain in the ass, aren't you?"

"I'm just getting warmed up."

They stared at each other as if waiting to see who would blink first, though no one had set the rules of the game.

After several seconds, Iris couldn't resist adding, "I want you to experience the full dose."

A smile began to tease the corners of Paula's lips. Iris pressed hers together to keep herself from smiling, but was losing control. Paula let loose an explosion of laughter. Iris followed right behind her. Paula slapped the bar and held her head in her hands. Iris held her aching ribs and wiped tears from her eyes. They began to calm down but got started all over again when Iris accidentally made a snorting noise when she inhaled. After a few minutes, their breathless laughter subsided into scattered chuckles.

Paula regarded Iris. "You look good, girlfriend."

"Thanks," Iris said.

"Real establishment."

"I've even voted Republican once or twice. So, ah, what have you been up to?"

"I know," Paula gestured toward herself with the cigarette. "I look like shit."

Iris laughed again. "What the hell have you been doing for the past twenty years?"

Paula languidly shook her head as if there were too many things to even mention. She abruptly grew serious, leaning her elbows against the bar and staring straight ahead. "I'd really hoped you'd forgiven me. Not just for that thing with your boyfriend and your money but, you know, for everything. I just couldn't stop hurting people I cared about. I hated myself for it, but I couldn't stop." She looked at Iris. "I'm sorry."

Iris regarded the dark circles under Paula's eyes and the deep lines in her face. "That's a lot to forgive, Paula. I don't think you've done anything to earn it."

Paula looked away and expelled air as if she was being deflated. "You really have turned into a tough broad, haven't you?"

Iris sipped her Coors. "I'm not trying to be tough. Just saying what's on my mind."

"I thought leaving made me tough. Every time things in my life got rough"—she jerked her thumb over her shoulder—"See ya!" She knocked ash from her cigarette with a flick of her middle finger and dragged hard on it again. "But some situations you just need to deal with. Walk through the fire, you know? And when you come out..." She clenched her fist and tapped her chest with it.

"Paula!" a man shouted from the pool tables at the back of the bar. "Hi, baby."

Paula raised her hand listlessly.

"I love you, baby! Is that your friend you were waiting for?"

"I told you her name's Iris."

"Hi, Iris!"

Paula explained, "That's Angus and his friend Bobby."

"Angus?" Iris asked.

"Yeah, well."

"Hi, Angus and Bobby," Iris shouted back through the cigarette smoke.

Paula said, "So what happened between you and Mr. Satisfaction after that night? I imagine you told him he could park his dick somewhere else."

Iris just smiled.

"Don't tell me. You took him back, didn't you?"

Iris held two fingers in the air.

"Peace?"

Iris raised the fingers again.

"Twice? You took him back twice? Jesus H. Christ, Iris. Can't you pick 'em better than that?"

"Don't worry, Paula. You haven't cornered the market on doing stupid things with your life. I'm great in business. Lousy in relationships."

"You married?"

"No. You?"

"I was, once or twice." She jerked her thumb toward the pool tables. "Not to him, though. Got any kids?"

"No. You?"

"Yeah, I got a couple. But they're not with me." Paula scratched at something on her face almost as if it might detract from what they were talking about. "So are you happy, Iris?"

Iris became thoughtful. Finally, she said, "Yeah. I'm happy."

"Being happy's like being in love. If you have to think too long about it, you're probably not."

"I'm happy," Iris insisted. "I'm being promoted into the job I've wanted for years. I've got a couple of new men on the horizon."

"Yeah, who?"

"Your brother, for one."

Paula blinked. "Thomas?"

"We're having dinner tomorrow night."

"You do have bad taste, don't you?"

"How do you know what he's like now? You haven't been around."

"A date isn't the only thing he wants, Iris."

"Paula!" Angus yelled from the back of the bar. "Baby, I'm lonely."

"I'm talking to Iris!"

Iris retorted, "I'm not going to fall into bed with him."

"That's not what I meant. He's only trying to use you to get to me."

Iris leaned away from the bar and folded her arms across her chest. "Why don't you illuminate this situation for me? Why did your father ask me to find you when he'd already been in contact with you?"

"Because he didn't want you to know about what I have that he wants. He thought you could sweet-talk me into showing up so he and I could have a little *mano a mano*. He doesn't know where I live, see? I've been moving around a lot just to keep him off base."

"What you have that he wants?"

Paula leaned close to her. "My grandfather's will, the *real* one."

"His will? What about the one that was read after his murder?"

"Didn't we all wonder why Gabriel left the rancho to both my mom and the old man? Everyone knew the last thing Gabriel wanted was my father to get his hands on Las Mariposas. So with Gabriel out of the picture, the old man forged his will. It would have been beautiful except the old man never got rid of the real will."

"How did you get it?"

"Remember when my mom flipped out and she made me take that picture of my grandparents' wedding? The will was hidden in the back. All these years, I never knew it until the picture broke in the earthquake." She chuckled throatily. "The old fart left the old man one square foot of *dirt*." She threw her head back and laughed, slapping the bar and clutching her ribs. She laughed harder and harder. Some of the other patrons couldn't help laughing with her.

Iris wasn't laughing.

"C'mon, Iris. It's funny!"

"I don't find anything funny."

Paula snapped her fingers as if an idea had occurred to her. "You can help me get the cash from the old man." She scratched her head. "How do they do that? You know, like when somebody's kidnapped somebody? You leave the person in one place and then you have them leave the money someplace else. Isn't that how it works?"

"Your mother left me a message right before she died. She thought your father was trying to kill her."

"So what? I thought he'd killed her years ago when he had her head fried."

"What's it like to go through life not giving a rat's ass about anyone but yourself?"

"Hey! No one ever cared about *me*, okay? Now it's my turn to do some taking."

Iris regarded Paula dispassionately. "You still haven't forgiven her, have you? She did the best she could."

"Well, it wasn't good enough."

"She reached out to you for help. She wanted you to have your grandfather's will. She was hoping you'd do the right thing."

"She was out of her head. She didn't know what the fuck she was doing."

"And you have the gall to ask me for forgiveness."

"Paula baby!" Angus yelled. "Let's go!"

"How much are you asking for the will?" Iris asked.

"Fifty thousand," Paula said in a manner intended to impress.

Iris made an unkind noise. "At least ask for something in the six figures."

Paula glared at her. "You think you always know more, don't you? But you don't. You don't know what it was like to live on that hill. You don't know. So don't get on your high horse and preach to me."

"Why do you hate them so much?"

"Just don't judge me. You're not me."

Iris slid off the barstool. "I'm not you, but I'm still going to form an opinion of you, whether you like it or not." She pushed the brown paper bag toward her. "Here. Your father wanted you to have this."

Paula tentatively unrolled the bag. She peered inside, then reached in, her expression still hard but without her previous conviction. She took out a small jewelry box covered in faded purple velvet and gold braid. The braid drooped in places where it had lost its adhesive.

"It's her good jewelry," Iris explained

"I remember. I'm not a complete idiot." She squared the box on the bar. "It was *for nice*. So she never wore it because she never went anyplace nice." She looked at Iris. "Did you open it?"

"Of course."

"I used to look at it when I was a kid, but she'd never let me play with it." Paula opened the hinged lid. She prodded the contents with her index finger, her jaw tightening, the finger jabbing in the box harder and harder. "That son of a bitch." She picked up a necklace with a pendant and waved it. "This is dime-store junk. It's not even gold." She slapped it on the bar and took out a charm bracelet, threw it on the bar, then picked up the box and turned it over, dumping out the last few pieces. "Bastard gave her crap and she kept it like it was something special. I was just a kid. I didn't know it was crap. Guess she didn't either. But he did." She leaned her elbows on the bar and buried her face in her hands.

The men at the bar glanced sideways at Paula and then stared down harder into their drinks, trying to pretend they weren't in the presence of a crying woman.

Iris had never seen Paula cry before. She reached out her hand but hesitated before touching her, recalling that Paula was never the touchy-feely type. She put her hand on her arm anyway.

At Iris's touch, Paula took her hands away from her face. She decorously picked up the jewelry and put it back in the box. "She's dead now anyway. What difference does it make?" She did not touch her face.

Angus and Bobby walked up.

"Are you crying, baby?" Angus's dull face rippled with concern.

"I'm not crying." Paula put the box back inside the paper bag.

"Whatcha got?" Angus asked.

"Something from my mother."

"That's nice. Let's go. Bobby and I have some business to take care of." He started to walk toward the door with Bobby following.

Paula rolled down the top of the bag, reached in her back pocket, and took out some cash.

"Forget it," Iris said.

"Paula!" Angus shouted from the doorway.

Paula picked up the bag and nodded at Iris. "See you in another twenty years."

Eighteen

Iris went shopping. She passed a billboard depicting her favorite mall, which now largely lay in ruins due to the earthquake. She headed to another mall instead. Small shops advertised "Earthquake Sale" or "Discount on Earthquake Mix" in an effort to hawk damaged or illogically sorted items. Spray-painted signs on stores with boarded-up windows cheerfully announced they were open for business, which was good news for Iris. She was in a mood to spend money and she did.

The mall was still suffering from the postquake slump and was almost empty save the few other shop-or-die kindred souls. She started with a swingy new dress for her date with Thomas. The new dress called for new shoes and the new shoes a new purse and new stockings. The new outfit cried out for new makeup and the new makeup a new fragrance. She couldn't wear her new look with tired lingerie, so she bought new, selecting lacy and silky nothings that skirted the edge of trashiness. The shopping spree soon took on a life of its own. A lot of things were on sale, things that were out of season, that she couldn't wear for months if at all, but she bought them anyway. Look at all the money she was saving. The store clerks scanned the tags as fast as she could pile the merchandise on the counter. This was the true meaning of disposable income. There was something about the delectable crinkling of the crisp shopping bags that tasted like freedom.

She loaded her packages into the Triumph, quickly filling the trunk and the storage area behind the seats. Sure enough, during her shopping spree, she'd formulated an action plan in relation to the DeLaceys. Some people go to gyms, some see their therapists, Iris shopped. Her method was tried and true and no more expensive, she figured, than regular visits to a Beverly Hills shrink.

She headed north on Pacific Coast Highway and east on Topanga Canyon Boulevard. Trees began to appear and minimalls disappeared as she headed further into the hills. Houses and apartments built cheek by jowl on the hillsides near the ocean were displaced by funky, woodsy affairs in the canyon. Licks of blackened areas appeared here and there between the trees. Soon she was in an ash-covered primeval landscape of crisp bushes, brooding tree skeletons, and cement stairs that led to nowhere. The odor of soot and burnt wood hung in the air and the earth itself was black.

Houses that had previously been shielded by the forest were now exposed. Chimneys still stood. Half-eaten walls revealed floor plans where kitchens and bathrooms were easily located by their porcelain fixtures. Some of the owners had completed the demolition of their homes, leaving behind just concrete foundations scraped clean. Rubble still cluttered others. Occasionally, a single house remained intact, only touched by the flames while everything around it burned. Maybe the owners were better prepared for fire or maybe they were just lucky, though it was guilt-inducing, odd luck to live in the only house standing in the neighborhood. Fire was fickle that way.

There were few trees, so there were few birds. The Triumph puttered obtrusively in the silence. She switched off her radio because it seemed inappropriately joyous. She turned on Cat Canyon, then on Withered Canyon, following a familiar route that she hadn't taken in months but was still fresh in her mind.

She drove higher until she could look across the burnt Santa Monica Mountains and see the Pacific, which had stopped the fire's westward progression, shining silver as the sun began to set. At the end of Withered Canyon, she parked in the flat clearing that had served as a visitors' parking lot. There were no visitors there now. All the houses in this canyon had been destroyed. She walked up the gravel road, her heels unsteady on the pebbles.

John Somers's house, built clinging to the side of the canyon wall, had not been visible from the road. Its only markers were a driveway and a mailbox. The steep driveway was still there but the mailbox was not. Iris stood at the top of the driveway and looked down. The large, woodsy, somewhat ramshackle redwood house was gone. In its place on the foundation was a large, jelly bean-shaped, aluminum Air Stream trailer. Two cheap white plastic chairs and a table stood in front of it. A jar on the table held bright carnations. It looked like a campsite in hell.

A sandbagging project was in progress. A wall of sandbags, three high, was placed in a V shape across the front of the property. A shovel, a pile of burlap sacks, and scattered mounds of sand were on the ground.

A dog began to bark and Iris caught her breath.

A muscular white bull terrier, his paws and the underside of his belly blackened with soot, charged from around the back of the trailer toward her. The stubby coarse hairs on the back of his neck were erect. He stopped short a few feet from her, his throat rumbling, and fixed her with one blue and one brown eye.

"Hi, Buster!" Iris exclaimed, glad to see this dog that had made it clear during the time she had been dating his owner that she was barely tolerated on his territory.

The dog turned his big head so that his warm brown eye faced her, then lowered his head compliantly and walked toward her. She reached her hand out and he licked her fingers once. She patted his hard skull and traced her fingernails across the short hair there. They both turned at the sound of a car engine. Buster bolted up the driveway, barking and wagging his tail.

A large, black Chevy pickup truck turned down the driveway and pulled onto the dirt near the sandbags. Its bed was full of sand. John Somers opened the door and stepped out. The large truck suited his long proportions. Wearing worn jeans, heavy boots, and a plaid flannel shirt, he looked as rugged as the surroundings. His coarse red hair was cut shorter than Iris remembered and he sported a neatly trimmed beard of a browner shade of red than the hair on his head.

"Is that Iris?" he half asked and half exclaimed. He stood next to the truck as if it made him feel safe.

"Hi, John." She held her hands open to indicate the scene.

"Yeah. Pretty weird, isn't it? I got your card. Thanks."

"Seems sort of a lame response to something like this."

"It was nice to know that you were thinking of me. You've had your own problems lately. Santa Monica was hard hit in the quake, wasn't it?"

"Yeah. The earth liquefied or turned to Jell-O or some damn thing."

"How'd you make out?"

She shrugged. "Not unscathed but not as bad as some people. The Homeowners Association is fighting over what they're going to fix and when and…" She shook her head as if the subject were repellent.

They met each other's eyes across the ash-covered dirt.

"You grew a beard. It's a bit more refined than the one you had in college."

"I'm on a leave of absence for a few months." He stroked his beard. "I'm taking advantage of my freedom."

"A leave of absence?"

"I just couldn't handle it. Investigating murders, then coming home to this. I've been seeing a therapist to help me figure things out."

"*You*, seeing a witch doctor?"

"Yeah, me. I've changed a lot. Had a lot of time to think." He looked at her meaningfully.

She pointed at the dog, changing the subject. "Buster came right up and licked my hand. Surprised the heck out me."

"He's been a kinder, gentler dog since the fire."

Buster walked to stand next to John, as if he knew he was being talked about.

John roughly scratched the dog's back. "Penny and Chloe couldn't find him when they had to evacuate. A few days later, I got a call from this guy who found him drinking from his pool. His fur was singed and his paws were blistered, but he was okay. He'd run all the way out of the canyon." He patted the dog, blinking as his eyes watered.

Iris also blinked back a tear at Buster's story.

John continued rubbing the dog, which seemed to have lapsed into a semihypnotic state. John glanced at Iris and pressed his lips together as if trying to hold back something that begged to be said. "She left me again. Penny."

"I heard. Tough luck. Chloe living with her?"

"Like before. Sometimes here, sometimes there. Chloe's going to be sixteen. Can you believe it?"

"She's going to catch up with me. I stopped counting at twenty-nine."

"You look like you're twenty-nine. You look great."

"Thanks."

She saw him inhale the air in her direction. It was a tiny gesture. He raised his head slightly and his nostrils flared for a moment. She'd spritzed herself so many times when she was shopping she probably smelled like the fragrance counter. She swayed back and forth slightly, feeling awkward. She scooped her hair behind her ear, just to be doing something, and looked at the Air Stream. "Did everything burn?"

"I saved some pictures and things. It makes you realize how little you really need. It's liberating, in a way. I lost a lot, but I gained a lot too."

He frowned at his shoes, then looked up with something settled, finalized in his eyes. He moved his leg as if he was about to take a step.

She virtually fled from him, turning and quickly walking toward the sandbags. She didn't want to hear it. She couldn't hear it. "What's going on here?" she asked conversationally.

He stood beside her, somewhat closer than necessary. "For the rain. There's no growth on the hillsides to hold the mud and water back. The V shape directs the water around the trailer." He casually rested his foot on top of the sandbag wall, but his body was tense.

She cringed slightly, sensing the inevitable. She hadn't come here for this, for revelations and explanations, but he seemed determined to seize the moment. She tried another tactic. "Hey! I'm being promoted to manager of the L.A. office."

"That's great, Iris! Congratulations."

"Thanks."

"I always knew you could accomplish anything you wanted." He sighed. "You're just terrific." He pressed his lips together like he had just before he spoke of Penny.

Here it comes, she thought.

"Iris, I've kicked my butt every day since I sent you away from me. I guess I really screwed it up for us."

"It's in the past."

"I agree. For the first time in a long time, I'm looking forward to the future. I hope with you."

He reached to take her hand. For some reason, she let him. She'd been lonely. She hadn't dwelt on it, but she was good at that, at forward motion, momentum, at not staying in one place too long and not looking back. His grasp felt warm and familiar. They had replayed this scene many times over the years. Him on bent knee, hat in hand, begging for forgiveness, and her swearing she'd never again go down that path. Two years ago, in spite of herself, she'd fallen in love with him again. A year ago, he'd told her he was going back to his ex-wife. She'd sworn it was the last time he'd break her heart. Her hand rested against his wrist and she felt his heartbeat. She immediately released him. She couldn't bear the intimacy.

"Let it go, John."

"I had hoped you'd forgiven me."

She looked across the barren landscape. "That's the second time someone's said that to me today. I have to go home and read my horoscope."

"I guess you haven't."

"I can't just set the pain aside. I've paid too dearly for it. I cried myself to sleep too many nights."

"If you don't make peace with the past, it'll pollute your present, Iris."

"Maybe it should."

He stroked his beard. "I want you to know that whatever happens between us, I'll always be your friend. You can always count on me. Call me if you ever need anything."

She changed the strap of her purse from one shoulder to the other. "Well, that's great because...umm...I do need something."

"Is that why you came?"

"Well...Yes."

He snickered and looked at his boots.

"I'm sorry. You started on this relationship thing before I had a chance—"

"You *held* my hand. I felt..." He bitterly shook his head. "I'm an idiot. I'm always an idiot."

She wished she could help him but she couldn't. He owned this one.

"So what can I do for you, Iris?"

It now embarrassed her to ask, but she hadn't come all this way for nothing. "I wondered if you could track down a car license number for me." She pulled a slip of paper from her purse. "It might belong to some guy named Angus or another guy, named Bobby, or to Paula DeLacey."

"Paula DeLacey. Why does that name sound familiar?"

"She's an old friend of mine. You met her when we were in college." She hoped he didn't remember the incident. She'd witnessed all the self-flagellation she could bear for one day.

He winced as he thought. "Oh, yeah. Paula. Of course." He took the paper and thankfully did not say another word on the subject but looked at her askance as if expecting a blow. "Give me a day to track this down."

"Great." She surveyed his new habitat again. "So I guess *everything* burned, huh?"

DIANNE EMLEY

"I just took some pictures and clothes and stuff, like I told you."

She chewed her lower lip. "Maybe it's best."

He rounded his eyes and mouth as if a thought had occurred to him. "You mean *that?*"

"Yeah, *that.*"

"So that's what you really came for." He grabbed a shovel which was leaning against the sandbags and started to walk past the Air Stream. He looked back. "Come and get it."

She followed. It was indeed what she had come for.

He walked past the foundation of his former house and down a slope to a level area where his fruit trees and garden once grew. The trees that were left were just stumps. He stood at the base of one of them and stepped five paces, then began to dig. After going down a couple of feet, he pulled a green plastic garbage bag from the hole. He dusted the dirt from it, then tore it open with his fingers. There was a second garbage bag inside. He tore that too. He pulled out a large overstuffed Louis Vuitton satchel and handed it to her.

She took it and looked inside.

"It's all there," he said. "What was it? About half a million dollars?"

"About four hundred thousand," she corrected him.

"I could never figure out why you left it on my doorstep."

"I wanted Penny to find it with the note I wrote. I knew how jealous she was. I did it to be a bitch."

"I found it before she got home."

"The best-laid plans…"

"Why didn't you keep it? I was the only one who knew you had it."

"It's unlaundered drug money from the mob. I couldn't spend that much cash without sending up a flare to the IRS. Plus some friends of mine died because of it. In my mind it's tainted."

"Why do you want it now?"

"I need a lot of cash for something and I got to thinking. If I use dirty money to do something dirty but morally right, maybe it makes the money clean."

"Two wrongs never make a right." He gave her a penetrating look.

"What?" she asked.

"You're not going to have somebody killed, are you?"

Her mouth gaped with delight. "It never occurred to me. Leave it to a cop to come up with a great idea like that. I could probably hire a real pro with this dough."

"Just don't get into trouble."

She gestured toward herself. "*Moi?*"

He laughed. It was good to see him laugh. It was a good time to leave. She turned and began trudging back up the sooty dirt. At the top of the rise, she turned to look at him one last time. "Thanks."

"Don't mention it. Say hi to your mother for me."

"Sure," she said, knowing it would be a cold day in hell.

Nineteen

Iris slapped the snooze button on the clock radio and remained horizontal. After ten minutes passed in a heartbeat, she slapped it again. When it buzzed the third time, she knew she'd be in serious trouble if she didn't haul her butt out of bed. She knew without looking at the clock that it was almost 5 a.m. She had fifteen minutes to get ready for work. She flew out of bed, leaving it unmade, plugged in the hot rollers, flung herself into the shower, barely patted herself dry, wound the rollers into her hair, burning her face and neck where they touched her skin, ran into her closet, struggled to pull on pantyhose over her damp skin, and snagged a work dress off a hanger. As she was buttoning it up, one of the buttons came off and flew into her forest of shoes. "Crap!"

She tore the dress off and grabbed her faithful herringbone-weave suit that was well overdue for a trip to the dry cleaners but never looked it. She rummaged in the closet, desperate to find a clean blouse. In the back, she found a blouse she disliked and hadn't worn in years. She fumbled with the buttons as she put it on, hoping that no one at the office would ask her if it was new.

Hearing the minutes tick by in her head, she spent a precious minute unzipping the garment bag in which she'd packed her new dress and accessories. She breathed a sigh of relief. That thing hadn't happened. That weird thing in which clothes that were "can't-live-without-it" in the heat of the shopping moment transformed into "what-was-I-thinking?" in the cool light of day. The outfit was still fabulous. She swooned.

She scooped makeup into her purse, grabbed her briefcase and the garment bag, poured already brewed coffee into her commuter mug, and ran out the door, down the stairs, and into the garage. She put on her makeup by the light of a flashlight held between her knees as the Triumph warmed up. At the on-ramp to the Ten, the light was green and she orange-lined the TR.

Forty-five minutes later, she walked into the McKinney Alitzer suite, composed and on time. She walked past the investment counselors' cubicles, her garment bag tossed over her shoulder, her briefcase held firmly in her hand, her posture erect and her stride certain.

"Rough night?" Kyle asked as she passed.

Warren Gray sniggered and Sean Bliss for once seemed to be staring at something in the vicinity of her face for a change. Amber raised her eyebrows.

What's their problem? Iris raised her chin to a regal angle, unlocked her door, and gave them an imperious glance when she turned to flip on her light switch. As she was taking files out of her briefcase, Amber Ambrose appeared in her doorway.

"Good morning," she chirped. She sauntered into Iris's office and casually leaned against her window.

"Good morning," Iris said tensely, having a natural aversion to and suspicion of early-morning enthusiasm. "What is everyone laughing about?"

"Have you looked in a mirror this morning?"

"Why?" Iris took a hand mirror from her filing cabinet and was examining her makeup when she saw it. "Son of a bitch!" She jerked the forgotten hot roller from her hair and sheepishly smiled. "A sign I have too much on my mind."

"Oh, really?"

The comment seemed innocent enough, but there was an eager edge to it that aroused Iris's suspicions. She started to tell her what was going on but thought better of it. "It's nothing."

"Hmmm." Amber spotted the garment bag that Iris had hung behind the door. "Going somewhere after work?"

"I have a date."

"Really? Someone new?"

"Actually, it's someone I've known for a long time, but this is our first date."

"Sounds interesting. Anyone I know?"

"You might have heard of him. Thomas Gaytan DeLacey. He's running for the City Council."

"No kidding? I've seen his picture in the paper. He's a fox."

Iris smiled crookedly. "Yeah." She continued taking folders from her briefcase and getting ready for the day.

"New blouse?" Amber asked.

"Ah, yeah." Well, it was almost new.

"Nice."

"Thanks." Iris couldn't figure out why Amber was being so unusually vociferous this morning.

"So, have you heard any dish about Dexter's leaving?"

Iris looked askance in spite of herself.

"You have, haven't you? Tell me, tell me." Amber's eyes sparkled.

Iris gritted her teeth and squinted in mock pain. "I wish I could."

"You know who Dexter's replacement is, don't you?"

Iris slid her eyes coquettishly to the corners. "I might." She beamed. She wasn't supposed to tell but she thought she'd burst if she couldn't at least throw out a hint.

"It's not you, is it?" Amber's demeanor changed from chatty to stern.

"If it *were* me, I'd hope you'd be a little happier about it than that."

"I would be if I thought you didn't get the promotion on your back, or was it on your knees?"

"What?" Iris shrieked.

"You know what I mean." She stomped out of Iris's office.

Iris stood speechlessly behind her desk.

Twenty

At the end of the workday, Iris changed into her date clothes in the women's rest room two floors above the McKinney Alitzer suite. She examined her tarty image in the mirror. "This is a side of you that's definitely not for McKinney Alitzer's consumption."

When she crossed the lobby to leave the building, the security guard with whom she was friendly shouted out, "Miss Exec-u-tive Woman! She's got it goin' on."

Iris waved her hand over herself, as if she was demonstrating a product. "Deal-making by day. Sinning by night. I'm every woman."

"Mmm… mm."

Iris retrieved the Triumph and puttered to the northeast side of town. The Gaytan DeLacey for City Council headquarters was a storefront operation on a busy street in the most populous and least prosperous part of the district.

The district boundaries zigzagged to the north and south and encompassed mostly lower-middle-class neighborhoods where the population was largely native Latino and immigrant Asian. The boundaries also included a small affluent pocket of primarily Caucasian conservatives who voted regularly and contributed generously to political campaigns. In the rest of the district, constituents over the age of fifty across all races tended to vote three times more regularly than those under fifty. Consequently, a steady stream of political moderates had occupied the Fourteenth District City Council seat even though the district's total population was inclined to be more liberal.

For the past twelve years, Gil Alvarez had successfully remained in office by focusing on the concerns of the older, vote-casting population. Gaytan DeLacey recognized the older voters' fierce loyalty to Alvarez and consequently had gone after the typically nonvoting younger and poorer constituents. Ironically, the land-owning Gaytan DeLacey was pitching himself as the representative of the common man and portraying Alvarez, the former cop, as an elitist.

Through the office's glass walls, Iris observed the hustle and bustle of Thomas's campaign volunteers, many of whom appeared to be young women. She saw Thomas exit an inner office at the rear, followed by a thirty-something Latina who was still dressing for success. She wore a dark, man-tailored business suit, an Oxford-cloth button-down shirt, a paisley bow tie, and round, plastic-framed glasses. Her attire seemed to plead for her to be recognized as a force to be reckoned with. Iris deducted points for trying too hard.

Red, white, and blue-themed campaign posters were hung in the large windows with Thomas's photograph prominent in each one. "A new generation of leadership for the new Los Angeles," Iris intoned. "Thomas Gaytan DeLacey is not a politician. He's a businessman, attorney, and lifelong resident of the Fourteenth District." Another poster showed Thomas as a young boy standing with Gabriel Gaytan in front of the Las Mariposas adobe ranch house. "Thomas Gaytan DeLacey respects our heritage yet recognizes the demands of the future."

She picked up a campaign button from a box on a table near the door and admired Thomas's face before slipping the button into her purse. The table was scattered with brochures. She picked up one that had a drawing of Gil Alvarez wearing a crown on his head and gazing into a mirror. The copy read: "He calls himself the lion of the Fourteenth. Isn't this how he *really* sees himself?"

Another brochure showed dollar bills floating in a river labeled "campaign contributions." It opened to a caricature of Alvarez done up like the Monopoly banker scooping the money from the river into a hole with question marks rising from it. The caption read: "Demand accountability. Demand Gaytan DeLacey."

From inside the campaign office, Thomas spotted Iris on the sidewalk. He pushed open the glass door and smiled as he walked toward her. The bow-tie woman was behind him.

"Welcome," he said.

"Pretty impressive, Thomas," Iris commented.

He shrugged diffidently. "Thanks. Hope they do the job."

"The camera certainly loves you."

"Critical in the television age," the woman stated. She was no-nonsense.

"Iris, this is my campaign manager, Sylvia Padilla. Sylvia, this is an old friend, Iris Thorne."

They shook hands, grasping firmly, like two graduates of the same assertiveness training class.

"TV?" Iris gave Thomas a provocative look. "That's right. You were the boy who wanted to be president."

"I still am that boy." His full lips had a defined edge and pulled away from his teeth at an angle when he smiled as he did now. He'd acquired the best features of both his parents. He had his father's height and long, stately bone structure and his mother's rich coloring and wide, dark brown eyes. "But my sole concern at this point is ensuring that the people of the Fourteenth are well represented in City Hall."

"I'm off," Padilla announced. "Thomas, tomorrow morning, Kiwanis Club breakfast at seven, PTA at nine, Senior Citizens Center at eleven, then All Saints Church for the carnival. In the afternoon, I think we should stump the commercial district down Huntington Drive and Eastern Avenue."

"Just dress me up and point me in the right direction."

"And don't forget the fund-raising dinner at the Mendozas'." She rapidly flipped through a datebook. "And we have to check out the American Legion Hall." She finally smiled. "I still can't believe that Alvarez agreed to a debate."

"We backed him into a corner."

"You're gonna bury him." She glowed. "See you tomorrow." She nodded at Iris. "Nice to have met you."

They watched her get into a practical Japanese coupe parked on the street and drive away.

"Wow," Iris said. "*I'm* exhausted."

"Sylvia's the best. She's absolutely committed to this campaign."

"Give her a tip and tell her to lose the little bow tie. It makes her look like she's been under a rock since the eighties."

He let his eyes travel over her. "Unlike yourself."

"Now I don't want to encroach on any situation between you and Ms. Padilla."

"She's involved with an organizer for the farm workers."

"My, she *is* a serious-minded citizen. And here I am, a lowly capitalist who's only concerned with making money and looking good."

"Somehow I doubt that."

They looked into each other's eyes.

"Little Thomas DeLacey," she said. "Boy, you were a pain in the rear when you were little. Always trying to kiss me and cop feels."

He smiled. "You can't blame a boy for trying."

"You were not a shy child."

He laughed. "I guess I've found the right forum for my personality. Although being in the public eye can be a burden. Sometimes I have to remind myself why I'm doing it."

"Why are you doing it?"

"Because I'm afraid of what would happen to the community if someone didn't stand up and do something."

She liked his answer. She took a good long look at him, wondering how he seemed to her away from the emotionally charged setting of Dolly's funeral. Very nice, she concluded.

"I don't collect rodents and spiders anymore, if that's what you're thinking."

It wasn't what she was thinking. She was thinking about his starched, crisp cotton shirt and imagining what it would feel like to run her fingers down it, pressing it against his chest. His silk tie was woven with a brilliantly hued abstract design. She imagined how it would feel to slide it between her fingers, how the silk would be smooth yet resistant to the touch. She caught a whiff of faded cologne. The green undertones had melded with his scent, creating something unique that could only be detected in close proximity. A bonus. She giggled and felt herself blushing.

"You're cute," he said. "You always were."

"Thanks. You're pretty cute yourself." She giggled again. He was making her feel giddy: a bad sign.

He straightened the knot in his tie, also appearing flustered.

Casting a glance at the window, she changed the subject. "So tell me about this campaign. Some of these materials are pretty controversial, don't you think?"

"It's necessary. The people have to see the real Gil Alvarez. Gil did a great job for eight years, but the past four have been a disgrace. His personal problems have destroyed his ability to lead. My family has long ties to this area and I won't see it dragged down."

He let his sable eyes rest on her. She wondered if he looked at every woman that way. If so, it was a guaranteed vote-getter. The atmosphere again grew prickly and she again moved past it to keep from acting like a schoolgirl.

"Thomas, *really*." Iris tapped the photo of him with Gabriel Gaytan. "Respecting our heritage? Isn't that the land your father wants to level for a housing project?"

"Low income housing," he corrected her. "It's a case of putting the needs of the community ahead of the benefit to an elite few, namely the Gaytan DeLaceys. Las Mariposas is prime real estate in a densely populated area, which can be used for the public good. My father is well experienced in low-income housing."

"*Thomas,*" Iris scolded. "Your father was fined and forced to live in one of his own rat- and roach-infested buildings for three months as punishment."

He took her comment in stride. "That was a case of poor communication on the part of a building manager whom my father has since fired. Now my father and brother oversee all the properties personally. I invite anyone to take a look at my father's buildings. They're clean and well run."

"You're *good,*" she goaded him.

He continued in the same dynamic tone of voice. "My being elected does not guarantee a go-ahead on my father's project. We're looking at a variety of ideas. On my desk right now there's a proposal from a firm that runs preschools and another from one that runs drug and alcohol rehab clinics for teenagers. The election of Thomas Gaytan DeLacey in no way means money in Bill DeLacey's pocket."

"Thomas, you can stop. I don't live here. I can't vote for you."

He rubbed his forehead and rolled his eyes. "Listen to me. The election's just a few weeks away and it's hard for me to switch gears. Sorry." His expression became almost shy. "Sometimes I'm too intense for my own good. Probably explains why no woman has been able to put up with me for very long."

"You've invested your time in building a career. It doesn't leave much left over for relationships. That's what I tell my mother about myself anyway."

"Does it work?"

"Nah. She still gets on my case."

Out of the blue he said, "Now that was an interesting time! My grandfather murdered, Humberto dying, my mother having a nervous breakdown, my sister running away from home, your father leaving, and the San Fernando quake."

"I've never heard anyone ask to do it all over again next Saturday night."

"You've never had any contact with your father after he left?"

"Not really."

"Didn't you ever wonder why he just left like that?"

"Yes." Iris shifted her feet. The topic made her uncomfortable.

A beat-up, small, red pickup truck pulled up next to the curb behind the Triumph. It was driven by Junior. The bed of the truck was full of sealed corrugated cardboard boxes.

Bill DeLacey pushed open the seriously dented passenger door with difficulty and climbed out of the truck's cab onto the sidewalk. The crablike bend of his legs made him look as if he were squatting. "Junior! I told you not to get so close to the curb."

Junior got out of the truck and began unlatching the tailgate. He was wearing an oversized T-shirt that his large belly still managed to raise in front. His dark curly hair had receded from his forehead. What remained was disheveled. He wore a neatly clipped moustache. It was the only neat thing about him. He didn't respond to his father but lifted a box off the truck bed and headed toward the front door of the office.

Thomas held the door open for him. "Good, the new mailers are done."

"Get a dolly, lame brain," DeLacey yelled after Junior. "Don't carry them in a box at a time."

"Lighten up, Dad," Thomas said.

DeLacey handed Thomas a large postcard printed on both sides.

"Hello, Mr. DeLacey," Iris said.

He ignored her. "I had them use the green instead. It's a lot better than the red you wanted."

Iris peeked around Thomas to see the postcard.

The front of the postcard showed a mock handwritten check made out to the Gil Alvarez Legal Defense Fund. The caption read: "Drunk driving. Wife battering. Gil's going to need every dime he can get."

"Looks terrific, doesn't it?" Thomas asked her.

Iris raised her eyebrows and responded diplomatically, "It's certainly an attention-grabber."

"Hear anything from Paula?" DeLacey finally acknowledged Iris.

"Actually, I've seen her."

Thomas stopped looking at the postcard. "You didn't tell me."

"Didn't come up." Iris added, "She was at the funeral."

DeLacey seemed amused. "Damned Paula. I spotted those guys in that Oldsmobile. I didn't think they looked like they belonged to our group."

Iris lied, trying to protect Paula. "She didn't have an Oldsmobile."

"I had Junior take a look," DeLacey continued. "Damned Paula."

"Mr. DeLacey," Iris said. "She came to the funeral. Aren't you pleased? Isn't that what you wanted?"

"How is she?" Thomas interjected.

"She told me about the will, if that's what you want to know."

DeLacey began to laugh, gasping air, his shoulders bouncing up and down.

Iris raised her chin in his direction. "I remember that about you, Mr. DeLacey. You laugh when things displease you, as if you can't quite believe what you're hearing, like it might be a joke."

"Well, you know old Paula. Always stirring the pot. Picking at the scab. You ever see a dog with a rag? You've got one end and he's got the other and he's turning his head back and forth..." DeLacey gritted his teeth and writhed his head to demonstrate.

Junior came out of the office pushing a dolly in front of him. He started loading boxes from the truck bed onto the dolly.

Thomas bristled. "Iris, you realize what this is about, don't you? Paula's always been jealous of me. Making up this will is a way for her to attract attention. I'm surprised she hasn't pitched the story to Alvarez."

"Frankly, Thomas," Iris responded, "I think it's simply a question of money."

DeLacey raised his index finger and opened his mouth at the same time. "Now, old Paula's mother, Dolores, was not the most mentally stable female, as you know. These things run in families. Now, Paula, while she's not exhibiting the schizophrenic aspects, she's definitely got a paranoid tendency…"

"Have you seen the will?" Thomas asked.

Iris shook her head. "No, but she was very specific about its contents. She said your grandfather left all his land to your mother with instructions that it was never to fall into your father's hands."

Junior was steadily working at unloading the boxes, giving no sign that he heard any of the conversation.

"…read a study a few years ago in *Psychology Today* about the effect of folic acid…"

Thomas continued, "You know as well as I do that Paula's an adept liar. My grandfather's will was filed after his death. It's a matter of public record."

"…and found a marked improvement in the subject's depression and paranoid tendencies. Now at the time that old Doc Osgood over at Casa La Propia Hospital was treating Dolores, he was convinced that the electroconvulsive therapy…"

Junior began working more slowly as if to linger so that he could listen.

Iris spotted him. "Junior, what's your take on this whole issue?"

He looked from Thomas to his father. "I don't know." He shrugged his shoulders very slightly. He was a big man capable of broad gestures but chose to use small ones, revealing little. He hurriedly pushed the dolly inside the office.

"That's one thing I can't figure out," Iris said. "Why a will? If Paula was going to fabricate a story, why something as dry as a will? It's unlike her."

"That's exactly what I've been standing here explaining to you," DeLacey said. "Old Doc Osgood over at the Casa La Propia Hospital, the psychiatrist who treated Dolores when she had her breakdown, says that the paranoid schizophrenic will fabricate stories to—"

"Mr. DeLacey, are you saying that Paula's crazy?"

"Based upon what you're telling me and what I've seen, that's the diagnosis I'd make."

"Your diagnosis?" She smiled at the ground. "Nice way to tie things up, isn't it? My wife's crazy, so don't believe her. My daughter's crazy, so don't believe her either."

"So did Paula say where she was living?" DeLacey asked.

"No, she didn't."

"Dad." Thomas put his hand out and patted the air soothingly. "I told you before, there's no need to get Iris involved in this." He took Iris's arm and began to walk with her toward the Triumph. "Why don't you go on to the restaurant? I'll catch up in a few minutes. I know my father can be a jerk, but he truly wants what's best for his children." He turned her to face him and put his hands on her shoulders. "Iris, no one loves Paula more than I do. But she's not content to destroy herself, she wants to drag the whole family with her. Sometimes I think my father's right about her having the crazy gene."

"She's not crazy, Thomas. She's sad and lost."

"Whatever her problem is, please don't help her ruin the DeLaceys. My father is an old man. He deserves better. My mother deserves better."

"You remember that check I wrote you?" Bill DeLacey called after Iris. He remained as he was, facing the campaign office. He spoke without turning his head in her direction. "There was no statute of limitations on it. It put you through school. You're still benefiting from that education, aren't you?"

Iris turned to face him. "Excuse me?"

"When I pay someone, I expect them to follow through on what I paid them for. You should have told me about Paula."

Iris pulled out her checkbook. She quickly scribbled on a check, ripped it out, and held it in his direction. "With interest, I figure two thousand ought to do it."

"Iris, this is unnecessary," Thomas protested.

"It's very necessary."

"Take it," DeLacey ordered Thomas.

She handed Thomas the check. "You're too big a boy to be under Daddy's thumb."

He tore the check in half and handed it back to her. "Meet you in an hour?"

"Why do you keep staring at me like that?"

"Like what?"

"Like you're trying to see through me or something."

"I'm sorry," Iris said. "I didn't realize it was making you uncomfortable."

"Is that why you went out with me, to satisfy your curiosity?"

She sipped her chardonnay and thought about that. "To be honest, I was curious. But I do find you very attractive."

"But you're not sure whether you like me." Thomas took a sip of his Campari and soda. "You seem cooler toward me than when we were talking on the street this afternoon. What's changed?"

Iris shook her head, even though she knew exactly what it was. She stabbed a poppy seed breadstick into a pat of butter and bit into it.

"I know what happened. My father and brother showed up."

"Seeing them today was a little jarring."

"I know. My father wasn't very pleasant to you. Iris, I can appreciate that you may not like my family, but I wish you'd give me a chance."

"Don't you think our families frame who we are?"

"Of course, but that cuts both ways. I've worked my whole life to be different from my family when it would have been easier just to go with the flow. I'm sure you of all people understand that."

She nodded ruefully.

He swirled the cranberry-colored cocktail in his glass. "But as hard as I've worked to make a life apart from the...shall we say, *eccentric* DeLaceys, I do love them. They're very important to me."

"Paula too?"

"I'm angry at her but I love her. I'd do anything in my power to protect and take care of my family." He abruptly stopped and took a sip of his drink as if his mouth had gone dry. He stared down into his glass. When he spoke again, his voice wavered. "I feel guilty about my mother and how she just slipped away. I can't shake the feeling that I should have done something." He quickly glanced up at her, then down again.

She reached her hand across the table and pressed it on top of his. "I know. I feel the same way. But maybe no one could have done anything."

"I don't really believe that but thanks."

The owner of the intimate restaurant, a small, neat man with a French accent and a balding pate, stopped by their table and topped off Iris's wine without asking. Iris started to pull her hand away from Thomas's but he held onto her fingers.

The owner casually rested his hand on Thomas's back. "I understand the campaign is going well, Thomas."

"Going great. We have a good shot at winning."

He patted Thomas's back and looked at Iris. "He's a good man, this one." He wandered away to another table.

Thomas looked at Iris almost shyly. "See, I'm not all bad."

She smiled. The candlelight was very flattering to him. She hoped it was as flattering to her.

They looked at each other in that searching way of people in love or angry. He rubbed his thumb across the tops of her fingers. "I loved it when you reached to touch my hand. It was a very warm gesture."

"Warm, huh? Pretty good for an Ice Princess. That's my nickname at the office."

"They wouldn't call you that if they knew you the way I do."

She slipped her hand away from his and touched his face, stroking a tiny mole on his cheekbone, then running her fingers down one side of his chin and up the other to his ear lobe. She started to pull her hand away but he grabbed it. With his other hand he shoved the candle out of the way, then pulled himself toward her. She tentatively eased toward him, aware of the diners at a nearby table who now seemed more interested in her and Thomas than their own conversation, but if it didn't bother him, it didn't bother her. She met his lips midway across the table. They kissed gently for what seemed like an indecent amount of time.

She was swept up in the moment and was tumbling down, fast and hard. She had wanton thoughts about following him anywhere, spending all her money, telling lies and bad jokes and living for the moment. Her relentless better angel didn't step in because she knew the most action Iris was about to see in the near future was the waiter arriving to take their dinner order.

Thomas ordered both their meals while she fixed her lipstick and gathered her wits. She noticed he was also wearing her lipstick and had half a mind not to tell him because it looked kind of cute.

"You have lipstick on you."

He picked up a napkin and wiped it off. "Miss Thorne, what a kiss. You're full of surprises."

"I surprise myself sometimes." So that she didn't surprise herself any further, she attempted a neutral subject. "So tell me, why did you leave one of L.A.'s top law firms to run for the City Council?" She still found herself looking at his lips.

"I wanted to give something to the community." He looked at her eyes, her hair, and the cleavage revealed by her low-cut dress. "My family's ties to the district go back four generations to when Las Mariposas was first settled. I saw how Alvarez was letting the area deteriorate and I couldn't stand by and do nothing. I'll admit I'm ambitious. I have political aspirations beyond the L.A. City Council."

Looking at his lips and eyes and only partially listening to what he was saying, she absentmindedly stroked the gold chain that lay on her chest.

"But that means I'll work hard to turn the Fourteenth around. Unlike Alvarez, my career doesn't end with the City

Council. To move on, I have to do a good job. And I want to. I owe it to the constituents and to all the generations of Gaytans who went before me." He gulped the last of his cocktail. "Please don't sit in the front row and do that at the debate."

"Do what?"

"You're running your fingers across your chest."

"I am?"

"It's very distracting."

Smiling crookedly, she clasped her hands in front of her on the table.

He leaned toward her on his elbows. "I'm really attracted to you. I'm getting a vibe that you might feel the same way about me."

She found him intoxicating. "There's something very squishy about this. It's like you're new but you're familiar too."

"It's very sexy."

"But I don't want to rush...I mean, I kinda do, but that little witch, my better angel, is telling me to slow down."

He took her hand between both of his. "You don't know how long I've waited for someone like you. I don't want to screw it up by rushing into something." He kissed each of her fingertips in turn. "So you're not involved with anyone right now?"

She shook her head.

"I'm surprised someone hasn't snapped you up."

"Men always think they want someone like me but when push comes to shove, most don't. It always comes down to power and who's going to be on top."

"I'd be very happy to let you be on top."

She blushed from the roots of her hair to her toes.

"I'm sorry." He tweaked her chin between his thumb and forefinger.

The waiter brought the first course.

They ate in silence for several minutes.

She stabbed her wilted spinach salad and tried a subject that was certain to douse their passion, "If this will thing is true..."

Thomas finished the sentence. "I can kiss the election good-bye. If the will does exist, I know there's a darn good explanation for it. But it wouldn't matter. The press would paint me with the same brush as my father."

"But Thomas, if it's a ruse, Paula deserves an Oscar for acting."

Thomas picked an anchovy from the top of his Caesar salad. "Until I have proof, in my mind there is no will. I don't know Paula. She left when I was eleven. But I know she feels venomous toward the family. She wrote some nasty letters to both my parents, blaming them for everything that went wrong with her life. I know she thinks I'm the favorite child and had it easy growing up. But she didn't know what it was like growing up under the burden of my father's expectations. He had it all planned out for me. Schools, jobs, family. Everything. He didn't want me to be an attorney. He didn't want me to study back East. I finally reach a point where I feel like I'm standing on my own accomplishments and all this trash about my grandfather's murder and my mother's suicide comes rushing out of nowhere, like some riptide, dragging me back." His voice was bitter. "If there is a will and I'm held accountable for things that happened when I was eleven…" He slowly shook his head. "I guess all my hard work and hopes and dreams were for nothing."

After dinner, Thomas walked Iris to her car.

"I had a lovely time," she said. "Thank you."

"So did I. When can we do it again?"

"Call me."

"I'll call you tomorrow. Call me when you get home to let me know you got there okay."

They kissed good-bye. It was brief, but it would be enough to keep Iris feeling warm and fuzzy through the night and most of the day.

He stood on the sidewalk until she was safely under way. At the end of the block, she looked in her rearview mirror and saw him still standing on the sidewalk, watching her depart. He looked very alone.

Twenty-One

You are on an airline and an executive from one of your competitors is sitting next to you. She gets up to use the rest room, leaving her firm's business plan on the seat. What do you do?

You are at an industry convention and are having a few drinks with an executive from one of your competitors. He becomes drunk and begins revealing information about his firm's upcoming product line. What do you do?

Iris refolded the brochure. The title was, "Ethics Seminar for Executives." She slipped the brochure into her briefcase and mused over a dilemma that was not among those mentioned in the brochure.

You have been asked to manage a valuable investment portfolio for a prominent City Council member. You know that the council member, a former police officer, was involved in the secret beating of a suspect in custody who later died. What do you do?

She picked up the manila folder that contained her research on Gil Alvarez's investment portfolio, slipped it into her briefcase, and flicked the brass fasteners closed. She pulled her suit jacket from the hanger behind the door, put it on, got her purse from the top drawer of the filing cabinet, hung the strap over her shoulder, grabbed her briefcase and left.

Gil Alvarez's secretary was filing her nails. She was sitting very erect in her desk chair, her breasts straining against the light fabric of her sleeveless sheath dress. She held her palm out to admire her nails, then bent her fingers toward her again and whacked the edges with the file.

Iris sat on a corner of the couch, flipping through but barely seeing a magazine. She smelled nail polish and looked up to see Alycia applying the final touch-up.

The office door burst open and Gil Alvarez entered, bustling and smiling and looking every bit like a man on top of the world. Jeff Rosen was close behind.

Iris leaped from the couch, virtually at attention. Alvarez breezed past her on his way to the inner office and as he did so, he grabbed her upper arm just above the elbow and whooshed her inside with him.

"So how's my favorite money manager?"

Iris smelled booze on Alvarez's breath.

Rosen followed, closing the door behind them. He excitedly rubbed his hands together and began pacing back and forth.

Iris stood her briefcase next to her feet. With all the good humor in the air, she distinctly felt like a party pooper. She grinned, pretending that some of their ardor had rubbed off on her. "What's all the excitement about?"

Rosen reached inside his jacket pocket, pulled out a folded piece of paper, and handed it to Iris. "We've just finished talking with a friend over at *The Los Angeles Times*. We got the *Times's* endorsement—"

Alvarez jutted two thumbs into the air.

"—which we were confident we'd get. And that article's going to run tomorrow morning."

Iris unfolded the paper.

WILLIAM DELACEY POSSIBLY INVOLVED IN MURDER COVER-UP
Did Developer's Plan for Historic Property Lead to Foul Play?

A recent reinvestigation into the 1971 murder of Gabriel Gaytan at the historic Rancho Las Mariposas has uncovered evidence that Humberto De la Garza, Gaytan's cousin, may have been falsely accused of the crime. A new examination of the case files revealed discrepancies in William DeLacey's description of the events surrounding the discovery of Gaytan's body the morning of February 9, 1971.

Alvarez opened an embossed leather box on his desk and took out a cigar and a chrome cutter. "We've got him on the run now." He tipped the box toward Rosen.

Rosen grinned. "Don't mind if I do."

Gilbert Alvarez and Ronald Cole were the first two police officers on the scene. Alvarez, now the incumbent in the race for the 14th District City Council seat, told reporters, "I've always been uneasy about the outcome of this case. De la Garza simply did not have a motive to murder Gaytan." Cole, currently an LAPD detective, refused to comment. Humberto De la Garza, who was arrested for Gaytan's murder, died in custody from injuries reportedly sustained in a fall that occurred when he resisted arrest.

Even after Rancho Las Mariposas fell into William DeLacey's hands, ground has yet to be broken on his DeLacey Gardens housing project. Environmental regulations and disagreements with the City Council have stalled the project for over twenty-five years.

Iris refolded the paper and handed it to Rosen. "That's quite an article."

Alvarez leaned back in his leather chair, put his feet on his desk, and waved his now lit cigar at her. "Gaytan DeLacey started it but we're going to finish it."

The phone rang. "Alycia, hold all calls except for the mayor's." Alvarez hung up and explained. "He should be giving me his endorsement any day now. How many endorsements does Gaytan DeLacey have? Hardly any."

"He's managed to get more than I thought he would," Rosen admitted.

Iris slowly walked to the window, carefully placing one foot in front of the other, buying time, trying to talk herself out of saying something that she'd regret. She turned to face them, leaning her hands and hips against the window frame.

Alvarez puffed on the cigar and looked at her in the same way he might have looked at a gemstone he was considering acquiring, assessing how it would look in the light, how it would look from a distance, how it would look on his arm.

"I was just a little kid at the time." Iris held her palm out to indicate her size then. "So my recollection is not great but I remember some discussion among the adults about Humberto and how he got hurt."

Alvarez rocked his chair back with his feet on his desk. He smiled indulgently as if he were now speaking to that small child. "What did they say, dear?"

"Well, as I recall, there was some speculation that you and your partner had beat him up."

Rosen sat on a small couch and crossed his legs. "The police are common targets for such accusations, but there's no basis for them in this case." He looked at Alvarez. Alvarez removed his feet from his desk and leaned forward. He centered the diamond ring on his finger. "Iris, you said something very important. *Speculation*. Just like Jeff said, a prisoner gets hurt, the police get blamed."

"Why are you bringing this up, Iris?" Rosen asked.

"Simply because I know the DeLaceys and I know they won't let this go unaddressed. The obvious area for counterattack is the issue of Humberto's death. The way I see it, you'll both end up slinging mud over things that can't be proved. Running this article might do you both more harm than good."

"Everything in that article is the truth," Alvarez said. "I'm not backing down from it."

"Do you think it's fair to hold Thomas Gaytan DeLacey accountable for something his father may have done when Thomas was just eleven years old?"

Alvarez squinted at her. "So that's what's behind all this. You're a Gaytan DeLacey fan now." He darted his cigar at Rosen. "Jeff, we've got a turncoat on our hands."

"Gil, c'mon." Iris smiled and tilted her head. "I'm only considering your best interests. This article takes the campaign to a new level of ugliness and it may not be a place you want to visit." She walked to a chair facing his desk, sat down, and slowly crossed her legs.

"Don't you think Gaytan DeLacey gleaned certain scruples from his father?" Rosen asked.

Iris looked at him. "What if he's spent his whole life trying to be unlike his father? And this is his reward."

"Life's tough, isn't it? Even for wealthy little boys like Thomas *Gaytan* DeLacey." Alvarez leaned back in his chair and leered at her. "I have nothing to hide, so I have nothing to fear from the DeLaceys."

She smiled back at him. "Then you're ready for anything."

"Absolutely."

She glanced at her watch. "My goodness! That late already? Let me quickly review what I have." She snapped open her briefcase, took out a manila file folder, leaned forward onto his desk, and flipped the file open. "I've taken a careful look at your portfolio and have come up with some excellent suggestions, if I say so myself."

He cooed, "I can hardly wait."

"They're all laid out in this report." She lifted a handful of stapled pages to show him, squared them in the folder, and closed the cover. She pushed the folder across his desk. "And it breaks my heart to tell you that I can't manage your money."

Alvarez's face dropped.

"Why not?" Rosen asked.

"I have some good news and some bad news." She cupped her hand against her cheek as if she was about to share a secret. "The good news is confidential so…"

Alvarez frowned in mock outrage. "It will not go outside these walls."

"I'm going to be promoted to manager of our L.A. office."

"Congratulations!" Alvarez reached his hand across his desk to shake hers vigorously.

"That's terrific, Iris," Rosen enthused.

"The bad news is, I simply cannot take on any new clients." She sadly shook her head, hoping she wasn't overdoing it. She was a terrible liar, but at least she knew it. Then she visualized the commission check that could have been and sincerely said, "I'm really sorry."

"Not as sorry as I am, pretty lady."

"That's sweet." She stood. "I tell you what. I'll make a list of some excellent money managers I know and fax it to you on Monday."

Alvarez and Rosen stood as well. Alvarez moved to walk her to the door. "I'm sure none of them can hold a light to you."

Iris touched her forehead. "All these compliments are going to go to my head."

"I'll send you an invitation to the inaugural party. I want you to come as my personal guest. And Jeff, let's invite Iris to the fund-raiser."

She smiled and extended her hand. Instead of shaking it, he grasped her fingers and pulled the back of her hand to his lips. She slipped out the door. As soon as she was in the outer office, she dropped the smile. By the time she'd reached the Triumph, she was smiling again but this time the smile was genuine. A stranger had offered her candy and she had resisted.

Twenty-Two

The circular electric saw shot sawdust from both sides of the blade as it cut through the wood plank. Les Thorne released the pressure on the C-clamp that held the plank against the sawhorse and fitted the angle he'd cut into the wood against a matching angle on another piece of wood.

Nearby, a teenage boy was drilling holes into a block of wood that had beveled edges. The boy looked up from his work when he saw Bill and Junior DeLacey enter the garage that served as a workshop. He called out, "Dad!"

Les looked up and nodded once to acknowledge them. He reached down to turn off the saw but did it slowly, without urgency, as if it were something he was going to do anyway, as if he wanted them to know that their presence hadn't disrupted his normal mode of activity in the least.

"Fine-looking boy, Les," DeLacey said.

"Thanks." Les was in his sixties but was fit and trim. His blond hair had gone white but it was still thick and contrasted starkly with his tanned, sun-weathered skin. He was still a handsome man.

Junior stood with his thick fingers tightly jammed into his jeans pockets and his weight on his heels so that his body was tilted slightly backward. His eyes followed the direction of his head so that his gaze fell at a point somewhere in the rafters of the garage roof. He was as removed as he could be without leaving the room.

"Brian," Les said to the boy. "Why don't you go see if your mother needs anything?"

The boy looked the two men over one last time, then left the garage.

"You doing carpentry as a trade, Les?" DeLacey asked as he roamed through the garage with his hands behind his back.

"Yeah. For a few years now."

"Honorable trade."

"Got a nice business built up."

DeLacey examined some cabinets that were lined against a wall, completed save for staining the wood. He intoned, "Wherever there is one alone, I am with him. Raise the stone, and there thou shalt find Me. Cleave the wood, and there am I." He ran his hand over the smooth, sanded surface of one of the cabinets. "Cleave the wood, and there am I."

"I had a feeling you'd show up, Bill." Les dusted his hands against his dungarees. On his left hand, half of the middle finger and the tip of the index finger were missing.

DeLacey frowned at Junior. "Go sit in the truck. You're just standing there like a lug anyway."

Junior took his hands from his pockets and took a step backward, as if to place himself beyond DeLacey's grasp. "I need to hear what you're going to say." He pursed his lips and defiantly stared at his father with eyes sunk deeply within fleshy lids.

DeLacey's shoulders began to quiver as he inhaled and exhaled laughter. "So you're ordering me around now?" He raised his index finger. "Let me tell you something, Junior. As long as you work for me, you'll do as I say."

Junior's cheeks became pink and blotchy. He trudged from the garage to sit in the pickup truck.

After he had left, Les said, "What is he now, forty years old? And you still talk to him like that?"

"Don't know what would have become of him if I hadn't been firm with him. I figure I've taken the raw materials and made the best of them. I hope us DeLaceys can leave our mark somehow before I'm dead and buried. Should have done what you did. Got a new wife and had more kids. It's a numbers game. Gotta have a lot just to get a few good ones."

"If you felt that way, why didn't you divorce Dolly?"

"You know I couldn't do that, Les."

"Why not?" Les smiled, squinting his blue eyes. "You loved her too much?" He grinned to himself as he picked up a sandpaper block and began striking it against the edge he'd just cut. "She leave any of that land to you?"

"She left it all to me, which is only right. I sacrificed a lot for her over the years."

Les stared at DeLacey. Suddenly, he began to laugh.

DeLacey gazed at him with rheumy, pale gray eyes.

"Bill, you're living proof that if you tell a lie often enough and long enough, you'll eventually believe it." Les put the plank down. "I know you're here because of that article in the paper about Gabe's murder. A couple of reporters have already called me. I told them the same thing I said back then. I wasn't around that night. I don't know anything that happened."

"It's not as simple as that, Les." DeLacey raised his gnarled index finger. "That was always just like you, simplifying. Simplifying things that are complicated. You see, Alvarez's people might try and get to you. Maybe even offer you money."

"They've already called. I told them I don't have anything else to tell them."

"That's not good enough. What I want you to do is—"

Les put his palm up. "No."

DeLacey drew down the sides of his long face, making the jowls of his cheeks dangle even further. "What do you mean, no?"

Les looked evenly at DeLacey. "I've done enough. You have some nerve talking about sacrifice. You've never done a single thing your entire life unless it somehow benefitted you."

DeLacey's breath hitched spasmodically in his throat as he laughed. "You'll never know the sacrifices I've made."

Les raised the sandpaper block toward DeLacey. "I'm not getting into a pissing contest with you, Bill." He started sanding the plank again. "I have to get back to work."

"What about Sonja?"

"You leave her out of this. I was with her that night. She doesn't have any reason to say anything else."

"See. You're oversimplifying again. Someone could give her a reason."

"Some things in this life are more valuable than money or power. I don't think you'll ever learn that, Bill."

"That's exactly why you're the weak link, Les. Everyone has their price. You just don't know what yours is yet."

"Please get off my property. I'll only ask you nicely once."

"Okay, if that's the way you feel about it." He started to shuffle out of the garage. As he left, the teenage boy returned. DeLacey asked him, "What do you want to be when you grow up, young man?"

The boy shrugged. "Maybe a fireman."

"Well, I guess there will always be fires to put out. You should get yourself a college education. Then when you can't put out fires anymore you can use your head." DeLacey looked at Les. "I've seen Iris and Lily."

Les put down the sand block. "Where?"

"At Dolly's funeral. Saw Rose too. She looked real good. Would have thought you might have at least kept up with them."

Les scratched his head.

DeLacey smiled slightly, apparently pleased to have made Les uncomfortable. "Thomas and Iris went out on a date." His shoulders bobbed as he laughed. "That Iris has turned into a good-looking female. Thomas and her seemed to get along real well. They're going out again."

Les's face became flaccid and his rich tan color paled.

"Course, you couldn't care less about that other family of yours anyway," DeLacey said. "You got yourself a new setup here, don't you?" He continued walking toward the truck.

Junior fired the engine when he saw his father heading down the driveway.

Brian watched the red pickup pull out of the driveway. He turned and looked at his father.

Les fitted a new plank under the C-clamp on the sawhorse, turned on the power saw, and began cutting the wood. The loud grinding noise precluded conversation.

Twenty-Three

Saturday morning, dressed in jeans, a plaid, lightweight flannel shirt, and tennis shoes, Iris packed some snacks in a paper bag, grabbed a liter of bottled water, and rechecked her map directions. She replayed the message that John Somers had left on her machine just to make sure she'd taken down the address correctly.

"Your blue nineteen seventy-eight Oldsmobile is registered to a Robert Bridewell. Address is eighty-seven forty-four Avenue K in Pearblossom out in the Mojave Desert. I checked his record. Has some prior arrests—two counts of possession of marijuana and cocaine for sale, three counts of burglary." The tape picked up a disheartened sigh. "I don't know what your angle is with this guy. Call me before you put yourself in a bad situation." There was a long pause where the tape just hissed quietly and it seemed as if what was unsaid hung portentously in the air. "Uh, bye."

"Don't worry about me, Johnny boy," Iris said to the machine as it rewound. "You know I'm perfectly capable of taking care of myself. Always have. Always will."

There was one last thing to do. She picked up the Louis Vuitton satchel and began packing the rubber-banded bundles of cash that were stacked on the dining room table.

She had counted it even though John had said it was all there. She told herself she had to replace the rotted rubber bands anyway. She stopped and considered another angle. "I don't need to take it all. A hundred grand should be plenty." She scolded herself. "Iris, you never wanted this money. You can't spend it. You don't even want to spend it. Get it the hell out of your life."

She put her hands on her hips and retorted, "Why are you so hard on yourself? None of that was *your* fault. The money just landed in your lap. Some people would consider themselves lucky. But not you. Unless you've sweated blood over something, you don't think you deserve it." She negotiated a compromise. "Okay, okay. I'll take half—two hundred grand. The rest of it goes in a safe deposit box for when I'm a doddering old lady. Okay, I'll just take a hundred grand."

Her route, which normally would have been straightforward, requiring only two or three freeway changes, had been complicated by the earthquake. The Antelope Valley Freeway, the Fourteen, had collapsed near the junction with the Five, causing a motorcycle police officer on his way to work to plunge to his death off the broken edge in the dark early morning of the quake. Sections of other freeways were closed for repairs or inspection.

Iris had dragged out maps and compared them with newspaper diagrams of damaged and otherwise closed freeways. She plotted a circuitous route that switched between undamaged stretches of freeway to surface streets, then back to freeways again. Now following her route, she was moving slowly. Traffic was terrible even though it was Saturday. This was postquake life.

After driving for three hours, she exited the freeway onto the flat, gridlike streets of Pearblossom. It was none too soon. The Triumph's temperature gauge had been steadily creeping up for the past hour and was now well past the midway mark.

Pearblossom's east-west streets were named with numbers and the north-south streets were named with letters. She drove down 22nd Street looking for Avenue K. The buildings were low, as if they could scarcely raise themselves from the street. Everything looked bare, sandy, windblown, and sun damaged, including the desert rat denizens. A large supermarket was on the corner of 22nd and K and Iris pulled the now-overheated Triumph into the parking lot. People were going about their Saturday-type affairs. The parking lot bulged with a preponderance of pickup trucks with camper shells and motorcycles.

She secured the Triumph as best she could, immobilizing the steering wheel by locking two bright red Club devices onto it. She looked at the car's bright, shiny red paint glinting innocently in the brutal sun and decided to drape it with the canvas cover stored in the trunk. A couple of locals were watching her. She stroked the Triumph as if it might be the last time she'd see it and again mentally promised to retire it and buy something plain Jane and practical for commuting.

Tightly clutching the Louis Vuitton satchel under one arm and her purse under the other, she began walking up Avenue K. According to the corner street sign, the address she was looking for should only be three blocks away. She was glad she'd dressed down.

She passed small wood-framed houses built on large plots of cheap desert land. For every well-maintained house, there were ten others with peeling paint, torn and rusted screens, pot-holed driveways, and threadbare roofs. There was an occasional green lawn, looking as lavish as a diamond tiara on one of the local biker babes. Some yards were covered in pebbles or colored rocks. Most were brown, sandy dirt. Some were cluttered with cars, some with artifacts hauled out of the desert such as wagon wheels, horse tackle, mining implements, or rubber tires used as flower beds. Some displayed colorfully painted plaster figures. There were deer, rabbits, wishing wells, Snow White and the Seven Dwarves, even a white-robed Jesus and a blue-robed

Virgin Mary. There were several collections of plastic pink flamingos.

Iris saw the faded blue Oldsmobile parked in the driveway of 8744 Avenue K on the corner of K and 18th. The house was small and rundown like the others in the neighborhood and the front yard had no lawn or plaster figures—just dirt.

She climbed the cement front porch steps. Through the sheer drapes covering the windows, she could see the bright flickering colors of a television set. The volume was high and she heard urgent, excited voices followed by applause and yelling, which elicited corresponding yelling from people inside the house. She knocked on the frame of a rust-stained screen door. The screen was pocked with small holes and rips. Her knock wasn't nearly loud enough to be heard over the television. She opened the screen, the spring that held it to the door frame stretching and creaking, and knocked against the flaking paint on the front door.

"Paula!" a male voice from inside the house yelled. "Someone's at the door."

Paula, somewhere farther off, yelled, "For Chrissakes, Angus. You're sitting right there!"

"Paula baby. Answer the fucking door!"

After a few seconds, the drapes near the door stirred.

Iris moved so that her face could be seen. "Hi!" She waved maniacally. "It's Iris."

"Who is it?" The man seemed to possess only one tone of voice—loud and abrasive.

"It's Iris from L.A."

There was the sound of metal sliding against metal and chains rattling as assorted locks were unfastened. The door opened and the scent of cigarettes and marijuana wafted out.

Paula stood with one hand on her hip and the other on the door frame and looked at Iris with a mixture of scorn and pleasure. "What the hell are you doing here?"

"Aren't you glad to see me?"

Paula smiled. Her full lips angled up to one corner, like Thomas's.

Iris took a step forward, inviting a hug or a handshake or something.

Paula didn't move but just swung back and forth against the door frame, using her flip-flop-clad foot as a pivot. "How the hell did you find me?"

"Friends in low places."

"You didn't tell my dad, did you?"

"No." Iris was offended.

Paula stepped aside and pulled open the front door. Iris walked into a sparsely furnished living room. A wide-screen television was against one wall. A football game was on. A worn sofa draped with an old bedspread stood perpendicular to the television. Bobby Bridewell, whom Iris remembered from the Last Call, was stretched out there. In front of the sofa was a scratched wood coffee table which held a bong, plastic lighters, a feathered roach clip, dirty glasses, beer cans, and several packages of cigarettes.

Angus was reclining in an adjustable easy chair that was angled toward the television. He held a can of beer against one chair arm. A remote control was balanced on the other. Both men were barefoot and wearing shorts and tank tops.

The living room was separated from the tiny dining room by a molded arch in the ceiling. A door off the dining room led to a kitchen that had a faded yellow linoleum floor. Another door off the living room's other wall probably led to the bedrooms and bathroom.

Angus leaned forward in the chair and peeked around the edge. "Hey, Iris." He waved clumsily at her. "How the hell are you?" Bobby stayed where he was on the couch and smiled dimly. They both moved slowly and fuzzily and had loose grins.

"You remember Angus and Bobby?" Paula asked.

"Paula, get Iris something to drink. She just drove here all the way from L.A."

Paula smirked facetiously but her back was to Angus so he didn't see her. "You want something?"

"Whatever you're having."

"Beer."

Iris noticed some framed photographs on top of the large-screen television. She asked Paula, "You mind if I look at these?"

"Go ahead."

Iris was careful to stand so that she didn't block the television. Among the photos of Paula, Angus, and their similarly ragged friends were a few family photos. There was one of Paula as a young teenager with her two brothers and her parents. Dolly sat with her hands tightly clasped in her lap. Her eyes were focused on something to the side of the camera and she was frowning, looking as if she had something on her mind. There was a photo of Dolly as a young girl with thick, braided hair. The braids were wrapped across the top of her head and woven with flowers. Her eyes were clear and attentive.

Paula returned with two cans of Budweiser and looked over Iris's shoulder.

"Don't tell me you're getting sentimental in your old age, Paula," Iris commented.

Paula shrugged. "I had to put something up there."

Iris picked up a photo of Paula and herself as toddlers wearing ruffled bathing suits on the front lawn of the ranch house. They were hugging each other and laughing, their eyes sparkling and their smiles broad and carefree. She glanced at Paula.

Paula smiled. "We were cute kids, huh?"

Iris picked up a black-and-white wedding picture of Gabriel and Isabella. "Is this the picture?"

"That's it."

Iris picked up the photo of the young Dolly. "Such bright eyes."

Paula held the beer out for Iris.

Iris slid the Louis Vuitton satchel off her shoulder onto the floor, took the can, and tipped it into her mouth.

"Paula, Iris!" Angus raised his beer toward them. "Baby dolls, can you talk outside, please? We're trying to watch the game."

Iris picked up the satchel. "So all those years, you never called your mom?"

"Is that why you're here? To try and make me feel guilty?"

"I came to conduct some business. The guilt's up to you."

Angus raised his beer can again. "Iris, if you came all the way out here because of the will, I'm sorry. Paula, sweetheart, tell her you're selling the will like we talked about."

"Just shut up, Angus." Paula set the beer on top of the television with a bang and faced him with her hands on her hips. "It's *my* will, okay? My mother gave it to me. I'm going to do with it what I want."

"That's what *you* think." Angus wormed around in the easy chair as if he were settling in for a long fight. "Who's the one who's been taking care of you for the past four years? Who's the one who bailed you out when you got picked up? Who's the one who gave you the idea of selling the will in the first place?"

Bobby, finding the argument more interesting than the football game, turned his attention from the television set and looked blearily from Paula to Angus.

Angus jabbed his hand, still holding the beer can, toward his chest. "Me! That's who. You're too goddamned stupid to figure out this stuff on your own."

Paula said in a low voice, "I am not stupid."

"The hell you aren't."

She screamed, holding her clenched fists in front of her. "Don't say that about me, you asshole!" Her voice grew shrill. "You're the one who's stupid, you stupid prick!"

A small smile played on Angus's lips, as if he were pleased to have gotten to her. He picked up the remote control and clicked the volume higher.

"Paula." Iris lightly touched Paula's arm to get her attention. "Let's go outside and talk, okay?"

Paula's eyes grew darker. She furrowed her forehead, rumpling the skin into well-practiced ridges. She turned her dark eyes onto Angus. "You motherfucker. I ought to slit your throat when you're asleep."

"Yeah, yeah." He clicked up the television volume again.

"Let's go for a walk, Paula." Iris tried to affect a cheerful tone.

Angus said, "Yeah, I think you need to go for a walk, Paula."

Saying nothing, Paula walked to the coffee table and picked up an open package of cigarettes and one of the plastic lighters.

Iris followed Paula as she walked through the dining room and into the dark kitchen which smelled of prepared food. A frying pan and several dishes stood upright in a dish drainer on one side of the sink. The cabinets, countertops, and floors were tired but clean. They went outside through a door at the end of the kitchen, which had a small curtained window at the top. The thin, lace-edged curtains were soiled around the edges as if they'd been opened frequently by dirty hands.

The backyard, mottled with patches of grass and dirt, was long and narrow and encircled by a chain-link fence. A detached garage was on one side. Through the fence, the backyards of the houses to the side and behind were visible. The third side of the fence bordered 18th Street.

Paula flopped onto a folding aluminum chair that was webbed with plastic tubing. She gestured for Iris to sit in a sister chair next to it, then tapped a cigarette out of its package and quickly lit it with the lighter. She set the lighter and cigarettes on a small white plastic table between the chairs. It held a round ashtray of amber glass that had a restaurant's logo printed in the middle. The ashtray was empty of cigarette butts but encrusted with ashes.

Iris took a swat at the chair, then examined her fingers. The chair was filthy but she sat on it anyway, not wanting to provoke further controversy.

It was late afternoon and the setting sun threw long shadows across the yard. Strains of a neighbor's heavy metal music floated on the air. Something rustled in a patch of dry grass next to the fence.

Paula dragged on her cigarette, making it glow bright. She picked at something invisible on her lip and said nothing. Iris sipped her beer and also said nothing.

The curtains in the back door window parted. Angus called out, "What are you talking about out there?"

"Nothing," Paula responded.

"You better not be talking about me." The curtains dropped closed.

Iris inhaled sharply, as if she were gasping for air.

"Just shaddup," Paula said.

"I didn't say a word."

"You didn't have to."

A minute of silence passed.

Paula dragged deeply on the cigarette, igniting the last of the tobacco. She tapped another from the pack and got a light off the old one before pressing it out in the ashtray. "He's not that bad. It's true, what he was saying. He's helped me out a lot. A lot of it's my fault, when he gets like this. I've been kind of weird lately. He'll apologize. He's real good about that."

"I'm sure he is."

"So you came here to talk about the will."

"It really exists?"

Paula sneered at Iris. "Of course it exists. What do you take me for?"

"Thomas and your father said it was a figment of your imagination."

"What did you expect them to say? Oh goody. Paula has the will."

"I want to buy it from you. I'll pay you a lot more than you were going to get from your dad."

"Angus wants to talk to this Gil Alvarez guy. Angus says he'll pay more than the old man."

"No!" Iris exclaimed.

Paula looked at her with surprise.

"Have you talked to him yet? Does he know about it?"

"No."

"Don't. Sell it to me. I'll pay you more than your dad or Alvarez." Iris picked up the satchel and put it on Paula's lap.

Paula unzipped it. "Damn! How much money is in here?"

Iris lowered her voice. "One hundred thousand, give or take a few bucks."

"Holy shit, Iris."

Just then, the back door burst open and Angus stumbled into the yard. "Let me see that." He ripped the satchel away from Paula, looked inside, then held it away from his body as if it might bite him. He stared at Iris. "How much, did you say?"

"I didn't say anything to you."

"A hundred thousand," Paula answered.

"Whoo-wee!" He looked in the satchel again and winced as if he were looking at a thing of great beauty. "A hundred grand," he whispered. "Baby, that could set us up for life." He pointed at Iris. "Lady, you bought yourself a will."

Iris was asleep on the shabby couch in Paula's living room. She and Paula had sat in the backyard talking until late. Although she didn't want to, she accepted Paula's offer to spend the night, not because she was especially tired but because it was late to be tooling along the desert roads alone in the Triumph. Not that she felt safe in the house where Angus and Bobby lived. Paula went with her to retrieve the Triumph. It was now parked in front of the house shrouded in its canvas cover.

Before Iris went to sleep, she'd taken off her shoes and belt but had left the rest of her clothes on, only undoing the top button of her jeans. In her arms she tightly clasped her purse that now held Gabriel's handwritten will.

Paula had taken the satchel with the money into the bedroom with her, managing to convince Angus that it wasn't a good idea to go around town with it, showing it off. He took a few hundred dollars and went out with Bobby. By the time Iris and Paula had turned in around midnight, they hadn't come home yet.

Iris was dreaming that Paula had left something in a frying pan on the stove and it had started to burn. Smoke rose from the frying pan and tendrils floated into the living room. They were dancing around her, she dreamt, caressing her but holding her too close. She was finding it harder and harder to breathe. She jolted awake. The room was full of smoke. The living room drapes were on fire.

She pulled the blanket from the couch and wrapped it over her head and around her body. "Paula!" She stepped on her purse, which had fallen. She put the strap over her head and diagonally across her chest and crawled to the bedroom. Smoke curled out from underneath and around the sides of the ill-fitting door. She touched the wood. It was warm. "Paula!"

She wrapped her hand in the blanket and was reaching for the doorknob when the door flew open. Paula stumbled out and fell on top of Iris. Smoke poured out and flames roared up, nourished by the new oxygen source.

"Let's get out of here!" Iris started to drag Paula down the hallway.

"Wait!" Paula yelled.

"Let's go."

"The money. It's on the floor near the dresser."

"Forget it."

"Forget you!"

Paula put her arm over her face and tried to walk back into the bedroom, but the heat was too intense. A spark flew onto her nylon nightgown and quickly ate a huge hole in the front. Paula madly swatted it.

"Get on the ground!" Iris pulled the blanket tightly around her, almost covering her face. "Hold onto my legs. Pull me out in ten seconds." Iris crawled into the room and Paula crawled behind her.

*This is stupid, Iris Ann! Stupid, stupid...*The heat was unbearable and she desperately needed to breathe but didn't dare lest she inhale smoke. *Stupid, stupid...*

The flames hadn't yet touched the satchel. She reached her hand from underneath the blanket. The heat singed the hair on her arm. She grabbed the satchel, but the vinyl was too hot for her bare hand, so she enveloped it in the blanket and dragged it with her as she slithered out of the room with Paula dragging her by the ankles.

The fire in the living room had spread, making the front door inaccessible. Paula grabbed the bedspread that was covering the couch and wrapped it around herself. The flames were near the television but Paula grabbed some of the pictures off the top anyway. Iris yanked on her arm and Paula reluctantly followed her through the kitchen and out the back door where they collapsed on the dirt, choking and gasping for breath.

Paula lay prone on the ground facing the fence that bordered 18th Street. She suddenly raised herself on her elbows and stared at the street. "Son of a bitch!"

"What?" Iris snapped her head around to look at the street but it was empty.

"A red pickup truck just drove away." She looked at Iris wide-eyed.

"So?"

"Didn't you say that Junior drove a red pickup? Get a clue, Iris. The old man must have seen me at the funeral in the Olds and tracked me down just like you did. See, he knows the will's not fake."

Iris unleashed her purse from around her chest and pulled out the will. "It certainly isn't." She reached in again and took out her cellular phone.

"What are you doing?"

"Calling the Fire Department."

"What for?"

Iris was befuddled. "What *for?*"

Paula reached into the Louis Vuitton satchel and took out Dolly's purple velvet jewelry box. She shoved the photographs into the bag and fit the jewelry box on top of them.

Iris watched her with surprise. "What was your mom's jewelry box doing in there?"

Paula shrugged. "Just a place to put it." She stood and slipped the satchel over her shoulder. "I've got everything I need. Let's get the hell out of here."

Iris stared at her speechlessly.

"Let's go!"

Twenty-Four

Paula was sitting on the floor in Iris's almost empty living room, wearing one of Iris's bathrobes. She was pouring handfuls of money over her head and rubbing it on her face and body.

Iris, also clad in a bathrobe, stopped in the doorway when she saw Paula.

Paula reclined on the money that was spread across the warped hardwood floor and writhed on top of it while scattering it over her. "I saw someone do this in a movie."

"That's really disgraceful," Iris said.

"It's fun. It's the most fun I've ever had in my entire life."

"Tomorrow, I'm putting the rest of my cash and the will into a safe-deposit box. I recommend you do the same with that."

Paula shook her head. "I don't trust banks. And I need to buy some clothes."

Iris raised her eyebrows.

"All my stuff burned, remember? And I need some wheels."

"You should put most of it away."

"You're a bore."

"Hey, I just spent a hundred grand to buy a will, so don't talk to me about spending money."

"Girl, I saw with my own eyes that you love money more than life itself."

"That'll come as no surprise to my coworkers." Iris walked to the dining room table where the remaining three hundred thousand was still piled. Next to it was Dolly's small purple velvet jewelry box. She opened the lid and took out a tarnished gold-tone charm bracelet. She undid the cheap clasp, put the bracelet around her wrist, then turned her wrist in front of her. "When are you going to tell me where you got this much cash?" Paula asked.

Iris dropped her wrist into her lap. "I can't."

Paula sat up on the floor. "C'mon. You think you're gonna shock me or something?"

"Frankly, I don't think I can trust you."

"Iris has a secret," Paula sang. "Tell me. You can trust me."

Iris looked at her skeptically.

"Believe it or not, Iris, I do have some principles."

"I had a friend who ran the mailroom at my office. Alley Muñoz. He was from Mexico and had polio when he was young so he had problems walking. He was deaf too. I taught hearing-impaired children for six years, so Alley and I bonded. He was talked into getting involved in a money-laundering scheme at my office and was murdered. He suspected he was going to be and before he was, he left me the cash. John Somers was the homicide detective on the case. That's how I got involved with him again. I tried to turn the money in to John, but he convinced me to keep it. He said that it didn't belong to anyone and it would probably be stolen by someone in the Police Department anyway. So, I kept it. And that's the story."

Paula nodded approvingly. "Not as sexy as I'd hoped, but it's pretty good."

Iris turned her attention to the burn on her arm. "This hurts like crazy." She took a tube from her pocket and dabbed on white cream. "When are you going to call Angus? Don't you think he's worried about you?"

"He's probably more worried about what happened to this." She tossed some of the money in the air.

"Is this your subtle way of leaving him?"

"I'd had it with him anyway. That thing with the will really pissed me off. I get one thing in my entire life that's worth something and he's got to put his claws on it. I can use this money to get set up. Get a little house or something. Maybe get my kids back." She seemed thoughtful.

"I don't know why you just let them go, Paula. It wasn't like the court took them or anything, or so you told me last night."

"Maybe that's *my* secret."

"So? Give it up."

Paula shook her head. She got up, walked to the newly replaced sliding glass door that led to the patio, and struggled to pull it open.

"I wouldn't stand on that terrace. I don't know how safe it is."

Paula pulled harder. "I need a cigarette."

Iris helped her with the door. "The wall's torqued." The door finally screeched open.

Paula nonchalantly walked onto the terrace, even though a large crack traversed the length of it. She leaned against the terrace wall with one bare foot on top of the other and pulled a package of cigarettes and a lighter from the bathrobe.

Iris pulled a dining room chair next to the sliding glass door track and sat down.

"What are you going to do with the will, Iris?"

"Don't know."

"Why did you buy it?"

"Figured it was safest in my hands. Seems like I'm the only one who wants to use it to put things right for Dolly. Plus, if it's authentic, it could cost Thomas the election if it got out. I wonder how he'll react when he finds out there really is a will. And I have it."

Paula looked at Iris soberly. "Thomas got to you, didn't he?"

"No one *got* to me."

"You're balling him, aren't you?"

"Balling him," Iris sneered. "Ever elegant Paula. What I am or am not doing is none of your business."

"You might as well be fucking my father."

"Thank you for that lovely image."

"You think it was Junior's idea to burn down my house? The old man pulls both Junior's and Thomas's strings."

"Thomas is his own man."

"*No one* who stays with my father can be their own man or woman. He sucks up everyone around him."

"Maybe Thomas found a way to master the situation. There are ways of dealing with problems other than just running away from them." Iris agitatedly recrossed her legs.

"Yeah. You can bash their heads in with a pickax."

"What are you saying?"

Paula dragged on the cigarette, tilted her head back, and blew out smoke. "I'm saying you'd better leave the DeLaceys alone before you find out things you don't want to know."

"That includes you."

"Especially me."

"I know you burned your house down. Is there something else I should know?"

Paula's jaw dropped in disbelief. "I didn't burn my house down. I told you I saw a red truck."

"I didn't see any truck."

"I can't help it if you're slow."

"It sure was lucky that you happened to slip your mother's jewelry box into the satchel with the money."

"And the satchel almost got burned up. If I planned the whole thing, why didn't I take it outside ahead of time? Why didn't I pack the pictures?" Paula let smoke trail from her mouth as she gazed at a corner of the terrace and shook her head derisively.

Iris got up and started to pace the floor. Her open-backed slippers quietly slapped her heels with each step. She turned mid-route and abruptly left the room. She returned with a handheld tape recorder. She stood next to the terrace door, refusing to step on the terrace, and played and rewound the tape until she got it in the right position.

She held the tape recorder toward Paula. "This is why I won't leave the DeLaceys alone." She pressed the play button and Dolly's message began to emanate scratchily from the machine.

"Iris! It's Dolly. Dolly DeLacey. I don't think he knows I know. I don't know who I can trust. He's turned my children against me. He knows everyone on the police department and at City Hall. I think he knows the governor and even the president and the president runs the FBI so who can I turn to?"

Paula fussed with the belt of the bathrobe and then busied herself looking for a place to put out her cigarette, as if she had tuned out the tape. She squatted down to press out the butt on the ground. But instead of getting up, she stayed down, wrapping her hands around her knees.

"Iris, he's trying to kill me. Bill's trying to kill me. There's a rope in the garage and some saws and poison, Iris! It says it's for rats but there's a skull and crossbones on the box. It's deadly poison! Then in his desk I found a metal box with my will in it. But I don't remember it, Iris! How could I leave him everything? What about my children? And my father's ring is there, too…It's him! There's his car! It's him! Oh my goodness!"

The message ended but Paula didn't move.

Iris dropped the recorder into her bathrobe pocket, then turned and walked into the kitchen. She was putting bread in the toaster when Paula came in. "Want something to eat?"

Paula opened the refrigerator door and stared inside. She reached in, moved some of the items around, then closed the door. "She finds a rope in the garage and she thinks he's trying to kill her? What kind of bullshit is that?"

Iris wiped low-cal spread on the toast. "When you were a teenager, you ran away because you were afraid of your father. Why are you discounting your mother's fears about him?"

"But rat poison? Lots of people have rat poison in their garages." Paula flung out her arms. "Can't you see how nuts she is?"

Iris bit into the toast. She poured more coffee into her mug and sat at the dining room table. "Was."

"What?"

"How nuts she was."

"Oh. Right."

"She does sound nuts. But that doesn't mean that someone wasn't trying to kill her."

Paula opened the refrigerator door again and took out a container of nonfat yogurt. She frowned at it. "Don't you have any food in this place?"

"What you see is what I've got."

Paula flipped the lid off the yogurt and began stirring the fruit up from the bottom.

Iris regarded Paula. "Maybe this is none of my business, but—"

"That hasn't stopped you yet."

"*But* why do you hate your mother?"

"I don't hate her."

"Let me rephrase that. You seem ambivalent about her. You went out of your way to go to her funeral. You leap into a fire to save her photos and jewelry but you always seem angry when you talk about her. After listening to the tape, you seem more upset about how crazy she sounded than about her accusing your father of trying to kill her."

Paula ate a spoonful of the yogurt and frowned at it. "That's what pisses me off. Whenever there was a problem, instead of dealing with it, she went off the deep end."

"She couldn't help it."

"That's bullshit. She took the easy way out."

"She didn't lose her mind for fun, Paula."

"You preach to me about how it's better to stand and fight when things get tough than to split. What did the old lady do? She mentally got the hell out."

Iris shook her head. "I don't get you. I don't know why you can't accept that your mother did the best she could with what she had."

Paula looked at Iris out of the corners of her eyes. "I told you before, you're not me."

"Fine. You don't give a damn about your mother or how your father might have murdered her to steal her assets or maybe to keep her quiet. Fine. No problem." She took a big bite of toast.

Paula still frowned at the yogurt.

Iris angrily chewed. "Wonder if she really lost her memory for that long. I guess it's possible. I read that that's one of the reasons shock therapy fell out of favor in the seventies. It's popular again, but they've learned a lot in twenty-five years. Who knows what they did to her head back then. I wonder if she forgot who killed Gabriel or if she managed to keep up the lie."

She crunched a corner of the toast between her teeth. "That's really blind devotion, isn't it? Lying to protect her husband even though he murdered her father." She fingered the cheap bracelet she was still wearing. "I don't understand why she did it. She would have done fine without Bill DeLacey. She had the land." Iris looked at Paula, who had sat down and was facing her across the table. "Unless she did it to protect someone else."

Paula got up and threw the half-empty yogurt container in the trash. "Who else could have killed him? There isn't anyone else."

"Sure there is. If it wasn't some stranger, it had to be one of us. Let's see…There was your father, Humberto, Dolly, Junior, Thomas, my father, my mother, Lily, you, me…"

"Don't forget Skippy and Perro."

"The problem is motive. Your father was the only one who had a motive."

"What if you start digging around and you end up finding out things you don't want to know?"

"Like what?"

"Like what if Thomas did it?"

"What would his motive have been?"

"To help the old man. You know what a kiss-ass Thomas was."

Iris bit into the second piece of toast. She shook her head. "Nah. That's not enough of a motive."

"Or Junior. The old man was always putting him down. What if Junior did it to show the old man that he was really a man? Or what about your own father? Maybe the old man paid him to get Gabe out of the way. You said he acted weird after that night."

"It was a coincidence. The two things are unrelated." Iris walked to the kitchen and put her plate and mug in the dishwasher.

"What if it wasn't a coincidence? Are you prepared to find that out? Why are you into this, Iris? It doesn't even have anything to do with you."

"Because a woman who was kind to me when I needed kindness asked me for help. Because a cop who participated in killing an unarmed man is sitting on the City Council. Because a greedy, controlling man is laying claim to land that belongs to his children. *Your* land, Paula. You said yourself that if you had a base, you could make a home for your kids."

"That still doesn't explain what's in it for you."

"I wouldn't be able to live with myself if I just stood by and did nothing."

"You've got the will. Why don't you just go to the police and say that the old man did it?"

"It wouldn't be fair to Thomas."

"Fair to Thomas," Paula snorted. She slapped her thighs and stood up. It marked the end of the conversation. She walked to the living room, dropped to her knees, and starting stacking her money.

"Off again? You'll have quite a ride on that stash until it runs out."

Paula sat back on her heels. "I think I know that metal box she was talking about. The old man used to keep one in his desk. I found it once when I was looking for money. He never throws anything away. I'll bet it's still there."

"I'd love to get my hands on it."

"Hell, I used to break into that house all the time. You know how the old man was about his ten o'clock curfew. If I was home one minute past ten, he'd lock me out."

"What are you saying?"

"Let's go home."

Twenty-Five

"Look at my poor old house," Iris said. "I knew the neighborhood had gone downhill…" She stopped the Triumph in the middle of the street. "My mother's roses and flowers are gone. My father's yard's all dirt and they've got cars parked on it."

"Looks like my house in Pearblossom." Paula looked up at the top of the hill. "Doesn't look like Las Mariposas has changed."

Iris parked the Triumph out of view on a side street across from the ranch's chain-link front gate. "Let's call and see if he's home."

"He won't be. He and Junior always went to the apartments on Sunday afternoons because the tenants are usually home. It's a good time to shake them down for the rent."

Iris took the cellular phone from her purse and called the ranch house. "No answer."

"Let's go. Looks like we're going to have to cut the fence with your wire cutters."

They got out of the car. From the trunk Iris grabbed a canvas bag that she'd packed with a few tools. They had started down the hill when Iris said, "I'd better cover up the car. Someone might recognize it."

She had started to walk back when she saw Paula jump behind a hedge bordering the front yard of one of the homes on the street.

"Iris, it's him!"

Iris ducked behind the Triumph.

Through the windows she saw Bill DeLacey get out of a cream-colored Cadillac that he'd stopped just inside the gate. He fiddled with a chain that held the gate closed, pushed it open, then got back inside the car. After he'd driven the car beyond the gate, he rolled down the driver's window and yelled, "Junior! Close the gate." Then he pointed the Cadillac's long nose down the hill and drove away with one hand on the steering wheel.

Paula and Iris looked at each other.

"Junior didn't go with him," Iris said. "Maybe we should do this some other time."

"I can handle Junior. Let's go before he comes out."

They ran across the street.

"What if they've got dogs?" Iris fretted.

"We'll deal with it." She looked at Iris and shook her head. "You're still a big sissy."

"I know."

They ducked into the citrus grove.

Paula pulled at the crotch of her jeans. "These are killing me. Thought you said they were big."

"Those are my fat jeans, darling. They're big on me."

"Bitch."

"Wonder if I can still find Skippy's grave. I buried him under an orange tree and put some stones on top to mark it. He lived to be sixteen. Great dog."

Iris lifted a string of Christmas lights dangling from a big grapefruit tree. She looked up at the sturdy branches and thought of Dolly's grisly end. "That's hardcore, to hang yourself."

Paula rubbed her hands up and down her arms as if cold. "Let's get out of here before Mr. Personality finally locks the gate. Junior, the original slacker."

They walked through the old citrus trees, which still held unpicked fruit from prior growing seasons. The ground was littered with fallen fruit in various stages of decay.

"Uhhh!" Iris inhaled sharply. "The Wall of Gaytan. It's still there!"

They walked into the clearing where the six-foot expanse of wall stood. It had several deep cracks and listed forward. The top remained unfinished with steel rods jutting from it.

"Looks like it'd come right down with one good shaker," Paula said.

"Wonder why your father never took it down," Iris mused.

"No deep dark secret there. The old man loves to save things." Paula squatted slightly and raised her index finger, imitating her father. "Don't throw that away! Might need it someday."

Iris looked at the wall and the lemon tree that still spread its branches above it and shook her head. "I never told you the real reason I was out here that night your mother drove into the wall. I was going to hang myself from that branch with the belt from my bathrobe."

Paula was stunned. "Really?"

"It was the night my dad left. Made sense at the time. But I couldn't do it." She looked at the limb again. "I never forgot being in that state of mind. Feeling such hopelessness and despair and not seeing any end."

"Why didn't you tell me?"

"Paula, you were gone with Mike all the time. When you took up with him, it was like I didn't exist."

Paula looked at the ground.

Iris gazed silently at the tree.

"I'll be over here." Paula turned and left.

After a while Iris walked in the direction Paula had gone and soon reached the toolshed. It was still run down and ramshackle looking and had been patched. It was smaller than Iris remembered. Paula was not around.

The toolshed door burst open.

Iris jumped backward and clasped her hand to her chest.

"Sorry," Paula said.

"You scared the life out of me!"

"*Sorry.*"

"What were you doing in there?"

"Nothing." She avoided Iris's eyes and started walking quickly. "Let's do this deal and get the hell out of here. This memory lane business is giving me a headache."

Iris followed.

They walked through the grove until they reached Gabriel Gaytan's old house. The red pickup truck was parked next to it. They heard the clatter of metal against metal and a whistling whine.

They stepped quietly past the house. The noise grew louder. When they reached the wooden lattice that formed the walls of the backyard patio, Paula threw her hand out, stopping Iris. She motioned for Iris to look through the lattice.

In a corner of the patio, Junior DeLacey was sitting on a chair, cleaning a handgun. Pieces of the gun were spread on cloths on the ground around him.

The green Amazon parrot and blue macaw were still alive. They were out of their cages and sitting on tall, T-shaped perches crammed against one wall of the crowded patio. Junior's model train set—arrayed on a platform that extended the length of the patio and halfway across it—was running full speed. It was quadruple the size it had been when Iris had last seen it in Junior's room. More villages had been added, with farms and forests in between. Throughout, there were tiny people going about their business, carrying bags of groceries, filling their cars with gas, waving at acquaintances, filing out of a steepled church, filing into a brick schoolhouse, and plowing their fields. A group of boys played baseball in a park. A cluster of children waved at the passing train, their arms permanently raised.

Junior wasn't looking at the train but was focused on his work, methodically rubbing a metal part with a stained cloth. The train provided background noise, like a radio.

When Junior bent over to set down the part he held and pick up another, the parrot strained forward on his perch and grabbed a hunk of flesh on Junior's neck just below the hairline. He cried out and swatted at the bird, who squawked and danced away from him on his perch.

"Stupid bird," Junior grumbled.

Iris and Paula clamped their hands over their mouths to stifle their laughter. They made the mistake of looking at each other, which made them laugh harder. They started to make their way around the patio, when Iris paused to get a closer look at something that had caught her eye. Paula kept going while Iris stayed frozen. The macaw spotted her and squawked, startling her and causing her to sprint behind the hill, leaving Paula in the dust.

Paula ran to catch her. "That bird still doesn't like him!" She was out of breath but was still laughing. "What's wrong?"

"Didn't you see it?"

"What?"

"Junior's train set. There was a figure of a woman with long dark hair in a braid down her back."

"So?"

"She was hanging by a rope from a tree in the middle of the town square. People were going to and fro and no one seemed to be paying any attention to her."

Paula snorted. "That really pisses me off. The old man lets him live here for free. He doesn't work. All he does is play with his guns and his trains. There were times when I could have used some help. But no. Everything for Junior and Thomas and nothing for Paula."

Iris put her hand on her hip. "Doesn't that seem weird to you? That model train set is Junior's perfect world. Everyone's happy, everyone's industrious, everything's beautiful, everything's everything. Why would he ruin it?"

"He's sick! So what else is new?" She started walking in the direction from which they had come. "I've had it with this place. Let's get out of here."

"We've come this far."

Paula sighed. "All right."

Iris resettled the bag of tools on her shoulder and started walking up the hill. She looked back at Paula, who was gazing at the crest.

"C'mon!" Iris urged. "We can't use the road. Somebody might see us."

"I don't remember it being so high."

Paula followed Iris, but the distance between them began to grow. Halfway up the hill, out of breath, Paula stopped and sat down with difficulty because of Iris's jeans.

"If you stopped smoking, you wouldn't be so out of breath."

"Thank you, Dr. Thorne."

They continued walking. They finally reached the grove of eucalyptus trees at the crest. The hard, helmet-shaped seed pods made a crunching noise underneath their feet. The trees' pale bark and slender, silver-gray leaves melded with the landscape's pastel palette.

"Let's sit here for a minute," Paula pleaded. The old man won't be home for a couple of hours."

Iris plopped beside her.

A gray cat lay curled at the base of one of the trees. A short distance away, two others, almost hidden in the tall grass, peered at them. Three more dozed in the sun.

"It's overrun with cats," Paula cried.

It was a clear day and they had good views of the downtown Los Angeles skyline to the west and the San Gabriel Mountains to the east.

"Been a long time," Iris said.

"Yeah. Funny. Everything here doesn't seem as big and everything out there doesn't seem as far away." Paula paused. "Except for the top of this hill."

Iris looked toward downtown. "I can see in this direction from one of the windows in my office. I look out it every workday and imagine I can see this hill. I know I can't really see it. It's too far and I don't think the direction's quite right but I like thinking I can. It grounds me somehow. It reminds me of who I was and how far I've come."

Paula leaned back on her elbows. "I don't like being reminded of who I was or who I am."

Curiosity had gotten the better of two kittens and they started taking tentative steps toward the women. Paula held her hand out and tried to get them to come closer. She made a sudden move and they darted away.

"Even the cats are telling me I'm not welcome." Paula got up and dusted off. "Let's go."

The ranch house's white paint was chipped and peeling. The wooden roof shingles were faded and warped and many were missing. A prickly pear cactus, some of its flat, green paddles as large as dinner plates, almost covered the wall to the right of the front door, obscuring the windows. Among the prickly pear, silver century plants had self-seeded until the area was spotted with dozens of them, some five feet in diameter. Their fleshy spiky leaves, lined with flat thorns along the edges, unfolded from the center like ominous roses. Several kittens chased each other through the cacti, elongating their backs to maneuver underneath the spines.

To the left of the door, a thorny bougainvillea grew, the vines in winter showing more spikes than green. The plant encased the wall up to the roof where the vines prevented a rain gutter that had pulled free from tumbling to the ground. The thick blanket of vines had been barely hacked away from the door.

The yard in front of the house was piled with junk. There was an old Ping-Pong table, scrap metal, bicycles, doors, window frames, weather-beaten corrugated boxes full of moldy clothing, and all manner of decrepit items.

"Let's do the deal and get the hell out of here," Paula said. "This is giving me the creeps."

They walked around to the back of the house.

"Here's my bedroom window. He never had it fixed." Paula carefully reached through a broken semicircle in the glass of the double-framed window, unlocked it, and pushed it open. "You go. I don't want to go in. I can't."

"Maybe he has an alarm."

"He doesn't even have a telephone answering machine."

"I'm not going in there!"

"Stop being such a sissy."

"You're calling *me* a sissy?" Iris fished a flashlight from the canvas bag. "Give me a boost." She clambered through the window. "It's wall-to-wall junk in here. I hope I don't get bit by something. Yell if anyone comes."

Paula went around to the front of the house. She tried to get the attention of some of the cats but they were practically wild and wouldn't come near her. She sat on the hillside in the direction that faced downtown L.A. and lit a cigarette. She looked at the skyscrapers that jutted incongruously from the flat basin. She looked at the citrus grove and the old Thorne house beyond it.

She leaned her head against her knees and soaked in the warm afternoon sun. She became lost in her thoughts and didn't hear the car until it had already rounded the first bend in the hill.

She ran to the front door and pounded on it. "Iris!" She ran back to the edge of the yard to get a look at the car as it rounded the second bend. It was the faded blue Oldsmobile. Paula ducked out of view but not before Angus, who was looking out the open passenger window, pointed right at her.

She ran to the back of the house to the open window. "Iris! It's Angus and Bobby." She heard the car pull up in front of the house and stop. "Oh shit."

Iris appeared on the other side of the window. She handed Paula a rectangular metal box.

"Angus and Bobby saw me! I knew he'd come looking for the money. I knew it."

Angus pounded on the front door. "Paula, baby doll. I know you're in there." He hooked a long wavy lock of hair that had pulled free from his ponytail behind his ear. "I saw her on the hill, man. She must be in the house. I told you she'd come here. She's going to try to sell the will again."

Bobby stood with his thumbs hooked in the belt loops of his jeans, making his angular pelvic bones jut against the fabric. "Find out what the fuck she did with your cash, man."

Angus pounded on the door again. "Just answer the door, baby. I forgive you for setting the fire."

He stepped back with surprise when he heard a lock in the door slide out of its casing.

The heavy old door was pulled open. Paula nonchalantly rested one hand on the doorknob. The other was behind her back. "Hi, Angus. Bobby. What are you guys up to?"

He pushed past her. "Where's the money, baby?"

"Money?" She maneuvered around him so that she stood in the doorway that led to the hall.

"Yeah, money! I don't know what you two broads think you're up to." He snatched at her arm.

She swung at him with the hammer she'd been concealing, grazing his knuckles. They lunged at her. She threw the hammer at them, then ran down the hall into her old bedroom. She slammed the door and shoved a stack of boxes in front of it, sending old dolls, toys, and books tumbling everywhere.

Angus managed to press the door open and squeeze through but stumbled on the junk that was barely visible in the dim light. Paula started to climb through the window just as Iris careened around the corner of the house with the blue Oldsmobile in reverse, swerving to avoid piles of refuse on the lawn.

As Paula hoisted herself through the bedroom window, Iris heard a sharp noise crack like a gunshot. "Hurry! Get in."

Angus and Bobby made it to the window just as Iris threw the car into drive.

Paula said, "Bobby, I always told you not to leave your keys in the car." The tires kicked up dust as they skidded around the house.

"I'm gonna get you, Paula," Angus yelled.

Bobby pulled on Angus's sleeve.

Junior stood just inside the door with his gun trained on them.

***

"Iris, slow down!"

When they rounded the last bend where the hill met the citrus grove, the Oldsmobile spun out on the loose dirt. It made one clean rotation on the narrow road. On the second one, it slammed into the Wall of Gaytan.

The Olds's engine cut out. The damaged metal creaked and groaned.

Paula gingerly touched her head where it had slammed against the passenger window. "Are you all right?"

Iris tried to start the engine but it just cranked dryly. "Yeah. C'mon, baby," she cooed to the Olds. "You?"

"Yeah."

The engine finally turned over and Iris backed up. The right front fender and quarter panel were smashed and the bent metal scraped loudly against the right front tire.

After she'd backed up a few feet and put the car in drive, she stopped to stare at the wall.

Paula looked around anxiously. "Let's get out of here!"

"I'm having one of those *déjà vu* things. I hate when that happens." Iris shook her head briskly, then peeled out on the dirt.

Finally outside Las Mariposas, they climbed the hill opposite, the Oldsmobile groaning. When it would go no further, its vital fluids streaming down the asphalt, Iris rolled it against the curb.

They climbed into the Triumph.

"My legs are shaking," Iris said. "When I heard that shot…"

"What shot?"

"I heard a noise like a gunshot."

"That was no gun, dingbat. I split your jeans."

Twenty-Six

It was Monday morning and Iris was bathed, dressed, caffeined, and at her desk with a fresh yellow pad squared in front of her and three freshly sharpened pencils lined up next to it. She was ready for war. There was a rumor that the Fed was going to lower the prime interest rate next week and the market was restless.

She managed to work feverishly but only for short gulps of time before her mind began to wander. She was fine as long as she was on the phone but once she hung up, the DeLaceys crept in. When the client with whom she was speaking now, a widow with two grown sons, began unloading on her about her problems with her children, which was probably the real reason she had called, Iris began to doodle on a yellow pad. She wrote: Bill DeLacey, Humberto, Dolly, Junior, Thomas, Paula, Dad. She crossed out Dad—the endearing term had a false ring—and wrote Les Thorne. She underlined it.

When her client hung up, she punched numbers that she pulled from memory onto her telephone keypad, crossed her legs, and leaned back into her leather desk chair. It was odd to call John Somers but more odd to find him home in the middle of the day. She supposed that was his life now as a damaged cop.

He was glad she'd called. He'd been worried about her. They chatted for a bit and she hoped that she hadn't arrived at the real purpose of her call too quickly.

"How easy is it to look at a file for a murder that happened in nineteen seventy-one in the Northeast Division?"

"I have a buddy who works out of the Northeast. I'll give him a call."

"Was your friend there in seventy-one?"

"Let's see." He paused. "Yeah, he probably was. What's up?"

"This is very confidential."

"You know I don't kiss and tell."

"Gabriel Gaytan was murdered in seventy-one and Humberto De la Garza took the rap for it. The only reason the case wasn't investigated further was because Humberto died after these two cops, Gil Alvarez and Ron Cole, beat him up when he resisted arrest. The case was closed to cover it up. I want to find out if there was any evidence that pointed to another suspect."

He agreed to look into it today. He seemed happy to have some police work to do.

Iris looked at her watch. Her bank was now open. She grabbed the strap of the small duffel bag that she'd stashed under her desk.

Kyle Tucker sauntered into her office. Iris quickly dropped the bag, then spotted her doodlings and tried to appear casual as she covered the yellow pad with a client file. Somewhat breathlessly, she said, "Hi, Kyle. What can I do for you?" She plastered a polite smile on her face and thought: *State your business and get the hell out.*

He flopped into one of the two chairs that faced her desk, resting the calf of one leg on the knee of the other, and cavalierly interlaced his fingers behind his head, elbows akimbo.

He said nothing but just grinned at her with his thin rubbery lips closed but stretched salaciously across his face.

Finally Iris said, "It's really not fair, Kyle. If I sat like that, I'd be accused of being unladylike."

"You might make some new friends." His already impossibly broad gash of a mouth stretched even further across his face.

"That's a shit-eating grin if ever I saw one."

"Want to know a secret?" His eyes twinkled, making it apparent that he had the beans and could hardly wait to spill them.

He was getting on her nerves. She decided to deny him what he wanted, just to be a brat. She decorously pulled herself erect in her chair and said, "I'm sorry, Kyle, but I am *really* busy right now." For good measure, she picked up a pencil and positioned it to write.

He persisted, her comment sliding off him like water off a duck's back. "I think you'll want to hear this." He paused and shot a quick glance through her door, as if checking for eavesdroppers. He lowered his hands from behind his head and leaned toward her with his elbows on his knees. "Truth or fiction? Amber Ambrose says she saw you and Garland Hughes kissing and holding hands on the street in front of the Edward Club."

Iris tried to remain poker-faced, but felt the corners of her mouth tighten. "What in the world would possess her to say something like that?"

His hands again went up behind his head. Now spent, he seemed more relaxed. "Truth or fiction?"

"That doesn't even merit a comment."

"C'mon, Iris. I thought we were friends."

"Let me teach you a few things about this business, Kyle. Rule number one: Trust no one. Rule number two: Hate everyone."

"Oooh. Tough talk, Iris. My nipples are getting hard."

She interlaced her fingers and clutched her knee between her hands. "What if it were true?"

"I'd say you were exercising rule number three: Use everyone." He got up and walked toward the door.

"Thank you for sharing, Kyle."

"What are friends for?" He winked at her. "Well, back to the veal-fattening pen."

Iris walked to the filing cabinet where she kept her purse. She gazed out of the window that overlooked the suite and watched Kyle duck into his cubicle. She lingered, gazing at Amber's pretty auburn-haired head, which was just visible above her cubicle wall. "Some friend you turned out to be."

Amber turned just then as if she sensed that someone was watching her. Iris averted her eyes and busily took her purse from the cabinet. She grabbed the duffel bag, made sure it was securely zipped, slung the long strap over her shoulder, and started to walk out of her office. She had her hand on the light switch when she changed her mind and ducked back inside. She flipped through her Rolodex, found the card she wanted, and slipped it into her suit jacket pocket.

"Iris is going to work out at the gym," Sean Bliss said with surprise as she walked by.

Iris turned but kept walking backward. "I'm going to drop-kick a few junior investment counselors, just to keep in shape."

At the elevator, she pressed the heat-sensitive call button, which glowed orange at her touch. Inside the car, she faced front and tilted her head to watch the illuminated numbers above the doors count off the floors, as did the other passengers. The elevator stopped a few times to pick up and discharge people during its descent.

By the time she'd reached the lobby, she had decided on a plan of action regarding the rumors. She voiced it aloud as if to solidify it. "Rule number four: Deny everything."

She waved to the security guard as she walked out the building onto the street. Her mood immediately improved. She loved the tall skyscrapers of downtown Los Angeles. They were new, sleek, and shiny and had lots of glass. Some of the front courtyards were decorated with sculptures, fountains, and fanciful gardens with palm trees and topiaries. Well-dressed people buzzed to and fro. She fit in. She was part of it. She was a player.

At the corner, she waited for the light to change, occupying herself by glancing at the other passersby and at the flow of traffic that buzzed through the busy intersection. Across the street, she saw two men who appeared to be homeless panhandlers talking to a suited businessman. The businessman pointed at the tall, black granite office tower where Iris worked. When the light changed, the men started walking to the corner diagonally across from Iris. She gasped when she realized it was Angus and Bobby.

She positioned herself behind a couple of tall men also waiting for the light to change and peeked around them. Angus and Bobby were still standing on the corner, talking to each other and looking out of place. When the light changed, Iris had to walk quickly to match the pace of the tall men. A car that was waiting to turn right impatiently nudged into the wave of pedestrians. Iris shot a glance across the street and saw Angus and Bobby crossing in the opposite direction from her.

Just then one of the men she was walking next to cut across her path, apparently not anticipating someone standing so close to him. He brought his large wingtip-clad foot down the length of her shin. She stumbled and the duffel bag slid from her shoulder onto the street. The car that had been steadily creeping into the intersection rolled onto the edge of the bag, the driver barely slamming on his brakes in time to avoid hitting her.

She pulled the strap but the duffel bag was hopelessly caught underneath the car's tires. She bared her teeth at the driver. "Back up!"

He shook his fist at her. "Why the hell don't you watch where you're going?"

"I have the right of way," she snarled.

The man who had stepped on her was holding his hands out, trying to placate everyone. "Let's just calm down. Sir, if you back up…"

Iris looked up and saw Angus and Bobby running across the street toward her through the oncoming traffic. She yanked on the bag's strap. "Back up! Back up! Those men are after me."

The driver spotted Angus and Bobby. "I don't want to be part of this." He backed his car up and the duffel bag popped free.

Iris looked for the man who had been helping her with the driver but he was long gone. She pointed at Angus and Bobby and yelled, "Help! They're after me."

She slung the duffel bag over her shoulder and started clumsily running down the street in her pumps and suit, the heavy bag slapping and swinging around her. "Help! Help!"

Pedestrians cut her a wide swath, but no one offered assistance. The heel of her pump broke and she stumbled, falling onto her hands and knees on the sidewalk. Grasping the broken shoe heel, she scrambled to her feet. They were close behind her. She tossed the heel in her hand.

Instead of running, she stood steadfastly, although unevenly, in the middle of the sidewalk and glared at Angus and Bobby. She muttered, "Damn two-hundred-and-thirty-dollar Anne Klein pumps."

Once they noticed that Iris had stopped running from them, Angus and Bobby slowed to a quick walk that grew less certain as they neared her.

"Why were you chasing me?" she demanded.

"Why were you running from us?"

"Because you were chasing me." She displayed her broken heel. "Look!"

Angus regarded it dispassionately, the significance lost on him. He mustered his bluster, took a step back, as if getting his footing, and demanded, "Where's Paula?"

"I don't know." It wasn't a complete lie. Iris didn't know where Paula was at that exact moment.

Angus absorbed the information and thrust again. "Where's the money?"

"Paula has it."

"Where's the will?"

"I have it." She began to speak excessively slowly, insinuating that he couldn't understand normal speech patterns. "I gave Paula the money and Paula gave me the will. It's called doing a deal." She fully expected him to smack her but she couldn't stop herself.

"What's in the bag?"

"My gym clothes."

"So where's the will?"

"In a safe place."

Angus glanced at Bobby as if to confer, but he shrugged cluelessly in response. Angus returned his attention to Iris, making a swipe at the air with his hand. An important point seemed imminent.

"You know, we could sell that will to this Gil Alvarez for two hundred thousand dollars, you know?"

Iris gaped at him. "Gil Alvarez knows about the will?"

"Yeah. I figured Paula took your money, then took the will and went to him. Thought for sure she was double-dipping. We just came from City Hall. Alvarez really wants it."

"I'll bet. Tell him it's not for sale."

"Why not? Two hundred grand is pretty awesome change."

"Because it's mine and it's not for sale."

He and Bobby exchanged a glance. Bobby was bobbing his head up and down as he looked around the street, seeming to approve of everything he set eyes on.

"Look." Angus dug his index finger inside his ear. "We're staying with some buddies in Hollywood. You know the crib got burned up." He examined his finger and wiped it against his jeans. "Here's the number where we're staying." He dug in his jeans pocket and took out a crumpled piece of paper. "If you see Paula, tell her that's where I am, will you?"

A shadow crossed his face when he mentioned Paula. Iris almost felt sorry for him. She took the paper and started to hobble away on her uneven shoes. Angus stopped her.

"Hey, you couldn't spot us a few bucks, could you? Everything got burned up, you know."

Iris reached in her purse and gave them all the bills she had. Twenty-three dollars.

Angus thanked her reticently.

She made sure they weren't following her before she continued to her destination.

She hobbled up the Great California Bank's worn marble steps and pulled open the heavy glass doors. The old bank, decorated with dark polished wood and brass, was dim and cool inside.

Iris walked to the door of the high-walled cubicle where safe-deposit box transactions were conducted and waved to Howard, the bank teller, who was occupied helping a customer. Weak-chinned, sweaty-palmed, turtle-bellied Howard always watched Iris with great interest, motivated by his unflagging, unrequited love.

Howard walked to the opposite side of the counter from where Iris stood and hit a hidden buzzer. Iris pushed open the tall door and entered the cubicle. She gave him her key and he returned with a large metal box.

The transaction had been blissfully wordless and Iris prayed it would remain that way.

No such luck.

Howard smiled at her in a way that perhaps was intended to look impish. "I'd give anything to be a fly on these walls and see what you put into and take out of that box."

She smiled politely at him.

"You seem to lead a very exciting life," he continued. "Much more exciting than mine."

"Don't let looks deceive you. I'm home every night by seven o'clock, reading Bible stories." Her polite smile turned tense as she waited for him to leave. As soon as he did, she unzipped the heavy duffel bag that rested on the floor by her feet.

First she layered in the three hundred thousand dollars, give or take a few bucks, that remained of her dirty money. Then she folded Gabe's will on top. She took out the small metal box she'd taken from Bill DeLacey's desk. From it she retrieved a gold wedding band. She read the inscription again: *Gabriel y Isabella 14 Junio 1934.*

She started to put it in the box, then changed her mind and shoved it into her skirt pocket. She closed the safe-deposit box, put Bill DeLacey's empty metal box inside the duffel bag and zipped it. She signaled Howard that she was finished and left.

Twenty-Seven

Iris went to the shoe repair shop, had her heel fixed, then drove the Triumph to Azusa. Azusa had been enthusiastically named by a founding father who saw everything from A to Z in the USA in this community at the base of the San Gabriel Mountains.

Her *Thomas Brothers' Guide* led her to the address she wanted. She parked the Triumph next to the curb in front of a modest house in a middle-class neighborhood, not unlike the one where she had grown up. She gazed at the house, examining its lawn and flowers and the contrasting trim painted around the windows and all the other little details. She was looking for something—but she didn't know what. A common thread. Something that linked her to this house in some way other than the most obvious one.

She stopped musing and focused on the task at hand. She combed her hair and fixed her makeup in the rearview mirror with firm, no-nonsense motions. She was going to get to the bottom of this DeLacey business. That was why she was here. That was what she was going to come away with. She didn't seek or expect anything more.

She was about to get out of the car when she spotted two young teenage girls walking down the street. They were talking animatedly to each other, probably gabbing about boys and best friends and dances and school and parties. A bit of life had been revealed to them, just enough to make them feel as if they knew everything and were qualified to speak of it with authority, cockily punctuating their words with dramatic hand and facial gestures.

Iris watched them, wistful for bygone days of walking home from school with friends, days when everything had seemed so complicated but in reality was deceptively simple. While she was watching them, she detected something eerily familiar about one girl, something that she couldn't quite put her finger on but was indelible. She suspected she knew the reason.

The girls split up and the familiar one walked up the path leading to the house in front of which Iris was parked. She cast a glance at Iris, one of curiosity more than suspicion, then eyed the Triumph. Before she reached the front door of the house, she dashed off the side of the lawn onto the driveway, as if she'd forgotten something.

"Daddy," she yelled. "I'm home!"

A man responded. "Okay, sweetheart."

Iris didn't know what made her do it. She had her questions to ask, her things to do all organized, but she found herself cranking the Triumph's engine for all it was worth. As soon as it turned over, she floored the accelerator and barreled down the street without looking back at her father's house.

Iris parked the Triumph in front of the Gaytan DeLacey for City Council headquarters. From her purse she pulled several cosmetic compacts, opened each one in turn, jammed their applicators into the different vats, and wiped the colors onto her face. She squeezed drops into her eyes, pulled a brush through her hair, and freshened her lipstick. She got out of the Triumph, smoothed her suit skirt, put on her jacket, and marched into Thomas's campaign office as if she had every reason to be there, as if she owned the place, as if someone had died and made her queen. The best defense is a good offense. She did everything she could to disguise the fact that she'd been crying.

She walked up to the first desk inside the door and asked the sweet, young, female campaign volunteer in a tone of voice that took no prisoners, "Thomas Gaytan DeLacey?"

"He's not here right now."

Iris sank. She spotted Sylvia Padilla, Thomas's campaign manager, avidly flipping through sheets of green-bar computer paper. She had half a mind to leave and go home and crawl into a Sara Lee butter pecan coffee cake with a chardonnay chaser. But her home was not her own right now—Paula was there—and Iris and Thomas did have a date. She would simply put her stupid emotional outburst behind her and follow through with her evening plans.

Iris stepped over to Padilla, hoping her repaired heel didn't break. She wondered how to address her: Ms., Miss, or just Sylvia. She opted for political correctness, assuming it would find a welcome reception here.

"Good afternoon, Ms. Padilla."

Padilla looked up through her thick glasses, which had slid down her nose. She reseated them with a push of her middle finger. A glimmer of a smile crossed her lips, as if she didn't want to smile but didn't recognize this intruder and didn't want to get off on the wrong foot.

"I'm Iris Thorne, a friend of Thomas's."

Padilla remembered, also remembering that this was no one whom she had to impress. The glimmer faded and she seemed to be anxious to get back to work. "He's walking the district with a reporter from the *L.A. Times*. I'm not sure when they're going to be back."

Iris glanced at her watch. "We had plans to meet at six."

"This interview came up suddenly." It was unstated: this more important than his date with you.

"How have you decided to handle Alvarez's accusations about the Gabriel Gaytan murder?"

Padilla released the page she was looking at and set down her pen. She warmed to this topic. "They're the wild ravings of a desperate and possibly unstable man. Alvarez has run this district like his own fiefdom for years. This is the first time he's had any real competition. Now the public has the chance to see what he's really made of."

"You don't think the allegations have any merit."

"Of course not. We've gone over the Police Department's file on the Gaytan murder with a fine-toothed comb. The only thing we've found that merits investigation is Humberto de la Garza's death, which was clearly caused by police brutality." She said the term with relish. "Unfortunately there wasn't a witness. Thomas's father is prepared to make a statement that Humberto appeared to have been beaten."

"Why didn't he say something when it happened?"

"It was a very traumatic time for Mr. DeLacey with the murder and his wife's subsequent illness. And, as a citizen, it didn't occur to him to question the police."

Iris nodded. "What if Alvarez produced evidence that implicates Bill DeLacey in Gaytan's murder?"

"Evidence? There isn't any evidence."

Either she didn't know about the will or she was a damn good liar.

Padilla continued, "If Alvarez's accusations had any merit, Mayor Riley wouldn't have given Gaytan DeLacey his endorsement today."

"He got the mayor's endorsement? Fantastic."

"It's unusual for a first-time candidate. The mayor could have remained silent on the issue. The fact he didn't shows the strength of this campaign." Padilla looked behind Iris and said, "Junior, just stack those against the wall. Thank you."

Iris turned to see Junior DeLacey rolling a dolly that was piled high with boxes. She was going to excuse herself from the conversation, but didn't need to: Padilla was again absorbed in her report. Iris walked outside, trailing Junior, who was pushing the dolly toward his red pickup truck parked at the curb.

"Hi, Junior." She attempted a friendly smile.

There were beads of perspiration on his forehead and dotting the top of his moustache. He uttered "Hi" without looking at her.

She didn't know how to begin.

He didn't dance around the issue. While continuing to move boxes from the truck to the dolly, he mumbled, "So now you've got that will, you think you can tell us what to do."

"How do you know I have it?"

"Two guys at the house said Paula sold it to you." He still wouldn't look into her eyes.

"I'm not sure it's authentic. It could even be an old version."

He was panting. He didn't seem to be working that hard. Maybe the human interaction was taxing him. His small eyes were almost buried within his fleshy lids, and watchful, as if sensing danger lurking nearby, danger visible only to him. He didn't say anything else.

She tried another tactic. "I'm sorry about your mother."

He furrowed his brow and climbed onto the truck bed.

She sensed she'd struck a nerve, so she continued pressing. "It was wonderful how you took care of her all those years. I didn't realize you were so devoted to her."

He hoisted a box to rest on his shoulder. His slack face grew compressed as if he were drawing into himself, as if the thing that was churning inside him were sucking him dry.

"Did she give any indication that she was suicidal?"

Iris ducked when the box sailed past her head. Astonished, she staggered backward to get away from him.

He still stood on the truck bed, clenching his fists. "Don't blame that on me."

Thomas and another man rounded the corner. Thomas appraised the scene but quickly banished the concerned look that passed over his face and continued talking. "Alvarez can't handle the fact that my campaign war chest books are open for audit. My father's contributions are well within the legal limit." He nodded at Iris and she gave a quick wave in greeting as she walked well away from the truck.

Junior rolled the dolly to the box on the sidewalk, loaded it, and went inside the office. Thomas continued, "DeLacey Gardens is a fine enterprise that will bring not only a much-needed facility to the community but many jobs as well. The fact that Alvarez opposes it demonstrates that he does not have the community's best interests in mind. He's acting out his private agenda against the DeLacey family."

The reporter said, "The election's only two weeks away and the latest polls show you and Alvarez neck and neck. You've risen ten points since the last poll, which seems to indicate that Alvarez's accusations haven't had any effect."

"In fact, they've had the opposite effect. They've only made him look desperate."

"The debate next week ought to be interesting."

Thomas ran his hand through his thick, wavy hair, smiling broadly. "It's a good forum for the public to evaluate the candidates."

The reporter shook Thomas's hand. "Mr. Gaytan DeLacey, it's been a pleasure. Or should I say Councilman Gaytan DeLacey?"

Thomas laughed disarmingly. "Let's not count our chickens..."

He waited until the reporter had gotten into his car and driven away before he walked up to Iris. "Hey, sweetness." He gave her a searching look. "Something wrong?"

Junior was still inside, out of earshot, but Iris whispered anyway. "I asked Junior whether Dolly had been suicidal and he flew off the handle and threw a box at me."

Junior came outside. He made a correct assumption about what they were talking about. "It just slipped out of my hands. Tell her to stop acting like she's part of the family." He got in the truck and drove off.

Thomas sighed, suddenly looking very tired.

Iris straightened the strap of her purse on her shoulder and pulled herself up. "I know we made plans tonight, Thomas, but I just..."

He gave her a look that was so sad and lost and lonely that it broke her heart. "Don't go."

Twenty-Eight

They had dinner at a little place nearby. Thomas had suggested going to Santa Monica with the implication that they'd go to her place afterward, but she gently and firmly nixed the idea.

"I'm curious to see how you live," he said.

She was also curious to see how she was living after Paula had been in residence for an entire day. She promised an evening *chez elle* in the near future.

"A home-cooked meal?" he asked hopefully.

"Well…The best home-ordered meal in town. Besides, I want to see this bachelor pad of yours."

She liked Thomas and everything she'd seen so far. She was ready to see more. This was their second official evening date, though they'd talked on the phone a lot and had twice met for a quick lunch. Thomas's campaign schedule hadn't allowed for anything more. She was glad that circumstances had forced them to take things slowly and Thomas had expressed the same idea to her. She wasn't eager to rush headfirst into a romantic entanglement. She'd made mistakes in the past. With Thomas, she found herself being more circumspect than usual and wasn't sure why.

She had fantasized about having sex with him. A lot, if the truth be known. After all, he was a definite turn-on. He was everything she wanted: handsome, sensual, charming, educated, accomplished, ambitious, kind, caring. But something told her to hold back. Maybe tonight she'd feel more at ease. Maybe tonight they'd get to know each other a little bit better.

They went to his place in separate cars.

He lived on a hillside facing the city in the tiny upscale section of the Fourteenth District. His house was built almost at a right angle with the hill and was supported by two stilts—a fragile structure built on even more fragile land. Such houses were popular in the hilly areas of Los Angeles even though they occasionally slid downhill after the earth had been weakened by floods or quakes. While they lasted, the view was spectacular.

Dinner had been quiet and noncontroversial with a litany of small talk about this and that. Iris contributed to the flow as much as he did, wanting to pretend that the whole big DeLacey issue didn't hang over them like a dark cloud. If only it could be just them and the whole rest of the world would go away. If only they didn't have all the DeLaceys and Thornes and Gaytans clinging to them like so many fleas. If only they could be who they were but different. Then everything would be perfect.

They sat on a couch facing the large picture windows across the rear of the house overlooking the city. He offered her a cup of coffee and she accepted.

While he was in the kitchen, she roamed around. What she saw confirmed her opinion of him. There was a variety of books and magazines. This was a well-read man. An office off the living room displayed framed diplomas and awards of all types. This was an ambitious man. There was an abundance of framed photographs of family and others, famous and anonymous. Although the decor revealed the hand of an interior decorator, there were small items that made the house homey. Mundane things that had been carried home and displayed on a shelf, each with their own little story. A tiny carved wood house. A smooth stone. A seedpod. This was a sentimental man. She liked it all. Then why was that little voice nagging her, telling her that something was amiss?

"Relax," she told herself. "Let whatever happens happen."

He returned from the kitchen carrying a tray with cups and saucers. There was also a small plate of Oreo cookies.

Her eyes must have betrayed her.

"You like Oreos?" he asked.

"They're my favorites."

"Really? Mine too."

She giggled nervously. "This is just too cute, isn't it?"

He kissed her. He just set the tray down and kissed her. They had kissed before, but nothing like this. He grabbed her around the small of the back and she leaned into his arms, her back arching until her feet barely touched the ground. Lights flashed behind her closed eyes. She felt weightless. She opened her eyes and looked at his, which were closed, his long lashes forming a dark fringe.

He opened his eyes and met hers. They stopped kissing but remained with their lips barely touching, their mouths open, breathing each other's air. He caressed her neck, chin, and ears. She recovered her feet. He took her hand and they wordlessly walked to the couch and sat holding hands, brushing knees, gazing at each other, looking at everything that was unique and on the way to becoming precious. They sat that way for a long time.

Then she said it. She didn't know why. It had been on her mind the whole night and cognition at the present time seemed to have yielded to instinct.

"I have the will."

"I know."

"What does it mean?" she said, now sorry that she had ended their interlude.

"I don't know." He got up and walked to the picture window and kneaded his forehead with his fingertips. "I don't like thinking about what it might mean."

"Alvarez knows about it, you know."

He looked alarmed. "No, I didn't know. How?"

"The two guys who told Junior about it, Angus and Bobby, told me that Alvarez offered them two hundred thousand dollars for it."

He grimaced. "I'm glad it's in your hands. What are you going to do with it?"

"Keep it for now. I didn't want it to come out during the election."

He looked at her warmly. "You do care about me."

"I do. But as soon as the election's over, I'm going to have the title to Las Mariposas investigated. I want Dolly's land returned to her."

"Doesn't matter. She left it to my father when she died."

"She told me in her phone message that she didn't remember making a will. If your father forged your grandfather's will, what would stop him from forging your mother's? If she died intestate, you and your siblings are entitled to part of her estate."

He shot a glance at her purse. "Where's this will you bought?"

"Not here."

"I want to see it. It's probably a fake."

"I don't think so, Thomas."

"How do you know? You wouldn't have any basis…"

She fished the ring from her skirt pocket. "Because of this."

He examined it, then asked coolly, "How did you get this?"

She couldn't lie to him but she couldn't tell him the truth either. "I'd rather not say."

"You were the woman with Paula when she broke into my father's house. Those guys thought it was you."

"I shouldn't have done that. I just had to see if there was any basis to what your mother told me in her phone message."

"I'm not notifying the police. I don't need my girlfriend arrested for breaking and entering."

"Bad for the campaign?" Iris suggested.

"Honey, I'm glad that someone cares about my mother as much as you do." He put the ring on the coffee table, then scooted close to her. The rough fibers of his gabardine suit pants rubbed against her skin. She noticed a single wild strand of gray hair at his temple.

She said, "Gabriel always wore that ring even though Isabella had died years before. I remember asking my mother why he still wore a wedding ring. It was missing from Gabriel's body when he was found in the toolshed. Your father's such a pack rat, he probably couldn't bear to bury a perfectly good ring. In any event, it indicates he tampered with the crime scene. What else did he tamper with?"

"Where's Paula?" he asked.

She frowned.

"That was why you didn't want me to go to your place."

She looked at him self-consciously. She was a terrible liar, especially when it involved someone she cared about.

"She's bad news, Iris. Stay away from her. She burned those two guys' house down. My father says she's capable of anything."

"I don't believe that."

"I just don't want you to get hurt."

"I'm not so sure my welfare is your only concern."

He took her hand between both of his. "Sweetheart, we both know that you and I have something special. But it's not going to go anywhere if you won't trust me."

"Trust isn't something that happens on demand, especially for me."

"But you trust Paula and she's the last person you should trust."

"I'm helping Paula."

"So help me!" He squeezed her hand tighter.

"I *am* helping you. You're one of the reasons I bought the will."

"It belongs to the family. Please return it to me."

He was mashing her hand. She tried to free herself. He became aware of what he was doing, loosened his grip, and moved to pull her hand to his lips.

She pulled her hand away from him. "The family. Now I know why Dolly called someone outside the family."

"Iris, you're dealing with mentally unstable people. It should be clear to you that both my mother and Paula—"

"You and your father keep playing that crazy card. It's not only getting old, but I'm finding it offensive." She stood and walked to the middle of the room. "Not to mention unconvincing. Dolly had enough wits to call me, to hide that will."

She regarded him skeptically. "Why aren't you more upset about the will and the ring? It implicates your father in your grandfather's murder and gives him a reason to keep your mother quiet. And what about Junior and his fit today? You took it in stride. Why was he concerned that I might think his mother's death was his fault?"

A look of profound sadness crossed his face. "Let my mother rest in peace. She killed herself. She'd tried before. Junior feels guilty about her suicide because he'd watched over her for so many years."

"He threw a box at me!" She pointed as if the box were in the room.

"I don't blame you for wanting to sort it out. The whole thing was all bound to come tumbling down anyway." He stared across the room. "And dragging everything with it. Everything I've worked for. It's unfair." He smiled sadly. "But as my father would say, who said life was fair?" He stood and started gathering the cups and saucers.

Iris chewed her lip. "Thomas, please just tell me one thing. Did your father kill Gabriel? If not, who did and why?"

Dark circles had appeared under his eyes. "Humberto de la Garza beat my grandfather to death with a pickax in a failed robbery attempt. That's the only explanation I know." He continued stacking the dishes on a tray. "I know that when the will and that ring are made public, my father will be formally accused of murdering my grandfather to get his land. My father is an old and a difficult man, but he's not a murderer. You know what the really sad part is?" He gave her a piercing look. "Those cops killed Humberto and they got away with it."

She picked at a ragged edge of a fingernail, then tore it between her teeth. She folded her arms across her chest to force herself to stop fidgeting.

He picked up the ring from the coffee table and handed it to her. "Take it. It's part of your evidence to bring down the DeLaceys. I don't know why you hate us so much. Is it still a boss-employee thing left over from your parents?"

"I don't want to bring down the DeLaceys. I want to find out the truth."

"What will it bring you? The whole truth will never come out. My family's reputation will be destroyed but those cops will go scot-free even though they murdered a man with their bare hands."

She didn't move to take the ring. "Give it back to your father."

He grasped it in his fist. "Why don't you trust me, Iris?" His eyes searched hers. "Have I ever done anything to hurt you?"

She couldn't answer. It wasn't something she could put into words.

"I guess your father's leaving really affected you."

"I suppose so," she admitted.

"Now I'm paying the price. I'm sorry, but I can't be involved with someone who doesn't trust me."

"If that's the way you feel..." She went to the door. "Look, this is who I am. It's not all pretty and it's not all perfect. If you can't give me the time I need to feel close to you, then maybe we shouldn't see each other." She put her hand on the doorknob.

"Iris, wait."

She looked at him hopefully.

"Did you see Humberto being beaten? That's what your mother told my father."

"She *told* him?" Iris fumed.

"Would you be willing to make a statement?"

"If Gabriel Gaytan's murder case is reopened, of course."

"No. I mean at the debate."

"I don't want to be part of that mudslinging."

"Iris, you already are. It started when you bought that will."

She didn't respond.

He took a step toward her. "If you come out about the beating, we'll finally be able to put this whole thing behind us. We can build something together."

"If you push the police-beating angle, the fact that Humberto was framed is going to be clear. There's bound to be a thorough investigation that may reveal the identity of the true murderer. Are you prepared for that?"

His voice grew stern. "Iris, if you won't help me, at least don't stand in my way. Give me the will."

"No," she said with finality. She opened the door and started to walk out. Just before she left, she turned and delivered the final blow. "I just want you to know that you had an excellent chance of getting lucky tonight and you blew it."

Twenty-Nine

Iris went into the lunchroom at McKinney Alitzer for another mug of coffee. She was toying with buying a second six-pack of Oreos when Kyle came in.

"Good morning." He flipped through the office copy of the *L.A. Times*, haphazardly pulling apart the sections. He freed the sports section—as was his routine—and held it in front of his face as he left the room.

A headline in the Metro section caught Iris's eye. AMBITION AND SENSE OF COMMUNITY DRIVE GAYTAN DELACEY. The article was accompanied by a photo of Thomas, looking handsome and dynamic, standing on a shabby street corner.

She folded the section and took it back to her office. She picked up the phone to call him. It would be reasonable to call him about having seen the article. She made herself set the receiver back in its cradle.

What was there to say? He had accused her of not trusting him. He was right.

"Another relationship bites the dust," she said aloud.

She started going through her mail. Work was a sure way to distract herself. She told herself she would just work harder until she felt better. But it didn't happen: she didn't feel any better. The phone rang. It was an outside call, so she answered formally. "Iris Thorne."

"Hi, it's John."

"Hi! How are you?"

He seemed surprised by her enthusiasm. "I'm good."

She was sad, susceptible to latching onto anyone vaguely resembling a friend.

"I talked to my friend over at the Northeast Division about the Gabriel Gaytan murder."

"Right." She'd forgotten she'd asked him for help. "What did you find out?"

"He said Ron Cole had a reputation for losing his cool. Alvarez was basically a good guy, but he and Cole were as thick as mud. When Humberto de la Garza died, everyone suspected Cole. There was an investigation, but there weren't any witnesses to contradict Cole and Alvarez's story. Since no one came forward to see that de la Garza's interests were served, the investigation was closed."

"Did he say anything about de la Garza being framed for Gaytan's murder?"

"The police reports said it looked as if the crime scene had been tampered with. There was a statement from Dolores DeLacey saying she saw de la Garza running from the toolshed. It was stiff and short. The detective who interviewed her made a note that Mrs. DeLacey was unresponsive and sobbing to the point that they couldn't get anything more from her."

She thanked him and hung up. She decided to send him a card to express her appreciation more formally. She wanted to thank him for more than just his help.

"He never bugged me about trust," she said aloud.

In her mail she found a small white envelope of good paper addressed to her in neat handwriting. It was an invitation to the fund-raiser that Gil Alvarez had told her about. The event was being held at Lunar, a hilltop restaurant in Northeast L.A. known less for its food than for the spectacular view from its outside garden terrace. It was a favorite wedding reception site. Even though this was going to be no ordinary party, it might lift her spirits. She started to have second thoughts about any interaction with Alvarez but shrugged them off. If he hadn't recognized her by now, he never would. He was too busy flirting with her and too full of himself to put two and two together. She'd just steer clear of him and hang around the fringes.

Iris called her condo. Paula answered the phone sleepily but abrasively. "Stop calling, asshole."

"What?"

"Oh, it's you."

"Want to be my date at a party tonight?"

"What time is it?"

"About seven this evening."

"No, now."

"It's nine fifteen."

"Nine fifteen? You didn't get home until two. When do you sleep?"

"I don't. It keeps me psychotic. Gil Alvarez is having a fund-raiser."

"Sounds like some free drinks."

"I thought you'd think so. I'll pick you up around three to go shopping for a dress."

"A dress?"

"The doo-wah's black tie. Who was calling?"

"I don't know. They'd just call and hang up. No heavy breathing, no nothing. If it's that stupid Angus, I swear to God I'll tear his throat out."

"Just do it in the living room. The floor there has to be replaced anyway. I'll see you at three. I'm in a mood to do some serious damage at the mall."

It was a chilly evening but Iris refused to cover up her new Donna Karan. It was hot pink and tight and backless and short and she didn't give a damn. Let 'em think the worst.

Hanging in her closet were several cocktail dresses that would have been perfectly acceptable, including the one she'd bought for her first date with Thomas. She'd flipped through the hangers as an exercise, knowing in advance that none of them would be any good. They were all tainted with other times, other events, other men. She was having yet another fresh start. That called for a new dress.

Paula had done their hair. She'd been a hairdresser in one of her previous lives. She'd pinned Iris's hair into a twist at the back of her head with tendrils dangling down her neck and teased her own thick mane into something big and glamorous to go with the black, knee-length, low-cut number she'd bought. With a little TLC Paula could still cut a striking figure.

At the party, Paula swept two champagne flutes from a tray carried by a waiter and handed one to Iris. "This ought to warm you up." Paula downed hers in two gulps and grabbed another.

Iris raised her eyebrows.

Paula shrugged. "They're free and you're driving." She scrutinized a tray of hors d'oeuvres carried by another waiter and piled several onto a small cocktail napkin. "Fancy schmantzy party, Iris Thorne."

Iris shrugged. "It's okay."

"Listen to you. Been there. Done that." With her eyes, Paula followed a waiter who had just entered the terrace from the kitchen. "I could really tie one on tonight. That stupid Angus calling all day really pissed me off."

"How do you know it was him?"

"It's just like something he would do. He treats me like crap all the years I'm with him, then I take off and he won't leave me alone. I'm not going to stand for him dogging me the whole rest of my life. No way. It'll be him or me."

Iris looked at her soberly.

"Hey, don't stress on it. I'm taking off. I'll go shopping for some wheels tomorrow, then"—she ran her hand in front of her like a car going down a road—"see ya!" She took off after the waiter.

Iris nibbled at a corner of toast and caviar. Her snug dress wouldn't allow her to eat much more. She eyed the crowd.

While Paula went in search of more hors d'oeuvres, Jeff Rosen energetically walked toward her with his hand outstretched. "Iris! I'm so glad you came."

"Hi, Jeff," Iris said guardedly, taking his hand. She assumed he knew about the will. "Nice turnout."

"Gil has loyal supporters. Their contributions might be small but at least it keeps him from being in the back pocket of a few large contributors like Gaytan DeLacey."

"Who's Gaytan DeLacey beholden to?" she asked.

"He never told you?"

"What do you mean?"

"I found out today that you've been dating him."

"News travels fast."

"Little goes unnoticed in a campaign like this."

"Apparently."

"Just so you know, Gaytan DeLacey's biggest contributors are real estate developers. They have their eyes on that five-hundred-acre ranch."

She gave him a blank look.

He gave her a smug one back. "There's a lot about Thomas Gaytan DeLacey that you may be unaware of."

Paula returned with a fresh glass of champagne and another napkin piled high with hors d'oeuvres. She popped a stuffed phyllo dough pillow into her mouth and licked the flaky crumbs from her fingers.

Rosen eyed her suspiciously, as if he thought she'd crashed the party.

Iris quickly made the introductions. "Jeff Rosen, this is my friend Paula...ah..."

"Molina," Paula volunteered.

"Very pleased to meet you, Paula."

She gave him her greasy hand. "Delighted, I'm sure." She slurred a bit. The champagne was taking effect. That didn't stop her from snagging another glass from a passing waiter.

"Paula?" Rosen widened his eyes. "You're Gaytan DeLacey's sister."

Paula pointed her hands to herself. "That would be me."

He looked at Iris. "Now this is interesting."

"Guess I'm just rotten with DeLaceys lately, Jeff."

"Mrs. Molina, we heard about your house burning down," Rosen said. "Do they know what caused the fire?"

"I don't know what *they* know, but I have some ideas," Paula said.

Rosen furtively looked around, then grabbed their arms and started guiding them away from the crowd. "Look. About that will. Gil's prepared to pay whatever it takes to get his hands on it." He looked from Paula to Iris.

"It's not mine to sell," Paula said. "Iris bought it from me."

"Iris?" he pleaded.

She shook her head.

He looked at her incredulously. "Why not?"

"I have my reasons."

"You think you're going to help Gaytan DeLacey win this campaign?" He pointed at Iris. "You'd be better off if you gave us the will now. Gil's about ready to have the Gaytan murder case reopened because of this new evidence. Then you'll be forced to turn it over. I wonder how the folks at McKinney Alitzer will feel about promoting you then."

Paula grabbed his hand and forced it to his side. "Didn't your mother tell you it was impolite to point?"

Iris looked at him evenly. "I'd advise you to get *all* your facts in order before you did that. Ask Gil about what really happened to Humberto de la Garza."

"I know what happened. He hurt himself falling down a hill when he resisted arrest."

"Really?" Iris scrutinized him out of the corner of her eye.

"There's no evidence to the contrary."

"Oh yeah?" Paula said. She staggered slightly on her high heels. "You'd better be pretty goddamned sure, mister." She punctuated her words by poking him in the arm with her finger.

He glared at her. "Excuse me?" Turning to Iris, he said, "What is she talking about?"

"Jeff, I suggest you have a heart-to-heart with Gil about what happened that day. If you don't, you'll see a political career crash and burn like you've never seen before. It won't be a shot in the arm for your career either."

There was robust laughter coming from the center of the terrace. Gil Alvarez was holding court.

Paula said, "That's him, isn't it?"

Iris nodded.

"I'll be damned." Paula shook her head and started walking toward him.

Iris quickly followed, with Rosen close behind.

Alvarez's face was slightly flushed. His eyes sparkled and his grin was broad. He was in his element. He spread his arms expansively, a lit cigar wedged between his fingers. "Considering how much he mentions the mayor's endorsement, he should give himself a third name, Thomas Gaytan DeLacey *Riley*."

Everyone within earshot laughed with delight.

"You would have thought that Mayor Riley adopted him or something."

More laughter.

A tall man stood next to Alvarez. He looked to be in his fifties and had a full head of wavy silver hair and a broad barrel chest. He wasn't wearing a tuxedo like most of the other men or even a dark suit, but had on a tweedy sports jacket over beige pants. His tie was broad and the material was cheap and stiff. He made Alvarez, who was wearing a black tuxedo, look downright elegant.

He casually looked over the crowd, almost as if out of habit, and immediately spotted Iris and Paula—nothing unusual about that since they were probably the most flashily dressed women there.

Alvarez took a sip of champagne and extended his arms again. "What my opponent doesn't realize is that getting the mayor's endorsement can actually be a liability. The mayor only has a forty percent approval rating in the Fourteenth. Most of the constituents see the mayor as elitist—not in touch with the needs of the people. This endorsement can end up being Gaytan DeLacey's boat anchor."

There was scattered applause and shouts of "Here, here!" and "Right on!"

Alvarez spotted Jeff Rosen waving at him, trying to get his attention, but ignored him. "Elitist," he sniffed. "I tried to give Gaytan DeLacey a tip. I told him, Thomas, stop telling people how you graduated from Yale. Doesn't make you connect to the Fourteenth, sitting there behind the velvet rope of the Yale Club."

There were murmurs of agreement.

Alvarez drained his glass.

"Oh no," Rosen moaned.

"I told him. Thomas, I said. Good thing you didn't take up sales as an occupation because, my friend, I don't think you could sell pussy on a troop train."

There were scattered guffaws, mostly from the men. Some of the women tittered uncomfortably. The tall silver-haired man slapped Alvarez on the back and laughed heartily.

Rosen looked aghast.

Iris grinned malevolently. "That's your candidate."

Alvarez was about to continue talking—a fresh glass of champagne in his hand, apparently having the time of his life—when Rosen took him by the arm and physically removed him from the scene. The silver-haired man tagged along.

"Miss Iris Thorne," Alvarez said. "How wonderful to see you." He bowed and kissed her hand. "You look delightful. I'm glad that Thomas Gaytan DeLacey at least has luck with the ladies."

Rosen indicated Paula. "And this is Paula Molina. Thomas's sister." He shot Alvarez a meaningful look.

Alvarez kissed her hand. "I must say that Bill and Dolores DeLacey certainly had very attractive children."

Paula nabbed another glass of champagne from a passing waiter.

Alvarez introduced the silver-haired man. "This is my old friend and former partner, Ron Cole."

Iris tried to keep her expression convivial as she shook his hand.

Paula was not as discreet. "I'll be damned. Ron Cole and Gil Alvarez. Who would have thought? What a small world. You two guys caught my grandfather's murderer. Thank goodness you got that dangerous Humberto off the streets."

Cole said, "Sure. I remember you girls." He looked them up and down. "Like I always say, thank heaven for little girls."

"Thank heaven," Alvarez agreed.

Cole asked, "So which one of you had the dog?"

Iris tugged on Paula's arm. "We'd better go."

Paula jerked her arm away. "What business is it of yours?"

"Let's go." Iris again latched onto Paula.

Paula walked sideways, dragged by Iris. "Are you a dog lover or something? Is that why you almost shot poor Skippy?"

Alvarez stopped smiling for the first time that night.

"Poor Skippy," Paula wailed. "You loved that dog, didn't you, Iris?"

Cole formed his hand into a gun and leveled it at Iris. He clicked his tongue against his teeth.

Iris tried to scurry away, but Paula was intent on taking her time, working the rear view for all it was worth.

Thirty

After work the next day, Iris drove to Casa La Propia Hospital, where Dolly had been a patient twenty-five years ago. The Woodland Hills hospital was on a large parcel of land that had once been in the middle of nowhere in the arid, sprawling San Fernando Valley. As the property steadily grew in value, pieces of its vast lawns were sold off by hospital directors seeking a quick budget fix. Now the once gated, very private psychiatric hospital stood facing a busy boulevard next to a large commercial-retail complex.

After Iris had cooled her heels in the hospital lobby for twenty minutes, a middle-aged woman wearing a sedate dress and low heels led her to a sparsely but elegantly decorated office. The walnut Colonial-style desk and credenza were spotlessly polished. The brass pulls gleamed. Many framed diplomas and certificates hung on the walls. On the credenza was a bust with the functions of the human brain delineated—language, memory, motor controls, body senses, and so forth. A bookcase was crammed with psychology books. There were no photographs or other items of a personal nature. A butler's table held an electric teakettle, disposable cups, and coffee and tea paraphernalia. An area to one side was furnished with a couch, a well-padded armchair, and a swivel-based, high-backed leather chair. Several clocks were situated around the room; one was visible from any seat. Each end table held a box of tissues.

"Doctor Osgood will be with you shortly. Please have a seat." The woman left.

Iris stood in the center of the room, wondering if the instruction was actually some sort of a test. She evaluated the available places to sit and took what she thought was the best one—the leather swivel chair. She could see the whole room from there and wouldn't have to tug at her skirt hem, which would ride up if she sat in the soft chair or couch.

A man entered the room, wearing a crisp white cotton short-sleeved wraparound smock with ties that circled around the back and were fastened in a bow in front. Underneath he wore dark suit pants and a light blue shirt with a button-down collar and a tie in a subdued print. He looked to be in his sixties and had thin but carefully styled silver hair frozen in place by some stiff concoction. He was barely as tall as Iris and had a large nose, small brown eyes with lids that drooped over the corners, and a big mouth with purplish lips and gums. He carried a thick manila folder.

Iris decided that even though appearance seemed to be important to this man, he had never been good-looking and had certainly always been short. She wondered what effect that had had on him through his life. He didn't seem to be very friendly. He had given her a distinctly disapproving look when he entered the room.

"I'm Dr. Randolph Osgood."

"Iris Thorne." She stood and shook his hand.

"Nice to meet you. Please sit down." He gestured to the couch and the other chair.

Iris got the idea. She sat on the end of the couch. Sitting in his chair was a small mistake. She felt like telling him to lighten up.

"You are a friend of the DeLacey family."

"Yes, I am."

He took a pair of half-glasses from the smock's breast pocket, set them on the end of his large nose, then gazed at Iris over the tops. "When you said you wanted to speak with me about Dolly DeLacey's illness and treatment, I took the liberty of calling Bill DeLacey."

Iris nodded.

"Is that problematic for you?"

"Not at all." She smiled pleasantly.

"You may or may not know that patient records are confidential and I'm not about to share them with whomever might call."

"Certainly not." *Arrogant ass*, she said to herself.

He opened the manila folder on his lap and began flipping through the pages, occasionally pausing to examine one in detail. All the while, he continued talking to her. "It's Bill DeLacey's opinion that I should speak with you about Dolly's illness and treatment in the most general terms. I conceded that I could do that without getting into specifics about Mrs. DeLacey's case. Mr. DeLacey feels you could benefit from some education about ECT, electroconvulsive therapy, and the depressed individual."

"Does he?"

"Hmmm…" He frowned at a page, then abruptly closed the folder and took off his half glasses. "He says that you are under the rather curious impression that Mrs. DeLacey did not die by her own hand." He held the glasses by one of the arms and spun them. "Furthermore, you believe that Mr. DeLacey was involved in her death. To support this position, you reference a telephone call that Mrs. DeLacey made to you a few days before she expired. Is that correct?"

"That's right. And she didn't leave a suicide note. And why would she hang herself? It's so grisly. Certainly she could have gotten her hands on drugs."

He refolded the glasses and returned them to the smock. "A suicidal person can be very resourceful, Miss Thorne. Anhedonia can reach such a level that an individual will seek almost any means of freeing themselves from it."

"Anhedonia?" She hated admitting he'd used a word that she didn't understand.

He raised his chin. "The state of deriving little or no pleasure from life. Furthermore, notes are left in only a quarter of all suicides. Mrs. DeLacey had attempted to kill herself at least once before, when she intentionally drove the family car into a cement wall in nineteen seventy-one."

"Were there other attempts?"

He flipped the glasses out, put them on, and reopened the folder. "The last time I saw Mrs. DeLacey was June, nineteen seventy-one. I'm unaware of any attempts after that."

"Why did you discontinue care?"

"I strongly encouraged Mr. DeLacey to continue with the follow-up drug therapy. Additionally, a program of follow-up shock treatments might have been in order. As I recall, there was a financial issue. ECT was quite expensive then, as it is today. I don't know what became of Mrs. DeLacey after she left my care."

Iris said, "Mr. DeLacey sent her to the family doctor. But a family practitioner certainly wouldn't be on the cutting edge of psychiatric care. Do you think that if she'd received proper care, she wouldn't have deteriorated the way she did?"

"I'm not in a position to comment on another physician's treatment plan, especially one I haven't reviewed."

"If Mr. DeLacey was concerned about the expense of ECT, why did he authorize it in the first place? And why did you administer it?" She scooted forward so that she was sitting on the edge of the couch. "By the early seventies, ECT had fallen out of favor."

He crossed his legs, settled into his chair, and again took off his glasses. "You are correct, Miss Thorne. That occurred partially as a result of abuse. In the fifties and sixties, ECT had been used to treat everything from schizophrenia to backaches, not to mention subduing problematic patients. Its popularity has returned in recent years. Nowadays, it's reserved for severely depressed patients who don't respond to drug therapy. But the technique has been greatly modified and humanized. Patients are anesthetized first, making the convulsions largely internal. Patients used to come out of ECT with bruises and even broken bones."

Iris said, "The problem is that, even when properly administered, ECT alters personalities and destroys memories. Short-term memory loss is common, but some people lose long-term memory and sometimes it never returns."

"It appears you've done some research on the subject."

"I have an interest."

"It is a popular but erroneous myth that ECT damages the brain. In some cases, it can be lifesaving. To see a depressed, cachectic, demented person return to active independent life is akin to witnessing a miracle." He held his palms out.

Iris said, "When Dolly DeLacey came back after her treatments she didn't know which way was up. She lost great portions of her memory for many years and *never* returned to active independent life, as you say. When I think about Dolly, I remember her being manic as often as she was depressed. ECT isn't an appropriate therapy for a manic-depressive. Why did you and DeLacey decide to do ECT right away without first trying drug therapy?"

"Miss Thorne, yours is a simplistic view. Mr. DeLacey was very well read on the subject and sought out my services because he knew I was a recognized expert in the field."

"Maybe he also knew that you were such a proponent of ECT you'd administer it whether it was indicated by her illness or not."

"ECT *was* indicated as an appropriate treatment for Mrs. DeLacey's illness." The glasses went on again. He flipped through the folder. "Dolores DeLacey suffered from recurrent and severe depression with agitation. Her condition worsened after the murder of her father, to the extent that she was a danger to herself and others. Mrs. DeLacey was psychotic, paranoid, and prone to hallucinations. For example, she insisted that her father had visited her hospital room and molested her."

"Molested her? Had he molested her in real life?"

"Clearly, electroconvulsive therapy was warranted in her case." He closed the file and stood. "I have other appointments to attend to."

"Had her father molested her?"

"I'm not at liberty to comment on that."

"Did she say who killed her father?"

"Miss Thorne, Dolores DeLacey was delusional. We do not give merit to patients' delusions. Furthermore, these are confidential patient records. Good day."

Thirty-One

Iris parked the Triumph in the garage of her condominium complex. There were still cars parked in a row down the middle of the street in front of the building, but people were slowly starting to use the garage again. They were either confident the building would not collapse or so tired that they no longer cared.

At the door of her condo, she noticed that only the small lock in the door handle was latched, but the bolt lock was open.

"At least she managed to close the door."

She walked across the parquet entryway, stepping around the empty squares where damaged tiles had been removed. She switched on the lamp on the small antique table in the entryway, set her purse on the table, and stood her briefcase on the floor next to it, just as she did every day after coming home from work.

"Paula?"

In the living room, she turned on a lamp with a crushed shade and broken base. Paula's hundred thousand dollars which she had left strewn across the damaged floor was gone. Instead there were empty shopping bags, mostly from discount stores where Iris never set foot unless she had to buy something like a broom or a flashlight.

In the kitchen, she opened a cupboard and grabbed an acrylic wine goblet. She poured a glass of chardonnay from an already open bottle, then took it into the living room, where she stood facing her new sliding glass doors and looked at the lights along the coast.

She thought she heard a noise. She cocked her head toward the hall. She heard it again. It was muffled and small like a whimper.

She set the goblet on the dining room table and walked to the broom closet in the kitchen, from which she took a wooden baseball bat. She hoisted the bat on her shoulder and walked toward the hall. Standing in the doorway of the guest bedroom with her hand on the light switch, she heard it again. A low moan was clearly coming from her bedroom. The door was closed.

She crept down the dark hall, the bat still poised against her shoulder, and pressed her ear against the door.

"Damn her."

She dropped the bat to her side and rapped sharply on the door. "Paula! I'd really like to use my bedroom."

The moaning grew louder.

"There's a whole empty bedroom down the hall."

She turned the doorknob, expecting it to be locked, but it turned easily. She pushed the door open. The lights were off and the room was dim, but she could make out a shape on the bed. The air was thick with a sweet, earthy smell.

Her heart began to pound. She took two steps into the room, knowing exactly how far it was to reach the lamp next to the bed. She turned the switch and a circle of pale, low-wattage light dispersed the darkness.

She gasped, dropped the bat then stumbled on it, her arms windmilling as she lost her balance. She fell on her behind in the doorway. Coordination abandoned her as she frantically swam against the carpet, trying to get out.

Angus lay on his back in bed. He had raised his bloody hand from where he had been clutching his blood-soaked chest and held it toward her as if he was begging. His moans had grown urgent and his eyes were desperate.

"Help me," he panted. "Iris."

"It's okay, Angus. It'll be okay." She got to her hands and knees. The small lamp now dimly illuminated the hall, revealing something that had been hidden by the darkness. Bloody footprints traced a path on the carpet.

She recovered her dropped bat and slowly stood, dragging her back against the wall. With the bat held by both hands in front of her, she eyed the dark guest bedroom and the hall that seemed excessively long. She crept to Angus, looking around furtively. "Is anyone else here?" He was motionless on the bed and his eyes were closed.

She put her ear near his face. He was breathing faintly. The condo seemed deathly quiet.

"Angus?"

No response.

She took a step down the hall and then another, barely able to make her feet move. She inched down the hall, her back to the wall, until she finally stood opposite the open door of the guest bedroom. She peered into the darkness, her breath a whisper. Then she bolted and flew across the living room to the front door. She fumbled with the lock, flung the door open, then spun into the hallway where two hands grabbed her. She futilely waved the bat and thrashed until she realized it was Bobby.

"What's goin' on?" he asked.

She gazed wild-eyed into the condo then at him. "Angus..."

"Yeah, I've been waiting for him. He came up to talk to Paula so I went down to the beach to walk around..."

"Angus is here. He's in the other room," Iris said with a glazed look on her face.

Thirty-Two

Rose Thorne sat in the breakfast nook in Lily and Jack Rossi's kitchen and nervously scraped at a design printed on a coffee mug. She was wearing a powder blue velour robe. Pink plastic rollers dotted her head. "I can't stop thinking about what might have happened! I just can't get it out of my mind, it's so awful to think...Oh my God, I can't get it out of my mind how..."

Iris pulled her worn terry cloth bathrobe more tightly around her. After the police had finished their work at her condo, she'd gathered a few articles of clothing and gone to Lily's. She didn't go to work that day. "Mom, try to put it out of your mind."

"But when I think about what might have happened, I just get sick to my stomach! You were so close..."

"Mom, drop it," Iris snapped. "You're obsessing over things that didn't even happen."

"But when I think about..."

Iris got up from the table and said in as lighthearted a voice as she could muster, "I'll be back."

In the living room, she passed Lily, who was helping her three kids get out the door for school. She leaned toward Lily and whispered, "I'm going to kill her."

Lily looked up from recombing eleven-year-old Gerald's hair. "I'll help."

"Aunt Iris," sixteen-year-old Vincent said as he was leaving. "How about lending me the TR to go to school?"

"No!"

"Okay, okay. Jeez, what a grouch."

Rose shouted from the kitchen, "I'm just worried about you, Iris. What kind of mother would I be if I didn't worry about my children?" Her voice took on an injured tone. "You know you children are my life."

Iris muttered, "Great, I have to live for me *and* my mother."

Lily put her hands on her hips and glared at Ashley, who was wearing Iris's hot pink short-sleeved pullover sweater. "Did Aunt Iris say you could wear that?"

Iris waved dismissively. "Go ahead. Enjoy."

Ashley sauntered past them, holding herself straighter than usual, and walked out the door.

Lily breathed a sigh of relief. "All gone."

They walked back into the kitchen. Lily poured more coffee.

"They don't really think that Paula shot that man, do they?" Lily asked.

"I guess she's a suspect. Frankly, I don't see how she could have done it either. But the fact is, she's gone and so is all her stuff. Hopefully Angus will regain consciousness and name his assailant."

Rose was turned around in the breakfast nook and straightening pictures thrown askew by the last aftershock.

Iris peered at her mother and inhaled sharply, as if she was about to say something but had to work up the nerve to do so. She bit her lip and frowned.

Rose glanced over her shoulder at her daughter. "What is it, Iris?" She sounded irritated.

"Did you ever hear anything about Gabriel Gaytan molesting Dolly?"

Rose looked horrified. "Who in the world would say a thing like that?"

"I talked to Dolly's psychiatrist."

Rose nervously fiddled with the neckline of her robe. "Dolly always thought people were after her or watching her or some such nonsense. Nothing she said would surprise me."

Iris said, "She wasn't completely bonkers. She'd be fine for long periods of time, then she'd have a bad patch."

Lily said, "If Gabe did molest Dolly, I wonder if he tried the same thing with Paula or even the boys."

Iris twirled a lock of hair around her finger. "Lily, was Gabe ever weird around you?"

"He always made me uncomfortable. I can't quite put my finger on it. But he never *did* anything. How about you?"

Iris shook her head. "I don't remember anything. Of course I was pretty clueless. I remember his putting me on his lap when I was as old as ten but I didn't think anything of it."

Rose said, "I personally refuse to believe any of it. Gabriel was a very nice man. He was always kind to us."

"I'm sure he was." Iris bit her lip again and peered at her mother.

"Now what, Iris?" Rose petulantly pursed her lips. "Not five minutes ago you didn't want to be in the same room with me. Now you can't leave me alone."

Iris let the comment slide. "Remember the night Gabriel was murdered?"

"Of course I remember," Rose replied. "I'm not that old."

"When Dad said he was with Sonja, did you have any reason to believe he wasn't?"

Rose's face grew long. "It was the first time he'd come out and admitted he'd been with that home wrecker. All the other times, I had to catch him. Remember that time we saw his car parked in front of her house all night?"

"I remember, Mom," Iris chafed. "I remember the pleasure of accompanying you as you cruised past Sonja's house half the night."

Lily stared into her coffee.

"Well, how else was I supposed to find out what your father was doing?" Rose continued scraping at the coffee mug.

"It was a school night too," Iris added.

Rose didn't seem to hear Iris's comment. "I wish I knew what that man saw in that overly made-up, dyed…" She straightened her posture, extended her neck proudly, and pressed her palm against her chest. "And me, always working hard to keep myself up. Guess he would have liked it better if I'd dressed like some streetwalker."

"I'm going to go talk to Dad today," Iris stated.

Lily looked at her with surprise. "Really? Why?"

"I think he knows something about that night. Why else would he have set up an alibi? He never admitted he had girlfriends. Even when Mom caught him outright, he'd have the gall to deny it."

Rose looked appalled. "Why would you want to go talk to him after the way he left you girls? Abandoned you. Left us in the lurch. What kind of a father is that?"

Lily said, "Mom, you're always telling us how we should have a relationship with Dad. Now you're telling us not to?"

"I'm not telling you not to. It's just that you girls don't appreciate all the sacrifices I've made for you." Rose began angrily to pull the rollers from her hair and slam them on the table. "All you ever talk about is Dad this and Dad that. You built him up like he's some sort of a hero or something. I'm the one who stayed and raised you. Don't I get any thanks?"

"Oh, Mom." Lily put her arms around her mother. She caught Iris's eye over their mother's shoulder and glared at her. "We love you."

Iris rolled her eyes and then put her arms around her mother too. "We do."

***

Iris parked the Triumph next to the curb in front of Les Thorne's house in the same spot she had previously.

"He's got five kids in that little house?" Lily peered around Iris from the passenger seat.

"You're sure you're okay with this?" Iris asked.

Lily nodded.

"You promise not to tell Mom anything I told you."

"I *promise*, Iris."

"She'll have a coronary if she thinks whoever killed Angus might have been after me."

"Do you really think Bill DeLacey would go that far?"

"It could have been Alvarez and Cole. I don't know what I've gotten into. I'm afraid. Just don't tell Mom, *please*."

"If you can't trust your own sister, who can you trust?"

Iris was mulling that over when Lily put her hand on her arm.

"There's something I've been thinking about lately." Her eyes were solemn. "I look at my daughter and I don't know how she could have handled what you went through when you were her age. It makes me feel really bad to think about it." Her eyes filled with tears.

Iris took her hand.

Lily sniffed. "All Dad cared about was screwing around. All Mom cared about was being angry. I was always gone. Then I got married, too young, just to get away. And you were left all by yourself."

"Well…" Iris sighed. "You know what they say, what doesn't kill you makes you stronger." She squeezed her sister's hand. "I don't blame you, Lil. You were just a kid too. We did the best we could. No one had anything to give to anyone else. Everyone was too busy just trying to get through the days and nights. Especially the nights."

"But I was your big sister." A tear rolled down her cheek. "I should have watched over you. I'm sorry. I'm sorry I wasn't there for you."

"It's okay." Iris pulled Lily toward her in the cramped car. "Apology accepted, but unnecessary."

Lily let go and busied herself by digging in her purse. "No tissues."

Iris taunted, "Mom would disapprove. You're always supposed to have tissues in your purse."

"And enough cash to get home."

"I wonder how much cash that is," Iris mused. She opened the glove compartment and took out a wad of paper towels that were streaked from being used to check the Triumph's oil. She tore off a somewhat clean corner and handed it to Lily. "Only the best for you, darling."

"I would expect nothing less."

A teenage boy came out the front door of the house and walked down the driveway toward the garage. Iris and Lily watched him.

"Think that's…?" Lily began.

Iris finished the sentence. "One of our brothers."

"He looks older than Vincent."

"Wonder if Sonja had him before Dad left Mom."

"Good Lord." Lily took a deep breath. "You ready?"

"Yeah."

Lily squinted at her image in the Triumph's clouded vanity mirror. "How do I look?"

"Fabulous."

They started down the path to the front door when they heard the sound of something electrical coming from the garage. They walked across the lawn to the driveway and stood beneath the open garage door.

The boy, who was varnishing a cabinet with a paintbrush, spotted them first. "Dad?"

"Yeah?" Les Thorne was leaning over a workbench, using a power saw to cut through a plank.

"Dad, there are two ladies here."

Les straightened, pressing his hand against the small of his back as if he were in pain. He pushed his protective glasses above his head. "Can I help you?"

Lily and Iris hadn't budged, as if their feet were rooted to the spot. They looked at one another, each waiting for the other to speak.

Les cocked his head at them with his mouth agape.

The boy rested the paintbrush across the top of the can and watched.

Iris said, "He doesn't even remember us. Let's go." She started to leave.

Lily hesitated, looking from her father to Iris.

Iris was halfway down the driveway when Les exclaimed, "It *is* you!" He walked toward Lily with his arms open.

Lily hugged him.

"It's the girls!" Les explained to the boy. He laughed. "You're hardly girls anymore. I'm so glad to see you."

The boy eyed Lily curiously and said nothing.

"Good to see you too, Dad," Lily said.

Iris hesitated at the end of the driveway. She quickly walked back, her body tilted forward as if she were walking into a storm.

Les moved to hug her but she thrust her palm out for a handshake instead. He brushed her hand aside and hugged her anyway. She barely tapped his back with her fingers.

"You two look wonderful," he gushed. "You're both so beautiful."

"You look terrific too," Lily said. "Doesn't he look good, Iris?"

"Terrific." Iris cleared her throat.

Les said, "This is your brother, Brian. Come and meet your sisters."

Brian slowly walked forward and awkwardly raised his hand in a wave.

"Nice to meet you, Brian," Lily enthused.

Iris smiled hesitantly at the boy. "Look, uhh…This is all nice and stuff, but I need to talk to you about something. That's why I, uh, we came."

"Why don't you come in the house and say hi to Sonja? Your brothers and sisters will be coming home from school soon. I hope you can stay to meet them. I talk to them about you girls, especially you, Iris. I tell them how you went to college and about your career. You're such a good example for them. Your aunts keep me up to date on what you girls have been doing."

Iris put her hands on her hips and stared at him. "Lily has kids you've never even seen. They're almost grown." She turned to Lily. "Doesn't that piss you off?"

Lily flinched. "We don't need to get into all that right now."

"When will we get into it?" Iris demanded. "Never? Just brush all that icky business about not having a father for the past twenty-five years under the table and start trading holidays like nothing happened? You host Christmas and I'll do Easter?"

Brian gaped at Iris.

Lily looked at her apprehensively. "Look, why don't we just tell Dad why we came?"

"Now, Iris," Les pleaded as he shuffled his feet uneasily. "Let's not get angry."

"No, *let's* get angry." Iris's words were clipped and her posture was rigid. "I think anger is very appropriate right now. I remember that about you, Dad. You always hated confrontation. I wonder if that's why I love it."

Lily stepped forward and began to rattle on without taking a breath. "Dad, remember when Gabriel Gaytan died? Well, Iris is all mixed up in something having to do with that and she needs your help. She might be in danger. Do you know anything about what happened that night?"

Les's pleasant demeanor turned cool. "I've already told everyone everything I know and that's all I have to say."

Iris stared at him. "So you're saying you won't help me. This is the only time I've asked you for anything my entire life and you won't help me."

He looked at her. "Did the DeLaceys send you? Stay away from that family. None of them are worth a damn."

"Is that why you stayed away from us? Because we weren't worth a damn?"

His eyes darkened sorrowfully. He suddenly seemed older. "I can't undo what I did. I'm sorry I left you girls, but it was for the best."

"Best for whom?" Iris snapped. "For you?"

Lily grimaced and stared at the sky.

"It was the hardest thing I've ever done, Iris."

"So you think that makes you a hero? Leaving's not courageous. *Staying* and working it out is courageous." She angrily paced back and forth. "Just do me a favor." She whipped her index finger through the air. "Do not talk about me. Do not take pride in the things I've accomplished. You played no role in my success. If anything, I am what I am in spite of you. You won't even help me now. You're too busy trying to protect this nice little life you've built. You're a selfish man, Les Thorne. A selfish, selfish man."

Les held his open palms toward Iris. "If I could only make you understand."

"I wish you could. I would really like to understand." Iris began to stomp down the driveway. After a few steps, she turned. "Don't worry, I'll never ask you for anything ever again."

Lily turned toward her father. "I'll call you in a few days." She patted his arm. "She'll calm down." She followed Iris.

Les returned to the garage and powered on the saw.

Brian watched Iris and Lily drive away, then walked to the garage. He stood silently next to his father as he worked. Les did not look up.

"Dad?"

Les still did not look up.

Brian pulled the saw's electrical cord from the socket.

Les finally looked at his son but still said nothing. He picked up the cord and began walking to the wall socket.

"Why won't you help her?" Brian demanded.

Les paused, then plugged in the cord and resumed his work.

Thirty-Three

The old storefront office stood on a street corner with a hair salon on one side and a discount shoe store on the other. The carved wood letters on the door were painted in black enamel and stood out from the chipped and bubbled white paint of the door. Some of the letters had fallen off. The sign now read: EV RETT C. VANDERSTA D, M.D.

Paula wobbled as she pulled the door open, then hung on it while she recovered her balance. She drew her hands through her long, unkempt hair and ran her tongue over her lips as if thirsty.

The dingy aqua-blue waiting room was furnished with maple Early American-style furniture. The upholstered pieces had been redone in sturdy light brown Naugahyde which looked incongruous with the gently curved legs and arms. Two halved wagon wheels formed the legs of a coffee table. A tall lamp with a ceramic eagle in flight as the base was topped with a ruffled plaid lamp shade. Venetian blinds covered the windows. The airless room smelled of mold and decay. Several patients were waiting, all gray haired, some with walkers or canes within arm's length.

Paula staggered to the sliding frosted-glass reception window and banged on it with her knuckles. She waited, her body swaying. Someone on the other side was talking on the phone. She banged on the window again.

It flew open, rattling in its frame, and a hefty woman of indeterminate age wearing a white, short-sleeved nurse's uniform scowled at Paula. Bright red broken veins snaked across her soft pink cheeks. Her cropped hair was dyed carrot red and tightly permed in a style that had been out of fashion for fifteen years. One hand was ready to slide the window back into place and the other held a telephone receiver against her ample chest where it was virtually buried. She barked, "I'll be with you in a minute."

When the nurse attempted to slide the window closed again, Paula stuck her hand in the opening. "I have to see Dr. Vanderstaad."

She regarded Paula critically. "Do you have an appointment?"

Paula churlishly wove her head. "No, I don't have an appointment."

The nurse leaned forward to inspect Paula's hands and the area around her feet, one corner of her pink-lipsticked lips raised almost in a snarl. "You're not selling something, are you?"

Paula lunged at the door to the left of the window. It was locked. The sliding glass door slid closed and something behind it snapped into place. Paula tried it. Now it was locked too. She pounded her fist on it.

"Ma'am!" the nurse shouted from behind the glass. "Are you going to calm down or do I have to notify the police?" She paused. "Ma'am?"

"I'm calm, I'm calm," Paula insisted.

"Are you under the influence?"

Paula stood with her legs spread for balance and rubbed her head. "Under the influence." She laughed and turned to look at the elderly patients in the waiting room to share the joke. They eyed her fearfully except for one man who didn't seem to notice her at all. "Yeah, I'm *always* under the influence."

Paula leaned her elbows against the counter, banging her head against the glass. "Look, nursey. I'm Paula DeLacey. The doctor brought me into this fucking world, okay? I have to talk to him. I'm not leaving until I talk to him. I have to…" She fainted dead away and slid to the floor.

Paula awoke lying on her back on an ancient examination table that was covered with a strip of tissue paper. A kidney-shaped bowl coated in chipped white enamel had been placed by her head, apparently by someone hopeful that Paula would use it if she felt nauseous. She picked the bowl up and started to throw it against the floor when she noticed an old-fashioned glass-doored cabinet against the wall.

She hoisted herself off the table, unsteadily found her balance, and tried to open the cabinet door. It was locked. Through the glass she could see small sample bottles and blister packs of drugs that were stored there. She rattled the door and looked around to see if there was something she could use to jimmy the lock when she heard footsteps approaching the examination room door. She quickly limped back onto the table.

"I see you're awake." Dr. Vanderstaad was wearing a rumpled, button-front white coat over snagged brown-checked slacks. He was a tall man but his spine had bowed with age and his head hung at an angle with the rest of his body, requiring him to turn it sideways or raise it in order to look a person in the eye. Large brown liver spots covered his head, which was virtually bald except for a dusting of fine white hair that looked as soft as a baby's.

He pulled a pen flashlight from his breast pocket, grasped Paula's head, and shone it in her eyes.

The red-haired nurse entered the room carrying a silver tray lined with a white scallop-edged paper. A syringe had been placed in the middle of it.

"Nurse will give you something to relax you."

"*Nurse* isn't going to give me a goddamned thing."

The doctor, unfazed, continued in his patronizing tone, "Now, Paula. We know what's best."

Paula stared at the nurse and ordered, "Get out."

The nurse raised her heavily penciled eyebrows in response.

"Velma," the doctor said, "let's comply with Paula's request."

"Certainly, Doctor." She turned on her rubber-soled shoes and padded from the room, the rubber squeaking against the linoleum floor.

The doctor folded his arms across his sunken chest and angled his head to eye Paula. He raised one overgrown eyebrow.

"Dr. Vanderstaad, just tell me one thing. How did my mother die?"

He moved his jaw as if he were tasting the question. "Your mother asphyxiated as a result of constriction of the trachea caused by the tightening of a rope around her neck."

"She hanged herself. I'm not ten fucking years old."

"I was only attempting to be clear. You seemed confused about the cause of death."

"I'm confused all right. I'm confused why you took the situation at face value. You were her doctor. Did she talk about killing herself? Or just all of a sudden, boom, she's swinging from a tree."

"What are you suggesting, Paula?"

"Didn't you think about looking at her blood to see if she'd been drugged or her head to see if she'd been hit, or did the old man convince you to help him out?"

The doctor set his jaw, making his loose jowls quiver. "Paula, I have practiced medicine for over fifty years. Fifty! It is my role as a physician to save lives, not to take them, and certainly not to assist people who do."

"You didn't wonder why my father called you and not the paramedics? Isn't it because he knew you'd slap a death certificate on her without questioning anything?"

"After Junior found your mother, your father called his family physician. He did everything he was supposed to do."

Paula hoisted herself off the table and unsteadily landed on her feet. "Thank you, Doctor. This has been very interesting."

He seemed alarmed. "I don't think you're well enough to leave, Paula. I think you should rest. I'll call Velma to give you something."

"I'm not taking *something*. Is that the way you treat patients who give you problems? Give them drugs to keep them quiet? Is that what you did to my mother all those years with the old man egging you on?"

"Dolores was prescribed drugs that are commonly used to treat anxiety and depression. Your father and I decided that was the best therapy for her."

"She was depressed, so you gave her a pill. She was anxious, so you gave her a pill. Did anyone ever think about finding out why she was anxious and depressed? Did anyone ever think about asking her what the hell was on her mind?"

An intercom on the wall buzzed. "Doctor, your next patient is waiting."

He fumbled with the button on the device, finally holding it down so he could respond. "I'll be there shortly."

"I think you should come now, Doctor."

The doctor turned to Paula. "Please stay a few minutes, Paula. When I come back, I'll tell you something you might find interesting about your mother."

He left the room and closed the door behind him.

In the reception area, Velma was methodically filing patient ledger cards. Bill DeLacey and Junior were crammed into the small area with her.

DeLacey was talking. "Now if you got yourself a computer, Velma, you wouldn't have to file your patient records by hand like that."

Velma kept working. "Bill, this is the way I've always run the doctor's office and this is how it's going to be run as long as I'm here."

"Even Junior has bought himself a computer, haven't you, Junior?"

Junior stood passively with his chunky arms folded across his chest. The skin on his face seemed perpetually moist.

DeLacey continued, "He's kinda slow on it. I get a kick out of sitting there and watching him trying to figure it out."

There were footsteps on the aged linoleum. Dr. Vanderstaad reached the reception area, his faced flushed from the short rapid walk. "Paula's in an examination room, but I don't think we can keep her long. I heard on the news that the police were looking for her in connection with a shooting. I thought it best if I called you first, Bill."

"Only it's more than just a shooting now," DeLacey said. "That boy died of his wounds."

Junior rubbed his nose with the back of his hand.

Vanderstaad looked nervously at DeLacey. "Oh dear. Maybe I should have called the police."

DeLacey frowned. "No, no, Doctor. You did the right thing. We'll see that everything's taken care of. Why don't you take us to her?"

They walked down the corridor and Vanderstaad opened the door to the examination room without knocking. Paula was standing against the wall next to the cabinet.

"Paula," the doctor said. "Look who came to see how you're doing." He moved to the side to let DeLacey and Junior in.

"Looks like you put on a few pounds," DeLacey said.

"Nice to see you too, Dad," Paula said. "Hi, Junior."

Junior was grim. "Why did you come back and start all this trouble?"

"Trouble?" Paula said. "I'm just trying to have some fun."

"Let's go home now, Paula," DeLacey said.

"I would except I don't have a home. Someone driving a red pickup truck burned it down." She looked at Junior.

His fleshy cheeks grew pink. "I didn't have anything to do with that."

"Junior, shut up," DeLacey said.

Junior exhaled loudly and stared at the ground.

"Stop bagging on him," Paula said.

"It's the only way he's going to improve himself. If you'd listened to me, you wouldn't be in the fix you're in right now."

"What would I be? Dead, like Mom? Or almost dead, like Junior? Or maybe I'd be like Thomas, Mr. Perfect, who never does *anything* wrong. Right." she sneered.

The doctor slipped out the door and returned with a syringe. "Paula, I really think you need something to relax. Bill, maybe you can help Paula by holding her."

Paula reached behind into the waistband of her jeans and pulled out a handgun. "You're determined to give me that shot, aren't you?"

"We're only trying to help you, Paula," DeLacey said. "I don't know where you get that distrustful streak from."

"Help me? You mean like you helped Angus? Just wait until he comes around, then you'll get yours."

"He's dead," DeLacey said.

Paula slammed the gun on a counter, making glass canisters rattle. She rapidly blinked, inhaling and exhaling deeply. Then she swept the gun across the counter, sending the canisters flying.

The men tried to leap out of the way. The canisters hit the walls and floor, spraying glass, swabs, cotton balls, and thermometers in their liquid blue bath across the room.

Paula was unfazed. She pointed the gun at her father. "Why do you take everything I love?"

He started to respond but she interrupted. "You think you're God or something and you can just give and take? Maybe it's my turn to do some taking."

She pointed the gun at Junior. He took a step backward. Then she pointed it at her father again. "Why do you love Thomas so much?"

"I guess he's easier to love, Paula."

"Easier to love." She nodded. "Why is that? Because he did whatever you wanted him to do? Because he became what you wanted to be? You made me suffer because I couldn't be who you wanted me to be. Wouldn't let me come home after I'd been on the road. What the hell was that about? You made me pay for things that weren't even my fault."

She put the gun to her own head and stared defiantly at her father. After several tense seconds, she lowered the gun to her side. "Had you going, huh? Everybody get a buzz off that?" She looked at her father. "Disappointed I didn't off myself, old man? Guess I'm not as easy to get rid of as Mom. I think I'll stick around a little longer to make your life miserable." She waved toward the door. "Out, single file."

Once they were all in the corridor, Paula ran the other way. She found the back door, just where she remembered it, opened it, and stepped into an alley. She ran to the street where an old white Dodge Dart was parked. She got into the car and started the engine.

The office back door swung open and DeLacey and Junior burst out after her.

Paula threw the car into reverse and swerved down the alley, heading toward them. They lurched out of the way.

She screeched to a stop, rolled down the window, and leaned out. "It's tit for tat time, old man. You took Angus from me. You took my house from me. Now I'm going to take something of yours. We'll see how easy Thomas is to love after I get through with him."

"You can't go on like this," DeLacey warned. "What are you doing with your life, Paula?"

"What I've always done, old man. Fucking it up."

Thirty-Four

Some of the members and guests of the Edward Club were having an informal lunch in the seventh-floor grill, some were squeezing in a workout in the fifth-floor gym, some were catching up with the daily papers in the second-floor library, and others were having a formal luncheon in the spacious third-floor dining room.

That's where Iris was seated with Herbert Dexter, the outgoing manager of the Los Angeles office, and his boss, Garland Hughes. They were at a table appointed with crisp white linen and sparkling crystal stemware, situated a discreet distance from the surrounding tables. Crystal chandeliers hung in a row down the length of the tall ceiling. Thick carpets and drapes muffled the diners' voices, which tended toward the polite rather than the boisterous anyway.

"I'm glad to see you're feeling better, Iris," Dexter said.

"I am, thank you. Must have been a twenty-four-hour thing."

"If you hadn't been in the pink by Friday, we would have delayed making the announcement," Garland smiled. He raised his glass of mineral water. "But now it's official. Congratulations, Iris Thorne, Manager of McKinney Alitzer's Los Angeles office."

Dexter raised his glass of iced tea. "A well-deserved promotion. Best of luck."

Iris met the other glasses with hers of mineral water. She beamed. "Thank you. I won't disappoint you."

Garland sliced into his lamb chop. "We have absolute confidence in you."

Dexter cut his New York strip steak. "Now that the promotion's official, I did want to mention something that's been floating around the office." He laughed and shook his head. "It's amazing how mean-spirited people can be. I'm only bringing it up, Iris, because I think you should be made aware of the existence of certain…saboteurs in the office."

Iris watched Dexter raptly, a forkful of her Cobb salad poised in midair. She became aware of her stiff pose, shoveled the salad into her mouth, and chewed. The Cobb might as well have been made of sawdust.

Garland was nonchalantly making short work of his garlic mashed potatoes.

"I heard that Amber Ambrose was going around the office saying that you and Garland are having an affair." Even though he started laughing, he eyed them sharply, as if trying to see if there was truth to the rumor.

Garland stopped chewing and glanced at Iris. She was trying not to gulp her water. Garland's already animated blue eyes began to gleam even more, echoing Dexter's amusement. "What in the world would possess her to say something like that?"

Dexter adjusted his fingerprint-blotted tortoiseshell-framed glasses. "Story is that Amber saw you and Iris holding hands and kissing on the street right here in front of the Edward Club."

"Well, Iris and I always like to share a good-bye kiss after lunching at the old E.C." He winked at Iris who was sitting stock still. "Don't we, Iris?"

"Of course." She chuckled tensely.

"I knew there was no truth to it," Dexter said. "I'm surprised at Amber, frankly. I thought you and she were *simpático*,

Iris." The use of Spanish sounded stilted on his lips. "Well, sometimes people don't like to see their peers move past them. They don't say it's lonely at the top for nothing. I just wanted you to be aware of the situation. It's your ball now."

"And run with it she will," Garland grinned.

The table lurched just then, as if someone had bumped into it. After a short pause, it lurched again. Soon the building began to quiver, the shaking slowly escalating. Conversation and eating stopped as everyone held their breath. Strangers met other strangers' eyes across the room and held their gaze, wondering if this person they'd never met before would now play a pivotal role in their destiny. Then it stopped. There was tense silence. Soon there was nervous laughter and animated talking.

"I'm not going to miss those when I move back to the East Coast," Dexter commented. "Or the fires or the mudslides or the droughts or the riots or the traffic or the smog. Have I left anything out?"

Both Dexter and Garland chuckled with a hint of smugness.

"Have you ever thought about leaving California, Iris?" Garland asked.

She looked at him with surprise. "No." Actually, she was grateful for the aftershock. It had changed the subject.

They finished lunch and walked down to the garage.

"I've got to leave for an appointment," Dexter said. "Forgive me for dashing off." A valet brought his Mercedes. He shouted from the window as he was leaving, "And no kissing on the sidewalk, you two."

They all laughed.

"You heading back to the office?" Garland asked.

She nodded. "I have to take care of a few things before the day's over."

"Mind if I walk with you?"

They left the quiet world of the Edward Club for the streets of downtown Los Angeles and began walking the several blocks to McKinney Alitzer.

"Look," Iris blurted. "That rumor *is* true. I *did* kiss you on the street. We *were* holding hands. I knew the rumor was going around the office but I didn't say anything because I was hoping it would go away before it reached you or Dexter. I guess I should have said something."

Garland dismissed it. "It's her word against yours and mine."

She stopped in the middle of the sidewalk and looked at him. "I got the job because I'm the most qualified, didn't I? I mean, you didn't promote me thinking I'd sleep with you or something, did you?"

"*You*, Iris Thorne, are the most qualified person for the job. I would never promote anyone to manage one of the firm's largest offices if I did not have absolute confidence in them. I am running a business here." He briskly rubbed his hand through his short hair, ruffling it. "Which doesn't mean that I don't find you very attractive."

She blushed but started talking quickly to disguise it. "We'd best put this incident behind us and make sure our relationship remains purely professional."

"Yes, ma'am." He smiled at her crookedly. "At least for the month that I'm going to be your boss."

"Your deal came through? Congratulations!"

"I'm going to be an entrepreneur for the first time in my life." He seemed thoughtful. "Well, like I've always said, go big or go home."

"Didn't you promise me dinner after all this came to pass?"

"I never renege on a commitment. Certainly not one as delightful as that. How about four weeks from this Saturday? You'll be in New York for your management training class."

"I'll put it in my datebook in ink."

Thirty-Five

The next morning, Iris sat in her office and waited. Through the window that overlooked the suite, she could see Dexter's secretary, Louise, soon to be her secretary, typing at her computer keyboard.

Louise's laser printer expelled a single sheet. She examined it and then took it into Dexter's office.

Dexter removed his Waterman pen from his breast pocket, uncapped it, and moved his hand below the line of his window, beyond Iris's view. Louise, middle-aged and the secretary to the manager of the L.A. office for over twenty years, retrieved the sheet and blew on the wet signature as she efficiently walked to the employee lunchroom. Everything Louise did seemed to be efficient.

Everyone else in the vicinity visually followed the route that Louise and the sheet of McKinney Alitzer stationery took through the suite. When she emerged from the lunchroom with the paper no longer in hand, the other employees found reasons to file into the lunchroom, one by one.

Louise walked to Iris's office and marched in with her hand outstretched. "Let me be the first to congratulate you. I couldn't be happier."

Iris stood and returned her firm handshake. "Thank you." She was relieved, afraid that Louise wouldn't be thrilled with the change. She beamed.

"You'll do a lot of good here." Louise looked around at Iris's walls and furniture. "I understand you want to stay in this office and not take Herb's."

"I like the view from here."

"You could do with some new furnishings. I'll bring you some catalogs."

"This stuff's fine. I didn't pick it out but..."

Louise leaned forward with her hand cupped to the side of her mouth. "Take it," she whispered. "Can I get you a cup of coffee?"

Iris was flustered. "I can get my own, really."

"I don't mind. How do you take it? Cream and sugar?"

"Black."

"That's easy."

Iris knew it would be impossible for her to concentrate long enough to get any work done today. The problem was, now that she was in charge, she had to work harder than ever. Tomorrow. Right now, she spread some additional papers and files across her desk. Making sure no one was watching, she stealthily pulled the daily newspaper from her briefcase, folded it so the article she wanted to read faced her, pulled open a drawer on the side of her desk, and set the newspaper on top. Now she could read the paper without any passersby detecting what she was doing.

CANDIDATE'S SISTER SOUGHT

The soap-opera campaign between twelve-year incumbent Gilbert Alvarez and challenger Thomas Gaytan DeLacey for the 14th District City Council seat has taken yet another twist. Gaytan DeLacey's sister Paula Molina is being sought by the police after having threatened physician Everett C. Vanderstaad, her father William DeLacey, and her brother William DeLacey Jr. with a handgun at Vanderstaad's office in the El Sereno neighborhood of Los Angeles yesterday afternoon. There were no injuries.

Molina is already being sought for questioning in the shooting death of a Pearblossom man at a Santa Monica condominium two days ago.

Oh Paula, what did you do? Suddenly considering yet another problem, Iris quickly scanned the article again. She breathed a sigh of relief. It didn't mention her name.

Kyle Tucker appeared in Iris's doorway, his elastic lips stretched into a broad, toothless grin that rolled like an agitated sea.

She quickly dropped the newspaper on the floor beneath her desk, closed the drawer, and picked up one of the file folders.

He scrutinized her, making no effort at decorum.

She couldn't help but laugh. "What's with you?"

"Just seeing if it's changed you."

"You'll soon know."

He entered her office with his hand outstretched. "Congratulations, boss."

"Thanks."

"I'm always happy to find out I've been brown-nosing the right people."

"Your broker's instinct was correct." She jerked her head toward the suite. "How's the temperature out there?"

He shrugged. "Hey, who cares? They don't shape up, you can fire their asses."

She became thoughtful. "Kyle, that's an excellent morale booster. My first official act will be to post a notice in the lunchroom: 'The beatings will continue until morale improves.'" She sniffed, "Signed, Iris A. Thorne, Empress."

"And they were worried it would go to your head." He winked at her and left.

A stream of well-wishers followed Kyle. Amber Ambrose was not among them.

The receptionist in the lobby buzzed her. Iris picked up the phone and realized Louise was already on the line.

"I changed your extension so it'll ring on mine, too," Louise said. "There're two men here to see you, Gil Alvarez and Ron Cole. They don't have an appointment. Isn't Mr. Alvarez running for City Council?"

"Yes."

"Do you want to see them?"

Iris exhaled with fatigue. "Sure."

"I can tell them you're busy. Herb does have meetings scheduled for you."

Iris pondered her offer. "Okay. Please do that."

After a few seconds, she heard a commotion in the lobby. She got up, closed and locked her door, then closed the blinds on the window that overlooked the suite. She leaned her ear against the door. There was angry shouting. After a few minutes, her telephone rang. It was Louise.

"They're gone. They were quite disagreeable. I had to call security."

"Thanks, Louise." Iris sat quietly at her desk, waiting. For what, she wasn't certain. It just seemed to be shaping up to be that kind of a day. She didn't have to wait long. When the phone rang again, she didn't answer it. Momentarily, Louise buzzed her.

"Would you like to take a call from Thomas Gaytan DeLacey?"

"Sure."

Thomas came on the line. "Hi, sweetness."

"Hello."

"I've missed you."

She didn't respond.

"Honey, I'm sorry for the way I acted. I was wrong. Can you forgive me?"

"Maybe."

He fell silent. Finally, he said, "I don't blame you. I was rotten to you the other night. I'm sorry. I'm under a lot of pressure."

"I know."

"Look, sweetheart, no one can expect to build a relationship in the middle of a political campaign. I'd like to give us another chance after everything settles down." He paused. "Would you?"

"Maybe," she said hesitantly.

"I'm glad to hear you say that." He lowered his voice to almost a whisper. "If we're going to make it, we have to stick together. We have to be a team. Don't you agree?"

"Sure."

"Then let's act like a team. Please come to the debate tonight. I'll call you to the podium and you'll tell everyone how you saw Alvarez and his partner beat Humberto. Then it'll be over. This terrible secret that you've had to live with for so long will be out. You'll finally be able to put those demons to rest. You'll be free."

"What about when Alvarez uses the opportunity to bring up your grandfather's will?"

"Just deny you ever saw the will. Easy."

"Thomas, I told you before that I'm prepared to talk about Humberto's beating but not at the debate. It's inappropriate. And I won't lie about the will."

His response was fast and clipped and unlike the warmth he'd expressed moments before. "Iris, you've started something that you're not prepared to finish. I thought you had more guts than that. I guess I was wrong about you."

"You're going to have to do better than that, Thomas. Maybe you're not as good a politician as you think you are."

"I can't figure you out. You bend over backward for someone like my sister, but you...Do you know that Paula wants to kill me? My father told me she made threats against me at that doctor's office yesterday. I never did anything to her. I never did anything to you either but you won't back me up. Everyone wants to drag me down. If people only understood—"

"Stop whining." Iris hung up on him.

She was agitatedly drumming her fingers against her desk, thinking about how close she'd come to getting serious with Thomas, when Louise buzzed her. "It's Mr. Gaytan DeLacey again."

"Please tell him I'm in a meeting." Iris settled back in her chair and contemplated her newly discovered executive power: inaccessibility. She liked it. There were people standing between her and the world, headed by the impenetrable Louise. After all, she had things to do. She didn't have time to be bothered by just *anyone*. Problem was, she couldn't stay in the protection of the office building forever.

At 2:00, Iris had a security guard escort her to the Triumph. She had parked it where she always did, in a remote corner of the parking structure where its doors were safe from dings.

The guard waited until she got inside and started the engine.

"Guess you'll be okay now," he said.

"Can you please wait a couple more minutes until the engine warms up? This car won't move unless it's warm."

He hesitated. "Ma'am, I've got to get back to the desk. The other guy went home early and there's no one up there. You said you have a cell phone."

"I do. You're right. Thanks." She watched his departure in her rearview mirror.

She adjusted the Triumph's choke and pressed the accelerator slightly. The temperature gauge still registered cold. She turned the radio on, but thought better of it and turned it off. She took her cellular phone from her purse and set it on the passenger seat. Finally, the needle on the temperature gauge registered just to the right of cold. The engine wasn't warm, but it would run. She threw the transmission into reverse and started to back up.

The car wouldn't move.

She tried again.

The rear wheels whizzed against the concrete as they futilely spun.

"Dammit."

She got out and looked at the car. A locking device used by the police to immobilize cars that were about to be towed had been clamped onto her left front tire. She rattled the bright orange metal lock, kicked it, then noticed a folded scrap of paper on her windshield.

"Iris, take a cab to my office. I'll give you the key to the wheel lock after we chat. Gil Alvarez."

"Screw you!" She angrily crumpled the paper and threw it on the ground.

She cut the Triumph's engine, grabbed her purse and cellular phone, locked the car, and walked to the bank of two elevators. She pressed the call button and stood with her back to the door and impatiently waited. She dug inside her purse to see if she could find any weapons.

"Wish I'd bought that pepper spray."

Her keys were the best she could find. So she waited, armed to the teeth with her Coach handbag over her shoulder, her cellular phone in one hand and her keys in the other.

Then the car came by.

It was a plain brown sedan that seemed selected to be so plain and nondescript that it virtually shouted "law enforcement." It cruised off the ramp leading from the parking level above, turned right, its fat tires squealing against the smooth concrete floor, and headed straight for the Triumph.

Iris didn't think she'd been spotted. She slinked to the far side of the square structure that housed the elevators and peeked around the corner.

The gears thudded as the driver slid the automatic transmission into park. Ron Cole got out, leaning his head down to keep from hitting it on the low roof. He looked at the wheel lock, saw the crumpled note on the ground and reached to pick it up.

The doors of one of the elevators opened.

Cole glanced up and Iris ducked back around the corner. She had a few seconds to decide before the elevator closed automatically. Should she stay where she was and hope he didn't see her or leave?

She left. She flew around the corner to the door, which had started to slide closed.

When Cole saw her, he broke into a run.

She frantically thrust her hand into the opening just as the doors almost closed. They shot open again. She got inside and pounded the Close Door button but there was a few seconds' delay. Finally, they began to slide together, but not fast enough.

She smacked the alarm button. A bell started loudly ringing.

Cole forced his arm into the opening, but the alarm system had frozen the doors. She cowered in the corner and tried to dial out but the cellular phone wouldn't connect. Cole had wedged his shoulder between the doors and was flailing his arm, trying to reach her. She was beyond his grasp but he was slowly forcing the doors apart.

The alarm didn't seem to have attracted any attention. She thought she'd heard the doors to the other elevator open, but apparently no one dared exit. She couldn't count on anyone bringing help in time or at all. She was on her own. There was a phone above the button panel, but she'd put herself within Cole's grasp if she went for it. She went for it. She grabbed her keys in her fist like a dagger and lunged at him, stabbing furiously.

He easily grabbed her arm and began pulling her through the opening, which had been too small for him but wasn't for her. When he reached to grab her around the waist, she swung her free hand up and stabbed him in the eye with the antenna of her cellular phone.

He yelled, clutched his eye, and staggered backward.

She pulled on the alarm button, disengaging it. The doors closed.

Thirty-Six

The American Legion Hall was on the corner of a busy intersection in El Sereno, looking even dingier than the rest of the dingy neighborhood. The street corner was crowded with people. Some were there for the debate, some were drawn by the bus stops flanking each corner, and some were just hanging out on the broad sidewalks that were unbroken by trees or scraps of greenery. The preponderance of waiting people gave a sense of too much time and not enough to do. That alone was enough to make the place look impoverished.

The old marquee announced the debate with mismatched plastic letters that appeared to have been culled from different sets.

CANDIDATES DEBATE TO-NITE!!

Gil Alvarez & Thomas Gaytan DeLacey

Vans from local radio and television stations lined the street in front of the hall. Thick black electrical cords snaked across the sidewalk and created a perilous mess in the hall's old lobby. A steady stream of people filed past the wooden double doors, pausing at tables set up inside to pick up bumper stickers, buttons, letter openers, key chains, and other campaign paraphernalia being handed out by volunteers from both sides.

Iris missed the first half hour of the debate. She'd waited in the lobby of her office building for the police to arrive before she dared return to the Triumph. After the two uniformed officers had discussed where the wheel lock had come from and why it had been put on and whether it needed to be on, she finally got them to call the people who could take it off. While they were discussing the lock, she snatched and read the new note she found on the windshield. It was short and sweet. "Don't do anything stupid."

It was the last straw. Since her presence at the debate seemed to be as anxiously sought after as Princess Di's at a charity function, she decided to give her public what they wanted.

"Don't have the guts to finish what I've started, huh, Thomas?"

After the Triumph was free, Iris just barely squeaked into the bank before it closed to retrieve the will. She couldn't think of a safe place to put it. She didn't want to put it in her car or purse since they could be easily taken from her, so she shoved it inside her panty hose, where it chafed uncomfortably against her belly. It was still far from the most uncomfortable thing she'd even worn, though. Any little number from her X-rated lingerie drawer would win hands down.

She drove to El Sereno as fast as she could through the relentless traffic. A vanity license plate on a car in front of her taunted: GIVE UP.

She entered the hall and walked down the aisle between rows of metal folding chairs. There didn't seem to be a single empty seat.

On the stage were two beat-up wood podiums angled toward each other. Thomas Gaytan DeLacey stood behind one and Gil Alvarez was behind the other.

Between the podiums were a steel table and chair where the moderator sat. Iris recognized a thin older woman with carefully coiffed blond hair and wearing a brown tweed suit as Mrs. Webster, her high school history teacher. A large glass fishbowl full of small slips of white paper was on the table.

Gil Alvarez was speaking. "I am against breaking up the L.A. Unified School District for the very reason that Mr. Gaytan DeLacey supports it." He stood with his hands resting on the podium, his expression convivial and relaxed, his demeanor confident. "Neighborhoods would gain more control over determining the direction of their local schools. However"—he paused dramatically—"this means the wealthier neighborhoods with a larger tax base will gain at the expense of poorer neighborhoods like those of the Fourteenth. For that reason, as your councilman, I have always opposed the breakup and will continue to do so."

There was scattered applause.

Mrs. Webster warned, "Audience, please hold your applause until the end." She turned to Thomas. "Mr. Gaytan DeLacey, your rebuttal."

Iris finally found an aisle seat three rows from the front near the side closest to Thomas. She sat behind a woman whom she recognized as a reporter from a local TV news program. The reporter was jotting notes on a small pad.

Both Alvarez and Thomas had spotted Iris. Alvarez continued smiling, but she felt his gaze coolly follow her. Thomas almost gleefully raised his eyebrows at her, apparently assuming that he'd won her over. His reaction caused the reporter sitting in front of her to turn around to see who was eliciting this response.

Once seated, Iris assessed the scene. Bill DeLacey and Junior were in the center of the front row. She was seated too far to the right to see backstage on that side but had a clear view of backstage left. There she saw Jeff Rosen glancing at a clipboard, checking his watch, and pacing nervously. She figured that Sylvia Padilla couldn't be far away.

Thomas sipped from a glass of ice water hidden in the podium, then smiled engagingly for a photographer at the foot of the stage. "I'm afraid my opponent has again oversimplified a complex issue. The possible dissolution of L.A. Unified merits more than Mr. Alvarez's typical knee-jerk response about haves and have-nots."

After shaking his head, as if to himself, Alvarez settled back on his heels and regarded DeLacey with haughty amusement.

Thomas balled his fist. "Decentralization of our public schools means that *all* children in *all* neighborhoods benefit." He punched the air. "If the Fourteenth is at a financial disadvantage, it's your councilmember's job to get the necessary funds. Instead of wringing our hands and moaning about the unfairness of life, why don't we ask ourselves what we can do to effect change in our schools? We citizens of the Fourteenth may be disadvantaged but we are not powerless." Thomas pounded the podium, causing a shock of his dark hair to fall onto his forehead.

There was resounding applause.

Thomas scraped his hair back. He was out of breath. He glanced in Iris's direction.

She gave him a thumbs-up.

He beamed at her.

"Ladies and gentlemen!" Mrs. Webster pounded the steel table with a gavel. "Please." In spite of her protestations, she seemed delighted by Thomas's speech. "Save your applause until the end so we can have more time for the candidates."

Alvarez raised his hands above the podium and applauded Thomas as well, thereby drawing the crowd's attention to himself. He nodded appreciatively. His mugging elicited scattered laughter.

"I would like to…" Thomas tried to shout over the noise. "I would like to close my comments…"

The audience settled down.

"I would like to close my comments by pointing out a man who has taught me a lot about prevailing in the face of adversity." Thomas held his palm to indicate the front row. "My dear father has spent his entire life overcoming adversity. Now in the twilight of his years, he has been forced to endure assaults upon his character by my opponent. But I know that in spite of his various health problems, he will prevail. And that's the same can-do attitude I'll bring to City Hall if I'm elected."

There was more applause. Some members of the audience leaped to their feet.

The reporter in front of Iris shot from her chair. "Mr. Alvarez, please comment on your accusations about the Gabriel Gaytan murder."

Jeff Rosen ducked from backstage and urgently talked into Alvarez's ear. They seemed to reach agreement about something. Rosen slapped Alvarez on the back, then disappeared backstage.

Alvarez regarded Thomas and nodded knowingly. "I would like to address that issue."

There were shouts of, "Let's hear it!" and "Who killed Gaytan?"

Sylvia Padilla slipped from backstage right and urgently talked into Thomas's ear. Both of them nodded eagerly before she disappeared backstage.

Mrs. Webster banged the gavel. "Order! Order, please." She fluttered her hands and then waved a sheath of papers. "That is not a discussion topic for this debate."

Thomas spoke. "Well, Mrs. Webster, maybe it should be. The public has a right to know."

There was applause and shouts of agreement from the audience.

Thomas again caught Iris's eye. She guardedly smiled at him.

"Gentlemen," Mrs. Webster pleaded. She dug her hand into the fishbowl. "The next question goes to Mr. Gaytan DeLacey." Her voice betrayed her nerves. "As you know, these questions have been compiled by the Friday Morning Club, our local ladies' group, which meets to discuss issues of the day." She pulled out a slip of paper, her hand trembling.

Alvarez ignored her. "There's someone here tonight who has solid proof that Bill DeLacey killed Gabriel Gaytan to get his hands on Las Mariposas."

More people leaped from their seats. Some in the back stood on their chairs in order to see. Reporters called out, demanding to know the identity of the mystery person and the nature of the proof. Camera lights scanned the crowd. The audience was growing increasingly restless.

Iris's face burned and her heart began to pound. Alvarez hadn't yet singled her out but she knew her moment in the spotlight was coming. She knew she should just stand up and speak out. Just stand up and proclaim, "I'm Iris Thorne and I have something to say," and have the truth about Humberto's beating and Gabriel's will out in the open. That was why she had come, after all. But the edgy energy of the crowd alarmed her. There were too many things that she should have talked about too long ago and she suspected that revealing her prolonged silence wouldn't play well in this audience. She'd had her reasons for keeping her mouth shut about the events in 1971, but it would be hard to explain her position while she was being confronted by a mob. She'd talk, but not here. It had been a mistake to come. She should have heeded her first instinct. Paula had always said she was a sissy. Fine. She could live with that.

Sylvia Padilla was now standing next to Thomas. Jeff Rosen appeared at Alvarez's side.

"You want to talk about my grandfather's murder and Humberto's arrest?" Thomas asked Alvarez. "You'd better be sure you want the truth heard."

Alvarez sneered, "You wouldn't know the truth if it bit you on the ass."

Thomas walked closer to Alvarez and jabbed his finger toward him. "Iris has a few things to say that'll make you change your tune."

Alvarez swatted Thomas's hand away. Thomas pushed Alvarez's shoulder. Before Alvarez could fully draw back his fist, Rosen grabbed him from behind and Padilla jumped between Alvarez and Thomas, holding her arms out to separate them.

Mrs. Webster tried to read her question over the pandemonium, apparently thinking that if she ignored it, it would go away. In a hesitant voice, she began: "Due to budgetary problems, the city has cut back on many basic…"

The crowd had caught the reference to Iris and it flew through the hall like wildfire. People were glancing around, trying to find Iris. Others were encouraging Thomas and Alvarez to have it out. Still others were demanding to hear the truth about Humberto and Gabriel.

Iris slid down in her chair and looked for an escape route. There were enough people and confusion that she thought she could slip out one of the side exits through which people were already beating a retreat in a steady stream.

She stood and started to drift to the side of the hall closest to her, thinking she'd just be pulled along with the flow, when someone grabbed her wrist. She turned to see Ron Cole.

His eye was bright red. She must have burst a blood vessel when she poked him with the cellular phone antenna. He leaned close and said, "You're not going anywhere, cupcake. You're too dangerous to be left on your own." He twisted her arm and pinned it behind her back.

Reporters, photographers, and TV cameramen had crept close to the stage. An inadequate number of frightened security guards tried to keep them and the audience members back. The noise and energy escalated.

"Somebody call the police!" Mrs. Webster cried. She then fled backstage.

Thomas and Alvarez were shouting at each other around Padilla and Rosen, who seemed to be losing their battle to keep them apart.

Bill DeLacey got up from his seat and stood still as the crowed swirled around him. He angrily shouted at the people who jostled him, apparently trying to restore order. Junior remained seated, clasping his arms tightly across his chest.

The stage was bathed in white-hot light from the TV cameras. Thomas and Alvarez had retreated behind their podiums, where they were each arguing with their managers who appeared to be trying to get them to leave. Padilla threw up her hands and stormed backstage and was soon followed by Rosen. Thomas and Alvarez leaned against their podiums and stared at each other. Neither wanted to be the first to go, not while the TV cameras rolled.

Scattered people had made it past the security guards and onto the stage, where most of them disappeared into the wings, looking for a back exit. Others were enjoying the spotlight, mugging for the TV cameras and saying hello to Mom at home. Others in the audience had started chanting, "Two murders! No justice!"

One of the security guards signaled to his buddy. They left their posts, hopped onto the stage, and retreated into the back. Alvarez yelled at them but they either didn't hear or didn't care. The remaining guard put one more call in to the police, then scooted backstage as well.

Cole was still holding Iris's arm pinned behind her back as they were pulled along with the crowd pressing close around them. Her purse strap was still on her shoulder but the handbag was suspended somewhere behind her. Her feet had been trampled time and again. She felt Cole's hot breath on her neck. She tried to spit out the hair of a woman in front of her. Finding it hard to breathe in the crush of people, she turned her face up and gasped sweat-filled air.

She twisted her arm and felt Cole's grip slipping. Just when she thought she could break free, he plunged forward, stepping on the people who separated them, grabbed her with both arms, and clutched her against his barrel chest.

"You want to leave?" he whispered into her ear, his lips unnecessarily touching her. "We're gonna leave." He plowed through the crowd, pushing and shoving with her in front of him, moving slowly toward the exit. Iris thought she would burst from the pressure of the bodies around her.

She screamed and dug her fingernails into his hand. She turned her head, the only thing she could easily move, and tried to bite him. None of it mattered. Her gyrations were lost in the pandemonium. But something about her struggle drew Thomas's attention to her.

He'd been scanning the crowd for her, as had Alvarez. When she screamed, he spotted her, almost buried by Cole. "Let her go!" he yelled into a microphone. "You'd better not hurt her."

The cameras soon found Iris and Cole. Someone extended a microphone on a pole in front of them.

"He's trying to kill me," Iris yelled. She wasn't certain whether that was Cole's intention, but this wasn't the time for subtlety.

"I'm just escorting her to safety," Cole droned. "This is the candidate's girlfriend." He changed direction and started shoving Iris toward the stage. People turned their heads to gawk at her.

Cole lifted Iris onto the stage where she ungracefully clambered to find her footing. Thomas grabbed her and pulled her into his arms.

"I'm so glad you're safe," he murmured.

Cole stood on the auditorium floor at the foot of the stage and pointed two fingers at his eyes, then at her, letting her know he was watching her.

Iris leaned against Thomas and tried to regain her balance, still feeling as if she were among the crowd. Television lights blinded her and she blinked to try and see. She shielded her eyes with her hands and looked at the crowd. People were in constant motion, like a wheat field in a breeze. Half the crowd was pushing to get out and the rest were clustered in groups, standing on folding chairs and in the aisles, stomping and yelling, "Two murders! No justice!"

Bill DeLacey stood at the bottom of the stage and shouted up to Alvarez, "You should check your facts before making accusations."

Junior had gotten up from his chair to stand next to his father, his face oddly void of emotion.

The reporter who'd been sitting in front of Iris was now on the stage. She shoved a microphone into Iris's face and started blabbing at her, not appearing to be fazed by the mob scene.

Iris didn't realize the reporter was talking to her and distractedly said, "What?" into the microphone.

The reporter scowled, elbowed closer to Iris, and spoke more loudly. "I asked, are you the one who has information about Gabriel Gaytan's murder?"

The camera crew's lights went dead. The reporter tapped her microphone which was also dead. "What's going on?"

Cole dropped the power cords that he had pulled apart.

"Hey!" the reporter snapped. "Leave that alone."

"Let's get out," the cameraman said.

"Like hell," the reporter answered. "I'm not going to miss this."

"Hasn't anyone called the police?" Iris asked.

"This is East L.A.," the reporter replied. "The cops think they have more important things to do."

"I'm out of here," the cameraman said. "I have a wife and kids at home to think about."

Someone in the crowd threw a chair. Somewhere else, glass was broken. Someone had found the controls for the stage lights. The stage went all blue, then red, then multicolored lights started spinning.

"Two murders! No justice!"

"Okay." The reporter relented. Let's go."

Thomas said, "Iris, do it now. Tell them about Humberto."

The people in the audience turned their attention to Iris. Some of them started yelling, "Speak!"

Iris wanted to shrink, but there was no escape. With the colored lights still spinning, she drew herself up and said loudly to the crowd, "When I was fourteen, I saw Gil Alvarez and Ron Cole beat Humberto de la Garza when they arrested him at Las Mariposas."

"Bullshit!" Alvarez spat.

Cole shouted from the auditorium floor, "She's lying. What do you expect from someone who's sleeping with Thomas Gaytan DeLacey?"

Thomas watched the response of the crowd with triumph.

"Pig cops!" someone yelled.

"This ain't over yet, Thomas," Alvarez warned. "It's just started."

DeLacey was standing next to Cole. "Wasn't too smart to have left a witness, was it?"

Cole retorted, "You got away with murder so don't preach to me."

Junior stood near his father. "He didn't murder anyone."

"Oh no?" Cole said.

The people on the floor shouted, "Police brutality! Who's going to pay?"

"It is not bullshit," Iris snarled at Alvarez. "I *saw* you."

"You say you saw this when you were fourteen and you're only talking about it now, after you started screwing my opponent?" Alvarez said. "Or are you pretending this is a repressed memory or something? No one's going to buy that."

"Pig!" a man yelled at Cole. "You beat my brother when he was a kid."

Cole shot back, "You're on drugs."

Someone else shouted, "Everyone in the hood knew about you, Cole."

"You think you can kill now and pay later?" A man climbed on top of a table that he'd pulled into the center of the auditorium and gesticulated toward the stage. "And later never comes? Well, now is later!"

The crowd took up the theme. "Now is later! Now is later!" The chanting escalated. The people who were trying to leave became more desperate. More chairs were thrown. A fist fight started. Still the crowd chanted, "Now is later!"

There was a gunshot.

Fear turned into panic. People were shoved. Some fell to the floor. Those near the exits were pinned to the walls. It seemed as if the police were never going to arrive. Screams and cries echoed in the old hall.

"Let's take it to the streets!" the mob's impromptu organizer shouted from his tabletop pulpit. "Now is later!"

There was a second gunshot.

Iris crouched on the stage floor with Thomas next to her. The wooden floor trembled with the footsteps of people running backstage to get out. The colored lights swirled.

Cole drew his gun.

Those near the stage scampered away from the shooter, clearing a circle. In the middle of the clearing stood Paula, her handgun pointed to the ceiling. She fired it a third time.

"Paula!" Thomas gasped.

"I said I wanted *quiet!*" Paula shouted.

The noise in the hall dimmed for a brief moment.

Bill DeLacey fearlessly approached his daughter. "Paula, what the hell are you doing?"

Junior trailed behind him, looking pale and damp.

The chanting resumed. "Now is later!"

Cole took a step toward Paula.

Paula turned her gun on him. "Get back. Throw the gun down."

Cole hesitated.

"I'll shoot you," Paula warned. "I don't give a damn."

He tossed his gun on the floor and raised his hands.

Paula stepped over to the gun and picked it up without lowering hers. She put it in her jacket pocket.

Alvarez said, "I refuse to stand here and—"

"You'll stand there!" Paula thundered.

Junior swatted his big hand against the perspiration that was trailing down his face.

Thomas nervously got to his feet.

Iris also stood and blinked at Paula in disbelief.

"Shoot the cops!" someone shouted. "The cops who killed Humberto!"

Alvarez clamped his mouth closed and took a step back.

Cole glared defiantly at the crowd.

"Justice for Humberto! Justice for Gabriel!"

"Now is later!"

The stage lights switched to steady red.

Cole shouted to Alvarez, "We'd better get out of here before we get lynched." He hoisted himself onto the stage.

"Go ahead and get out," Paula said. "It's not you I want." She aimed her gun at Thomas.

Cole ducked as a Vote for Alvarez key chain, thrown by someone in the audience, sailed past his head.

"Not before I get my hands on that will," Alvarez said.

Bill DeLacey, standing beside Paula, shook his head, his shoulders bouncing as he silently laughed. "Paula, I always said that if you had just a little more brains, you'd be really dangerous."

"Don't underestimate me, Dad," Paula said. "Not when I have a gun on your precious little boy."

People continued to flood the exits. As the auditorium emptied, the action moved to the street. More people had taken up the chant, "Now is later!" People were breaking car windows. Through the auditorium's open doors, Iris saw police in riot gear, the scene outside taking precedence over the one inside the hall. Something was burning. Iris glimpsed a police car that had been turned over and set aflame.

"What do you want?" Thomas asked Paula as he stared at the gun barrel. He then ducked and held his hands up to avoid being hit by campaign buttons thrown by someone in the dwindling crowd.

Iris, Alvarez, and Cole ducked as well while the buttons showered over them.

"Answers," Paula said.

"Give us some answers!" someone shouted.

Paula continued to hold the gun on Thomas. "Which one of you A-holes killed my mother because she knew too much? Go ahead. Don't be shy."

Bill DeLacey slowly raised his gnarled hand and pointed his index finger. "Paula, stop looking for skeletons in the closet."

"Then explain this, Mr. DeLacey." Iris turned her back, reached inside the waistband of her skirt, pulled the will from her panty hose, and waved it.

Alvarez exclaimed, "The will!" He lunged and grabbed it.

Iris held on.

Thomas tried to pry Alvarez's hand from the document. He reared his fist back and slugged Alvarez, sending him to the floor.

The people who had been taunting Alvarez and Cole let out a whoop when they saw Alvarez down. "Get him!" They started to rush the stage.

"Gil, let's go." Cole helped Alvarez to his feet and pulled him toward the back door, leaving Iris and Thomas on the stage. Junior, Bill DeLacey, and Paula were on the auditorium floor just below.

Paula waved the gun at the crowd. "Stay back." She released a shot into the air.

Iris was clutching the will in both hands when Thomas grabbed it and yanked it from her. "Thomas!"

Some of the crowd called Paula's bluff and pushed past her onto the stage to follow Cole and Alvarez.

People jostled Bill DeLacey and Junior, who were still below the stage. Junior tried to shield his father with his body. He climbed onto the stage and held his hand out for his father to join him. "Dad, let's go out the back."

Iris tried to grab the will.

"It's DeLacey property, Iris." Thomas blocked her with his elbow.

"You stinking son of a bitch." Paula turned the gun on him again. "You're done."

Thomas grabbed Iris and pulled her in front of him. "Go ahead and shoot now, Paula."

Iris struggled in his grasp.

Paula waved the gun, trying to take aim at Thomas without hitting Iris.

"Paula," Iris yelped.

In the commotion, no one had noticed a man quietly making his way to the front of the auditorium.

"Dad?" Iris whispered.

Paula kept her gun pointed on Thomas, but turned to look at Les Thorne.

"Thomas, let her go," Les said.

Thomas released Iris.

Iris glared at him. "You creep." She snatched the will from him.

"Paula, give me the gun," Les said.

She handed it to him. "It was empty anyway."

"Empty," Thomas said. "I knew that."

Junior took a few steps backward as if to put space between himself and Les. "What does he want, Dad?"

"You've got no business here, Les," Bill DeLacey said.

Their voices sounded loud in the hall that was almost empty save a few people who had come in to take refuge from the riot outside and others who were trying to recover from the earlier stampede.

"I'm here to help my daughter and to do what I should have done years ago," Les said. "It's time people knew the truth about who murdered Gabriel Gaytan."

"You know who did it?" Paula asked.

Before Les could answer, a gunshot rang out from the stage. Les crumpled to his knees.

Iris jumped from the stage to the auditorium floor. "Dad!" Her father bled from his abdomen. "Somebody call an ambulance," she pleaded, clutching her father's hand.

DeLacey suddenly grabbed hold of Paula as he frantically scanned the stage. "Find Junior." He clutched his chest and grew pale and breathless. The old man didn't seem able to stand on his own.

Paula put her arm around him to hold him up. "Thomas! Something's wrong."

Thomas climbed down from the stage. "Dad, sit down." He tried to edge his father to a folding chair but Bill DeLacey wouldn't move.

"Find Junior," he rasped.

Paula lowered her father to the floor. "I think he's having a heart attack."

"Find Junior," DeLacey repeated, panting. "Please. He thinks everyone knows he killed Gabriel. I'm afraid of what he might do."

Outside, the chanting subsided and was replaced by the sound of broken glass as the protest that was born of a search for justice quickly disintegrated into mindless looting.

Thirty-Seven

Paula and Thomas sat next to Bill DeLacey's hospital bed, where DeLacey was lying motionless on his back, his eyes closed. Tubes fed in and out. Monitors blipped. A television mounted to the wall hummed quietly.

"I suppose Iris and I are finished," Thomas said.

Paula stared at him, as if to make sure he was serious, then sniggered.

Thomas ignored her. "Wonder what happened to Alvarez and Cole."

"Keep your fingers crossed. Maybe you'll win the election by default."

"I haven't heard anything on the news about them. I guess they got away from the crowd unharmed." He gazed down at his father. "He looks old, doesn't he?"

"He is old," Paula responded.

"Wonder where Junior is."

"He's bound to turn up. "He's never been more than a hundred miles from home his whole life." Paula looked at Thomas. "You never knew that Junior killed Gabriel?"

"I always thought it was Humberto. When the will surfaced, I realized there was more to it but frankly, I didn't want to know the truth. I hated thinking it was Dad. The way you were acting the past few weeks, I began to believe it was you. But I couldn't figure out why you would have killed Grandpa."

"I wanted him dead all right."

"Why?"

"You don't know?" Paula winced in disbelief. "Damn. You don't know, do you?" She shook her head. "The favorite son. Sheltered from all life's nasties."

On another floor in the same hospital, Iris and Lily paced up and down the hall, sipping paper cups of machine-brewed coffee. They passed a waiting room where five children were sprawled on the couches and chairs watching television. The eldest boy was seventeen. The youngest, a girl, was eight. There were two boys and another girl in between.

Earlier, Lily had been chatting with them. She had a better rapport with children than Iris, who had tried to make idle conversation with her half brothers and sisters. They all ended up covertly glancing at each other, checking each other out, until she could stand it no longer and made Lily walk with her.

"I'm surprised Mom's still in there with him," Lily said.

"Isn't Sonja still in there too?"

"Sure is."

They both chuckled.

"I don't think Mom's leaving until Sonja leaves," Iris said. "It's a question of seniority. Mom and Dad were married two years longer than Sonja and Dad."

"Plus, Mom was the first wife," Lily said momentously.

Iris said, "She married a man who changed her name from Rose Bell to Rose Thorne. She had two girls who she named after flowers. Let's give her a break."

"Absolutely."

They walked a few feet in silence.

Lily said, "So I guess last night was the end of you and Thomas."

"Duh. Just as well. He's too self-absorbed. Too much like me. We probably would have had mutant children."

A door of one of the patient rooms opened and Rose Thorne came out.

Iris and Lily exchanged a glance.

Sonja came out on Rose's heels. In her middle forties, she had a mountain of blond hair styled in loose curls that cascaded to her shoulders. She was wearing a long, loose, black knit top over leggings.

"Sonja's still pretty," Lily remarked to Iris.

"If you like that overly made-up look."

"I guess you and Mom agree on something."

Sonja and Rose walked down the hall together until they reached the sitting room, at which point Sonja left to join her children.

Rose stood between Lily and Iris and put an arm around each of them. "The doctor said he's going to be fine. The wound isn't serious."

"What a relief," Lily said.

"I'm so glad you girls have reconciled with your father," Rose gushed.

"Well," Iris said, "it's a start."

Rose glanced at Sonja as they walked past the waiting room. "She's really not that bad, you know."

"I don't imagine she is," Iris said.

Rose looked meaningfully at Iris.

"Something on your mind?" Iris asked with suspicion.

"Have you talked to Thomas?"

"No."

"You know he's here in the hospital sitting with his father. He's got a good future ahead of him, Iris. A man like that's hard to find."

"Mom, he tried to use me as a human shield."

"Stop being so critical of people, Iris, or you're never going to find anyone to marry you."

Iris was about to respond when Lily tugged on her arm. "Let's say good-bye to Dad."

Iris cast a disbelieving look at her mother, who was toddling off toward the waiting room.

"I thought you'd just decided to give Mom a break," Lily said.

"It's going to take some practice. It doesn't come naturally."

When Iris and Lily entered their father's room, he extended his hands on each side of the bed. Lily walked to the far side and took his left hand and Iris took his right.

"I'm glad you're going to be okay," Iris said.

Les squeezed her hand. "How's Bill doing?"

"Not well," Lily answered.

"I can't get over how Bill protected Junior all these years," Iris said. "I guess he really loved Junior."

"You'd never know by the way he treated him," Lily said.

"Why did you help Bill DeLacey cover up the murder?" Iris asked her father.

"Well, Bill told me Junior killed Gabe in self-defense. That Gabe had attacked Junior as a way of getting back at Bill. I told Bill to tell the police, but Dolly became hysterical. Made me promise I wouldn't tell. She said Junior would die if he went to prison and she was probably right. Then Bill made some insinuations about me keeping my job.

"But that wasn't the only reason I helped. Junior was a young kid. He was terrified. Thought I'd give him the benefit of the doubt. I agreed to help Bill make it look like some stranger had done it. I went off to bury the hammer and Junior's bloody clothes. When I came back I saw Bill breaking open Gabe's head with a pickax. He told me it was best if the police found a murder weapon so he was giving them one. At the time I didn't know he was setting up Humberto. Then when Humberto died, I realized what I had participated in."

"That's when you left," Iris said, pressing her lips into a thin line.

"That's when I left. I couldn't stay. I don't know how to explain it to you. After Humberto died and Bill got his hands on Las Mariposas, the walls just seemed to close in. I almost told the cops, but I after I saw what Bill was capable of, I started to worry about you girls and Rose. So I left. I guess leaving wasn't the best thing to do. Wasn't the honorable thing to do, but it was what I did."

He looked at Iris and Lily in turn. "I thought about you girls every day. If I could undo the past, I would."

Lily reached over to hug his shoulders. Iris followed.

"I wonder if we'll ever find out the whole truth about why Junior killed Gabe," Iris said.

"What happens to you now, Dad?" Lily asked.

"It's time for me to accept responsibility for my role in covering up Gabe's murder. The police already told me they want to talk to me."

"While you were in surgery, I called a friend of mine who practices criminal law," Iris said. "You've got options available. No need to worry about it right now. Just try and get better."

"Did Junior kill Angus?" Lily asked.

"The police should know something soon," Iris responded. "Everything points to Junior. Supposedly Angus came to my condo to find Paula. When Junior showed up, maybe to get the will, he panicked and shot him."

"I'm glad you weren't there," Les said.

Iris patted his hand, "Thanks for helping me out."

He smiled at her. "Don't mention it."

"Stop the sibling rivalry crap and tell me what you're talking about," Thomas said to Paula.

"Guess the old fart didn't go for little boys. Unless he kicked before you got old enough."

Thomas looked at her evenly. "Are you saying that Grandpa molested you?"

"Molest." Paula savored the sound. "That word always seemed too polite to describe what went on in that toolshed."

"My God." Thomas ran his hand through his hair. "When?"

Paula twisted a strand of her long, dark brown hair. "Started when I was about eleven. Ended when the bastard died." Her eyes teared.

Thomas reached to touch her. "Paula, I'm sorry. I never…"

Paula shrugged. "Well, now you know."

"Did Mom know what was going on?"

"I never told her. I figured she'd tell Dad and somehow it would end up being my fault. But I think she knew. When it began was when she started to lose her grip big time. At first, I thought Mom killed Gabriel. Then I decided she didn't have the guts to do something like that. But she knew Junior killed Gabriel and she managed to find the guts to protect him. Why didn't she do anything to keep that filthy old fool away from me?" Her voice was plaintive.

"But none of this explains why Junior killed Grandpa," Thomas said.

"You ever see a cat squatting while it's taking a crap?"

Both Paula and Thomas gaped at their father.

"You're awake," Thomas said. "How do you feel?"

DeLacey turned his head on the pillow to look at them. "You see the cat grunting and straining." He screwed up his face and made his voice thin to demonstrate. "That's what you two remind me of. You're focused so hard on one thing, you're ignoring everything else."

"Like what?" Paula asked.

DeLacey pointed at the television. It was broadcasting clips from the debate. "Is that me? I'll be damned! I always knew I'd be on TV someday. I used to always say that, remember? I always said I'd be on TV." He glanced around. "Where's Junior?"

Thomas answered. "They're still looking for him."

The door opened and a police officer stuck his head in. "Mrs. Molina, we have to go downtown now."

"Can't you let me be for five minutes? My father is dying."

"Don't hold your breath, Paula," DeLacey retorted.

Paula stood and pointed at her father. "Aren't we going to get any answers from you? Or are you just going to die and leave us with this mess?"

"Why are you so eager to have me dead and buried?" DeLacey asked. "Think you're going to get your hands on Las Mariposas?"

"Why did Junior kill Gabriel?" Paula demanded.

He feebly raised his hand from the bed and pointed his index finger. "Now each of you kids is different. Paula was the headstrong and stubborn one."

"I'm right here, old man," Paula said. "You're talking like I'm not even here."

"I'm not finished. Thomas was the smart and ambitious one. Junior wasn't the brightest and wasn't glued together too well but he had a good heart."

"Jesus H. Christ," Paula cursed. "You don't know why Junior did it, is that it?"

"Wait!" Thomas rose from his chair and pointed at the television.

Paula covered her mouth with her hands.

DeLacey inhaled sharply.

It was a live broadcast of a fire burning wildly across a hillside. While a brush fire burning out of control was not an uncommon news story in California, it was unusual for February. But the weather had been dry and windy, the sort of weather that tugged at an arsonist's heartstrings.

A helicopter-mounted camera flew over the scene. Yellow flames marched across the land, leaving a trail of blackened flora and white-hot embers. The helicopter camera showed the citrus grove and the workers' house, which had already been consumed. Two heavily dressed fire fighters came out of the ruined house carrying what appeared to be Junior's blackened body between them.

DeLacey slowly let out the long breath he had been holding. His eyes were still dully focused on the television screen.

"Old man?" Paula said, nudging him. "Dad?"

Bill DeLacey was dead.

Thirty-Eight

Iris returned to the office after grabbing a quick sandwich by herself. She pondered whether having no one to eat lunch with was one of the prices she was paying for climbing the corporate ladder. She figured she'd have to join the Edward Club and cultivate new friends. She decided to ask Garland Hughes to nominate her for membership.

She rode in the elevator with a nicely suited businessman who was glancing at a daily newspaper as they ascended.

Thomas's picture was on the front page. The headline said: GAYTAN DELACEY SQUEAKS TO VICTORY. Another headline on the same page trumpeted: ALVAREZ AND COLE DENY EXCESSIVE FORCE IN OLD ARREST—Inquiry to be Reopened. Yet a third announced: SUICIDE CAUSE OF JUNIOR DELACEY'S DEATH—New Councilmember's Brother Torched Historic Ranch Then Shot Self.

The businessman saw Iris reading the paper. He folded it to look at the front page. "Is this beyond belief? This Alvarez almost won the City Council seat." He guffawed. "He was arrested twice for drunk driving, in a city vehicle, mind you. His wife's accused him of beating her and now it's come out that he and his old partner on the police force kicked this poor slob to death." He flicked his hand at the newspaper. "And he gets forty-eight percent of the vote. What's this world coming to?"

"Go figure."

"And this DeLacey's not much better. Did you see how he pulled that woman in front of him to protect himself from being shot?"

"Amazing, wasn't it?"

Just before the elevator reached the twelfth floor, Iris hurriedly took a brush from her handbag and swatted her hair with it. She took a second to freshen her lipstick. The doors opened.

There were several reporters waiting. Camera lights went on and microphones were shoved in her face.

"No comment," she said, smiling pleasantly. After all, she was on TV.

She rapped on one of the suite's heavy glass doors, which were now kept locked to keep the reporters out. The receptionist let her in. The day before, she had returned from lunch to find two reporters had snuck unobserved into her private office and were going through her trash.

She walked across the lobby's thick carpet and turned left to enter the sales department. Previously, she would have furtively glanced around to see which of her peers had worked through lunch, to see who was on top of their game, who was working harder, who was more driven than she was. Now, she surveyed the department to make sure all of her flock were at their desks, hard at work improving her bottom line.

She nodded at Kyle Tucker, who winked and grinned crookedly at her. She noted that Warren Gray's cubicle was still empty. She raised her eyebrows at Sean Bliss, who did not look at her legs or chest but just smiled at a point beyond her left shoulder. She smiled tensely at Amber Ambrose, who gave a small, sheepish smile back. She was startled when Warren Gray approached her from behind as he returned to his cubicle from the lunchroom.

"Afternoon, Iris," he said cheerfully. "Got a hot lead on a big new client."

"Terrific," she said as she unlocked her door, which she now kept locked at all times. As she put her purse away in the filing cabinet, she peered through her window at Herbert Dexter's office in the opposite corner, where she saw Louise busily packing boxes. One reason for the bonhomie on the part of her employees occurred to her—Dexter's empty office was up for grabs.

She let the filing cabinet drawer slam closed. *I expect some major ass-kissing before I assign that corner office to someone.*

She took a second to look out her western-facing window, which gave her a wide view across Los Angeles. The post-earthquake sky was still crystal clear and painfully blue. On the horizon, a thin sliver of the ocean glinted. Beyond that, easily missed by the untrained eye, was a pale silhouette of Santa Catalina Island.

A sharp rapping on the metal door frame roused her.

"Nice lunch?" Louise asked. She carried several manila file folders and a green steno pad from which she began reading and checking off items as she reviewed them, looking through half glasses perched on the end of her nose.

"Garland Hughes's weekly managers' conference call is at nine o'clock. Herb would like you to participate." She placed one of the manila folders on Iris's desk. "Here are your airline tickets, itinerary, agenda, and background materials that you need to read *before* you leave for your management training class in New York the week after next. The class starts *promptly* at eight on Monday morning, so you depart L.A. on Sunday. Sorry about ruining your weekend." She tossed another folder on her desk. "These are financial reports that Herb would like to review with you tomorrow morning." A third thick folder landed on the stack. "These are employee salary evaluations that Herb wants to review with you by the end of today. The fourth file hit the pile.

"Per your request, I sent flowers to the funeral home, two sprays, one for William DeLacey and one for William DeLacey Jr. I had the cards signed, 'Condolences from Iris Thorne, Rose Thorne, and Lily Rossi.' I charged them to the credit card number you gave me." She glanced at Iris. "Do they expect a crowd at the funerals today?"

"Hopefully not. The family tried to keep the location quiet, but these media people are amazingly resourceful."

"Your fifteen minutes of fame should be about up."

"I hope so." Iris picked up one of the heavy folders from her desk. "Guess I better get to work. Does wonders for keeping your mind off things." She gazed out the window again. "My mother used to always tell me, don't wish too hard for what you want, Iris Ann—"

"Because you just might get it," Louise said.

"I could never understand why someone wouldn't want to get what they wanted."

Louise glanced at her steno pad one last time. "Oh. Thomas Gaytan DeLacey called. He wanted to thank you for your card. No need to call him back because he said he was looking forward to seeing you this afternoon."

"He must need a bodyguard. If things don't work out here, I might have a new profession."

When Louise left, Iris pulled out her desk chair. There was a red rose lying across the seat on top of an envelope from which she pulled a card. The cover said "Congratulations" and was illustrated with balloons rising into the air. Iris opened it and read the handwritten note:

Congratulations on your promotion, Iris. I couldn't be happier for you. I apologize for behaving the way I did. I had a long talk with myself and realized I was jealous and acting unprofessionally. I hope we can continue to be friends. Amber

Iris picked up the telephone and punched in three numbers. "Thank you for your note, Amber," she said distantly. "That was very thoughtful."

"I meant everything I wrote," Amber gushed.

"I know, and I appreciate it. I'm going to need everyone's support and good wishes. Thanks again." Iris hung up. She twirled the rose in her hand. "Too little, too late, *amiga*."

Louise buzzed her. "I have Garland Hughes on the line."

"Now *that's* a call I'll take!"

Thirty-Nine

Iris drove the Triumph past the chain-link fence around Las Mariposas.

The citrus grove looked as if it had been drenched in acid. The remaining fruit had been reduced to unlucky eight balls. The ground was thick with gray ash.

The Wall of Gaytan still stood, undamaged, its surface marked with soot blown onto it by the powerful flames. The citrus trees' evergreen foliage had once shrouded the toolshed and small workers' house, but now the structures' blackened skeletons were painfully exposed. Any remaining walls leaned precariously, their windows popped by the force of the heat.

Iris drove up the road that spiraled around the hill. A light breeze blew, kicking up soot and ash and coating the car with a fine powder. She rolled up the windows and continued up the curbless road, which grew increasingly narrow as she ascended.

At the crest of the hill, she drove through the remains of the eucalyptus grove. The fire had whipped through the base of the trees, leaving the towering tips untouched. Several cats roamed, looking lost.

The old adobe ranch house fared slightly better. A black residue of flames was visible around the arched doorway and small square windows. Corners of the roof had been eaten away. The detached wood garage was in ruins.

A white Dodge Dart was parked in front of the garage. Next to it was a rented moving van.

As Iris parked the Triumph, Paula came out of the ranch house's front door pushing a wheelbarrow that was piled high.

Iris waved the leather work gloves she'd brought. "How's it going?"

"Exhausted."

Iris peeked in the van. "You've already got some furniture loaded."

"We rented a storage garage not far from here. Thomas sent a couple of guys over yesterday to help. I'm just taking the antiques and a few other things, like my mother's sewing machine. The old adobe part in the front did okay, but the back got burned up pretty good. What didn't get burned got water damaged. I wanted to get as much done as I could before I have to go to court for that little incident at the debate."

"Does your attorney think you'll go to jail?"

"Nah. Because of the personal issues and stress and the strings Thomas can pull downtown, I'll probably just get probation."

"At the funeral, Thomas told me your father hadn't left a will."

"Believe it or not. All the wills he forged and he didn't write one for himself. Guess he figured he wasn't going to die. Must have come as a real surprise to him."

"How long are you going to stay with Thomas?"

Paula shrugged. "The lovey-dovey brother-sister act is already wearing thin. Angus's friend Bobby called me. Wanted to know if him and me could work something out. Share a place or let him live here or something. No way. I'm done with that lifestyle. Turning over a new leaf. What's up with you?"

"The Homeowners Association finally decided to go forward with the repairs. I'm going to patch up my condo and put it on the market. Probably lose my shirt, but I don't want to live there anymore. I rented an apartment downtown in one of the Bunker Hill buildings. The commute's short. It'll do until I get things straightened out. I've got plenty of room. You're welcome to bunk with me."

"Thanks. I haven't decided yet what I'm going to do."

"Gonna stay around?"

"I'm thinking about it."

"What are you and Thomas going to do with Las Mariposas?"

"We're going to bulldoze everything except the old adobe. I'm hoping it can be restored. Other than that, I don't know. Thomas was hot to sell it, but I think I've made him feel guilty enough to drop the idea. Real estate developers have been in my face nonstop. I called the cops on one guy. He was going on about some promise Thomas made during his campaign. I said, 'Buddy, I ain't got nothing to do with that.'"

"At least you've got some cash. Should last you awhile."

Paula raised her eyebrows. "I just paid out sixty thousand dollars in back property taxes."

Iris whistled. "Thomas pay part?"

"Are you kidding? He's hocked to the hilt because of the campaign."

"You gave them cash? Weren't they suspicious?"

"Said I found it hidden in a safe. Told them the old man didn't trust bankers. Everyone knew he was a lunatic so they bought it." Paula rubbed the back of her neck. "The way I've been shelling out dough for this and for that I'll be back to zero before I know it."

"If you need money, let me know."

"Thanks."

Iris sniffed the air in Paula's direction.

Paula frowned at her. "What?"

"What's that smell?"

Paula sniffed the air. "I don't smell anything."

"Sure, it's…" Iris sniffed again. "It's the stench of respectability."

"Shaddup." Paula loosened and replaced one of the bobby pins holding her thick hair in a bun at the back of her head. "Guess I could always pitch a tent here. After all, the property belongs to me and Thomas. I don't think the ghosts would mind."

"Ghosts?"

"Yesterday I saw my mother sitting at her sewing machine. Last night when I was leaving, I saw a ball of light moving through the grove."

Iris's eyes were wide. "Weren't you scared?"

"Nah. I didn't get any bad vibes. I imagine this place has always been rotten with ghosts. Maybe I just couldn't see them until now."

"Speaking of ghosts..." Paula turned and walked into the house. "I want to show you something."

They walked through the burnt and water-soaked rooms, stepping over rubble and squishing on the wet carpet. Iris imagined she heard strange noises and periodically swiveled her head to check for ghosts creeping behind her.

They went into Bill DeLacey's office. The flames had been stopped before they reached this remote room, but water had seeped onto the floor underneath the piles of newspapers, books, magazines, and other junk. The room smelled of mildew and smoke. Dim light filtered through the small paned window.

Iris, eager not to be in the dark, flipped the light switch on the wall several times.

"Electricity's out." Paula sat behind the cluttered desk, opened a top drawer, and took out a folded piece of paper. She handed it to Iris.

Iris opened it. It was a sheet of DeLacey Properties stationery. The note was written in blue ballpoint pen in a wildly slanted and florid handwriting style. It said:

Dear Bill,

Please don't forget to pay the electric and the telephone bills. I put them in the middle of the kitchen table. Last time you forgot and they turned everything off.

The cat food is under the kitchen sink. I know you don't like the cats, but they don't hurt anything and they don't take much to take care of. You might even get to like them a little bit.

Tell Paula I said hello if you see her again. This will be better for Thomas because I know he's ashamed to have me for his mother, the way I am now.

Please take care of Junior. I worry about him the most. Please take care of him. I know you always have. You have always treated him like your own son. I always wondered how things might have been different if Daddy hadn't told him. I don't know why Daddy wanted him to know. Daddy started to want everyone to know. I still don't know why. Junior was afraid I wouldn't be able to take it if everyone knew.

I don't want anything fancy for a funeral. It's not worth spending the money on me. It's easier this way for everyone. I know you are tired of having me around. This way I will be out of the way and you can have the house to yourself. I have had enough. I don't want any more.

Dolly

Iris sat on a pile of newspapers and reread the note. She looked at Paula. "Gabriel was Junior's father?"

Paula shrugged. "Guess Gabe balled his own daughter. The old lady had more to deal with than I realized."

"And your father hid Dolly's suicide note because he didn't want anyone to know who Junior's real father was."

"You like the message she left for me? Tell Paula hello. That's all she had to say?"

"You're never going to let your anger toward her go, are you? She wasn't well. Can't you accept that and move on?"

"That's no excuse. It still makes me mad. She was well enough to protect Junior his whole life. And he watched out for her. Junior and my father looked out for each other. Thomas and my father were thick as mud. Everyone's watching out for everyone else. Except for me."

"Paula, let it go."

Paula stood. "Let's get out of here."

They walked into the bright sunshine and crossed the lawn to the edge of the hill.

Iris took a few deep breaths.

"That's why I left my kids, you know." Paula was staring into the distance. "I didn't think I could protect them. She couldn't keep me safe, so I wondered how I could protect my own. You would have thought she could have at least kept him away from me. It wouldn't have taken much, but she couldn't do it. When I had kids, I figured, this is something that's mine. Finally something that's mine. But I got scared it was going to happen to them and I wouldn't be strong enough to stop it. So I sent them away. I figured they were better off without me."

She crouched down and dragged her fingers through the sooty soil. "Now I guess all I've got is this hunk of dirt." She looked at the damaged landscape.

"And an old friend." Iris crouched down next to her and put her arm around Paula's shoulders.

"Yeah, I guess I'm stuck with you whether I like it or not." Paula smiled.

Iris smiled back.

Paula stood as if to cut the moment short. "The old man always said that idle hands are the devil's workshop."

Iris slapped her work gloves against her palm. "Then we'd better get busy."

BONUS: EXCERPT FROM

FOOLPROOF

The fourth Iris Thorne mystery

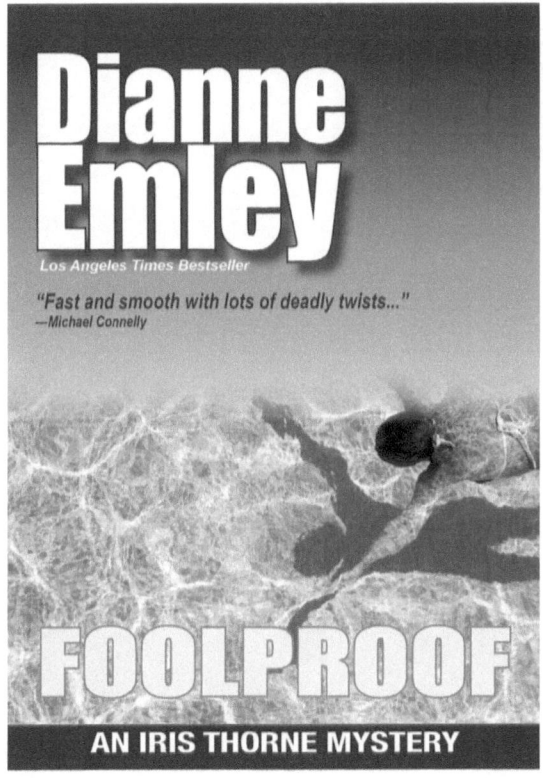

Dianne Emley

Los Angeles Times Bestseller

"Fast and smooth with lots of deadly twists..."
—Michael Connelly

FOOLPROOF

AN IRIS THORNE MYSTERY

One

"What makes you so sure he *wouldn't* try to kill you?"

"Alexa," Bridget Cross chided her friend. "Kip's not like that."

"Desperate people sometimes do desperate things."

"I've been married to Kip a long time. There are no surprises left."

"You've never seen him like this, with his back against the wall."

Shaking her head with amusement, Bridget gazed at her five-year-old daughter, who was leading the family German shepherd by a leash far enough ahead on the packed-dirt path to be out of earshot.

"Stetson, fetch!" Brianna threw a stick and the dog ran after it, his leash dragging on the ground. He picked up the stick but playfully dodged away whenever the child tried to take it from him.

Alexa added, "You never thought he'd cheat on you."

Bridget stopped smiling.

"The *nerve* of him, screwing around right under your nose with that Toni person at the office. Of course, you're the last to find out." Apparently oblivious to her friend's uneasiness, Alexa went on. "You think she was the only one? Did you ask him?"

"I would prefer not talking about it."

Coldwater Canyon Park was almost deserted in the middle of a weekday afternoon. It was January in Los Angeles and hot, sunny, and windy thanks to a Santa Ana that had kicked up the day before, blowing dry desert air westward to the ocean. The women and child were bare-armed, the dog was panting, and the sky was as blue and brittle as glacier ice.

A gust of wind ruffled the dog's fur and blew Brianna Cross's long, dark hair, the crown gathered at the back of her head with a bright ribbon, over her shoulder and into her face. She decorously scraped it from her cheeks and patted it back into place while her mother watched, touched by the young child's newly grown-up demeanor.

"When are you going to tell him?" Alexa Platt asked.

Bridget sighed, almost with despair. "I don't know. I keep thinking we can work it out."

"You could, if he were willing. Seems he's made it clear he's not."

"The last thing I wanted was Brianna to be the product of a broken home, but I'm at my wit's end." Bridget grew pensive as she watched her daughter instruct the dog to sit and shake hands. "Maybe it'd be easier if Brianna and I moved out."

"No way! He's the one who should move out." Alexa flicked back her long, blonde hair and planted her hands on her slender hips. "Why are you acting like such a wuss?" she complained. "You *are* afraid of him, aren't you?"

Bridget suddenly put out a warning hand for her friend to stop talking. She turned and frowned at the empty lane behind them.

The child, oblivious, continued playing and chatting to herself and the dog several yards away. Stetson, however, was looking in the same direction as Bridget, his ears pricked.

"What's wrong?" Alexa peered down the path but didn't see anyone.

The dog cocked his head and began to whimper at the sound of heavy footsteps on the sandy dirt.

A man with stringy, shoulder-length hair dressed in a khaki uniform rounded the curve.

"It's that grounds-keeper guy," Alexa remarked under her breath.

Bridget exhaled with relief. "Afternoon."

He mumbled a greeting as he passed, not meeting their eyes. They watched as he disappeared around a bend in the path ahead of them.

"Ugh," Alexa commented. "He was staring at me when I was waiting for you in the parking lot. Gives me the creeps."

Bridget shook her head and resumed walking.

"What?" Alexa stroked her friend's arm. "Is there something you're not telling me?"

Bridget paused, as if debating whether to respond. "Lately, I've felt like someone's been following me. Watching me."

Alexa frowned. "When?"

"Last week, in the parking lot at the office. Then, a few days later, at home outside the French doors."

"On the patio? Did you see anyone?"

"No. Just movement, a shape silhouetted by the pool light. The dog started barking, so I know I wasn't imagining it."

"Was Kip home?"

"He was at Pandora, working late on the new release…he claimed."

"You think it could have been him?"

"Why would Kip spy on me?"

"Maybe it was one of Kip's scorned lovers," Alexa said excitedly. "Maybe Toni."

Bridget raked her hand through her close-cropped hair. "The noise in the parking lot was probably my imagination. On the patio, it was probably a coyote, maybe the same one who jumped the fence and got our cat. Anyway, let's not talk about Kip's…" She looked askance.

"Keep the alarm on."

"I do now."

"You and Kip still have that gun?"

"I don't know how to use it."

"That wasn't what I was thinking."

"*Alexa*," Bridget scolded.

A strong gust of warm wind blew, sending dry leaves and loose dirt scuttling down the path, pushing the women and the child to take a few quick steps. The dog, more surefooted and lower to the ground, was not affected.

"You have to admit that Kip has changed a lot over the past few years." Alexa blinked at a speck of dirt that had flown into her eye. "One minute, he's a…" She searched for the appropriate word.

"Geek?"

Alexa laughed. "I was going to say, loner. But, okay, a geek. The next minute, he has groupies. I went through that, 'you may kiss my ring thing' with Jim. But Kip's forgotten one thing—you made him what he is."

Bridget dismissed the comment with a shrug.

"C'mon, B, everyone knows it."

"We built the company together."

"You said you didn't want to talk about it, but," Alexa persisted, "I think Kip slept with Toni to punish you for taking the company in a direction he doesn't want it to go."

"That's occurred to me. But I can't worry about Kip's need for control." Bridget's tone was determined. "I have my daughter's welfare to consider. I'm not going to throw away her financial security just because her father doesn't want to answer to stockholders."

"Bottom line, it doesn't matter what Kip wants," Alexa added. "He gave you control of Pandora Software. He couldn't be bothered with all that icky business stuff. He wants to spend his time being Mr. Creative Genius."

"I never thought it would matter unless push came to shove."

"It has. No wonder you're looking over your shoulder."

* * *

After admiring Alexa's new Jaguar convertible, the women said good-bye in the gravel parking lot near the park entrance. Bridget and Brianna pulled out first, rushing to avoid being late for the little girl's ballet class. Alexa, holding her car keys, waved until Bridget's Volvo had turned down the hill and slipped out of sight.

When Alexa had not returned home by 1:00 a.m., her husband called the police.

ABOUT THE AUTHOR

Dianne Emley is a *Los Angeles Times* bestselling author and has received critical acclaim for her books which include the Detective Nan Vining thrillers: *The First Cut, Cut to the Quick, The Deepest Cut,* and *Love Kills* and the Iris Thorne mysteries: *Cold Call, Slow Squeeze, Fast Friends, Foolproof and Pushover.* Her books have been translated into six languages. A Los Angeles native, she's never lived more than ten minutes away except for the year she lived in Southern France. She now lives in a hundred-year-old house near L.A. with her husband. Learn more at www.DianneEmley.com.